SCHOOL'S OUT

It was more than an hour before Joe reported in again.

"Carol! Molly! There is a problem here. I've found what attracted our robots, and it is a little disconcerting."

"What is it?" Molly responded.

"It seems to be two suits of environmental armor, designed for different species. One I do not recognize by name. The other would fit a Kantrick. You could get into it, Charley, except for one fact."

"What's that?" Charley called.

"It's already occupied . . ."

By Hal Clement
Published by Ballantine Books:

CLOSE TO CRITICAL

THE CYCLE OF FIRE

ICEWORLD

MISSION OF GRAVITY

STAR LIGHT

STILL RIVER

THROUGH THE EYE OF A NEEDLE

STILL RIVER

Hal Clement

A Del Rey Book

BALLANTINE BOOKS • NEW YORK

A Del Rey Book
Published by Ballantine Books

 Published in the United States of America by Ballantine Books, a division of Random House, Inc., New York, and simultaneously in Canada by Random House of Canada Limited, Toronto.

Library of Congress Catalog Card Number: 86-26603

ISBN 0-345-32917-1

Printed in Canada

First Hardcover Edition: June 1987
First Mass Market Edition: February 1989

Cover Art by Don Dixon

To George, Rick, and Christy,
our children—whose advent
had me naively expecting to
learn a lot about alien minds,
but whose real lives have only
shown that no mind one loves
can be really alien

PERSONAE

The following students, all candidates for the Respected Opinion degree at the institution called by the Human name Golden Fleece University (apparently from a rather remote association, through Human mythology and the constellation name Argus, with its location near the Leinster site at Eta Carinae), formed the voluntary associate team assigned to examine the standard laboratory object Enigma 88. This had been left untouched long enough to be sure that any casual memory of it would no longer be circulating in the School, and of course earlier laboratory reports had been sealed.

The names of the nonhuman students are given as carried by Human interpreter equipment. All had met, both socially and in connection with course and laboratory work, and appeared to like and respect each other sufficiently to be able to form an effective work group. They are:

(1) Joe, Nethneen. Home planet Dinar, orbiting an M0 main sequence sun, normal temperature range 220–260K, gravity 0.18 Earth standard, atmosphere inert at about 50 millibars. Body fluid ammonia based, nonbreathing. Spheroidal body, four equally spaced limbs of which two are adapted for handling and two for locomotion. Immobile head on top of body, four pairs of eyes covering full circle.

(2) Molly (Mary Warrender Chmenici), Human. Home planet technically Earth, circling a G2 main sequence sun, temperature range 260–310K, but, like most of her species, born, raised, and educated on other planets and on board spacecraft. Body fluid water based, oxygen breather. Age 27 Earth years, 165 centimeters tall, mass 57 kilograms. Married to another student, one six-year-old son.

(3) Charley, Kantrick. Home planet Merrvar, circling an M5 main sequence sun, temperature range 200–250K, gravity 0.87 Earth normal, atmosphere inert at about 850 millibars. Body fluid ammonia based, nonbreathing type. Physical shape roughly similar to Joe's but considerably larger. His body is covered by an exoskeleton and therefore does not show Joe's rubbery texture; he has four single eyes, covering, like Joe's, the full circle. His prehensile organs are four-digited nippers rather than Joe's delicate tendrils.

(4) Carol, Shervah. Home planet Krekka circles M2 main sequence flare star; temperature range 240–250K, gravity 0.83 Earth normal, normal atmospheric pressure 2700 millibars, partial pressure of NOCl 210–330 millibars. Body fluid ammonia based, NOCl breather. Shape humanoid, but very small by human standards; height 137 centimeters, mass 32 kilograms. Face repulsive to human taste; no chin, mouth almost out of sight, large independently mobile eyes on opposite sides of head able to cover full circle. Covered with dense brown fur.

(5) Jenny, Rimmore. Planet Hrimm, sun an M2 main sequence star, temperature range 220–260K, gravity 1.85 Earth normal, atmospheric pressure 4300 millibars, oxygen partial pressure about 320 millibars, rest mostly nitrogen and carbon dioxide. Body fluids ammonia based, oxygen breather. Physical shape, two-meter-long centipede, front three of eighteen limb pairs modified for handling. Two large eyes on sides of head.

DATUM ONE: JOE

Joe, for the first time in weeks, felt really comfortable. True, the gravity was only half what it should be, but it was real gravity, and in a moment he would be outdoors. Not, of course, that he could feel any difference between acceleration and gravity—there wasn't any—but having to compromise with beings who walked or slithered or crawled or even flew around weighing two or five or ten times what anything of their size should weigh was uncomfortable. It could even be dangerous, after a while.

There was gas outside, too. More than enough, actually, but gas couldn't do any real damage, even if the pressure was rather high. These people who had to breathe did tend to be quite choosy about their gas mixtures; it was a nuisance having to wear a sealed garment just for their comfort. Some day he would have to find out just what compounds his skin gave off that made the Human and Rimmore so uncomfortable. Once outside now, he might even shed the suit and feel really free.

Waiting to calm Molly's worries had been a nuisance, but probably worth doing, and Jenny had certainly been quick enough with her analysis. Of course there was nothing dangerous outside. No oxygen, no chlorine, none of Carol's stinging nitrosyl chloride. Carbon dioxide, methane, and ammonia were all harmless. The ammonium carbamate and other dusts that the gases were constantly forming seemed inactive enough.

He opened the inner lock door, speaking reassuringly as he went—the Human still looked anxious. As quickly as possible without actual rudeness he closed it behind him and keyed open the outer valve. The ship trembled slightly as he did so, and simultaneously the voices of the high-gravity women roared confusingly through his translator.

Even if he could have untangled the messages, they would have been too late. There was no word for *wind* in Joe's vocabulary or that of his communication device. His home world wasn't quite airless—there was pressure enough to keep body fluids liquid—but no one had ever been blown away.

Until now. It was surprising that gas could transfer so much momentum, he thought rather blurrily as the landing boat spun out of sight.

Of course, his species had not used rockets for a long, long time.

DATUM TWO: CAROL

The little Shervah dashed through the near-darkness at the top of her speed. With so little gravity, this meant an awkward series of leaps rather than a graceful run, but she could see ahead well enough in the beam of her hand light to be willing to risk that. There was no time to waste; there was life, however unlikely that might be, and, if her own eyes could be believed, all competing explanations for Enigma's retention of atmosphere had to take second place. Biology just did too many improbable things.

She had no idea at the moment what life might be doing, or what sort of ecological pattern would have to be worked out before the little planet made sense. Life, however, could do things like make oxygen and ammonia co-exist in large quantities on Hrimm, or oxygen and cellulose on so many other worlds. This was even odder than having the oxygen, one of the most savagely active elements in the universe, existing free, as it did—thanks to life—in so many environments.

She had to see more. Finding Molly was also desirable, of course, taking reasonable care of her own safety should be given some sort of weight, but a possibility like this simply *had to be* checked out.

There was that sparkling, metallic stuff, too; now that she remembered, that could be living. She knew perfectly well there were races made of high-conducting hydrocarbons. Molly had collected some of this, of course, but Carol wanted to see for herself. Hurrying, even under near-zero gravity, was safe enough as long as one could see well ahead . . .

And as long as one looked underfoot.

Her mind did not work as fast as Joe's. He would probably have thought about hydrogen bonds being characteristic of life even while he was spinning through the air; he would have reasoned that *that* might be what made the sticky stuff that Molly had reported so sticky; he would have expected it to produce slippery material, too.

Carol didn't. She was very annoyed with herself as she spun, but none of the explanations got to her consciousness until somewhat later. Instead, her memory flashed back to an incident months before on Pearl, the inner planet of Smoke, where most of the Humans lived because of the gravity. She had only recently met Molly, and the high-temperature family was engaged in teaching Carol's group the sport of skating—ammonia, which does not expand when it freezes, is consequently not slippery. The rink had shop facilities, and skates had been quickly provided for the Shervah family, with interesting and challenging consequences.

Carol and one of her Others had seriously considered mastering the art of figure skating . . .

Contact with the cavern floor brought her mind back to the present.

Even then, she didn't discuss either hydrogen bonds or ice with the others; speed was not the only way in which her mind differed from Joe's.

OF COURSE I SAID THAT

Joe felt a very slight, unfamiliar sensation. He knew that it was about time for reality interface, and wanted to believe that this was merely the effect of a strange drive system, but he somehow couldn't feel completely sure. There was an odd touch of disorientation, as though his walking flaps and handling tendrils might not be exactly where they seemed; and he felt oddly reluctant to move so as to find out.

It was encouraging that there had been no change in the display before him; even the most minor error as a carrier penetrates the interface between real and unreal space-time usually kills sensing apparatus completely. As it was, the terrifying image on the screen had not even flickered. Perhaps it had all been his own state of mind; a star like Arc could unsettle anyone.

Or almost anyone. He had forgotten for an instant the giant seated at her own instruments beside him. For a moment he hesitated to look at her; his standards of courtesy would have made it an intrusion, since she was presumably busy. Then he remembered—this always took a moment—that the human being would not even be aware of his glance; her only eyes were inside the hood surrounding her vision screen. Reminding himself firmly that he really wasn't doing anything improper, he let his right-side pair of optics center on her hands.

The fingers, which the Nethneen simultaneously envied for their strength and pitied for their clumsiness, rested motionless at the key bank. If she had been bothered by the jolt, the worry was not being translated into action so far.

Whether that meant she hadn't felt it or was too familiar with what she had felt to be bothered by it was impossible to tell; asking would be intrusion even by Human standards as long as she appeared to be working. He could, of course, get her readings onto his own screen without disturbing the giant, but there were two objections to this. The first was that it probably wouldn't answer his question, and the second that it could easily be dangerous. If she were looking at Arc in anything like its natural color . . .

Joe shivered. There were usually five or six hundred species at any one time at the Eta Carinae establishment, and these tended to be fairly sophisticated about alien life forms; but the recent arrival of human beings had startled most of them badly. It had been casually accepted by the community that life could not be expected near suns hotter than about K8. One of the reasons for the face-fitting mask around the Human student's screen was protection of her classmates from the short-wave radiation she used for vision.

Joe gave up useless speculation for the moment and went back to particle counting. It was less unnerving than examining an O-type star would be. He could ask Molly if she had felt the whatever-it-was later on.

Mary Warrender Chmenici felt the jolt, but paid no real attention to it; it was less noticeable than the interface transitions she was used to, and she interpreted it as merely another of these.

She was not even as conscious as she should have been of the display on her screen, though this was not of very great importance. In principle, students were supposed to be observing while on watch; in practice, even the stuffiest of the Faculty would not expect much useful material to be picked up before the traveling classroom got a lot closer to Enigma. If anyone had known that Molly had already formed a working hypothesis and used it to plan her operations for the next few weeks, there would have been criticism; most of the red-sun races, if the individuals she had met so far were typical, were conservative in their ideas of where reasonable organization ended and wild speculation began. Even these, however, might have made allowance for her youth.

If asked, she could have claimed she was searching for Enigma at the moment. Presumably the body would be emitting the long waves characteristic of planetary temperatures, combined with reflected light from Arc; she had set her equipment to respond to such a combination and to center her screen on the source and shift to maximum resolution if it were found. Her mind, however, was elsewhere—though her eyes, like Joe's side and rear ones, would put in a call for attention if their input pattern changed significantly. She was taking for granted, from the barely detectable sensation that had bothered her little Nethneen friend so greatly, that they were back on the real side of interface, but that left a couple of her days of ordinary flight before the laboratory site could be examined in any detail. Arc and its almost equally huge companion formed too massive a system to permit interface transfer at planetary distances; real space-time was too badly warped in their vicinity.

Enigma. Did the Faculty member of centuries past who had named the little planet have a sense of humor? Most intelligent beings did, of course. Actually, it was Enigma 88 in decimal notation—which, she reminded herself, was not used at the School. One of the things that had made her feel more at home, during her first weeks at Eta Carinae, had been the story of a major administrative upheaval, during the establishment of the place, over the question of octal or duodecimal time units.

The Faculty had a file of Enigmas for student investigation, she knew, within reasonably short distances from the Leinster site. Molly thought she could guess why this one had been given to a team containing a Human student. The guess assumed that the Faculty had already learned a good deal about her species, but this was likely enough. Any red-sun native would have been curious about the combination of a high-energy star and a fairly habitable—from their point of view—world like Titan, and even more so about a place like Earth. In asking the Human students about these, they could hardly have failed to learn a lot about the beings they were questioning.

But that was really letting her mind wander. The assigned exercise was to produce an explanation for the basically surprising fact that Enigma, with far less mass than Earth's moon, had a very substantial atmosphere. The team was to present observational support for its solution with an absolute minimum of items taken for granted; and here was the trouble. Ten months at Eta Carinae, and a really close friendship with Joe, had certainly not supplied her with a complete list of what even one red-star type took for granted. This was bad enough. Worse, twenty-seven Earth years of life and a good education still left her unsure of which of her own everyday assumptions would need supporting evidence to nonhuman minds. Science was science, physical evidence was evidence, but there are spaces between the points on any graph. To her, the explanation demanded by the exercise seemed obvious to the point of being trivial: the planet was too young to have lost its initial atmosphere. She was sure, however, that supporting evidence was going to have to be very carefully handled indeed. She was not normally inclined to worry, but dealing with minds of such different background still made her uneasy. They certainly weren't all like Joe.

The hull trembled again, much more noticeably this time, snapping her attention back to her instruments. Back into false-space? Why? It didn't feel like that, though she knew there were scores of different faster-than-light techniques and she was not really used to the one employed by *Classroom*. No, she was seeing directly, not by relay. Solid matter—meteoroid? It was hard to believe that any spacecraft could not handle such an incident without attracting the attention of the passengers, though in a system as young as Arc's must be there were no doubt lots of unaccreted particles. Her fingers played over her console, shifting from simple visual imaging to build a tridimensional model of the space around the craft for a kilometer radius.

There was matter, of course—the Eta Carinae region is rich in nebulosity; but material at a density measured in atoms, or even billions of atoms, per liter does not jolt several million tons of spacecraft. The matter was unusually rich in heavy atoms, since it had cycled through more generations of star formation than even Molly's part of space; but this seemed irrelevant, too.

There was energy. Arc was still hundreds of astronomical units away, and its companion even farther, but both radiated fiercely in their appropriate spectral ranges. None of Molly's fellow students would have dreamed of exposing themselves to the flux outside the hull—she herself would have been uneasy about the X-ray component. Still, there seemed nothing to account for the ship's behavior.

She frowned in thought for a moment, then flicked off her screen and removed her face from the viewing mask. Beside her, Joe made a gesture indicating that he was aware of her motion and willing to converse, though he kept his front eyes at his monitor.

"Joe, did you recognize that last bump? We went real two or three minutes ago and still are; it couldn't have been interface."

"Not sure. I wasn't sure about the earlier one—it didn't feel like faces I've been through, but if that's what it seemed like to you, you're probably right. This was some sort of real acceleration, then. Have you checked our surroundings? I've been concentrating on ion counts, and nothing has changed much there."

"I made a quick sweep out to about a kilo for gross matter and obvious EM and particle radiation without spotting any immediate answer. Would any of our fellow teams be doing something that could account for it?"

Joe failed to answer at once, and for a moment Molly wondered whether she had violated one of the courtesy rules again. Some of the red-star races carried the mind-your-own-business attitude to what she considered an extreme, but her question could hardly have been an intrusion even by Nethneen standards. Scientific research was a matter of general interest, especially when several projects were working out of the same unit and likely to use the same resources. Besides, Joe would make allowances; he knew Molly and her husband very well, and several other human beings slightly.

"It's possible," he said at last. "There was some work to be done that involved leaving monitors adrift to gather data, and they would have to be dropped at velocities very precisely measured with respect to Arc and its companion. I suppose . . ." His voice trailed off. The translator Molly carried had been well programmed in the last few months, and she got the distinct impression from the tone structure that he had been about to say more but couldn't bring himself to do it. She remembered that the crew of the vessel consisted largely of students, too. Joe would not have wanted to say anything that reflected on the personal competence of one of these. It occurred to her that the student pilot might be a bit heavy-handed, and stopped worrying.

It was the first time she had thought even momentarily of personal danger in connection with the project, and had no trouble dismissing it from her mind at once. Space is, of course, a dangerous environment for a planetary species, but so is a world for which the organism has not evolved; and Mary Chmenici did belong to a race whose ancestors, only a few generations earlier, had casually accepted manually controlled and individually directed vehicular traffic.

Maybe some other people on watch would have ideas and be willing to discuss them, though for the most part they shared Joe's ethical standards. At the moment, of course, everyone in the conning room was busy; this included pairs from ten different teams, whose usual membership was four, though her own group had five. She and Joe were the only ones from the Enigma Exercise now on watch.

She keyed a clock onto a corner of her screen. Looking at it directly meant that her translator was no help, and it took several seconds to interpret the dial, even ignoring the sweep-mike needle that was a little too fast for her eyesight, and work the reading into time units in which she could think comfortably. They would be relaxing in a little less than half an hour. She would spend the first ten minutes in her own decently lit cabin, thinking of personal matters like the husband and son she wouldn't be seeing for several weeks; then she would go to the team's office and spend some more time persuading Charley and Jenny that geochemical dating was really all that had to be done to solve their problem. Charley seemed nearly convinced already, and with luck she could get him to work on Joe, who was oddly hard to persuade. Then—

Then the weight went off. No one had come up with artificial gravity yet; weight on a spacecraft came from real acceleration in real space and its unreal mathematical equivalent in false-space. As a matter of safety, passengers were warned when either was about to be changed deliberately; there had been no warning this time. Main power? Molly thought. No, there was still light, and instruments were still functioning. Only drive seemed affected. No alarms, either visual or auditory, were making themselves obvious. The heavy-handed student pilot again? If so, there should be acceleration warning and a resumption of weight in, at the outside, a few seconds. Molly held her chair arm and waited.

No warning. No weight. For fully a minute, no word. The students in the conning room remained at their instruments, but a faint murmur of conversation began to interrupt the sacrosanct work atmosphere—some pairs present didn't need translators, and the neutral gas mixture did carry sound—and faces lifted from monitor screens. Molly looked down at the Nethneen beside her and could tell that his right pair of eyes was meeting her own. Even Joe was willing to talk.

"What's going on?" She hoped her translator was not betraying her uneasiness; she had done her best, over the last few months, to condition it to convey to her any innuendo it could read in incoming messages, but would be just as glad now to have that a one-way operation. Joe's answer seemed free of worry, but that could be due to similar management at his own end of the communication link.

"I don't know. No normal sequence within my experience is running, but I have never ridden in a craft of this type before, so that is not very meaningful. I can suggest nothing but to wait a reasonable time and, if no information is received, to follow standard emergency usage."

"I know the emergency procedures. What's a reasonable time?"

The Nethneen was spared the need to answer. Another voice, inhumanly calm, sounded in both their translators.

"Permanent crew to Condition Four stations. Research students to your assigned lifecraft, Salvage Status Four. Crew students to your assigned permanent crew monitors." The orders were not repeated, giving Molly for the first time in some days a sharp awareness that she was not among human beings. This was reinforced by the absence of chatter among the students in the conning room. A few quick, short sentences from senior team members, establishing who was present and who was not, and a cloud of weirdly shaped forms had pushed away from their stools, chairs, wrapping posts, couches, and other stations and were floating rapidly toward the room's dozen exits. In the dusky, rubrous light of the place, the Human student was reminded of a picture she had once seen of a stream of bats entering a cave on the home world she had never visited.

She joined one of the streams, her left hand held by Joe's tendrils. Although accustomed to a gravity over five times as great as his, she had spent fully half her life on spacecraft and was much more adept at weightless maneuvering than he. The Nethneen knew it and allowed her to transport them both; his twenty-one kilograms of mass gave her no problems as long as he accepted responsibility for holding on.

As they approached their chosen corridor, the crowd grew denser; there was no way to avoid personal contact, since very few of the beings were equipped by nature to fly. Courtesy ruled, however, and only gentle pushes, needed for steering, were used. Molly had transferred Joe to her back, below her life-support pack, by this time, and had both hands free; and as they swung into the cavernous space that led for most of the length of the flying schoolhouse she found and grasped the first of a series of handholds along what would have been a ceiling under normal acceleration. The passage was much wider than the door that had led into it, and the crowd proportionally thinner. Also, people were spreading out along the line of travel as their different speeds took effect. Molly did not yet use her full strength.

"Joe, is your armor in the boat or in your quarters?"

"Boat. Don't worry about me."

"All right. So is mine. Hang on." She repeated rapidly, and as hard as she could without losing directional control, the one-hand-after-another chinning motion that carried her from one hold to the next, and accelerated their bodies to a speed that made the Nethneen feel a little tense. He said nothing, however; this did not seem a good time to question his companion's strength or coordination. As long as she didn't panic, of course, he amended the thought; these beings who had to breathe sometimes did when their gas supply was threatened, and the transparent affair she was wearing was no defense against vacuum. He decided not to say anything about that, either. Molly presumably had either thought of it and was controlling herself, or one could hope she wouldn't think of it until they reached the boat.

Two Rimmore passed them too fast for Joe to tell whether either might be Jenny; they were even better adapted for this sort of climbing than human beings, and as amphibians were more casual about lack of effective gravity. He had time for only a brief and passing thought about the matter; a turn was coming up. He wound his limbs as best he could about the giant's trunk, avoiding her refrigerator's heat exhaust with great care, and concentrated on holding on.

Molly seized a rung at the edge of a side passage and held firmly, swinging into the smaller corridor and letting go at the critical moment. Joe was still with her, but broke contact as they floated free—there were no more course changes, the hatch that led to their own vessel was only fifty meters ahead, and he was uncomfortably warm from the output of her heat pump. The Human had aimed perfectly; they drifted through both air-lock doors and brought up against the far wall of the main compartment beyond.

Apparently Jenny had not been one of the centipedelike figures that had passed them earlier; the only person already in the room was shaped much like Molly but little more than three quarters of the Human's meter-and-two-thirds height. It was already encased in armor and as they entered greeted them by pushing their own safety equipment toward them, Joe's gaping clamshell-fashion and Molly's unzipped. Both combined their thanks with fast motion; the Nethneen was encased more quickly, as his nearly spherical body and serpentine limbs were far easier to fit. He was sealed in time to help Molly with her helmet.

"You made quick time, Carol," the giant remarked as she checked her last snaps. "Thanks for getting the suits out."

"I was here already," replied the Shervah. "I was pretty sure you two would be first, since I knew you were on watch. The others must have their armor in their quarters; it isn't here. If that's the case, they won't be hurrying."

"Charley wouldn't hurry anyway," Molly remarked, "but you're probably right. Is there anything useful on the board, or is this just another drill?"

"Nothing graphic. I heard an audible signal—probably the same one that started you here from Con, judging by the time—and put my big batteries on. Then I got your stuff out, opened it up, and waited."

"Thanks again, Carol," said Joe. "It sounds like a drill, but we'd better get to launch stations." Neither he nor Molly needed to comment on the fact that the Shervah had only to power her armor; her normal air pressure was so much higher than that maintained in *Classroom* that the usual flexible envelopes worn by most of the other air-breathing students were hopelessly inadequate for her. Joe needed no protection from the relatively inert nitrogen around them, and would normally have gone uncovered if others had not objected to the mercaptans his skin evaporated. Molly used an oxygen-nitrogen mix at ship's total pressure. Her body temperature, murderously high to most of the red-sun species, was handled by cooling fluid circulating through the suit skin and well refrigerated—in spite of the low ambient temperature, her body generated heat faster than the insulation of her garment would pass it—by a small unit between her shoulders. Carol, on the other hand, usually wore full pressure armor outside her private quarters; this needed only additional power for long-time life-support use.

None of the three was considering this point consciously; there were more immediate problems, starting with the two missing members of the team, but by no means ending with them.

"How much project equipment is loaded, if we do have to launch?" Joe queried in a soft voice.

"Most of mine," replied Molly. "That is, most of what I absolutely need. I can use more, of course—the faster I can collect and date samples of crust, the better—but I can make do with what's already on board."

"I'd be happier staying near *Classroom* and salvaging from it for a while." Carol's voice, as Molly had programmed it in her own translator, was rather deep, in deliberate contrast to the speaker's small size.

"We can't do that," the Human student pointed out. "If we have to launch at all, it will be because engines or power supplies have become unstable, or something like that. We can't even stay nearby. We'll have to head for Enigma in order to have a reasonable chance of being picked up alive."

"Carol knows that. It was a statement of feeling." Joe uttered the words with no obvious emotion of his own. "As it happens, you will both be far better off than I, if it comes to waiting on the planet without wasting time. I have only one master unit on my air-current trackers completed, of the twenty I am planning to use, and only four slaves for it. The amount of data I could secure in a reasonable time would hardly be worth the trip, and would certainly not make an impressive report."

"I still think you should both focus on my dating method," Molly pointed out. "The only problem they've really set us is ridiculously simple. Unless someone has set it up as a deliberate student trap, I can see no explanation except that the world is so young it hasn't had time to lose its original gases, or at least the immediate secondary ones. That fits in with the suns of the system—with their luminosity, they can't possibly be very old, either. It still seems to me that a good set of crustal dates, backed up by careful gas analysis down to isotope level, will let us make a good, solid case for that idea. Charley thinks so, too, and he agreed to help me get and date rock samples."

"Or ice samples—don't you human beings distinguish the two rather carefully?" interjected Joe.

"Of course, I—"

"Not *of course* to some of us. I admit the liquid water you drink isn't quite the same as lava, but the distinction is a bit academic."

"I didn't mean the *of course* that way; I was conceding your point."

"I hope Charley isn't compromising his independence of thought," Carol remarked. "He should have come up with some notion of his own, like the rest of us."

"I doubt that any of us can be really original." A new voice cut into the conversation, and two more armored figures floated into the chamber. Molly would have known that Charley was the speaker even without the identifying tone pattern supplied by her translator. The smaller newcomer, who looked in his armor like a slightly larger version of Joe, brought up against a wall and continued to express opinion. "That world has been known for a good many thousands of years—more than a hundred thousand—and about all that you can find out about it is what you've just said about the atmosphere."

"That's a bit exaggerated," said Joe mildly.

"Only a bit. They've been using it as a lab subject all that time, and all the reports that come in get sealed. They want to keep on using it; it's nearby, and convenient, and does make people think a little. I had a lot of ideas about it, but I'm quite sure Molly's is the right one, so I'm doing her isotope analyses while she gets crust samples for dating."

"You said it that way on your preliminary report?" Even Joe's voice, Molly thought, showed a bit of doubt.

"Of course. How else should I have said it?"

"I'd have tried to find words suggesting that my own imagination had been at work," replied Carol frankly.

"Even if it hadn't?"

"Are you changing the subject, or admitting that yours wasn't?"

"Neither. I was just a little surprised at the suggestion of using words to convey a misleading idea."

"Or, at least, contrary to one's own hopes for the fact."

If Charley grasped Carol's sarcasm, which was quite obvious to Molly, he gave no sign. "Anyway," he said, reverting to the earlier point, "I submitted my exercise plan supporting Molly's work, as I said; and they *did* approve it."

OF COURSE IT'S SAFE

Molly was tempted to say something, and strongly suspected that Joe felt the same. The mere fact that permission had been given for a project did not mean that any of the Faculty thought it was good research, but only that the student was unlikely to be killed by it. Neither had a chance to utter a word, however; the Kantrick kept talking.

"If this drill gets over with in a decent time, we can certainly help Joe make up his wind-chasers. Information can always be useful, and if it doesn't tie into our team report it may be even more helpful—perhaps they won't seal it the way they have the earlier student reports on the planet. It would have been nice to be able to find out more about this place when we were first doing our planning."

"Maybe they wanted to find out who would go ahead and theorize on what little we *were* told." Jenny's raspy voice had not been heard before, but this surprised no one; she listened much more than she talked. Molly's translator carried more than a hint of sarcasm in the rebroadcast tone, and the human being thought it was probably right, though she did not really trust this bit of programming.

If Charley detected the Rimmore's feeling, it did not seem to affect his self-confidence. "Who's theorizing?" he returned. "You don't make any plans without *some* idea of what's going on."

"Including the casual assumption that we're here because of a drill, so you didn't see fit to make any decent speed on the way to this boat?"

"With Rimmore ideas of what's decent speed along a set

of ladders, who could?" retorted Charley. Molly decided the discussion needed an orbit shift.

"Are you really sure it's a drill?" she asked. "Have you heard or seen anything but the order to report to the boats?"

"No, of course not," replied the Kantrick, waving his front arm casually. Unlike the others, he had allowed himself to drift away from all support and had nothing within reach of push or grasp. "If it were a real emergency, we'd have heard plenty by this time. We—"

"Do you propose that we leave the boat, or delay any longer in manning its launch stations?" Molly was rather surprised; interrupting was decidedly unlike Joe, however justified it might seem to be.

"Oh, no—not at all." Charley's response was quick and emphatic. "Jenny, you were last in—get the 'all aboard' signal out and seal the lock. The rest of us know what to do."

Jenny, who knew equally well, said nothing; Molly would have been quite annoyed in her place. The Rimmore had been last because of Charley's dalliance, and everyone present knew it. Neither Human nor Rimmore was really adept at reading body language or facial expression of the other, especially through environment gear, but Molly's brown eyes tracked with Jenny's much larger green ones for a moment, and each knew what the other was thinking. The four who were holding on were at their stations in seconds. Charley took some time to thrash his way into contact with a surface that would serve to get him moving in the right direction, but the others carefully refrained from noticing this.

Molly had time to speculate on the possible reasons for the nearly universal illogical response to incongruity called a sense of humor, and why beings who knew what laughter was and who enjoyed using it nevertheless often resented being laughed *at*. Even Human courtesy was enough to keep her attention strictly on her assigned instruments until the Kantrick was properly stationed. Joe and the others were equally absorbed in their own business, of course, and silence fell in the craft as its crew went through power-up and prelaunch checks.

They were able to complete these, and were in full standby status for long minutes, before any additional information came through. When it did arrive, Molly was almost annoyed to hear it support Charley's contention, and wondered whether Joe were Human enough to have a touch of similar feeling.

The same calm voice that had ordered them to the boats sounded again in their individual receivers. "Acceleration will resume in about twenty minutes. You may power down all auxiliary craft. Shift change will phase in at the acceleration signal. The interruption occurred near the end of Shift C; Shift A will start at that time. First drop-off is anticipated at Enigma 88 in about seventy-five hours."

Molly glanced at a clock; her translator had turned the time periods into her own units, of course, but she wanted to calculate what the dial reading would be when acceleration resumed. Twenty minutes would be slightly over half a soon in Station units, which was probably what the speaker had actually said. There would be another warning just before the actual time, but no one wanted to be away from support when that came—not even Charley; like the others, she noticed, he was checking the clock. His head, like Joe's, was an immobile dome on his nearly spherical body, but his eyes, which were single rather than paired, were a good deal larger than the Nethneen's and it was easy to see even from Molly's distance that one of them was covering that part of the room.

She turned head and attention back to her board, and went through the appropriate operations. It took her only half a minute to finish, but Charley was done first.

"That was a waste of time!" he practically growled. "I was almost ready to load the last of Molly's analyzers. Now we won't get to it until Watch B unless she wants to do it alone, and that doesn't seem quite fair."

"Actually, I thought it would be better to help Joe with his equipment," the Human woman said quietly. "There's more of it still to be made than any of the rest of us have to worry about, and having another operator in the shop should save several hours. I thank you for saving me so much effort, Charley; but since we won't be casting off for three of my days anyway, it seems best to be sure that we're all set as we want to be. I know you have everything you want, Charley. How about you, Jenny?"

The woman curled a meter or so of her centipedelike body away from her station, holding position with her last five pairs of climbing legs and bringing her eyes toward Molly. "I think I can manage, thanks. I'll be sure by about halfway through the next shift and will be very glad of any help you can give, if it proves to be needed then. Thanks for the offer."

"How about you, Carol?"

"No problems, thanks. I'll be able to help with Joe's machines after next shift."

"Thank you all," said Joe. "I am personally grateful, of course, and probably should remind all of us that we are a team and should all be completely familiar with all procedures and equipment anyway. The process of mutual help will move us in this direction, of course, but any apparatus anyone does not understand by the time we reach Enigma will have to be very familiar before we start work there—understood by *everyone*. The time taken to achieve this will have to come out of the hours we have on the planet, or the time before we reach it. The latter seems preferable to me."

"Good point," conceded Charley. "I'll help with your wind-trackers, too, as soon as Molly's gear is on board here."

The others expressed agreement, less hastily than the Kantrick, and they waited with their varying levels of patience for the acceleration warning.

Enigma became visible during the next watch, and by the time Molly was back on Con duty, the little world could be seen in some detail. The only trouble was that there were no real details to see. Its surface was largely hidden by a blanket of cloud, though not quite as completely as those of Venus and Titan in her own system. The veil glowed even whiter than that of the former planet in the glare of Arc and its companion. Neither the clouds nor their gaps provided patterns that offered meaning to the Human mind.

That, she reminded herself, was in what she considered proper lighting. The atmosphere—obviously there was one—could be supporting clouds of water or ammonia droplets, solid crystals of either substance, or light-colored dust—really light-colored; salts of alkali or alkaline-earth metals, possibly silica or rutile, but, except for the last, probably nothing from the transition metal part of the table that would absorb what to her was visible light. She shifted her instrument through the spectrum experimentally to see whether any albedo features might show at other wavelengths. There was some streakiness in the ultraviolet that reminded her of Venus in the same range, but interpreting this as wind was probably premature. A little work indicated that the cloud tops were at a temperature of about two hundred Kelvin, moderately comfortable for most of her friends but too cold to narrow down the chemical possibilities for the clouds themselves.

She cut off her screen and sat back to think.

"I tried a Doppler display, Molly." It was Jenny's harsh voice; the Rimmore woman was on watch instead of Joe, who was still manufacturing wind-robots. She was as diffident as the Nethneen about interrupting someone at work, but less likely to interpret physical inactivity as mental labor.

"Does it suggest anything? May I look?" asked Molly.

"I was hoping you would. I think so." Jenny keyed her monitor controls to the general output circuits, and the other woman shifted hers to take the picture. She had to modify the presentation colors, of course, but this took only a few seconds, and once she had a visible image she could see immediately that the other had some useful information.

"It *is* wind—I thought it might be from the cloud pattern."

"I've had practice with this," replied the Rimmore. "There's one big difference between Ivory and Hrimm, you know. Ivory has decent gravity and general temperature, and even a breathable atmosphere—"

"Yes. There aren't many people at the School who can walk around on one of its planets with no environment armor. But what's the difference?"

"Climate—that is, the way weather changes with time. At home on Hrimm, the equatorial and orbital planes are only fifteen degrees apart, and Hrimm rotates in about eighteen hours. Ivory has a forty-degree inclination and a thirty-seven-hour rotation. Air circulation is simply weird, and I did a lot of work on it, both from the surface and from space."

"Good for you, Jen. There's some more work to be done

here, but I'd guess offhand that this place has seasons. The rotation axis is somewhere near *there*, the end toward us out of sunlight, the one having winter. Does your world have seasons of that sort?"

"Yes."

"Then I'd say you're picking up high-altitude winds from the winter hemisphere to the summer one, running two or three hundred kilometers an hour at the cloud tops. Cool air would be—hey, that doesn't make sense. High circulation ought to be the other way, shouldn't it?"

"I would have thought so." Jenny shifted sinuously at her station, her iridescent scales shimmering through her transparent air-suit.

"Rotation is—let's see—by my criteria, the northern hemisphere is having summer now. We'll need more orbit data to see how long it's been so and how much longer it will be. As I remember size, rotation must be—no, forget that. There's no way to tell how much of the east-west component of those winds can be credited to the solid planet."

"Not until we have surface imaging," agreed Jenny. "There are some old maps available, as I recall the original notes we were given. Radar ones from space; anything students did on the surface in earlier exercises has been sealed, I suppose."

"So Charley insists." Molly thought for a moment. "We'd better call up the orbit data; we're going to have to think about seasons here. Surely they haven't sealed that—it's information anyone could get in seconds with ordinary navigation equipment."

"They may expect us to get it from the student crew," Jenny pointed out, "and sealed it from them."

Molly nodded absently and played with her console. The other woman followed on her own screen. Both made gestures equivalent to a head nod as the requested information appeared. The Faculty was not expecting them to waste time, it seemed.

"Good," rasped Jenny. "Very slow rotation—about twenty-three days." Molly started to glance at the clock, then remembered that the translator would have turned whatever the Rimmore had actually said into her own days. "Nothing to affect our Doppler wind reading seriously. Joe will want this; it will help him plan the initial setup of his air-current monitors."

"Right," agreed Molly. "You'd better do the saving—it was your idea, and I'm likely to pick colors he couldn't distinguish on the display. I'll be looking for records of surface structure; someone must have given it a going over in radar."

"We can do that ourselves."

"Not from here, with any decent resolution. We will if we have to when we get close in."

"We'd better anyway. Surfaces change," Molly agreed absently; she was already keying through records for anything there might be about Enigma's topography. It was a young planet, of course; it had to be—stars like Arc and its companion were too massive and luminous to last more than a million years or two. The surprising thing was that a planet existed at all; material that had not been incorporated into the two stars should still have been in the form of protoplanetary junk, and most of that should by rights be ejected from the binary system before it ever managed to coalesce.

No other planets. Correction: no record of other *known* planets. Probably a safe datum; from Enigma's well-lit neighborhood forty-odd astronomical units from Arc, anything of decent size would be clearly visible even against a rich star background. Not even Charley would suggest that such records would have been sealed to make a more complex exercise for future students.

Especially since there *was* a map available. Molly recorded it with pleasure, and began looking it over in detail. It was entirely topographic, with no clue to surface composition; there were fairly large areas that appeared smooth to within the resolving limits of whatever instrument had been used, but whether these might be liquid, seas or lakes, could only be guessed.

She would have to do better than guess. There should be some order to her own planning—where would it be best to take samples for dating? Where would the oldest specimens show? The object was far too small—less than three thousand kilometers in diameter, smaller than Earth's moon—to have crustal plate motion, but there were irregularities. Volcanoes? Possibly; silicate bodies that large could generate plenty of radioactive heat in the Solar system, and the

Eta Carinae region was even richer in heavy elements than Molly's own part of space.

The map, annoyingly, had a purely arbitrary coordinate system; no one had tied the physical surface shapes in with the rotation axis. Change or no change, the team would have to remap as they approached Enigma, as Jenny had said.

The watch ended with no further data, except for minor changes in the wind patterns that neither woman tried to analyze. Both of them spent the time planning.

"That's all the wind-tracers I want," Joe said thankfully, dropping his tendrils from the shop's console. "Even with Jenny's very helpful high-altitude Doppler map, there seems no reason to do any more regions simultaneously. Twenty masters started at symmetrically spaced sites, each with five subordinate units covering altitudes from surface up to two hundred kilometers or so, should gather enough air-current information in the time we have. As soon as Molly and Charley finish the radar map they're doing now and decide where to do their mineral sampling, we'll be ready for dropoff. The tent has been checked both by us and the regular crew, and will give us work space besides the boat until *Classroom* gets back. All apparatus except the units we have just finished is on the boat; so is the tent. I think we're about ready to go."

"I hope so." Carol got up from her own board, walking around the shop rather uneasily—her home gravity was nearly as great as Molly's and about four times *Classroom*'s real-space acceleration. Only Joe was really comfortable in that respect. "I hope so. The more I think about my own part of the project, the sillier it seems. I agree with Molly—Enigma has to be a very young planet, and that may be the only reason it has any air left at all. Still, it's sort of ideal in temperature and atmosphere for prelife conditions, it seems to me, and there could be some very unusual chemistry contributing to the problem we've been handed. The chances, though, when I actually try to evaluate them—"

"You can't evaluate them, dear," cut in Jenny. "You know that. I think you did much better chancing a low-probability item to check than Charley did in following Molly blindly—with all due respect to Molly. I agree that the chance of actual life on a world like Enigma is essentially zero, but you're quite right about the prelife. It's above the melting point of ammonia at the surface, and the pressure seems high enough to allow liquid. There is certainly a lot of photochemistry in the clouds and above them—no, your only trouble will be deciding where to stop collecting data. I rather wish I'd done a Charley with your project—I will help, as much as I have time for, of course."

"Of course." Joe had waited for the Rimmore to finish but not long enough for anyone else to start. "The actual work planning will have to be done without regard to who is doing who's job but entirely on who has time available. There will, we must remember, also be work not directly connected with the research but with keeping us all alive, which will also have to be done. You will note that nothing was said in the final approval form about who would do any task, or about government or leadership. None of us had mentioned this in his or her proposal, and the Faculty is quite capable of leaving us to discover for ourselves the need for such organization. I mention this now, before dropoff, only as a reminder; I am sure we are all ready to cooperate fully in all tasks that we agree to be desirable and necessary."

Both women looked at the Nethneen thoughtfully.

"I did rather overlook that point," grated Jenny. "The Human seems to have the most forceful personality, but I am not sure whether all of us . . ." She did not complete the sentence.

"I'm a little surprised that Charley overlooked it—if he did," remarked Carol.

"It's more surprising still that he hasn't mentioned it," returned Jenny.

"I am quite willing to leave the matter open for the time being, once I am sure that everyone has given thought to the necessity." Joe's quiet tones resumed. "Should I mention it again when the others join us from their mapping task, or should I wait and speak to them one at a time, or would one of you prefer to handle the matter? I do consider it vital that everyone be aware of the need for cooperation, and I know that there is a wide range of opinion in the School about the best way to assure this."

There was silence for a moment while the others thought.

Then the Shervah spoke. "Either of us can speak to Molly. Maybe you'd better take it up with Charley in private, Joe. I don't think I understand him as well as I do the Human, and I'm pretty sure Jenny feels the same." A ripple of agreement flowed along the Rimmore's body.

"Very well. We have nearly twenty hours before drop-off; I can find an appropriate occasion during that interval, I am sure. Let's get this last stuff to the boat."

"And I want some time out of this suit, for a shampoo. Molly's insulation may be longer, but at least it's only on her head, not all over," added Carol.

Drop-off itself was uneventful; unlike the emergency drill, they were given plenty of time to board the boat, complete all checks, and separate from the huge bulk of *Classroom*. By this time they were only a few thousand kilometers from Enigma, though no attempt had been made to match velocities with the little world. It would be up to the students to do this, or, more accurately, to let their machinery do it for them; they were not student pilots and had only the normal educated grasp of the vector problem involved.

Not even Molly was looking outside directly. She might have been able to view the white half-moon of the planet without injury, but even she wanted nothing to do with the direct output from the O-type supergiant called Arc by the Human students. The other four not only contented themselves with false-color screen images of their surroundings but by common consent let Molly do the "piloting." Hot stars were her normal environment, they considered, though they would have admitted, if asked, that there was really more difference between Arc and her G-type sun than between the latter and any of theirs. Unfortunately, they had without exception an almost Human tendency to be more impressed by qualitative analogies and symbols than by quantitative reality. Molly was detached enough, at the moment, to be amused.

Velocity matching took some time, mostly because of Joe's low acceleration tolerance; the Nethneen home world had about eighteen percent of Earth's surface gravity. It had been decided that there was no real reason to pick one landing spot over another, with one exception; the arctic zone was to be avoided. That polar region was currently having summer, and even shielded by the heavy clouds, the students would require extra protection from Arc's scattered light. Otherwise, the surface was uniform enough so that any general topography it offered could be found within a few hundred kilometers of any given spot. This greatly simplified landing maneuvers, even with ship's brain essentially in control.

In a way, it might have been better had a living pilot—even a student one—handled the last part of the landing. The boat itself had such perfect inertial sensing and such quick response that neither Molly nor any of the others felt the wind. The craft's guidance equipment had already detected the planet's solid surface and was allowing for air currents, and the faint trembling of the structure that they all felt was assumed to be normal aerodynamic stress—even Joe and Charley had made landings on planets with atmosphere, virtually airless though their own worlds were.

Once into the white clouds, Jenny paid no attention to the boat's behavior; she was occupied in collecting samples for analysis. Molly kept her attention outside, shifting the sensors that fed her vision screen up and down the spectrum, but for some minutes was unable to tell whether the lack of view was due to lack of penetration or lack of anything to see. The other three remained apparently calm; all were accustomed to automatically controlled flight under varying conditions, though this was certainly different from space.

The pilot screen eventually cleared. They seemed to be beneath the solid cloud deck, but in either a snow or dust storm—Molly was using what she considered ordinary light, so the stuff must have been *really* white. All that was getting through the clouds was a dim glow, crepuscular even to the other team members. Visibility was fair, perhaps ten kilometers, and in another minute or two ground appeared below.

It looked about the way the radar map had implied: ripply, with an occasional peak strongly suggestive of a volcano. None of the hills was large—none had been on the map, either. Neither she nor Charley had had any success whatever in matching the charts they had made during approach with those they had obtained from the records. There had been no large-scale features for guidance; one might as well have tried to match two areas of pebble sidewalk that did not include ends or edges. Even an hour of computer comparison did no good; either there were more possible scales and orientations than the machine could handle in that time, or the surface had made significant and general changes in its detailed topography since the earlier map had been produced. Knowing the machine, Molly was inclined to the latter view.

This had interesting implications, even if a few thousand of her years had passed since the previous map had been made. The implications were even more interesting if the time were much shorter. There seemed no way to tell from the records.

The boat's two-hundred-meter hull settled to the surface and sank some meters into it—Molly still could not decide whether the material was soil, sand, or snow.

"First requirement is a life center independent of the ship," Joe pointed out. "I'll go outside to see whether the ground is suitable for the tent."

"But shouldn't we—" Molly started. Then she remembered and smiled.

"You're too environment conscious, Molly." The Nethneen chuckled. "The temperature is quite comfortable, and I don't care what the air is made of. The pressure is high enough to keep me from boiling—a good deal higher than normal"—he gestured toward the instrument panel— "and for once the gravity is respectable."

Jenny gave a snort through several sets of breathing vents at once. "I'm glad there's someone here who can feel gravity," she muttered. "As far as I'm concerned, we're still floating." Molly felt much the same, though her home gravity was little more than half that of the Rimmore, and nodded in sympathy.

"Joe, it still seems to me that checking outside details would make a lot of sense before anyone stepped out. We don't know that the air isn't corrosive—there are worlds like Jenny's or mine with free oxygen, and that wouldn't be good for your skin even if you don't ingest it, would it?"

"I've spent time in oxygen atmospheres," the Nethneen replied, "and even without analysis I refuse to worry about that element here. It is thermodynamically unstable, strictly a product of life, and if there is any life on a planet this young, I'll be delighted to take the risk of an oxygen burn just to see it."

"But how about the stuff that's blowing? Surely you're not claiming that *no* chemical can hurt you."

Joe hesitated for several seconds. "Perhaps that would be a bit excessive," he said at last. "Jenny, have you made anything of the cloud composition and of this precipitate that presumably is coming from them?"

The centipedelike form turned back to her instruments and was busy for a minute or so.

"Not a simple substance," she said at last. "Largely ammonium salts; carbamate, carbonate, amide, traces of water ice, urea, and a lot more—it will take a long time to run a complete list. A good deal of what you'd expect from reactions between gases in this atmosphere."

"But nothing clearly dangerous."

"Nothing that waves a flag to me."

Joe gave the rippling arm gesture that was his equivalent of an affirmative head nod and was at the door in two long, gliding steps, something his tentacular legs could not have managed under decent gravity, Molly reflected. "We'll keep lock protocol," he said as he opened it. "Outer atmosphere could be a nuisance to some of the rest of you." He closed the valve behind him, and Molly activated the screen showing the inside of the air lock. The Nethneen had already opened a bleeder valve and was letting outside air in to bring the pressure up. This was causing him no visible distress.

The team watched him reach for the key that opened the outer door, and as he did so the ship trembled very slightly.

Jenny, Molly, and Carol simultaneously shouted a warning.

"Joe! No! Wait!"

They were too late.

OF COURSE THE BOAT WON'T LAST

"You knew what was going to happen!" cried Charley.

Molly shook her head. "We should have. Any air breather should have, but we were too slow. It didn't occur to either of us—to any of us—" she included Carol with her glance—"that he would never think of wind, or what wind would do on a low-gravity world like this. Blame me or us all you want, but let's decide what to do."

"Ask him what condition he is in, I would say" was the suggestion from the Shervah.

"How—? Oh, of course. His translator should still be in touch. Joe? Can you hear us? Are you hurt?"

"Clearly enough. I am not hurt but greatly embarrassed. I was thinking only of the chemical effects of gases and had forgotten their physical potentialities."

"Where are you? Are you still being blown away?"

"I can offer no answer to the first question, even assuming the boat's location as starting coordinate. I traveled for an unknown but brief time at an unknown speed in whatever direction the gas carried me. Just now I am no longer traveling. I struck a sloping surface composed of powdery material, was carried up it and over the top. I fell down the farther side, where the gas was not moving nearly so rapidly but much more erratically. I have dug my way into the surface, to avoid further involuntary travel, since I don't know that the gas speed will remain low. I am presumably not very far from the boat. Since we have no absolute direction reference as yet, I suggest that you find which way the gas is moving now, as soon as you can; I would judge that its inertia would prevent a really great velocity change in this short time. This should provide the only clue I can think of at the moment to my direction."

"How do we do that?" asked Charley. "I don't think we have an instrument that would . . ." His voice trailed off. The three women were at the console, using the outside screens, looking first in one direction and then another.

"There's a hill about half a kilometer away," Carol pointed out. "There'll be some eddying."

"Do what we can," replied Molly. "The sand, or snow, or whatever it is seems to be coming from about there." She had her screen centered some thirty degrees to the right of Carol's hill. After a few moments' checking with their own viewers, the others agreed.

"Then Joe should be in the opposite direction." Carol lined up her pickup as she spoke. "There does seem to be a broad, low hill that way. Maybe it's the one you went over, Joe. I wish this stuff would stop blowing; we could see more clearly and maybe come after you."

"If it would stop blowing, I could get back by myself," the Nethneen pointed out. "How about it, you heavy-atmosphere types; do we expect this to go on indefinitely, or will it stop reasonably soon? Or does the fact that this planet rotates make prediction impossible?"

"Difficult," replied Molly. "There isn't time for a talk about weather and forecasting just now. I don't know whether this wind is a local storm good for a few hours, or something that will last for the next twenty or thirty years until the season changes. Any planning we do had better include the breeze, and we'll just be grateful for the luck if it drops." The other air-breathers gestured agreement.

Charley, not used to feeling helpless and disliking the sensation, made a suggestion. "Couldn't we take the ship to the other side of the hill?"

"We could," answered Molly slowly, "if we were sure we could avoid putting it down on Joe if he's there and getting back to this spot to restore his only possible reference point if he turns out not to be."

Jenny suddenly straightened and elevated the front half of her two meter body. "We could send one of his own wind-robots after him!" she exclaimed. "They're inertially guided and supposed to hold position or travel on a predetermined path regardless of the air current—"

"That sounds hopeful" came Joe's voice. "But reprogramming will be needed first. They are programmed to fly into the wind—I wanted them to determine sources, not sinks. That can be changed, of course. Someone will have to make them go *with* the current, but at a very restricted speed so that I can catch it if it does come close—no, I won't be able even to see it unless it comes pretty close. Someone will have to ride with it, using it as a vehicle, and alter its course or stop it when and as needed. You all know the machinery well enough to do the control changes; I think Jenny's thought is excellent."

"The idea is good, but offers practical difficulties," pointed out Molly. "Your controls are easily keyed by your tendrils. Charley and Jenny and I can't even get handlers in to them, and even if I could reach them, I don't think my fingers are delicate enough to—"

"True," cut in Carol. "Not to be critical, dear, but Humans are clumsy. You drop crumbs from your cake. Also you are large and massive, which may not mean too much in this gravity, but since the robots were not designed to carry anything and the driver will have to be fastened to the machine to keep from being blown away like Joe, it probably is significant. Let's get one of those machines. I'll rework the program."

All four started to leave the conning room; Jenny stopped before they reached the door. "Charley, you're enough to help Carol if she needs any. Molly and I had better stay here and observe. Our first trouble seems to have happened because we acted without learning enough about this place."

"A good thought" came Joe's voice. Charley seemed hesitant, but when Molly nodded and turned back with the Rimmore he swallowed whatever he had been about to say and went on with the small woman.

"Carol had better wear full environmental armor when she goes out," the Human remarked as they settled back in the observing stations. "I think we'd better act as though we didn't know how long we were going to be out *whenever* we go outside on this world."

"No one thinks of everything." Jenny performed her equivalent of a shrug.

"True, but I'd come to think of Joe as a bit above that sort of slip."

"Maybe he had, too." For a moment Molly wondered how the Nethneen would be affected by that remark; then she remembered that both translators would have shifted to private channels in response to the tones of the speakers. Most of the team members had established such links when the group first formed, though none existed between Charley and the two nonhuman women. Molly had been rather disturbed by this at the time, but decided that there was nothing she could say that would be better than silence. Some species, of course, had a strongly negative attitude toward the idea of privacy in any form—though this could not be Charley's reason, since he had set up channels with Joe and Molly on his own initiative.

In any case, the remark had been made, Joe had probably not heard it, and if he had, he was either detached enough not to resent it or a good enough actor not to show it. Perhaps more important was the likelihood that Charley had not heard it, either.

Those thoughts flickered through Molly's mind too quickly to interfere with important questions; she didn't even miss Jenny's next point.

"Carol will have to take Joe's armor along."

"I thought of that" came the Shervah's voice. "Charley is getting it ready and will figure out some way of fastening it to the machine."

"I'm afraid I was not foresighted enough to provide the bodies with convenient points of attachment," Joe remarked. "I should have made more allowance for the unforeseen. I begin to see why the Faculty insists on a certain amount of laboratory and field work before granting any sort of rating."

"That annoyed me when I first got here," remarked Molly. "I had a perfectly good doctorate in structure from a place on New Pembroke and was quite ready to make clear how much I knew to anyone who cared. They let me take charge of a lab group doing an exercise on Sink—"

"I know that one," remarked Jenny.

"—and I started to set up some outside equipment in ordinary space armor. All that kept me from losing my feet was the fact that the gravity was low enough to let me walk fifty meters on my hands. My brains had nothing to do with it. An ice ball at a temperature of about six Kelvins can really suck heat from a suit; even my hands were losing their feeling by the time I got back to safety. The worst of it was that I couldn't say anything to my six-year-old except that I'd been stupid, and his father had to agree with me."

"Do you think the child will be able to profit by the lesson?" Jenny asked with interest.

"I can only hope. I certainly did. This Faculty knows enough about teaching to let us make our own mistakes, I found out. At least your robots can be reprogrammed, Joe," pointed out Molly.

"When I was designing them, I had not made up my mind about the best way to use them. As you've already noticed, I did not give thought enough to who might have to do the programming."

"Are conditions still the same where you are, Joe?" Jenny cut in. "I know you've buried yourself, but with this wind it might be wise to make sure you're not getting buried even more deeply. That hill you were carried over sounded suspiciously like a dune, and if you can't get to the surface when Carol is near you she might as well stay here."

"My translator has no symbol for dune, but the concept of blowing sand makes sense. A moment while I try. It's just as well this happened to me rather than you, Jenny; I can see nothing while buried, and for you the gravity is so weak you probably couldn't tell which way is up." He fell silent for a few seconds. "I'm uncovered. I don't think I was any deeper, though I admit I hadn't measured. I do have an impression that the slope of the hill that I descended is a trifle closer than when I dug in; is that the sort of thing you had in mind?"

"Precisely. I suggest you measure the distance from the nearest point now, give us the figure, and dig in again if you wish for another quarter hour. We'll call you at that time to come out and make another measurement. I won't be at all surprised if the dune is crawling toward you; they do that. Right, Molly? On your world, too?"

"Yes, or so I've read. I have no firsthand experience, and wouldn't know what speed to expect."

"I have." Jenny's tone was grim, over and above its usual grating sound.

"I am four meters from the slope, as nearly as I can judge" came Joe's voice. "Something is starting to itch; I must dig in again."

"Get a couple of meters farther, first," snapped the Rimmore.

"All right." Silence fell again. The two observers collected what data they could; Molly was a little surprised at the lack of basic instrumentation. There was no direct way to obtain wind velocity, for example. Granted that this was a space-craft, it was also supposed to be part of a research facility. Even if the makers had not themselves been native to a planet with a reasonable atmosphere, anyone around a Leinster site—a place like Eta Carinae likely to attract spacefaring species because it was a scientific curiosity—should have at least heard of *wind*.

Of course, Joe hadn't remembered it. And this was a *student* facility, designed to teach people not to take too much for granted, she must remember. She'd simply have to improvise. She and Jenny analyzed the gas around them, refined the work Jenny had already done on the dust/sand/snow, set up a computer watch on the inertial navigation system to get a more precise measure of the planet's rotation rate and their latitude, located the sun by judicious selection of wavelengths in the boat's sensors, established their present location arbitrarily as longitude zero for convenience in future work, and determined that astronomically they must be in the southern hemisphere. Just how far south, in both angular and linear units, would come with increasing precision over the next few minutes as the computer compared inertial data with Arc's apparent motion.

Presently Jenny stopped work and called to Joe. "Dig out and see how far the hill is, please. I should have reminded you earlier but got absorbed."

"I was thinking myself," replied the Nethneen. "Just a moment." It was rather more than the implied quarter of a minute, but the answer was a relief. "As far as I can tell, the slope is very little nearer—certainly not more than half a meter, and I think less. I must remember to keep a measuring device attached to my person in the future; this estimating is most unsatisfactory."

"At least you're not about to be buried alive," responded Molly. "Dig in again if you want. Carol must be nearly ready to go out."

"Just starting" came the voice of the tiny humanoid. "Charley has sealed up Joe's armor so it won't fill with sand before we get it to him and roped it to the robot so that it'll stick—Joe and I may have trouble detaching it, but it won't blow away."

"Will you need help getting out?" asked Molly.

"No more than Charley can supply, I'd say. Watch from where you are, and make sure nothing goes wrong; you can keep Joe informed as long as I'm in sight. I'll use one of the ports down here, as soon as Charley has his armor on, too. He's not taking chances, either. Two or three minutes now. If you're really as close as you think, I should be with you very quickly, Joe."

The two observers switched active sensors to cover the ground where they expected Carol to appear, and waited, eyes on screens. There was no way to pick up the port itself, either from inside or out, and they both selected surface viewpoints a little downwind of its location—if anything did go wrong, they would catch it promptly.

Nothing did, however. "All right, close up again!" came Carol's voice. "This thing is holding steady. Let me key in—there; one. Downwind drift at about a third of a meter a second—you should be seeing me any moment, up in Con. Let me know."

Three or four seconds later both observers called out simultaneously. "There you are." "Steady as a ground roller," added Jenny. Molly was not sure whether the reference was to a vehicle or some animal native to Jenny's world, but was equally satisfied with the situation. The robot was a vertical cylinder about a meter in diameter and three quarters as high, with the projecting rim of its field shaper forming a platform eighteen or twenty centimeters wide around the bottom. Carol was standing on one side of this and Joe's armor sprawled on the other, both attached with festoons of rope that looped around the entire structure. The machine hung some ten centimeters clear of the ground, rock-steady in the still-violent wind; as its rider had said, its motion was perfectly smooth, controlled by its own inertial system, sensors, and drive fields. Carol's thirty-plus kilograms on one side, poorly balanced by Joe's empty suit on the other, did not seem to bother the drive system at all.

Molly and Jenny watched silently as the figure shrank with distance. The latter keyed in a ranging sensor and set automatic magnification to keep the image large enough for details; Molly kept her scale unchanged, preferring to see directly how Carol was approaching the dune, if dune it was, that lay downwind. It occurred to her that the robot might try to plow into the surface as the latter rose, but either Joe or Carol had anticipated that in the program; the Shervah started to ride up the hill without incident.

As she neared the top, Molly called out, "I don't know whether you can tell slope very well from where you are, Carol, but it looks from here as though you were about to go over the edge that Joe described, if you're really following his track. If the far side is really steep, will the robot stay upright? I don't recall the guidance program well enough."

"It should" came the Nethneen's voice. "Tell me when she disappears—or Carol, you tell me when you start downhill—and I'll dig out and watch for you."

"I'm at the edge" was Carol's immediate response. "The slope in front of me is very steep and loose. Sand is blowing past me and falling over—I can see why the hill is crawling toward you. Here I come."

"Then it *is* a dune," Jenny remarked with audible satisfaction.

"Not only that, it's Joe's dune," replied Carol. "There he is, seventy or eighty meters to my right."

"Can you see her, Joe?" asked Jenny.

"Not against the sky glare. It's painful even to look up. The main question is whether she can see me, and that she's answered."

"Does that machine ride downhill all right?" asked Molly.

"It doesn't know the difference," the Shervah assured her. "I'll be at the bottom in a few seconds. Joe, you can cover up again for a moment or two if the blowing stuff hurts; I know where you are but will have to redirect this thing. As you said, the air currents here are irregular, and I'll have to cut the wind sensor out of the guidance plan and just travel—let's see—this will take some time—no, not so long at that—there, that should do it. Come up again when I call out—now! Good! You can see me this time, surely."

"Yes. Here you are. Let's get that armor ready. Charley, did you improvise with these ropes, or do you have experience?"

"Well, I have used them before, but not very much. Is there some trouble?"

"With all due recognition that a knot should not untie itself, it should be possible for someone to untie it. This one—there, it's coming now. Can you come around to this side yet, Carol?"

"Not yet. There was more than one knot. I have one here—now it's coming—I'll be right with you—there, it's loose. WATCH OUT!"

"What's the matter?" cried Molly.

"The armor is loose—it's blowing away—even in this wind where we can stand!"

"Don't worry," said Joe. "There's another rope holding it. Just don't untie that one until I'm inside—it's fastened to a leg piece, and I can open up without undoing it."

"Some things don't need experience," Charley remarked complacently. "A little foresight is enough."

"Your foresight is appreciated. The thought of chasing that suit at full wind speed—"

"We could have brought the ship over, now that we know where you are. We still can, if you want," Molly cut in.

"I'd rather like to try riding the robot upwind, as it was meant to go, if Carol doesn't object. We'll have to change positions, Carol, so that I can get at the access panel. You don't seem to have had any trouble with redirecting; I'd better make sure I can do it as easily."

"All right. This last rope seems to go all the way around; we'll stay inside it and work our way to the right simultaneously. It's lucky we're not as big as Molly or Jenny."

"The drive would support them easily enough."

"They'd have trouble fitting, though maybe one of them could balance on top. There, can you reach in?"

"Yes, thank you. There is another trouble that I had not thought of, though. The blowing sand is getting in when the access panel is open. If it packs too tightly, I will not be able to get at the controls themselves. There, I think we are all right. Hold on. We should now head upwind, at about the same speed you came down."

The observers looked at each other. There was a faint grin on the Human face and an equivalent twist to the Rimmore body. Neither said anything, but Molly moved over to the boat's main controls. Silence continued for another minute or more, to be broken finally by Joe's quiet tones.

"Do any of you air breathers have a word for a wind that goes around in small circles?"

"We call such a current an eddy, Joe," replied Molly. "Shall I bring the boat over, or do you want to reprogram without using the pressure sensors?"

"Bring the boat. I don't think I'd better open the panel again." The translator was doing a good job; Joe's tone carried resignation.

"Interesting but a bit anticlimactic." Rather to Molly's surprise, the remark was Carol's. The little woman was back in the conning room, her armor shed; she had found time at last to improvise a simple transparent envelope that held her high pressure and showed her gleaming dark-brown fur. As far as could be told from appearance she was feeling no more excitement than her words suggested. Joe had no eyebrows to raise, but he shifted his body position enough to bring two pairs of his optics to bear on the speaker.

"If you are here for emotional release," Joe said, "I wish you luck; but I must admit that I don't plan to cooperate. I also admit that while that experience was educational—defining education as anything one lives through to profit by—I look back on it with much more embarrassment than pleasure. I can attribute the event to nothing but my own lack of thought."

"As Molly said the time that I made a fool of myself, no one can foresee everything. Those of us who haven't done something as silly so far will probably manage it before we finish here."

"I hope you are wrong, Charley. Where are you now? The rest of us are ready to get the planned program going, I think. We should settle finally our personal schedules of activity."

"All right. I can hear you. I'm trying to be foresighted again."

"In what way?" rasped Jenny. "Where are you, anyway?"

"In the shop. I'm making handholds and tie rings to put on all the master robots, and distributing a hundred meters of rope on each."

"Did you check with Joe?"

"I'm not harming his machinery, just cementing things to the outer shells, away from gas intakes, pressure sensors, and the like. In view of what just happened, I'm sure Joe would be the last to object."

"A good thought. I should have done it myself," admitted the Nethneen. "I strongly suggest, however, that no one leave the boat in future without very detailed planning and without taking as much potentially useful material as can conveniently be carried."

Molly shook her head. "A standard emergency kit is one thing," she said. "Everything one *might* need is hopeless."

"Of course," agreed Joe. "I realize that—there would be no upper limit, especially for beings who regard the creation of an imaginary series of events as an art form. You take me too literally."

Molly smiled to herself but made no answer. Her first acquaintance with Joe and Charley, nearly a year before, had been during a School routine translator check. The institution's central data handler on Think, one of the common planets of the Fire-Smoke binary, was still somewhat limited in Human-language figures of speech, and a Faculty group working on the problem had asked her to describe any of the students who happened to be near her at the moment, for the translator's benefit. Charley had been a dozen meters away, and she had taken him as her subject; the computer had returned a symbol set that gave the Faculty analysts the impression that she had meant Joe, who was also in the neighborhood. The two *did* have a superficial resemblance, and neither student, when brought into the conversation, seemed to be offended by the mistake. Charley, after pointing out a dozen detail differences, emphasizing size, had closed with a commiserating "Even if he does grow up, he'll never have a decent shell!"

Joe, much later in a private conversation with Molly and her husband, had explained why he hadn't made the obvious answer, though by then the Humans knew him well enough to guess the reason. "It might have offended you, Molly; you have hard parts, too, even if they are inside. Like the main translator, I didn't know about Human figurative expression—even irony—then."

"I don't know." Charley's voice brought Molly back to the present. "I've been thinking of quite a few things that might go wrong in this environment, and—"

"By all means design an emergency kit around them. One that *I* can carry—in a high wind combined with low gravity!" snapped Carol. The Kantrick made no answer, but Molly felt pretty sure that he wasn't bothered. Here, too, he would probably take the suggestion literally.

After a brief pause that no one seemed inclined to interrupt, Jenny resumed the situation summary.

"We've just been reminded that we can not only fail in this exercise, we can get injured or killed while trying. I don't know how many of your languages distinguish among terms for lab exercise, research, and exploration; if anyone got the same codes for any two of those, we'd better spend some time with the translators." She paused, but no one spoke. "Good. This is not just an exercise, no matter what earlier students found out about this place that we haven't been told. If nothing else, no machine is perfect, and if something serious goes wrong with the boat before the *Classroom* gets back, we'll have to live with the results."

"We have the tent, which we're supposed to set up first thing," pointed out Charley.

"Precisely. If there were anyone else around to snatch us out of trouble, we wouldn't have been supplied with so much emergency equipment. There are reaction dampers in a student chemistry lab, but not environmental armor unless reactions that even the instructors can't handle are expected. Think it over. Joe was lucky. We can't count on luck consistently."

Molly noticed that there was no code break here, either; everyone's translator had some term for *luck*. The real question, she thought, was whether it meant quite the same to all of them.

There was another pause, broken this time by Joe.

"Your points are well made, Jenny. The only precaution

I can see for setting up the tent is that it not be too close downwind to any of those dunes. It is strong but might not take too large a hill climbing over it even in this gravity. As far as I can see, the ship's present location should be all right, and Molly and Jenny have already started the coordinate system from here. Any other thoughts?"

"Should we check a few more spots on the planet to see whether this wind is universal?" asked Jenny. "A quieter region might be better and safer for the tent."

"Could we be sure such a region would remain windless?"

The air breathers, even Jenny, all made emphatic negative gestures.

"Then the time spent looking for such a spot would probably be wasted. I propose we unload and set up here. Were you listening, Charley? Do you agree?"

"I heard. This is perfectly good for the tent, if that's what you meant about my agreeing. We should get at it quickly, too; of course the boat isn't going to last."

OF COURSE IT WILL

Charley refused to elaborate on his remark, though he did not seem bothered at having made it. "Just a hypothesis. Perhaps the *of course* was a bit excessive, but we'll see" was all he would say. Since he was still out of sight there was no way to check his expression, even if any of them had felt confident reading Kantrick body language. Joe, perhaps—no. Molly had to remind herself consciously that the resemblance between Charley and Joe was really little greater than that between herself and Carol; she could probably read any of the others, including Charley, just as well as he.

Carol was less restrained. "If that talking *thramm*—sorry, Joe, I know the shape is irrelevant—has any real reason to believe there's something wrong with this boat, hypothesis or better, he has no business keeping it to himself. If he's afraid of looking silly because it turns out to be wrong, he'll be a lot sillier if he keeps quiet and is right, and we failed to—"

"Sorry, Carol," the Kantrick assured her, "but it isn't at that level at all. There is nothing for you or the rest of us to worry about, no matter what I said or think of the boat. I'm sorry I said anything."

"But if this craft fails, there's *plenty* for us to worry about. You're talking nonsense."

"No, I'm not," Charley responded. "You'll see why, if I'm right, and if I'm not there's no danger, either. Let's get the tent out, unless we should rest and eat first." Carol sputtered into silence. Jenny changed the subject.

"It looks a little as though the wind were going down. Maybe we should set up one of Joe's machines outside, programmed to keep station and report ram pressure readings to us. If it's a real decrease, and we can be sure of it before the tent is ready to go out, it might be worth scheduling a rest period before actually setting it up. Wind won't bother the tent, but it would be a lot easier for us to have quiet air while we're outside."

"Good idea." Charley was clearly eager to discuss something besides his remark. "If Joe or Carol will do the programming, I'm still in armor down here and can put the thing out."

With six hours of sleep and a good meal, Molly found that she didn't care much whether the storm had ended. She trimmed her mahogany hair, which was getting a little long for air suit and armor, and joined the others, eager to face what Enigma had to offer. By the time anyone went outside again, however, the wind had dropped so far that even the smallest and lightest of them had little trouble walking. The tent was no trouble in any case; it was basically a set of six small but massive field generators that could be travel-programmed like Joe's robots. Once in position at the corners of a hexagon a dozen meters on an edge, these sprayed out a cloud of highly specialized molecules that were maintained as a film by the fields, rather as a cloud of iron particles might be held in a given pattern by a properly arranged magnetic system. The same field anchored the generators to the ground, and there was no question of blowing away—though, as the group well knew, having the structure buried in an advancing dune might be another matter.

The tent gave much more room for work, and the research equipment was readied well before local sunset, twenty hours after their landing. Jenny had already done a lot more chemistry. The atmosphere's composition was now firmly established; methane, nitrogen, ammonia, and carbon dioxide accounted for ninety-five percent of it. Most of the rest was carbon monoxide and argon. Molly nodded thoughtfully as the Rimmore dealt off this list of words and numbers. It fitted with her own idea of vaporized comet ices and with the fact that there seemed to be no other planets in the system.

"As I suggested, it's just an oversized comet, still vaporizing."

"As you also suggested, a nice prelife mixture," remarked Joe, "with lots of energy available from the sun. If I could think of a way to do it, I'd have my robots check their areas for prebiotic compounds for you when we get them stationed, Jenny."

"I can use parts of Molly's and Charley's samples. They're picking up solids from the same sites."

"Or liquids. In this pressure and temperature range you could have ammonia oceans."

"My translator didn't handle that last word. It gave me a new code. Can anyone clarify?"

"How about *lake* or *river*?" asked Molly.

"Neither one. Both new," replied the Rimmore. The Human woman described the behavior of water and ammonia on planets whose temperature and pressure permitted large amounts of either liquid.

"I see. That doesn't happen on Hrimm. The biological liquid is ammonia, of course, but with a lot of free oxygen in the atmosphere that's not stable—it exists at all only because life forms are constantly producing it. The same, of course, is true of the oxygen, as it must be on your world, Molly. We have ammonia bogs and swamps—did your translators handle those?—but no lakes or oceans."

"So there'd be no oxygen here, either," suggested Carol. "No reason to expect life on a world this young, even with lots of ammonia."

"How about the clouds?" asked Carol.

"Largely ammonium carbamate, which you'd expect to be produced from ammonia and carbon dioxide. Some water-ice crystals, some carbonates of ammonium and alkali metals. The difference between the clouds aloft and the dust down here seems to be a quibble. In connection with your other point, I found only a trace of oxygen, and with all the hard radiation from this sun, that was probably produced from the carbon dioxide," replied Jenny.

"Then we know what we're doing," Joe summed up. "We've picked twenty sites, symmetrically spaced around the planet, starting right here. We drop a drift robot at each and collect samples for analysis, then come back here to the tent, signal the robots to start all at once—not really necessary, but may simplify calculation later—and monitor them and their slaves, doing our analyses from here. By the time *Classroom* gets back, we should have enough data for all our needs—possibly even some that will support our various favorite hypotheses."

Molly felt herself blush at the last remark, and wondered what the equivalent reaction was with the others. The Rimmore watched with interest as the changing background color briefly hid her Human friend's freckles. They both rather expected Charley to give some sort of retort, but it was Carol who made her feelings known, and these seemed unconnected with the Nethneen's gentle gibe.

"Assuming, of course, that the boat gets us back to the tent to work over our data—or is that inconsistent with a favorite hypothesis?"

"Are you worried?" asked Charley. The Shervah turned her head so that both her side-placed eyes could cover the speaker at once; then she rolled them both away from him in opposite directions.

"No." The eye that had come to rest covering Molly winked. The Human wondered what that could mean; her translator had no way of handling gestures. Even with a private channel available, she decided, this was not a good time to ask. She glanced toward Joe.

"All that I need there is on the boat," Joe responded.

"Your robots, too? Everybody else ready to go?"

"One drifter and its slaves are in the tent. I'll set them out when we get back. I'm ready, yes." The others spoke or gestured agreement, and Molly keyed the boat off the surface.

Even without the wind, there was still precipitate; visibility in short waves—short enough for Molly—was only a kilometer or two. This was not dangerous, since the radar maps had shown very little relief on the planet's surface and they were flying high enough to clear all of this, but it was boring. Molly shifted her pickup farther into the infrared, converting it at the screen to light that she could see but that was not short enough in wavelength to bother the others. It would have been possible to hood the screen and keep her face buried in it, but with only her own personal friends present she preferred to feel free to look around. The others, she saw, were also examining the surface flowing past below them. Not real work, by Joe's standards.

So far there was no sign of liquid, in spite of Jenny's pressure report; they might have been over Enigma's Arabian Desert. Dunes, easily recognized from above by their crescent shape, were numerous when they started, but before reaching the first vertex of Joe's imaginary dodecahedron, the sand gave way to what looked more like bare rock. Molly was tempted to land for a sample, but decided against it; she would be busy enough with the scheduled stops, and more specimens could always be obtained if needed. She did not like to display impatience, especially before Joe. She knew he would understand, but didn't want him to have to.

The boat announced the approach to the first site, and a few seconds later came to a halt a few hundred meters above the ground. The five spent only seconds examining the surface, which was not very impressive: bare rock, very smooth on the finer scale, rippled and hummocked with larger irregularities averaging a few dozen meters across and one or two in height. Nothing showed any sign that liquid had ever flowed there, but the surface might well have been polished by wind-blown sand. Without waiting for suggestions from anyone else, Molly keyed the boat to slow descent. It settled to the rock half a minute later.

Joe had already resumed his armor and was out of the conning room before they were down. Carol went with him. Three minutes later the robot—much taller than the one the Shervah had ridden to Joe's rescue, since its slaves were now riding its top—was standing on the polished stone. Charley was outside cutting samples from the hard parts of the surface and scooping up bits of loose material that were lying in smaller hollows. Each went into a separate container, carefully labeled, and Molly recorded the whole procedure visually from on board. Carol was back inside before the Kantrick had finished, but Joe remained beside his machine, fussing with its various controls, until everything else scheduled for the site had been done.

By the tenth landing, everything was both routine and, for

some of the students, boring. Twice they had put down on lakes. Sampling was more interesting there; Jenny had gladly submerged and obtained liquid, solid, and mud specimens. Any of them could have done the same, as their armor was quite adequate for such an environment, but she was the only one used to a liquid environment, and the others felt the usual discomfort at not being able to see normally below the surface. Even Jenny was a little unhappy at so much *clear* liquid; she was used to the tangled vegetation of the swamps of Hrimm, where the combination of climbing and swimming for which her form was so well suited was the standard way to get around.

The twelfth stop was desert again, this time with little evidence of wind. They were on the night side of Enigma now. As they descended, Molly wondered whether really different material would ever turn up. She was getting a little puzzled; the overall size and gravity of the world had matched her comet hypothesis, as had the atmosphere, but the specimens collected so far had not.

The planet's average density, from size and gravity, was about five thirds that of water, which by any reasonable standards suggested that a good deal of its makeup was ice—water, ammonia, carbon dioxide, or methane. The atmosphere strongly supported this notion, but the rocks, at nearly twice the planet's average density, did not. Molly, very prematurely—before coming within sight of the place, in fact—had convinced herself and Charley that Enigma was simply a young ice-and-silicate body that any decently programmed translator would call a comet, but which was far too big and had far too high an escape velocity to show a tail even in Arc's impressive stellar wind.

The ice, it was beginning to appear, was already largely gone from much of the surface; it looked as though she would have to drill for it, and she had not come prepared to do any such thing.

This was embarrassing. She had been given laboratory assignments at School obviously intended to remind her of the need to be prepared for the unexpected. Worse, her present companions had taken the assignments with her. Worse yet, she had done well on them, receiving even Joe's commendation on the way she had gotten the group out of trouble when it had looked for a time as though they had done a prematurely destructive test on a problem sample.

The present situation was not only embarrassing but hard to believe. She had encountered plenty of ice bodies, small and large. There had been comets; there had been Pluto and Titan and Callisto in the Solar system, and Think and Sink in the School one. She knew what ice could do, given a set of temperature and pressure parameters.

If it were all buried, it could not be contributing very rapidly to the atmosphere, and the latter had no business being anything like as dense as it was. At cloud-top temperature, methane and ammonia would escape in a few decades at the outside, even without bothering to consider Arc's ultraviolet and the still faster loss of free hydrogen. The Human did not really enjoy mathematical modeling, but it looked as though she were going to have to play at it.

After the present supply of data had been gathered and organized, of course. There might be easier explanations.

"We're coming down in a crater." Joe's quiet tones cut into Molly's cogitation. Her fingers moved on the keys.

"There don't seem to be any real craters here," objected Jenny. "Nothing suggesting them showed on the radar maps."

"Nothing suggesting impact features," admitted Joe. "The hole we are just avoiding would look volcanic except that there is very little buildup around its edge, and the bottom is well below the surrounding ground level. There were many such on both the original map and the one we made during approach. If they had been mentioned in the original description we had of Enigma, we would certainly have been expected to offer an explanation for them."

"Shouldn't we anyway?" asked Jenny.

"If you can think of one, and the requisite work doesn't interfere too greatly with what is already planned. Allowing oneself to become distracted by the unexpected is one of the more certain ways to keep from finishing any task, it seems to me."

"And ignoring the unexpected is one of the surest ways to have your solution outdated before you report it," retorted Carol. "The explanation of these holes may have nothing to do with the official question of why Enigma has an atmosphere in spite of its small size, but I think a good, detailed map of a group of these things, and a close examination of a few of them, is in order."

"The map is available. Pick your area from the radar record and have it plotted at any scale you like. When do you want to do the examination?"

"Well, I hate to delay the start of your own run. I don't think there were any of these things near the tent—"

"We can check that easily enough," pointed out Charley.

"And even if there aren't we can get back here, or to some better site if the record shows one, quickly enough," admitted Carol.

"On the other hand, you could take a quick look right now, while Joe's robot is being set out," suggested Molly. "You can see well enough even if it is night, can't you?"

"Certainly, with this sky glow."

Molly had been unaware of any sky glow and assumed it was too far in the infrared for her eyesight, but stuck to the main theme. "Do you have a pretty good idea of what you want to check?"

"Yes, I think so."

"Then for goodness' sake get outside and get your data. It won't delay us worth mentioning. Can any of us help you?"

"You might need a camera for what I can remember, but if you want to take one, I'd be glad of the material. Get sizes and especially inner slopes, and outer slopes if any, of all these holes you have time for. You take the left side of the ship, so you can start the moment you're outside; I can move faster and will only have to look to remember, so I'll go around to the other side."

"All right. We're down; let's go." Molly seized a camera, thankful that there was *some* basic equipment aboard that no one had specifically had to arrange, and the two women headed for the exit lock that was already opening.

Outside, the Human realized that she had forgotten an important point. She had been seeing the landscape on infrared pickup, converted on the screen to frequencies she could use. Now she was looking directly, and seeing was much harder. It was not totally dark; the sky produced some glow that even Human eyes could detect. Possibly Arc's companion was above the horizon, though she would have been hard put to prove it at the moment, and a little of its radiation was getting through the dust. This was no time to theorize, however; there was work to do. The camera's finder could be adjusted to convert to more comfortable light, though walking around with one eye glued to its small aperture was inconvenient and deprived her of depth perception.

She walked slowly toward a low ridge fifty meters away, climbed it, and saw that it did indeed mark the rim of one of Carol's craters. She took photos in both directions along the rim and toward the far side; these would be enough for the slope measurements, since the instrument was holographic.

After some search through the finder, she thought she could see another feature some two hundred meters away. This proved to be an error; the ridge was simply a ridge, no more. The next two tries were successful, however.

Then Joe's voice sounded. "The robot is out and set. Have you recorded what you need, Molly and Carol?"

"I have three sets of pictures," replied the Human. "I'll hope that's enough for now. Carol has probably done a lot better."

Carol made no answer. Joe, being Joe, did not repeat his call at once; Molly, not being Joe, waited for scarcely ten seconds before she did.

"Carol! Did you hear us?"

Still no answer.

"Joe, we're not on private for some weird reason, are we? Can you others hear us?"

Charley and Jenny both acknowledged at once.

"Can either of you hear Carol? We can't."

"Neither can we."

"Can anything go wrong with the translator channels? Joe, you'd know better than I—so would you other two. How about it?"

"It is hard to believe. The receivers and transmitters that you carry yourselves, and the ones at the central translation computer in the boat, are extremely redundant; so are the internal works of the computers. The channels use achronic radiation, not electromagnetic, so they can't be blocked by matter, though their range is only a few thousand kilometers, and of course they can't be sensed directionally; that's why I couldn't use that system on these robots. Gross destruction of a translator would of course stop its transmission, but that would—"

"Stop the lecture and let's find Carol!" snapped Charley. "Molly, come inside; you can't possibly see well enough out there to be useful in a search. Jenny and I will come out. Joe, you stay there. Molly, come up to Con and guide us on the screens."

Before anyone could respond to these instructions, the Shervah's voice came through to all of them. "You needn't all come. Jenny, you're the heaviest of the ones who can see well. Bring some rope, fifty meters at least. *Don't* hurry; crawl. That was my mistake. I know this gravity is silly, but don't let it fool you."

"Where are you?" asked Molly, making toward the boat, the only thing she could see reasonably well without the camera finder.

"I am at the bottom of a hole about half a kilometer from the ship, two hundred grads from the bow direction to the right. I was in a hurry to get to it and jumped over the edge. I can't jump out again."

"Why not?" asked Charley. "This gravity is weaker to you than it is to me, and I could do it."

"I'm tempted to suggest that you come and try," said the Shervah bitterly. "If there were a *knevreh* at the bottom to eat you, I think I would."

Molly was inside now and able to move much faster. She didn't know what a *knevreh* was, but the context suggested an answer.

"I take it the sand inside is very loose, and at angle of repose," she said.

Carol was silent for a moment. "Your translator couldn't have handled that!" she said at last. "Or have you been spending time studying our worlds, since the team was set up?"

"Neither," admitted Molly. "You said enough for inference. When we get back to *Classroom* try the main translator with *ant-lion*. Ecology is an interesting field, and a lot of

Human information has been filed there by now, though I don't suppose the boat's unit carries it. Jenny has just passed me with a coil of rope; you'll be with us in a few minutes."

"If she doesn't make an equally big fool of herself. Watch the gravity, Jen; stopping isn't easy, even on rock, and these holes are full of the loosest stuff you ever handled. I don't think even eighteen pairs of legs, or whatever your count is, would give traction enough."

"Only fifteen for traveling. I'll be careful," promised the Rimmore.

Conversation ceased for a minute or so, and Molly was able to reach the Con room and bring a vision screen to bear in the appropriate direction. She had not bothered to remove her armor, except for helmet and gloves. The centipedelike form of Jenny was easily located; the Rimmore might be traveling slowly by her own standards, but Molly felt uneasy as she watched. She tried to locate the hole, presumably somewhere ahead of Jenny, in which Carol was trapped, but even the highest of the boat's pickups was too low to give her a good landscape. Designed primarily for use in space, the screens were not holographic.

The Shervah had said half a kilometer—but that would have been a translation, and the translator did round to levels of accuracy implied by the speaker's own choice of words. Two hundred meters more or less might easily have been meant, even though Carol's highly precise distance judgment and incredible memory would have given her a far more exact knowledge of the real figure. There was no useful way for Molly to guide the rescuer, even though the boat's sensors could tell her the latter's distance to the centimeter.

Jenny needed no guidance, however. Carol's words had been enough—they might have come through in more helpful form to the Rimmore, Molly realized. Near the limit of vision set by the boat's geometry and the local topography, Jenny stopped, quickly enough to prove she was in control and not speeding recklessly, and elevated the front half of her long body. After a moment she dropped back to the ground, crawled another ten meters in a direction slightly to the right of her original course, and stopped again.

"There you are" came the grating voice. "I can see why a place like that would get anyone in trouble. Don't pull on the rope until I've moved away from the edge and onto solid rock, here; the traction is poor, and I don't want to be pulled in, too."

"All right. I'll tell you when the rope reaches me but won't pull at all. You can do that when you're ready."

There was pause; Molly assumed that the Rimmore was checking the coiling of the rope, but could not see her clearly enough to be sure. Then the rough voice resumed.

"Ready now to throw. I have no weight to attach to it; I've fastened one end around my body, made an open coil of the rest, and will try to throw that over you. I wish my arms were longer; maybe I should have brought Joe or Charley along."

"In this gravity it shouldn't take much," pointed out Carol. "Give it a try."

There followed an almost Human grunt.

"Told you it would be easy. Fine for distance, a couple of meters to one side."

"I'll coil and try again, unless you think you can climb that far."

"That far, yes. Wait a minute." Pause. "There—no, missed it, and I'm back at the bottom—but the rope came a little way, too, with the sliding sand. One more try—there. I have it. Let me tie it around me; there. I'm no more of a knot expert than Charley, but we can get it off later. There'll be no hurry. You can pull whenever you want."

"A minute. I'm getting as far from the edge as the rope will let me—there. That's something to hold on to, though I feel as though I were floating anyway. I'm pulling—very slowly. I'm not moving, I'm glad to say. Are you?"

"Yes. Upward bound at last. There's an upward wind through the sand at the bottom, for some weird reason, which helps a little. Steady does it. I'm not wiggling at all; I'd do more harm than good. Halfway up now. Are you coiling the rope or backing away?"

"Coiling. I don't dare move a leg; I've got a grip with each foot and don't dare shift a single one. Nearly up?"

"Nearly up. Ten more meters. Five. Two. Over the edge, thanks. I'd jump over to hug you but don't think I'll do any more jumping on this planet. Wait till I get this rope untied."

"Why untie it?" came Charley's voice. "Seems to me

you'll be a lot safer connected. Come on back to the boat; there are still some robots to put out."

The rope did have to be untied before the women could remove their armor, but the Kantrick's sensible suggestion was followed. The untying was done in the conning room, by Joe's nimble tendrils.

"That makes two of us," the Nethneen remarked as he recoiled the rope. "Experience has its uses, however valuable foresight may be, Charley. I hope you were less frightened than I, Carol."

"For just a moment it was bad," the little humanoid admitted. "Falling into a hole means nothing in this gravity, of course, but the pit did remind me of the *knevreh*—antlion, Molly called it, which is quite a dangerous creature at home. For just a moment I thought of that. Then of course I remembered that whatever may be on Enigma, including interesting prelife chemistry, it won't be life."

"Of course it won't," agreed Joe.

"Of course it will," grated Jenny.

OF COURSE I SEE IT'S GONE

There was a moment of silence, and several sets and patterns of eyes focused on the speaker. She sprawled relaxed, in the corner of the room that had been fitted with a tangle of pipes, bars, and ropes for her comfort.

"I should have thought of it when I did the first analysis," Jenny continued calmly. "I should *certainly* have thought of it when we were talking about the possibility of free oxygen."

"But there isn't any oxygen, you said. At least, no more than could be explained by hard light from Arc on the other gases." Charley's tone was indignant, through Molly's translator.

"Quite true; there isn't. However, there is a large amount of carbon dioxide, and that is just as improbable—at least, with activation energy—mixed with ammonia as the oxygen is. They would have reacted to produce ammonium carbamate."

"Of which there is plenty around, you said," Molly pointed out.

"Yes. So there is evidently nothing to block the reaction. But there must be something to reverse it, up the energy hill, or one of the gases would be gone. There is plenty of energy, of course; but how is it applied? All I can think of is the sort of thing that supplies free oxygen on your world and mine, Molly, and nitrosyl chloride on Carol's, and high-energy nitrogen and chlorine compounds on Joe's and Charley's: biological catabolism."

"But this place can't possibly be old enough to have life at that organization level."

"As far as our experience goes, no, Carol. I fully agree. Nevertheless, I am happier about my wild-shot project than I have been since it was approved. At the moment, the best working suggestion I can make is that there is something analogous to vegetation here that uses energy from Arc to break down ammonium compounds and release gaseous ammonia and carbon dioxide, and maybe water ice. Whether there is anything using the reverse reaction to power itself I would not presume to guess; this is, as you point out, a very young planet—we feel sure."

"It has a very young sun," insisted Joe.

"I accept that."

"What do we *do*?" asked Charley.

"My first thought is to watch the ground we pass over much more carefully than we have been, looking for any unusual coloration. We should be particularly attentive near bodies of liquid, which will presumably be ammonia. Once your robots have started work, Joe, I want to return to the lakes we have already seen and do much more sampling and much more careful analysis of what we get. I set up for only simple compounds, I am ashamed to admit, on the earlier runs."

"If you hadn't, would you have finished any of them yet?" asked Joe.

"Very few."

"Then there seems no need for shame. You were doing what seemed needed. Now more seems needed. We can live with that. Molly, perhaps the time has come when your different color sense will be of help. We could of course set each screen to different selection and different false-color representation, but I have the impression that you can do more by watching your whole natural range. Do you mind riding with your screen hooded? Or would it be better if we stayed elsewhere in the boat and let you watch in comfort?"

"I don't mind the hood, if one of you doesn't mind looking ahead while I look down. The assumption that we have been flying higher than any hills agrees with the radar data, but I still prefer to trust living eyes this close to the ground. The catch is that except in areas where the clouds are thin or nonexistent, and we haven't hit any of those on the day side yet, my eyes are no better than yours; the light is very faint, fainter even if whiter than on most of your worlds, I'd guess, but if anything you can probably see better. The clearest region was around the south pole, and it's having winter. No daylight. As I recall, Arc's companion is shining on that area, and I'll certainly be glad to watch it in white light when we get there."

"I will be glad to con while—"

"I'll do it!" Charley cut in. Joe made no attempt to argue; Molly would have been surprised if he had. She was a little startled at Charley—not at his willingness to interrupt, which all were getting used to, but at the strength of the feeling that seemed to have prompted the interruption.

"It might be better," suggested Carol, "that we finish setting out the wind-robots as planned; then Molly, and Charley, if he wants to help her, can take a really close look at the short-wave region."

"There is certainly little point in all of us being there; the originally scheduled work should go on as far as possible," agreed Joe.

"And none of you will be very happy with no clouds between you and even that companion star," added Molly. "All right, we'll do it that way. I can look for Jenny's life as well as for my ice—though, of course, Jenny's idea may mean that the ice is less likely—I'll have to think about that."

"If you see any, sample it!" said Jenny.

"Of course. Also any off-colored surface areas."

"What would you consider off-color?" asked Joe pointedly.

"Well, the sand is practically white to me by daylight—it's mostly ammonium salts, Jenny says. The hard rock has all been darker, and I suppose that would be silicates with heavy metals. This part of space seems to have been through more stellar life cycles even than mine. The School planets run pretty high in heavy metals, don't they, except for the way-out common ones like Sink?"

"Even the dust in those is iron-rich," Jenny confirmed.

"Thanks. It goes along with the brand-new stars and nebulosity here at Eta Carinae, after all. Let me know when you finish some of those rock analyses, please, Jen. I guess anything that isn't either practically white or practically black will need a closer look. There's no point in trying to put other color words through the translators; we respond too differently to various wavelength mixtures. Two samples that looked alike to me might be very different to some or all of you, and conversely."

"Any further thoughts?" Joe was still asking the key questions. No one said anything, and the boring aspect of the flight was resumed.

Molly spent much of the time wondering who would be next to make a dangerous or ridiculous mistake, and suspected that Charley was thinking along the same lines. The difference between them, she reflected, was that the Kantrick was probably hoping for it to happen—to someone else, of course. His sense of humor seemed to work best in situations that made him look better than others—though to do him justice, as Molly suddenly realized, he had never displayed it in a really serious situation like the present one. At parties, on picnics—if an outing where everyone wore environmental armor could be given such a name—even in class, he could be objectionable; in the lab he had been different, and he might well be so in the field. She'd give him the benefit of the doubt until something did happen.

Disappointingly, the surface showed nothing surprising or encouraging to Molly's eyes, and only the regular samples were taken at the three sites where robots were left in open starlight. Jenny's enthusiasm waned visibly.

As had been predicted, the sun was almost gone when they got back to the tent, though it took long-wave sensors to prove it.

Charley had decided entirely on his own, as both Nethneen and Human had been very careful not to say anything that might have been taken as a suggestion, that he would also accompany Molly to the heavily clouded arctic. He gave no special reason, but suddenly broached the idea toward the end of the search around the other pole. This area had proved to be mostly bare rock; there were no lakes or rivers, and very little loose sand or dust, but a very irregular, mountainous topography. Molly suspected that something about this fact had set the Kantrick thinking, and the report certainly bothered Carol. She couldn't see why there should be mountains.

Molly herself spent some of the unloading time rigging a hood around her conning screen, and now she lifted the boat and headed it north, still hoping for something that looked more or less like a natural landscape instead of the dim orange-red patterns of which her eyes were so tired. She had not completely forgotten Charley's prediction about the boat, but if he was willing to ride in it, she saw no reason to worry.

Molly had never seen Earth except from a distance, of course, being far short of retirement age. However, she was familiar enough with holograms and other images of what was technically her home world, as well as of many others. This was not exactly like any of them, but not wholly new, either.

The dunes in the region where they had landed were too light in color to be any sand she knew, but not light enough to be snow. Where these ceased, as they did before the boat had gone a hundred kilometers, the surface texture remained about the same for a while. Then increasing areas of bare solid that might be rock—it couldn't be ice; it was far too dark—began to show. It was not really black in color. There were dark browns, traces of what to Human eyes looked reddish brown and occasionally a real red, and sometimes there showed bits of what she suspected might have been greenish or even lighter yellow patches if the light getting through the clouds had been bright enough to give her more confidence in her color sense.

Several times she was tempted to land for samples, but reflected that if she did this every time the surface tint changed she would never cover ten percent of the planet. For the present job, it would be best to wait until liquid could be seen—unless, of course, some unmistakable ice showed up.

Neither did, for hundreds of kilometers. She was flying slowly, to get a good look at the ground below, in spite of her desire to reach daylight, and time had shifted to a slow crawl.

She herself was still interested in the endlessly varying landscape below; Charley, who was taking seriously his duty of looking where they were going, was getting bored and was quite willing to say so. There were clouds and dust devils and real sandstorms, sometimes above their flight level and sometimes below, but he didn't find their patterns at all interesting.

Conversation with the three back at the tent did not help, as all were too busy to say much. Joe had started his robots; the slaves had lifted to their assigned altitudes, and everything was obediently moving slowly upwind, whatever the local wind might be, according to the monitors. A worldwide map of air currents at five altitudes was under construction, but since no robot was yet more than ten kilometers from its starting point little could be read from it so far.

Jenny was deeply buried in chemical analysis but had not yet reported evidence either of the prelife compounds she had originally hoped or the photosynthetic life more recently inferred. Carol was equally silent; Molly supposed she was doing more with the radar maps or the data they had picked up around the "craters," or perhaps just brooding about the arctic mountains. Joe of course said nothing and Molly herself did not like to interrupt with questions. Some of Joe's ethical code had rubbed off on her. She regretted it slightly; chattering during lab work seemed more comfortable, but with Joe actually present she felt a little uneasy about unessential talk. It was certainly not that she disliked or feared the little Nethneen; somehow she just didn't want to merit his disapproval. She wished something would appear on her own screen that would give excuse for a report—a real report, not just a periodic statement that the boat was still all right, as Charley was making.

But it was several hours more before this happened. The equipment indicated that they were over a thousand kilometers from the others when a lake—no, it was a chain of lakes—came into view. They were near the edge of the heavy arctic cloud cap, and the light was getting white enough if not bright enough to make Charley a little unhappy. The clouds were evidently of fairly coarse particles. The general landscape had been smoother for some time, and she had speeded up their flight, not expecting to find anything interesting; and for some minutes she and Charley had been arguing on private channel about this. He could not grasp the Human emotional attitude that because nothing had happened for some time, nothing was likely to. Being bored, he insisted, was quite different from being unreasonable.

The argument ended as the gray-blue patches that had to be liquid made themselves obvious. The Kantrick aimed his own screen downward as their horizontal motion practically ceased, and began calling out to the others.

"It looks as though we had some liquid here—lakes, ponds, whatever—I don't see any rivers, so ponds may be it, though they're pretty big; one is a dozen or more kilometers across, I estimate. Any new colors, Molly?"

"Yes, right around the edges, but so uniform I can't help suspecting it just means the ground is wet."

"Is the surface the salt-sand we're used to, or bare rock, or something different?" asked Joe.

"It looks pretty much like the former, but I can't be sure. We'll be down in a moment. Will you get my armor, too, Charley?"

The Kantrick did even more. By the time the boat was grounded and controls safely capped, he was back in Con with his own armor, the Human's, and a coil of rope. Molly decided not to ask him the purpose of the last until she had finished checking the gas tightness and temperature controls of her own equipment. She then started for the main lock and, as she had expected, was stopped by her companion.

"Wait, Molly. We'd better fasten ourselves together. I know there doesn't seem to be any wind, and I don't see any holes, but we don't know what it's like out there. If the ground is wet, there might be quicksand or something like that."

"And if we both got pulled in?"

"We stay safely apart. One of us goes out first, and goes the full length of the rope before the other follows, then we keep that length apart until we're reasonably sure the surface is trustworthy."

"That still doesn't answer what we do if we both get in trouble."

"The others—oh."

"Yes. The others aren't here. Sorry, Charley. You stay inside and take the boat back to the tent for help if I get in trouble."

The spheroidal figure stood motionless for several seconds, passing the coil of rope from one four-digited hand to the other, its forward eye fixed on Molly's at about the same level and the two others that she could see roving aimlessly about the con room. Then the rope was tossed to one side and the transparent helmet dome of the armor slowly removed. "You're right, of course. I'll watch. Please keep talking whenever you think I may not be able to see you."

"That would only be right next to the boat. I'll keep a running report, though, anyway. And I'll be careful of quicksand; did you have some special reason to be afraid of that?"

"Well—nothing special. It was the first thing I could think of that wouldn't be as obvious as high winds or holes."

"Have you ever had experience with such a thing?" asked Joe.

"Not personally. I've read about it."

"All right," said Molly, "I'll step carefully, and in this gravity I don't think I need really worry about that, either. No, don't say it, I know I'd sink just as deeply into any liquid here as on my home world, but I can use inertial effects more constructively here, I'd think. We'll hope I don't have to find out, though. I won't be long; I'll get water and mud for analysis and be right back."

Charley made no answer, but settled down at his dimly lit screen and keyed it to cover the area just outside the nearest lock. Molly quickly rechecked her armor and went out.

There was more light than before; the clouds seemed to be thinner for a moment. She had already mastered the coordination needed for walking in seven-percent gravity, of course, and required no conscious thought for that problem, so she could focus full attention on the landscape before her.

The nearest lake was about two hundred meters away. There was just enough wind to make its liquid state obvious by ruffling the surface into small waves, which moved with eye-catching slowness in Enigma's gravity. Considering the temperature and pressure, its main constituent was presumably ammonia, but there was no reason to suppose it was very pure.

The ground at her feet was mostly the light-colored material that Jenny claimed to be ammonium salts, but now it could be seen that smaller, darker pebbles were scattered through it. Molly collected several of these, finding that they were filled with tiny, sparkling metallic-looking particles when examined closely. She reported this to Jenny, and walked slowly on toward the lake.

"Everything all right?" asked Charley.

"Eh? Oh, yes. Sorry—I promised to keep reporting, didn't I? So far nothing special. The surface holds me up well enough and seems perfectly dry so far. As you can see, I'm heading toward the lake now."

"Not too fast. You don't have Jenny's traction, and you want to be able to stop."

"True. I'll watch it, though getting wet with ammonia shouldn't hurt me in this suit. My batteries are up, and I could boil a lot of it away from around me before getting frostbite."

"But I couldn't see you under the surface."

"I'm not sure I'd sink; I've never stopped to figure out my density in armor, and would have to look up that of the ammonia. In any case, if I go under for any reason, I'll keep talking to you. In fact, now that I think of it, getting mud from the lake bed might be a good idea; if there's any sort of microlife on this world, the bottom of a shallow body of liquid with some decent light shining on it would seem to be the best place to look for it. Now stop worrying, Charley. I can't guarantee there's nothing dangerous, but I'm not going to take any unreasonable chances. I want to see my husband and little boy again, the sooner the better as long as this job is properly done. *Do* calm down."

"All right. I didn't mean to be giving orders. It's just that I was so surprised when Joe blew—"

"So was I, and so was he. The universe is full of surprises, thank goodness. Some of my ancestors believed in an evil god they called Satan, but his real name was Boredom. Hold on a minute, here's a patch of something that looks different. Sort of pink, no, more orange, with little veins of yellow. Its texture is slimy, of all things. This is encouraging; maybe we have Jenny's life already. I'll can some of it . . . there. It sticks to my gloves. Probably I can rinse them off in the lake. Wait a minute." She took a long, gliding step that brought her ankle deep in the liquid. "It doesn't shelve off too quickly. I'll get some of the bottom stuff in another can while I'm here. There; at least the gloves *look* clean. I'll rinse them off again with a couple of different solvents when I get back to the boat, and Jenny can play with those washings, too. Now I'll go out a little farther and get some deeper stuff."

"Do you have to?"

"Why are we here? If it will make you feel better, I'll come back to the boat and let you do it, but that seems a waste of time with me here already."

"Well—I'll go out next time."

"Fine. I was going to suggest that anyway."

Molly waded away from shore and boat, occasionally pushing her faceplate below the surface to get a clearer view of the bottom. It looked like plain mud or sand; there was nothing that suggested living beings, plant or animal, protist or argilloid, though she could hardly expect to see either of the last two except in colony form. She finally reached waist depth.

"I'm going to get some stuff from the bottom. One liquid sample, one mud or whatever. I'll be down less than fifteen seconds, if I can get down at all."

"All right." Charley tensed himself at his station. He was extremely uneasy in one way at losing sight of his partner, though he still had faith in the Faculty that had set their problem.

He needn't have worried. Molly had been able to immerse her face when she wanted to see the bottom, but getting entirely below the surface was another matter. She couldn't sink, and her center of buoyancy was if anything below her center of mass. She just couldn't reach the bottom. Getting her feet back down after lifting them off took some doing. Even Charley was amused. Swimming was not an art with his species; as he had said, they floated even in liquid ammonia, and with no need to breathe they had never regarded staying up as a problem. Their shape and mass distribution made it easy to stay right side—head pole—up if they *were* floating; Molly's present need to go head down, coupled with her already weird shape, made the situation really funny.

"Blast!" exclaimed the Human when she was finally standing again. "I know ammonia's a lot less dense than water, but so am I with this suit. The recycling gear takes up too much room. I ought to have designed it with the batteries in the feet. I should have learned more than organometallics when I was taking that course with Jenny on Ivory. The gravity made me spend a lot of time swimming there, and of course I didn't use real armor—just good insulation, which bulked enough to let me float in the ammonia but didn't keep me from diving."

Charley knew what she meant; he, too, had taken courses on the high-gravity fourth planet of Smoke, the fainter star of the binary system whose planets had been taken over almost completely by the University.

"I'll have to make do with shallow-water samples this time and rig up some sort of long-handled scoop for the future. I'm coming back. Don't gloat."

"I've been listening, Molly" came the grating Rimmore tones. "If you need to make more equipment, how about coming back to the tent with the specimens you already have? I can't wait to work on that slime you were talking about."

"Well—all right, Jenny." Molly had intended to use the shop on the boat but could sympathize with her friend's curiosity. "I wouldn't mind knowing what the stuff is myself. You don't mind waiting for stuff from other lakes?" She splashed out on the shore, noting that the material underfoot was more mud than sand; it clung to her feet and ankles. She made no great effort to get rid of it; specimens were specimens, even if they collected themselves.

Actually, most of it had dried and fallen away by the time she reached the little spacecraft; her trail was marked not only by the indentations of her footprints but by the fragments of hardened mud. She did not stop to think of any implications of this rapid evaporation; after all, her armor was heated to keep her alive.

"You might as well fly, Charley," she remarked as she closed the outer lock behind her. "I'll have to get this stuff properly recorded." Her companion made no objection, and by the time they were back at the tent—a far shorter trip than the outbound one, since neither of them was bothering to observe and the Kantrick used far higher speed than before—she had labeled her specimen containers more completely, described each with a brief note covering its reason for collection and location, canned several of the flakes of sediment still adhering to her armor, and topped off the batteries of the latter.

Jenny received the material with eager nippers, listened to Molly's backup information, and settled down happily to work. Charley and his Human friend went to see the beginnings of Joe's air-current map; the Kantrick remained to watch it grow, though there was still little sense to be made of it. Molly retired to the shop to make a shovel. This was completed in a few minutes, the shop resources being what they were, and she then suddenly realized that she could use some sleep. No one had set up a watch system as yet; the students were doing what came to hand. There was no objection to further delay in the inspection of the daylit region.

Sleep was rather uneasy this time; Enigma's gravity was a great deal less than the normal *Classroom* acceleration, low as that was by Human standards, and Molly woke up several times from a falling dream.

Her conscience eventually decided that she had rested enough, and she took a quick meal before going back to the tent. Her translator had of course blocked all non-emergency communication while she slept, and the first words to come through when contact was resumed rather surprised her.

"Joe, I would never have thought it of you!" The voice was Carol's; the machine was using the tone of honest surprise, but Molly rather suspected sarcasm. She was not yet in sight of the others, being twenty or thirty meters from the lock that led to the tent, and found herself at a loss for the motive behind the Shervah's words. Had Joe actually interrupted someone at work, or what?

She hurried, making full use of the handholds, but her first view of the tent occupants told her nothing. All four were gathered around Joe's map, but there had been no more words and no one appeared to be doing anything but look. Molly joined them as quickly as she could, and looked the map over silently from all sides, hoping to learn what had provoked Carol's remark; but she saw nothing surprising.

The map itself was a holographic projection of the planet, about two meters in diameter. The sunlit side was indicated by what to the Human was slightly brighter illumination, and a coarse coordinate grid indicated the rotation axis. Faint reddish and orange lines, all so far extremely short, marked the paths that had been followed by the robots, and the locations of each of these were indicated by slightly brighter sparks of light at the appropriate end of each line. In each case, the starting point could easily be identified as the spot from which the trails of each robot and its five slaves radiated. Presumably, as the lines lengthened, it would become possible to make some sense out of their pattern, but Molly could see nothing organized so far.

There was, of course, no meaningful connection between the starting points and the coordinate system. One of the twenty was at the arbitrarily chosen zero longitude, and neither rotation pole was anywhere near one of them, since chance had not brought them to the ground at an appropriate latitude—Molly realized with some embarrassment that she would have had some trouble calculating in her head just what an appropriate latitude would be. How many degrees apart on the circumscribed sphere were the vertices of a dodecahedron? She put that one firmly out of her mind, and returned to the possibly more immediate question.

What had Joe done or said to surprise Carol? Of course, he would never have made a remark about the pattern's already supporting his hypothesis—not Joe.

"Does this make sense to anyone yet?" Molly asked.

"Notice the summer end of the axis," replied the Nethneen. What Molly actually noticed was that he had not really answered her question; but she backed a little farther from the globe image to get a better view of the area in question, and examined it more closely.

The true arctic circle had not been located yet, since no one had bothered to check the orientation of the rotation axis with the planet's current radius vector; but presumably it was farther from the pole than the circle now in total daylight. Within that circle were only two of the robot tracks, and Molly examined these very carefully. It was the area they knew to be more heavily clouded and that she and Charley had been examining more closely, but the map showed nothing of the clouds.

"I don't see anything very different about them," she admitted at last. She was embarrassed again; if Joe had spotted a difference, surely there must be one. What could be expected to show this quickly? The region was presumably getting more heat, of course—potentially higher winds; but if anything the patterns of radiating lines were smaller, suggesting slower air currents. It couldn't be that.

"See the wind strength?" Carol still sounded sarcastic. Would Joe be drawing conclusions already about general circulation? It was a temptation common to Human minds—she wasn't sure about many of the other species—to notice things that supported one's own preconceived ideas. Surely Joe was above that, though; or was he? Did the robots measure vertical components? She tried to remember.

Then she suddenly saw the larger pattern. "Oh! Of course! What can have happened? When did it happen?"

"I only noticed it a few minutes ago," replied Joe. "I've had to take some readings from other sensors on the slaves to make sure, but the air is generally rising over that area, and—"

"But I meant the other thing—the missing robot!" exclaimed Molly. "Isn't that what you were talking about?"

"Oh, no. That couldn't happen. Of course they're all—" Joe fell silent as he realized that Molly was quite right.

OF COURSE IT'LL BE SOFT

The boat hovered a hundred meters above Enigma's surface, with all five occupants staring intently into their screens. It was daylight, though dim, even by Molly's standards, since they were close to the summer pole, and all were using the light that most nearly suited their own eyes. Meter by square meter they were searching the landscape for the missing robot.

The surface was different here. Rock and sand were interspersed, as they had been elsewhere, but crater-topped cones were scattered freely; they had seen dozens in the last two or three hundred kilometers as they approached the final recorded position of the lost machine, and five were visible from where they now hung. Nobody wanted to believe in active vulcanism on a planet this small and young, but nobody could think of another name, or another explanation, for the cones.

And nobody could see the glint of metal against the sand or the rock. Joe, dividing his attention between his visual screen and receivers set for the robot's telemetry broadcast, had had nothing to report, either. Jenny had put her chemical work aside and was searching as earnestly as Molly, but neither had seen anything worthy of comment. Carol was very interested in the local topography and might conceivably have been paying more attention to the hills than to possible metal cylinders, but she was tactful enough not to make irrelevant comments. Charley was the least restrained, as usual.

"Joe, have you picked up anything from the slaves of the missing unit?" he asked after many minutes of futile circling.

"I haven't tried. They were on a different frequency and were transmitting to the master to be relayed from it. Naturally, we lost touch with them when it went out."

"But if they are anywhere around broadcasting, couldn't we pick them up directly?"

"We should be able to. I'll try it." The Nethneen operated his keys briefly, and his voice showed emotion that might have been enthusiasm or might have been annoyance—Molly could have sympathized with the latter. Why did *Charley* have to be right? "Yes. They're radiating—all five of them."

"Where are they?" came several voices at once.

"That will take some work. The original setup was designed to locate them relative to the master. We may have to get directions and go back to crude triangulation . . ." Joe fell silent and his tendrils worked keys again.

"What were their heights?" asked Molly from the boat controls. "I'll get us level, or nearly level, with each of them in turn, and we can home in on it if you can get direction." She sent the craft floating upward as she waited for Joe's reply, knowing that the lowest of the slaves was at five or six kilometers. She also set up an outside pressure reading for her own screen, remembering that the things had been set for pressure rather than absolute altitudes.

Twenty minutes located all five of the devices, since Joe elected not to bother to bring them aboard. Horizontally, they were all within about fifteen kilometers of the spot where the master robot had last indicated its position, and very much closer than that to each other. There was still no sign of it in that neighborhood, however, and no obvious place where it could have been hidden. Enigma showed no evidence of tectonic activity hereabout unless the "volcanos" counted; there were no canyons, caves, or cliffs with landslide evidence—or without, for that matter. There were no lakes within ten kilometers, and the few that lay within twice that distance seemed at casual inspection to be shallow, though this might have to be checked. There were no biological hiding places like forests.

"Will radar get through ammonia far enough to check

those lakes, or will we have to do each one personally?" queried Joe.

"Depends on their depth," replied Carol. "It won't go very deep. The ammonia must have electrolytes in it—right, Jenny?—and will be a fairly good conductor. We'll try. Who's densest?"

"I'm made of water," replied Molly, "and we can add enough weight to my armor to let me submerge. I can almost certainly see farther than any of you through the stuff, with my short-wave eyes. That would let me do a search most quickly."

"That is all true," replied Joe, "but any of the rest of us, except perhaps Carol, would be safer. Jenny's done it so far, with no trouble. The ammonia is, for us, at a relatively comfortable temperature. While your armor should keep you alive, if anything should go wrong with it you would be in far more danger than one of us. I suggest that Jenny and I search the lakes, weighting our armor as she did before; I because it is my problem, and Jenny because she would be able to observe and sample the lake bottoms, in connection with her own work, at the same time."

The Rimmore grated strong approval, and no one else objected. Four hours later Jenny was happily burdened with bottom samples from every lake within twenty kilometers—some of them had been over fifty meters deep—and Joe's tendrils were empty.

The raspy voice was more enthusiastic than Molly had ever heard its owner before. "Look at this stuff! Clay minerals—a real likelihood of protolife compounds on their surfaces! I was hoping for a chance to do some structures. A lot of this sparkly stuff—it must really catch *your* eyes, Molly—you know, I have some ideas about that. It could be prelife stuff, too; remember the Dendender, and the Pahrveng, and—oh, at least a dozen others you sometimes meet at the School. They all look metallic, but its really carbon compounds with free electron channels in their structures that make them shiny and gives them real electric conductivity in their nervous systems. Some of them can handle this temperature range. I'll have to get at that stuff I thought was free metal. And look at this slime! Beautiful! Does somebody want to look it over with a simple microscope—I'll bet it won't take chemistry to tell the story here!"

"But who walked off with Joe's robot?" asked Charley.

"You mean what happened to it?"

"Of course."

"I don't know. If it's in any of those lakes, it's sunk into the mud. It was dense enough for that, wasn't it, Joe?"

"Yes, in principle. I don't know how long it would take in this gravity. I'll have to rig up some sort of metal detector and look for it under the mud, I suppose."

"I've thought of a way to narrow the search," Molly put in rather diffidently.

"How?" Again several voices sounded together.

"It would mean interrupting part of your mapping project. You could start another robot at the same place the first one was and watch to see where it went."

"We don't know that the air currents haven't changed. It's been hours now, and that storm that blew me away when we first landed certainly wasn't permanent."

"I realize that. I still think it's worth trying. Even if the second robot doesn't go to the same place, it will be investigating currents in the area where the first vanished; and that would seem to me to be worth doing in any case."

"It would mean staying here, away from the tent and the main work."

"Not for all of us. We could take turns—or just one of us budget a few hours, since that's all it took the first one to vanish. You could stay at the tent and watch your map grow—maybe other information would appear there that would help—and Jenny of course must get back to her chemistry; but Charley or I could stay here for a while, and Carol might enjoy it—except she might forget to watch the robot if the landscape got too interesting."

"Wouldn't that interfere with your work?" asked Joe.

"I don't think so. Much of my thinking is going to depend on what Jenny's analyses tell me. I'm sort of hung up until I can either find ice or get some evidence that it's just not here. Charley has been working along with me, unless that new idea that he won't describe is a branch-off. I'll be glad to ride herd on a robot for a few hours. Which one do you think would be best to pull out of your pattern?"

A little more than three hours later, the boat settled back to the ground at the starting site of the lost machine. Joe, after some vacillation, had decided which of the robots to pull from his pattern, and the group had collected it and its slaves. This had taken most of the time, as the slaves were by now scattered over a fairly large area.

The device was placed precisely where its predecessor had been, Carol's memory serving as the final check, and Joe made sure that the original programming was still set up. None of them could be sure whether the local wind was just as it had been before; Carol had not been outside to feel it. Since no one had been present when the first one had started to move, only the original instrument log could have been used as a check; and, as Charley remarked—no one else bothered to—if that had been to a large enough scale, the present reenactment would not have been necessary anyway.

Possibly.

"All right, it's ready," said Molly as Joe closed the access plate of the metal cylinder and stepped away. "Charley, you take the others back to the tent and then come back to keep an eye on me. It shouldn't take you very long, maybe three quarters of an hour. It was much longer than that before we lost track of the other one, so there's no need to worry about me. My batteries are charged, emergency chemical cells loaded—I'd be all right for days if I had to. Don't worry, just get the others back to their work."

Charley, rather to her surprise, made no objection, and she watched the two-hundred-meter torpedo lift from the rock and vanish into the bright dust clouds.

She did not keep her eyes fixed on the robot, though she watched with some interest as the slaves detached themselves from its top and drifted upward. She knew the master would not start its motion until they had all reached their planned altitudes, so she spent some minutes looking over the ground in the hope of finding some evidence of the ice she so badly needed for her theory—no, she corrected herself, her hypothesis; at the present rate she would have to be very lucky for it to graduate to theory status.

Still, there had to be ice somewhere; the surface material Jenny had analyzed up to this point was far above Enigma's average density. More and more it seemed likely that the stuff was inside; that Enigma, like a middle-aged comet, had lost much of its outer ice and concentrated the silicate to a real crust. If all the surface had been sand, or salt, or dust, this would be easy to believe; but *rock*? She found an exposed patch of the dark, hard stuff and examined it as closely as she could by eye. She had ordinary tools, and chipped off a few more pieces with laser and hammer; but there was nothing about them, or the flare as they vaporized under the laser beam, to suggest that these were any different from the earlier ones. Sodium, of course, as any human eye could tell, but that ubiquitous element was not very informative.

She glanced up at the robot. It had started to move, so she suspended her planetological research for the moment. The metal cylinder drifted along, into the wind as planned, its base a few centimeters from the ground, much more slowly than a comfortable walk. She amused herself by marking its path with her own footprints whenever it passed over anything soft enough, and by the time Charley came back with the boat she had decided that the wind was fairly steady. While she could locate the foggily visible sun at times—the combination of filters and eyeshades that even she had to use to protect skin and eyesight from the tiny, blazing disc had startled her friends considerably—she was at a latitude where it was above the horizon all day and was in no position to judge absolute direction.

The situation was getting rather boring by the time the boat settled down near her again. She was, for once, as glad to see Charley as he was presumably relieved to see her.

"Let's establish some direction around here!" was her greeting. "Will you get the inertial system to line up the boat's long axis with the local meridian? I feel lost not knowing which way is north."

"No problem," replied the Kantrick. "Are you sure you'll feel any less lost when you do, though? You don't know what there may be in any direction, whether the latter is named or not."

"Maybe not, but I'd feel happier knowing whether I'm walking azimuth twenty or three hundred twenty. I admit it would also be nicer to know where I've been—well, I do; I was at Joe's Station Fifteen—and where I'm going, but knowing which way is some help. Don't be so individual,

Charley. Haven't you ever tackled an idle problem when you were bored?"

"I prefer to find an important one. However . . ." The craft lifted, swung slowly, and settled once more. "To within a grad or so, the axis is pointing along a great circle through the planet's poles of rotation, with the bow toward the nearer one."

"Good. Thanks. By my convention, that's north—it's northern hemisphere summer. The robot is drifting toward azimuth sixty-five or so, not that my line of footprints is very precise. What can we do now to keep busy? It didn't occur to me that this job would be simple snail-watching. If this thing is going to disappear, I wish it would get about it."

Charley was of course able to infer something about snails from the context, but giving him more details killed a little time. Molly was rather amused at part of his reaction; he was not quite sure whether to add the words in question to his translator's vocabulary, vast as the memory capacity of the equipment was. He wasn't convinced that they were worth the space. The Human had calculated long before that she could add words as fast as she was likely to be able to talk for the rest of her life without reaching the storage limit of the fifty or so cubic centimeters of doped synthetic diamond at her throat. This was one reason she had deliberately made the attempt to program the device to handle tone inflections—or whatever Nethneen, Rimmore, and the other team members used instead of tones—as well as formal symbols.

She spent some time at this now, chatting idly with Charley, trying to read likely emotions into his answers and assigning different tonal values to them. She had no real confidence in the result, but it was fun.

One kilometer. Two kilometers. Time out for food, still watching from the Con room. It was much more pleasant to eat in the boat than to depend on the recycled material provided by the armor. Charley felt the same, and while there seemed no possibility of either's ever tasting the other's foods, a discussion of taste and of food preparation as an art form entertained both of them for some time. Both, as it happened, knew something of each other's culinary customs; they had attended social gatherings at the School often enough. These were normally interspecies, and it was customary for guests to bring their own refreshments. Even beings with common temperature range and using the same body-fluid base, such as the usual ammonia, were seldom similar enough chemically to share each other's foods. Demonstrations were not unusual—a Human consuming corn on the cob or lobster, or a Kantrick everting his stomach starfish style around an artistically prepared and decorated delicacy of nearly his own size. The typical student had learned to be tolerant and even casual about sights that would have revolted a less sophisticated member of his or her race. Charley and Molly were able to be critical on a reasonably artistic level.

The robot, disappointingly, had ceased to follow a straight line. After some eight kilometers of annoyingly slow travel, it was approaching one of the conical "volcanoes"—not directly, but working its way closer in rather erratic style.

"You know, if there are eddies around the lee side of that thing, the machine is just going to spend the rest of the term going around in circles," Molly remarked as the hill loomed closer.

"Could that be—no, we'd have found it; or rather, we'd never have had any reason to wonder where it was."

"We'd have wondered why it wasn't traveling, after a while," pointed out Molly.

"I admit it was an afterthought, but I did cover the eddy problem in the program" came Joe's voice. "If the present chase leads you to one, watch what happens after three trips around the circle."

"I apologize, Joe," replied Molly.

"No need; I have already made sillier mistakes—or, at least, mistakes equally attributable to inexperience, I suppose."

"How is your map growing?"

"Convincingly. I still have no suggestion as to what may have happened in your area, however, so please don't lose track of the machine. I would hate to have to spare another from the pattern."

"We're watching. I won't need sleep for a while yet, and Charley for a lot longer. By the way, Joe, how closely has the map pattern made by this robot and its slaves matched the first?"

"So far they are indistinguishable on the map scale. I am very encouraged that the same thing is likely to happen again."

"Do you mean encouraged or hopeful?"

"I should have used the latter term, of course. Has the robot shown its response to an eddy yet?"

"Not yet. I think there may be one soon; we're near a hill. But something occurred to me, Joe. Wouldn't it be possible to get some sort of idea how constant Enigma's wind patterns are, or at least whether they change with seasons, by comparing earlier pictures of the planet? Right now, for example, the south pole is having winter and is just about free of clouds; here it's summer and almost solidly decked over. That's not what I would expect—maybe Jenny mentioned that to you earlier; we noticed it from *Classroom*."

"She did, but it gave me no ideas. I did secure a set of early pictures, but I—"

"They let you have them?" asked Charley.

"Yes. I have not yet made sense out of them, however. Some of the rest of you should try when you have time."

"I think we're getting to an eddy zone," Molly cut in tactfully.

She was right, but the watching required some waiting as well; it took the machine fully ten minutes to get around each swing of the eddy. Molly had to remind herself that the speed of the robot had nothing to do with the speed of the wind; the latter was registered on the map by the pressure sensors in the cylinder's skin, the former was determined by the preset program. The boat had no equipment for measuring wind directly, and unless there was something like sand or precipitate blowing around visibly there was no way of judging air currents from inside.

Molly decided, well before the third traverse of the eddy pattern, to go out and judge for herself. Charley made only a halfhearted objection; he was rather impatient for something to happen himself, and would have suggested that he be the one to go out if he had not had so much private reason to follow Molly's lead in most matters. He settled himself more alertly at his screen while the Human rechecked her armor.

Outside, she could barely feel the wind, light as she herself was. They had grounded the boat several hundred meters from the robot to avoid complicating the winds in the latter's neighborhood, and by the time she had walked carefully to a point perhaps fifty meters from the cylinder, it had completed its third trip around the eddy. The response that Joe had built into it was immediate and obvious. Molly reported for the Nethneen's information.

"The robot's lifting straight up—the wind's so light I can't tell whether it's holding station for the moment or still going against the current."

"I set it to hold" came Joe's voice. "Integrating all the velocity contributions during the lift into the map would have been more of a complication than it was worth."

"How high should it go?"

"Nine or ten meters. Then if it follows more than an eighth of a circle around the same eddy course it will rise again, and so on until there is a significant difference."

"It's about ten meters up now. I think it's drifting more nearly straight toward the hill than it was before." Molly paused for perhaps a minute. "Yes, it's definitely closer—it's over the base of the cone now. Its course is changing, I think—yes—it was making a slanting climb; now it's heading straight toward the top. I'll follow it."

"Better do it in the boat," cautioned Charley.

"No need. I can go a lot faster than its set speed on foot. Fly over the hill if you like and see where it's going. It looks like one of Carol's 'volcanoes.' "

Molly moved as quickly as the gravity permitted to the base of the slope and started to climb after the robot. She promptly encountered the same difficulty that Carol had faced some hours before. The hill was of loose, sandy material at its angle of repose; the stuff slid down under her, refusing to support even her few kilograms of weight. Fine powder rose around her, cutting off her vision completely until it drifted slowly away from the hill in the negligible breeze.

"It's a crater, all right," Charley reported from overhead. "It's not quite like the ones we got involved with before. It looks as though the hill were a heap of sand on a flat table of rock. It seems to be a little deeper inside than it is high from without, but the sand doesn't come together the way Carol's did. There's a definite hole that goes down into darkness where I can't see. If there is gas coming out, that will explain what happened to the other robot; it must have followed its program into the hole."

"But these aren't real volcanoes. How could wind be coming out of a hole in the ground?" asked Joe. Molly had a flash of inspiration, remembering the wind Carol had noticed in her trap.

"My ice!" she called. With no more words, she retreated a score of meters from the hill and then "ran" toward it as rapidly as her negligible weight permitted. As she reached the slope she jumped toward the robot as hard as she could.

She flew over it, spinning awkwardly, and struck the slope almost flat on her back four or five meters above the drifting cylinder. The sand here was no more able to support her than that at the base had been, and she slipped downward. Her aim had been good, however, and she met the machine within a few seconds. There might have been time for another leap if she had missed, she reflected later; she was never sure whether she would have recovered her common sense in time not to make it.

"Molly! What are you up to?" cried Charley.

"I'm getting a look at that hole in the ground, and I'm getting gas samples out of it." she replied firmly. "Besides, if the robot tries to go out of sight, shouldn't we stop it?"

"How?" came the pointed query in at least two voices. The Human thought as quickly as she could.

"If I block its pressure sensors except on one side, won't it suppose that way is upwind?"

"No," replied Joe. "The actual sensors are inside, fed by microscopic openings in the shell. You couldn't block them all without wrapping the whole machine in something. You probably can't even see them. If a few are totally blocked, the controller will assume that that's what's happened and omit them accordingly from the wind calculation. How do you suppose Carol and I were able to ride one awhile ago, without upsetting its guidance?"

"Get off while you're still on the outer slope!" cried Charley. "We can figure out how to follow the machines later, if we decide it's worth the risk."

"Wait till I get to the top," retorted Molly firmly. "At least I'm going to get a look at that hole. Bring the boat down so I can reach some of the climbing grips on the hull; that will be better than rolling back down the hillside and maybe getting buried in the sand."

Again Charley made no vocal objection. The boat was now almost over the center of the crater. He lowered it until the bow entrance port was about level with the rim of the cone and worked his way slowly toward the point where his friend should appear over the edge in a few seconds.

He judged the position properly, unfortunately. Suit and cylinder appeared directly in front of him. At almost the same moment, the wind from below, deflected by the hull, raised another puff of blinding dust; the Kantrick was using long-wave pickup for his screen, but not long enough. Both he and the Human were cut off from view of each other. Simultaneously the robot swerved, in response to the change of wind, in the direction in which Molly had stepped to avoid its path. Its push was gentle—too gentle to feel at first, or in time. Joe would probably have realized he was falling soon enough to react properly; the Human, already at only a fifteenth of her normal weight, did not. By the time either she or Charley could see clearly, she was sliding down the inner sand slope, well ahead of the robot.

The latter was following, and she made every effort to scramble up toward it, or at least to slow her descent enough to let it catch up. Charley moved the boat ahead of them and tried to lower it so as to block the paths of both, but the craft was too big. Its stern, two hundred meters away, encountered the far side of the pit and caused an unplanned dip at the bow end; Charley frantically manipulated keys to level off, forgetting for a moment that there was no absolute need to be level and that he could have blocked the hole at the bottom with the vessel's bow. By the time this occurred to him, Molly was out of sight of his screen, and he did not dare lower for fear of crushing her with the hull until he could find her again. This took perhaps half a minute.

She was now at the very bottom of the slope, apparently standing on something solid, with sand that she had displaced still pouring past her feet and vanishing below and the wind from the crater now marked by another rising plume of fine dust. The robot was half a dozen meters up the slope, descending straight toward her in its unhurried fashion.

Charley manipulated keys, ignoring the items in the boat that were not fastened down; the stern went up, the bow down, until its long axis was vertical. Gingerly he eased the craft toward his friend, trying to keep its central axis over the hole. Again the change in wind caused by the ship ruined his good intentions.

As the nose of the vessel entered the nearly circular opening, it left a smaller and rapidly decreasing annular space for the emerging gas to use. Molly realized what was happening, since she could see the wind, but not in time.

"Charley! Wait! Stop!" she screamed. The Kantrick obeyed, but the damage was done. The wind lifted another cloud of sand and dust, as well as Molly herself, partway up the slope. "I'm blowing away! The boat's funneling the wind!" she called. It might have been better for her to keep quiet; if Charley had lowered enough to bring the hull against at least part of the hole's rim, she would have had a good chance of catching some handhold.

As it was, her friend hastily reversed the descent. The blast of local air dropped. So did Molly, nearly buried in falling sand and invisible in the dust anyway. She missed both boat and robot as she went over the edge.

Of course, she thought as she finally realized she was falling, there'll be a lot of sand where I hit, and in this gravity I needn't worry. Still, I hope it's not level . . .

OF COURSE I'M COLLECTING IT

Even on Enigma, Molly's fall wasn't long enough for her to formulate any more thoughts, or for that matter to come out with any words. The passage feeding the "volcano's" crater was not vertical; its slope was so small that she struck the bottom in a few seconds, and in a few more was able to bring herself to a halt. Irritated but still in control of her temper, she started to climb back toward the faint light she could still see.

Then something pushed her gently but firmly in the opposite direction, knocking her off her feet again. She guessed that this must be the robot, but with practically no help either from her eyes or her semicircular canals she had trouble making either her feet or her hands steer her in the right direction. She was only partly on her feet when she was bowled over again in slow motion.

This time she bounced gently twice, taking much longer to hit the ground the second time, and realized that the floor had become steeper. She eventually collected enough of her senses to use the hand lamp that was part of her armor's equipment.

By this time Charley's frantic voice was clamoring for attention.

"Molly! I can't see you! There's sand still flowing into the hole; are you buried? Can you tell if you're moving? I don't dare bring the boat down again until I know where you are!"

"I'm not buried, and you needn't worry about crushing me," the Human answered as calmly as she could. "I'm down the hole, apparently. I can see no light but my own,

I'm sliding and rolling down a bare rock slope, and I seem to be well ahead of the robot. I don't think I can have come very far, but I don't at the moment see how I'm going to get back. The boat will certainly never get in here, I can't reprogram the robot to carry me back downwind, and I don't think I can climb back on my own; there isn't enough traction. Any ideas?"

"Just to do what you said if you got in trouble—head back for the others at top speed. Do the rest of you know what's happened?"

"It seems pretty clear," said Joe. "Carol's trouble, amplified, I gather. It would seem best to stay near or even on the robot if you can, Molly; at the moment I am still picking up its broadcast, though if this is what happened to the other one we must expect it to get far enough below the surface to lose the telemeter waves eventually."

"At the moment I can't see it, and I think I'm going downhill faster than it does."

"We'll have to hope that downhill is also upwind. Keep looking for it, and if you do see it, do your best to get hold of it. Charley's ropes should be extremely useful. Charley, I assume you're on your way back for us. I'll check out the receiver I used for finding the other robots, and we'll try to get back to your neighborhood in time to measure how far from the original entrance you may have traveled. It should be possible to make a long enough rope in the shop to let one of us follow you and help you climb back, regardless of traction and slope. Jenny, will you see about that?"

The Nethneen's calm efficiency slowed Molly's heartbeat to something near normal, though no Human tumbling through darkness in near-free fall is ever likely to be completely at ease.

A gradual realization that her fall had ceased helped even more to restore her equanimity. At least, she reflected, there was one good point to Enigma: the worst thing about a fall was *not* the sudden stop at the end. Both the light and her sense of touch, through her thin gloves, told her that she was on sand once more. The rock must have leveled, or even formed a hollow, where the blowing grains could collect. First things first, however; where was the robot?

She twisted the lamp control to narrow beam and swept

it back and forth in the direction from which she thought she must have come, widening the search angle more and more as she saw nothing and grew less and less sure of her own sense of direction. After several tense minutes, there was a gleam of light on metal nearly ninety degrees from where she had thought to find it. She nearly panicked again as it occurred to her that she might have been right and the robot was now passing her to one side, but she retained enough self-control not to leap toward it. Holding the light beam as steadily as she could, she finally decided that the cylinder was coming almost straight toward her and reported the fact to the others, receiving a variety of nonverbal sounds of relief in response.

"You know," Molly added, "if you folks get back soon enough, it might be worth trying to block that hole completely with the ship. If the wind stops, the robot will also, I suppose, and I won't get any farther in."

"But don't you want to find your ice?" asked Charley innocently. Molly, for once, found herself with no answer ready.

"It may be worth trying." Joe also ignored the Kantrick's question. "That won't start the machine back this way, though."

"But if it turns out that it's not too far from the hole, you or Carol could come and fix the controls. You could go on down to the ice with me, or at least look for it for a reasonable time. Would either of you be willing?"

"Of course, it's planetary structure," Carol remarked thoughtfully. "I don't really suppose Joe wants to spend more time than he can help away from his map, but it certainly sounds like fun to me. We'll see what things look like when we get there."

"But how—" began the Kantrick.

"'Scuse me a minute, Charley," Molly cut in. "Sorry to interrupt, but the robot is getting close and I'm going to have to travel a little to be sure I'm in its path. With no horizon, I'm even less sure of up and down than usual, and walking is awkward. Remember I'm out of control when I'm off the ground, just as everyone but Joe is. Please let me concentrate for a minute."

"Please keep us informed."

It was Joe who uttered the words and Charley rather than Molly who was surprised at his doing so after her request. He must have good reason, she assumed, and started talking.

"It's about fifteen meters away, still traveling at its set pace. I think I'm right in front of it now, and it's heading right at me. It's back at its basic height above the ground, Joe; it must have decided it was past the eddy. Here it comes. I'm getting onto its field shaper—no, I think it will be easier to ride right on top. I see you put some tie-downs there, too, Charley, and I'll use some of this rope—there. You can talk now. I'm safely aboard, and riding with the thing wherever it's going."

"Can you see where?" asked Carol. "What sort of place are you in? Is it more of a tunnel or a real cave?"

Molly swept her beam around. "Tunnel fits it better so far, though it's a very big one—forty or fifty meters high and three times or more that width. I'm fairly close to one side."

"Is the robot following a straight path?" asked Joe.

"I can't be sure. It doesn't leave any track even in the sand, of course, and we're over plain rock again."

"Would it be convenient for you to drag a foot and leave an occasional mark, if you do cross any more sand, so that we—I—could get some idea of your actual track? I admit I should set up some larger-scale recording procedures here, but I may not have time to do that before the boat arrives and we have to come for you; and of course I am to blame for not thinking to do it beforehand, anyway."

"If any of us gets to the end of this operation without bumping our heads on something we've left undone, he or she will be very lonely," replied Molly. "Sure, I'll make tracks whenever I can, and look back at them for as long as the light allows. At the moment it doesn't look promising; the floor is getting steeper again, and there doesn't seem much chance of sand or anything else loose collecting on it. I'll watch, though. I certainly don't want to fall asleep."

"Better tie yourself on, just in case."

"Thanks, I've already done that, Charley. Do I really need to keep talking? There's nothing new to see or to say for the time being, and so far at least you can keep track of the robot."

"All right, relax unless you really have something to say," agreed Joe. "One of us will call you every few minutes to make sure nothing has taken you by surprise; please answer."

"Of course."

Nothing visible occurred before the party lifted off on its way back to the Molly-trap, as Carol was calling it, though more and more things were going on in the Human's mind. She knew she was not traveling rapidly, but the passage never lost at least some downward slope; she was getting farther and farther below the surface. This was good in a way, as it was presumably bringing her closer and closer to the ice that she was still sure must be somewhere below; but as time went on, she began to think more and more often how nice it would be to have company in this vast expanse of darkness. Not just talking company, but touching company. Rovor, her husband, for first choice, or little Buzz, but they were parsecs away; and of course it didn't have to be Human. Joe or Carol would have been quite acceptable, not merely because they could control the robot.

"We're well on the way." It was Carol's voice this time. "Joe is a little worried."

"I suppose the signal from the robot is getting lost," Molly answered.

"I'm afraid so," said Joe himself. "I am doing everything I can with the sensitivity of the equipment on the boat, and I have already calculated as well as possible how far you are from the place where you fell."

"What's your answer?"

"About two kilometers."

"That's reasonable, assuming it's been a fairly straight line—which is something I wouldn't have guaranteed. Have you any idea of the uncertainty?"

"About the same, I'm afraid."

"Why? Electromagnetic timing is good to millimeters at planetary ranges."

"My fault again. I sacrificed resolving power for speed, and wanted only broad measures of the winds. It seemed likely that small local ripples would be more nuisance than help in working out planetary circulation."

Molly had to admit that he was probably right. "A two-kilo uncertainty still seems pretty big, though."

"It does to me, as well," replied the Nethneen, "but inconsistencies in the measurements of the last hour or so force me to admit the figure."

For the first time, Mary Warrender Chmenici began to feel real worry about her own safety. Two minutes later the anxiety deepened.

"Joe! All of you! There's nothing around me!" she suddenly cried out.

"You mean your light failed?" asked Charley. The prosaic question steadied her, and she actually checked by turning the beam on the robot under her.

"You would think of something like that. The light seems to be all right, but there is no ground under the robot. It's supposed to stay only a few centimeters up, Joe!"

"Yes. Look in other directions than what you think is down."

"I can't be wrong about that, unless the robot's guidance system has quit. Upward—I think there is rock, but it's too far to be sure. What has been ahead all along, nothing. Behind—that's better. Rock. Only a hundred meters or so away, I think, though I don't trust my depth perception at that range and there's nothing to give me scale. I'm going down, slowly."

"You've entered a cavern at a point well above its floor, I'd say. The robot is going straight down, ignoring wind, just as it went straight up for the eddy. Can you guess how long it was after you actually entered this space before you noticed it? Was your light on?"

"It was on, I assure you. I missed the floor right away and yelled within a split second."

"Good. Let us know when you get to the bottom, and we'll be able to figure the depth; the descent rate is set."

For the first time in their acquaintance, Molly felt an urge to tie knots in Joe's appendages; then she realized that he was probably not really indifferent to her feelings, but deliberately helping her to control them. She forced herself to slacken the death-grip she had taken on two of Charley's improvised handholds. The robot wouldn't fall, and if it did, there wasn't much damage likely to result here, she reminded herself firmly. A cave could hardly be more than a few tens, or perhaps a few hundred, meters deep, without collapsing.

Of course, with Enigma's gravity, that figure might have to be refined upward, depending on how the cave might have formed. Lava bubble? Solution space? Carol's question, really, and the little woman would need data. The question of getting herself back to the surface could be faced later; her armor was good. This was not an emergency, just an unexpected research incident.

So far. She dismissed that codicil from her mind, emphatically.

"All right. Nothing in sight yet below. Joe, this robot must be sensing ground distance. Can't you tell how far we're going to—well, fall?"

"Yes, it does, and no, I can't. I arranged no readout for that information. Given time, I suppose I could do so, but I did not foresee any such need."

"Carol, you should have ridden him harder; you could have used that sort of information."

"Next time," replied the Shervah. "This one just counts as educational experience." The sarcasm was again evident; Molly felt more and more confidence in her translator's handling of Carol's tones. She wished she were more certain of Joe's.

"Still nothing visible?" Charley's voice cut into her thoughts. Molly leaned over the edge of the cylinder and directed her light downward.

"Not sure. Very vague brightness; just a moment. It disappears when I turn the light out, so it must be real reflection."

"Anything horizontal?" asked Carol. "I can't for the moment imagine what could happen on a planet like this to form a cavern."

"I couldn't imagine what could form solid rock, either," Molly replied. "We both have a touch of revision to do on our ideas. To answer your question, I can't see anything at my own level in any direction, and the glow below doesn't seem to be getting brighter with any speed. This place is pretty big."

"But you can guess what might be light-colored underneath!" remarked Charley.

"As long as we call it a guess, sure. Just let's not say it until I get there," replied his Human friend. Molly was learning caution.

"Is the glow uniform, or can you make out features?" asked Carol.

"It's still hard to be sure, but there seem to be lighter and darker patches when my light beam is fairly wide. When I narrow it down and sweep it around, it's harder to compare."

"Keep watching with the wider beam, and let us know when you feel sure the features are increasing in size. That will tell us you're near the bottom, whatever the bottom is," Joe pointed out.

"All right. I rather hope there's no wind down there; I'm starting to feel cramped on this thing. It would be nice to take a walk."

"There's good reason to hope the wind will be straight up from whatever you land on, isn't there?" came Charley's voice.

"There's hope. I'm not going to claim *good* reason." Molly did not feel like mentioning the word *ice* for the time being; she was still on the emotional backswing from the jump at a conclusion that had carried her into her present trouble. If Charley wanted to keep his optimism, all right.

There *were* features below, spreading and growing more distinct as she approached. Nothing really clear yet; just some places a little darker—really darker, or a little deeper?—than others. Her mind came back to full concentration on business, and she reported tersely to the others as the picture clarified.

"It's not a level bottom. I thought for a minute the dark places must be deeper—farther from the light—but it's the other way. One of them is higher than I am now—"

"Which way?"

"*That* way. Please, Charley; what possible direction reference do I have? Even if this cylinder hasn't turned during descent, and I'm willing to believe it hasn't, *I* have, often enough to forget which way I was originally facing. The lighter stuff is coming up now, and I'm going to meet what seems to be a steep slope close to a fairly sharp boundary between light and dark. There. Descent has stopped, Joe. How far down did I go? At least roughly, in kilometers."

"About six hundred fifty meters." Still no detectable emotion, but the Nethneen had to be laughing; Molly herself was. "Are you moving at all? Is there still wind?"

"Yes, apparently. I can't feel it through armor, and I don't plan to step off as long as this thing is traveling, but it is traveling, so I assume it senses impact pressure."

"What's the ground like?" cut in Jenny. "Any visible difference from what we've already analyzed?"

Molly swung her light downward and looked carefully for the first time, and a grin spread on her freckled face. "I can't see the ground, Jen," she said softly. "It's covered with feathery, silvery-looking crystals."

"What?" Carol almost screamed.

"Yes, dear. I—"

"Get some! Are they really dense, like an actual metal, or could they be conducting hydrocarbon—the stuff Jenny mentioned earlier?"

"I can't tell the density, for several reasons. Even if there were decent gravity, I have no way of telling how loose or open the structure of this fluffy stuff may be; even its inertia won't tell me anything. It's bound to be low. Maybe if I'm here long enough I can tell you whether it's growing or not, but I rather hope to get specimens back to you for that sort of check."

"What are the temperature and pressure? Not much different from the surface, I'd suppose."

Molly consulted the environment checkers on her armor. "No significant pressure difference—in this gravity and with this gas mixture that would take several kilometers change in altitude, I'd think. The temperature may be a trace higher; unfortunately I didn't think to record it to a hundredth of a Kelvin before I started down. It's a hair over two thirty-five. For practical purposes, you have surface conditions here except for light."

"And that difference would be in favor of life!" said Carol happily.

"Why?" asked Molly. "Wouldn't the life need some sort of energy source?"

"Of course, but not something as destructive as Arc's light—oh, I forgot for a moment. We'll worry about the energy later, when we have specimens."

"Good," said the Human, suddenly remembering her own situation. "Is there any practical way in anyone's mind for getting me out of here?"

"Oh, I'll come after you," said the Shervah enthusiastically. "Jenny has started a rope in the shop; there's plenty of carbon in the air, so there's no limit on raw material. In this gravity, we can carry kilometers of cord strong enough to lift both of us, if we have to."

"And how are you going to find me?"

"Simple. I'll ride another of Joe's robots, and set it to go upwind at higher speed than the one you're riding. Sooner or later I'll catch you, and I can reset both robots to come back downwind. Actually we shouldn't need the rope, but I'll play it safe; that seems the sensible way—we could be taken by surprise by something else, after all."

"Have you consulted with Joe about taking another of his robots from the mapping project?"

"No, but this is important; and we have to save you, too. I know your armor should be good for a long time, but as he said awhile ago, the environment is really bad for a Human. You'd freeze to death in seconds if your power failed—or maybe boil; I know you have good insulation and your body produces an incredible amount of heat."

"The atmosphere study is important, too," Molly pointed out in some amusement.

"Well, yes, of course. Maybe it would be quicker for Joe to make a new robot in the shop than to go off and pull another from the mapping. How about it, Joe? You must have all the patterns."

"Yes, I do. I am not quite so sure about raw materials, however; the boat doesn't carry much in the way of spare metal. If I improvised by making the shell from some carbon polymer, manual replanning would be needed, and that would take awhile. I fear it would be quicker to take another from the mapping job."

"Joe," said Molly softly, "I don't consider myself an emergency case yet. I admit I'd be relieved to be back among you, but getting specimens for Carol and Jenny and me is also part of the job, and this is a part of the planet we'd never have seen—never have suspected, probably—if I hadn't been so silly about making that jump a little while ago. I haven't heard of armor failure in my lifetime, and I don't mind a few days of mild discomfort. If Carol wants to come along and see the place for herself, and collect her own specimens, and that fits into any plan for getting me back, fine; but I don't see why parts of the project already planned and underway need to suffer."

"Charley, let me at the keys." Joe spoke quietly, but for the first time a thrill of real fear—not just the sudden, brief panic that had come with a fall—seized Molly. If Joe were taking over the flying, and especially if he were changing flight path, he was not making a new robot; he was going after one of the others. That meant he considered the situation more serious than she had allowed herself to believe; and Joe's opinion, for reasons none of the group could have stated clearly, always carried more weight than his negligible physical size warranted. Maybe it was his species; the first Nethneen Molly had met was also the first instructor at the Eta Carinae institution whose ability to get abstractions across to a student was not hampered by translators. She had given the being the translator name of Sklodowska, after one of her own classical heroes, and had been rather careful never to learn whether it was male or female. Molly herself had not, until meeting this being, really expected to learn much from lectures at the School. The incredibly informative combination of verbal symbols with animated and still graphic presentations had given her a completely new realization of what could be done with the art of communication, and left her with a respect for the teacher that, perhaps unjustly, tended to rub off on all Nethneen. If Joe thought she was in danger, then—

Then she needed to keep control of her own feelings. There was nothing any of them could do to get her out of where she was for some time yet. In the meantime, sitting on a metal cylinder and thinking about her own troubles would do no one any good. She, and Jenny, and Carol could all use specimens, so the thing to do right now was collect specimens.

Making sure that she was tied to the robot, she lowered her feet to the field rim at the lower edge. Then she set her light to a diffuse glow and clipped it to her helmet so that it would shine in whatever general direction she was looking, took hold of one of the grips installed by the Kantrick, and reached down with her other hand into the fluffy mass below. It had no strength at all; the crystals disintegrated into sparkling dust at her touch. She made several efforts to get intact samples into a specimen can, but had to settle for the microscopic fragments. She called Carol and described the problem, leaving possible solutions to her and the boat's resources.

"How deep is this stuff?" asked Jenny. "Can you reach

any substrate? Is it the usual sand or rock, or something we haven't seen yet?"

"Whatever it is is lower than I can reach from here," replied Molly. "Just a moment while I check this safety line."

"What do you think you're doing?" asked Charley.

"Stepping off, of course. How else do I find how deep these crystals are?"

"Lower a rope through them, of course!"

"Using what for a weight to carry it down? I'm less than four kilos here myself. I have two safety lines tied to different eyes on the robot, if that makes you feel easier. I'm letting myself down on one of them. I'm about half my height in the fluff—getting a new hold lower on the rope—down again—I'm not sure I want to go under it completely; I won't be able to see. A little lower though—there. Yukh!"

"No symbol!" came the response in four voices.

"My feet have touched something. Something sort of between slippery and sticky. The symbol implied distaste, but nothing seems to be doing any damage. I was almost pulled loose from my grip on the rope—don't worry, it's tied around me as well. I'm trying to walk along behind the robot holding the line, but my feet sink in and are hard to move. I'm climbing back up—if I can pull them free—there. Loose. I'm back on top of the robot again."

"*What's on your feet?*" Carol almost shrieked.

"It's hard to tell; it's all covered with the metallic dust. I wish I could blow it off; brushing doesn't do much good. There are big gobs of it on each boot; maybe I can pry enough of the outer part off to see whether the shiny stuff is part of it, or was picked up on the way up." She paused.

"Well?" Carol had waited for much less than a minute.

"Still far from sure. I can't completely get rid of the metal, if that's what it is, but there's certainly less of it inside the lumps. Have you ever tried to get aluminum powder off something? Anyway, as best I can tell, the rest of the stuff is a brownish—to my eyes, of course—very sticky jelly."

"Collect it!" cried Carol. "If you have no more cans, dump something you've already picked up and collect this!"

"Of course," replied Molly gently. "Even if it isn't ice, I'm collecting it. Are you ready to come and get it—and me?"

OF COURSE YOU DIDN'T

Carol, to do her justice, was embarrassed when she thought back over her recent words, but could not really believe that the others, even Molly herself, wouldn't have felt the same.

"Of course we'll get you! But when I get there, you'll want to go on and find your ice, won't you?"

Molly admitted that she probably would, but that there might be qualifying factors. The Shervah felt some doubt about this, her own pit adventure having been too brief to impress her emotions greatly, but she said nothing else tactless.

"It's a pity you didn't see everything along your path. You could have described it, and I wouldn't need to ride another robot; I could follow on foot."

"Down the slope where I couldn't keep from falling and into this cavern from the top?"

"With rope, and tools to secure it along the way, sure."

"I'm afraid that even if I'd seen enough, I wouldn't remember it with anything like your standards. I hate to do it to Joe, but I think another robot is the answer."

"Oh, yes. We're picking one up right now. Joe has gone out for it and commanded the slaves to come back as quickly as possible. We should be at the Molly-trap in a few more minutes."

"Joe?"

"Yes, Molly?"

"It didn't take you so long to decide which robot to use this time, did it?"

There was the barest hesitation before the Nethneen answered.

"I took the closest one to our flight path."

"I thought that might be it. Thanks a lot. I'll help somehow with the map to make it up."

"Your own work is as likely as mine to provide the help. It is all one picture—one pattern—we are trying to assemble, remember."

"You've been thinking of more than that," the Human insisted. Joe made no answer.

After a minute or two of silence, Charley resumed standard procedure. "Anything different at your end, Molly? I take it you're still traveling."

"Yes. Both up and down; the cave floor is very irregular, and I can't even guess whether I'm higher or lower than where I first reached it. It's certainly not a straight line; I've been able to leave tracks in the crystals. There's no pattern I can work out; sometimes it's fairly straight for a while, then a turn in either direction. If there's any cause at all, I'd say the wind was being affected to some extent by the irregularities in the floor, but that's not very informative and certainly not surprising. About all that's helpful at the moment is that I can tell which way I'm going and look ahead to see if anything is coming up. So far, nothing seems to be."

"We'll be over your hill in another minute or two," Joe commented. "I have this receiver at its highest practical amplification. Conceivably, if we're close enough to straight above you, there'll be little enough rock in the way to let some radiation through. That would depend at least partly on the shape of your cave, of course."

"Especially of its ceiling, which I never did see," agreed Molly. "Anything coming through?"

"I think—no—yes, there are traces on the right frequency, and . . ." His voice trailed off for a moment.

"And just about straight down?" asked Molly eagerly.

"Nearly so. The direction indication is not too definite. Charley, fly along this heading until I tell you to stop; then swing one-third circle to the right, and straight again. Keep doing that until I give you a new pattern."

The Kantrick took over the keys without comment, and silence fell for several more minutes.

"Without meaning to be insulting, you're allowing for my motion, of course," Molly remarked at last.

"I am allowing for the certainty that you are moving," replied the Nethneen much more precisely. "I would love to have an independent report on the actual vector. I *think* I have it worked out, actually, but distance readings for that read depth, of course—are still inconsistent. You appear to be radiating from between four and six kilometers underground, which I find hard to believe considering the total time, the known horizontal speed of the robot, and the other information you have sent."

"I'd just as soon not believe it myself," responded Molly.

"Well, it's the best I can do. There are sudden variations in direction that force me to conclude the measurements themselves are unreliable. There seems nothing to do but descend and let Carol or me start after you. Jenny, how much rope have you completed?"

"Five kilometers, nearly" was the chemist's reply. "I doubt that Carol or even I could carry it all—because of the bulk rather than the weight."

"The robot will, if it's neatly enough stowed," pointed out the planetologist. "Is that your hill, Charley?"

"Yes."

"All right, let us down right beside it."

"Not right into the crater?"

"If Molly will forgive me, I'm going to devote another minute or two to practicing with the robot controls. I'd rather do that out here where a mistake won't be quite so critical. I'm going to leave the slaves on the boat, coil the rope on top of the cylinder—the whole five kilos of it—with an end fastened to a weight or a post or something right here in the sand, rigged to pay off from the center of the coil as I travel. At least I can get back from five kilometers even if something goes wrong with the robot or my handling of it. I'm hoping with both lobes and all my blood pressure that Joe's depth measure really is wrong. Down, Charley. Jenny, if you'll bring the rope to the hold where the robot is, I'll meet you there."

"I'm there already. I had the spinnerets coil the rope as it was made, of course. It should pull out from one end without tangling."

"Good. Recoiling that much by hand might have let Molly get more than five kilos away even if Joe *is* wrong. I'll be right there."

Molly found herself much more able to examine her surroundings after hearing the other women settle this matter. She had been in full armor this long before; most of the planets of the Fire-Smoke binary system, even Pearl, where the Human colony had centered because of the gravity, had environments where no Human could survive. She had done laboratory and course work on most of them at one time or another, often with no Human-conditioned station anywhere nearby. Then, however, the interest of the work itself usually kept her from considering personal comfort for very long at a time.

Now, though, she found herself thinking more and more of the simple comfort of being able to relax, move her limbs freely, and breathe without hearing an echo in her helmet. Decent gravity would also have been nice, though she had been aboard *Classroom* long enough to be less concerned with this aspect of life. With safety now a smaller problem than comfort, however, she could concentrate for a while longer on the job.

"Not much change yet," she reported. "Still no sign of any wall to this cave, and the stuff underneath is about the same. Not enough pressure or temperature change to read. Did you find any reasonable prelife compounds in the earlier samples, Jenny?"

"I haven't had time to work on them yet. I haven't been able to think of any other explanation for the atmosphere, either. That clay is going to get a real working over, as soon as we get you out of there."

"Along with a few other things. Sorry to have delayed you."

"Forgiven, considering what you'll be bringing back with you."

"It's a pity, isn't it?" remarked Charley.

"What?" asked all three women.

"That all this stuff has probably been worked out already, and we just haven't been allowed to see the answers."

"Are you sure it has?" asked Jenny.

"Enigma has been known for tens of thousands of years.

It must have been used for a lab exercise for just about all that time. Do you really think there's much chance that we're doing or finding anything new? The School just seals the student reports—if they even keep them. It would be more fun if we were allowed to start where the earlier ones left off. Don't you think so, Molly? Then we'd have reasonable hope of coming up with something actually new."

"Personally," remarked the Rimmore without waiting for Molly's answer, "I'm happier not having my imagination limited by what someone has decided is the right answer. I know some discipline is needed for that particular tool, that's why we were educated in the first place; but if I'm going to be confronted, back on *Classroom*, with a 'gramful of other people's notions of why this place still has atmosphere, I want the one I come up with—or *we* come up with—to show up decently in the list."

"Do you feel that way, too, Molly?" repeated the Kantrick.

"Yes, I think I do. Personally, I *can* believe that no one has been down in this cave before; I discovered it in such a silly fashion, and surely no one could have expected it."

"Wind from the hole. For that matter, the wind from Carol's trap, come to think of it."

"Well, maybe, Joe. Anyway, I agree with Jenny about doing our own thinking, and it's probably a good idea for a few more years for us to do it with lots of independent checkers. Anyway, I'm not worried about the philosophy just now. Work—data collecting and thinking—first; worry about getting back to the rest of you alive, second—and maybe that will climb to first later; worry about what the Faculty thinks of my work, and what my friends think of it, not to mention what I think of it myself, third. First point, Joe—the wind is getting stronger, I think."

"You can feel it?"

"I'm pretty sure. Just a minute while I get a handful of this stuff." Molly reached down and collected some of the powdery crystals, tossing them upward. "Yes, they're drifting backward quite a bit faster than before."

"Is it strong enough to do anything to the undisturbed crystals?" asked Jenny.

"Just a minute. Not generally—but yes, around the base

of the robot itself, where there are eddies, some of the stuff is being blown away. I'm starting to leave a blowing dust trail—a pretty, sparking one—behind me."

"Suggestion. You could be approaching a wall of the cave, with the wind coming from a narrow, or relatively narrow, passage," the chemist returned.

"Good thought. I'll go back to narrow beam and look ahead as far as I can." The others waited silently. Carol, now outside with the rope-laden robot, continued her work on its controls, but even her attention was divided. "Nothing in sight yet." Three more times, at roughly one-minute intervals, Molly repeated this message. The situation was not really boring, of course; merely tense. A well-remembered chemistry exercise in the isolation lab on Beryl had been similar. There had been automatic dampers, of course, that *might* work in time to forestall an explosion; but the lab itself was on tall stilts, which combined with the little world's lack of atmosphere to prevent the transmission of shock to surrounding structures if they didn't. Molly had wondered at the time why she had not been allowed to perform the experiment by remote control; Rovor had been quite indignant about it. Now she thought she knew the reason. Here there was no equivalent to the dampers, but she found herself quite free of panic. The tendency for familiarity to breed calmness, if not actual contempt, was almost universal, not a Human peculiarity.

Carol by this time had satisfied herself about the key responses and was riding up the hill at some five times the pace her vehicle's predecessor, or predecessors, had taken. She could have set in a still higher speed, but prudently used one within her own running capabilities. She was not planning to get off, but she had not planned to fall into a crater before, and Molly had not planned to go underground.

And Joe had certainly not planned to blow away, she was sure.

She watched everything around her carefully as she went; if the rope failed for any reason, her memory would serve one of its functions. The cord, which Molly would have thought of more as fishline than rope, had been fastened to a rod driven into the ground near the base of the hill and was paying out comfortably from the top of the cylinder;

Carol kept carefully clear of it. It was thin material, but far too strong for her to break if she became tangled in it. She had a knife, of course, but felt strongly that having to use it would be glaring evidence of carelessness.

"Still nothing in sight" came Molly's voice.

Over the edge of the crater. It occurred to Carol that the air from below must be cooler than surface atmosphere; it would not have poured down the side of the cone to guide the robots otherwise. Down the slope, over the central hole. A straight letdown into the hole; she had not altered Joe's original programming on this point. Almost at once a steep slope that the machine treated as a surface, flying into the wind—down the slope—at its set speed. Carol herself could feel the wind at first; then it decreased rapidly. She could still see fairly well without her hand light and was not surprised that the passage was growing larger.

"Still nothing in sight."

Now it was a good deal steeper, and the little Shervah could picture her giant friend helplessly rolling down into the darkness ahead. Within seconds she had to use her own lamp, and before long the surface leveled and was covered with the same sort of sand as that composing the cone above. Carol was not surprised; she had guessed how the cone had been formed.

"Molly, I'm about at the place where you must have let the robot catch up with you. It's past a steep slope of rock where you certainly couldn't have stopped yourself, and I can see marks in the sand that you probably left."

"Good. It's awhile yet to the cave. Joe, I suppose you're tracking Carol's machine as carefully as possible."

"I am indeed. I already suspect the cause of the earlier reading uncertainties. I should have thought of it earlier."

"I'd welcome you to the club, if you weren't the founder. What's the answer?"

"Refraction index. The electromagnetic waves—radio waves—are not only absorbed by the rock but slowed by it, so both timing and direction measurements are affected. The rock of course is not uniform, and every time either the transmitter or the receiver moved, the beam was going through a different length of different medium. Hence kilometers of probable error."

"Have any of you studied enough about Humanity to have gotten the term 'twenty-twenty hindsight' into your translators?" asked Molly.

"I have," said Charley. "Very appropriate."

The Human did not have time to express her surprise; her attention was taken up by something more immediate.

"Cave wall ahead, I think!" she called suddenly. "The wind is a lot harder. I should have told you earlier the floor is bare rock; it looks as though the crystals couldn't hold up in the draft."

"Bare rock, or the sticky stuff?" asked Jenny promptly.

"Rock. I'm sorry; I should have made more checks under the crystals. We can do it on the way back, or if Carol has time she can pause coming over—but watch out, Carol; remember the crystals are a good deal deeper than your height, at least in some places, and the stuff at the bottom is quite adhesive. You're not as strong as I am, and if you couldn't pull loose the situation would become rather awkward."

"I'll control myself," the Shervah assured her listeners. "Are you close enough to the cave wall to see where the wind is coming from?"

"Quite close—two or three hundred meters, I'd guess—but I can't see any passages or openings in it yet. I should go right to whatever it is, so I'm looking straight ahead, but still just dark rock. That may be the trouble, of course; the passage won't be much, if any, darker. I'm very close now—fifty meters—less; still nothing—uh-oh. Joe!"

"Yes, Molly?"

"I should have paid more attention to the programs in these things. What will they do if they *can't* go forward?"

"How can that happen?"

"Meaning you didn't consider it in the program. The wind is coming through a horizontal crack that seems to start thirty or forty meters to my left and is about thirty centimeters high at the point I'm approaching. It continues to get higher to my right, as far as my light will let me see. This machine won't fit into a crack of this height. It's going to run into the rock and stop, and either the controls are going to do something about the situation, or something is going to break. Which will it be, Joe?"

The Nethneen was silent for a number of seconds, and Molly resumed her report.

"About ten meters to go. Should I get off? Will anything burn out if it tries to push the planet out of the way? This machine has a fusion unit in it, after all."

"No. It won't push hard enough to damage its drive or its shell; that's basic to the control system, and I had nothing to do with it," the little being finally said. "Nothing should burn out, blow up, or break. I'll have to think out whether being held motionless will be treated like an eddy—let's see—it can't count the number of times around, obviously—"

"Contact," reported the Human. Silence followed.

"If you're just staying there, I'll be able to catch you that much quicker," Carol had time to say.

"I'm not. It's going to the right, just scraping against the wall. That's the way the crack is getting wider. If that continues, the machine will fit in pretty soon and I'll be scraped off the top. Why is it doing this, Joe?"

"At the moment, I have no idea. Please keep reporting."

"What's the rock like?" asked Carol. "Is the crack a fault, or an erosion product, or what?"

"I wouldn't know even if I could see it better, I'm afraid. Obviously wind goes through it; if that ever carries sand, it would explain any amount of erosion. I haven't seen any liquid yet. The top of the crack is nearly up to the top of the robot; the bottom has been a continuation of the cave floor all along, not that that makes it very level. I'm getting off and following on foot. If the thing does go in, I can too, though not very comfortably. The top rises rather suddenly to nearly my own height, about eight or ten meters ahead, and then levels off, and then the crack comes to an end as far as I can see. It would be nice if your mystery controller showed enough liking for a Human to go over to that point before going in, Joe."

"I don't see why it should—nothing personal, of course—but then I don't see why it's doing this anyway. If it goes to the high part—hmmm. Let's see."

"Don't start calculating yet. That's not even a hypothesis, dear colleague. Wait."

"For how long?"

"Ten . . . five, four, three, two, sorry—speed not as constant as I thought. Wall's curved. We're there, and it's going in. I don't like the idea, but I guess I'd better follow."

"Wouldn't it be wiser to wait for me?" asked Carol.

"If there were no doubt that you'd avoid all trouble on the way, and I suppose it *is* a pretty safe bet, yes. However, if you don't get here—if you run out of rope because measures were off, or your robot doesn't follow the same track as this one because the underground winds aren't as steady as we're hoping, or something none of us has thought of yet—then I'd better stay in reach of that machine. My armor has battery power for a few days—just how long depends on what it has to do in the way of temperature control—but any longer and I'll have to recharge. The robot has a fuser, and I can plug into the slave feeder on the top. That machine could be air, food, and drink to me for months, much as I hate the thought of being in here anything like that long."

"You're not really serious about that, are you?" Charley's tone was as protesting as his choice of words.

"Very serious about not wanting it. I consider the possibility too serious to ignore. I'm staying with the machine until Carol catches me, though I'm nearly certain that she will. I'm not going to report for a while, unless it's something urgent. I'm still connected by rope, but this passage isn't quite high enough for real walking, and even in this gravity I don't want my armor to be dragged."

"If you have a chance to turn your light to both sides, Molly, you might tell me something about the shape of the passage you're in. I know where you entered it was higher than it had previously been; the portion passed, which I judge is now to your left, was at that time lower. Might I hazard a guess that you are now under a rather low roof and that it gets *higher* to your left, and that there is very little of the passage at all to your right?"

"Wait a minute. If you're right, I could go to my left and stand up, which would be a relief—all right, you diminutive genius, how did you work that one out?"

"I claim no more than a guess—there probably was, and remains, a vast number of possibilities that have not yet occurred to me. However, there must have been a small wind component, or a pressure effect that the robot would interpret as one, to the right along the cave wall outside, or it would not have traveled in that direction. If the outward wind speed was higher where the crack was low and decreasing as you went along, Bernoulli effect would produce a slightly lower pressure on the left of the robot as you faced the wall. To have such a velocity change, there should be a relatively large chamber or passage beyond the crack. There were really too many possible variables. I repeat, it was a guess, and I should prefer not to make another such."

Joe, the women knew, was genuinely embarrassed; Charley might have been less aware of his colleague's feelings, but even he recognized that it was better to let the subject drop.

"Carol," called the Kantrick, "have you reached that long drop yet?"

"Almost at its edge. I was just going to call you so Joe could check his timing. I'm over emptiness . . . now!"

"Any trouble with the rope?"

"None. We should have thought to provide some regular marking system along it, so that a really good measurement of distance could be obtained."

"Welcome to the club!" came three voices.

"It would have added some time to that needed for making it, though," added Jenny.

"I suspect even Molly, at the wrong end of the road, would admit that it would have been time well spent," retorted the little planetologist. "Wouldn't you, big friend?"

The Human's answer was affirmative, but possibly not as immediate or enthusiastic as the Shervah would have liked. Joe was the one to alter the subject this time.

"I'm losing touch with your robot, too, Carol. I have been getting the same sort of depth measurements by triangulation that I did with Molly and feel quite sure that the uncertainties are due to the rock effects. If we really want to map your underground regions, we'll have to make a new robot with a really good inertial system equipped to integrate its readings."

"Fine! Let's do it, as soon as Molly's out of trouble!" exclaimed Jenny.

"Remember, friends—wind maps!" called Molly softly. "We have plans, which are already somewhat out of shape, and we have only so much time before *Classroom* gets back."

"If we get something really new, as you seem to hope, Molly, maybe we could stay here longer; they could fit Eighty-eight into the next run, I should think, without too much trouble, and pick us up then."

"We'd better not plan on it, Charley," replied the Human,

"though I agree it's a tempting idea. My impression is that *Classroom* is scheduled years ahead, and making a change would have an avalanche effect on other schedules. What we really need is a breakthrough—something that will convince the Faculty that this isn't just a matter of adding trivial details to a picture whose outline is known. That might persuade them to arrange a special investigator of its own for Enigma. Unfortunately, we don't know that we have one here. I'd like to believe that sort of thing could happen, but I'm not conceited enough to expect that I'll be the one to do it."

"Why not?" Charley asked in honest surprise. "Someone has to, and it does occur—sometimes every few years, always every few centuries. The Faculty knows that, don't they? And the School is just the place for it to happen."

"More likely in a physics lab than a planetology one, though," Molly returned. She was about to ask Joe whether he didn't agree with this point, when she remembered that it would not be tactful to suggest that he take sides in their debate. She was a little surprised to hear his voice anyway.

"We can't afford to forget how the disciplines interlock," he pointed out quietly. "Our studies here are no less physics than are those in a particle lab. If anything, we have more factors operating at once on any given observation; our problem would be to recognize the breakthrough when we encountered it, I fear."

"Well, Charley's right on one point, anyway. If I could write this up for home and bypass the School sealing, somehow—no, I can see why that wouldn't be very popular. Bottom in sight yet, Carol?"

"Just. With my light, I think my eyes do better here than yours, though I'm certainly not sure. I'm definitely getting closer, and I can see light and dark as you did, though I'll have to wait to be sure my light isn't your dark, I suppose."

"Not too likely, if her light areas were the metal crystals," pointed out Jenny.

"True. Here we come. I can't see where you hit the fluff, Molly, but the stuff is so irregular that it might be any of the hollows. One trouble is that I can't get this light very far away from myself, so there's no shadow perspective to speak of. Depth is hard to judge. I won't try to make any collections until I'm at the edge of the crystals; then maybe I'll get some of your sticky stuff. No, skip that; I'll catch up to you and reset your robot first, and we'll do the research coming back. All right?"

"All right. I hope it won't be too much longer. This passage is opening out larger and larger, and the wind has dropped so I can't feel it any more, and the floor is bare rock—the whole thing is boring, and I'm getting rather tired of it for the moment."

It was still a number of minutes, in spite of her higher speed, before Carol could report the cavern wall in sight ahead of her.

"Have you left the crystal region? I had before I could see the wall."

"The fluff is gone, yes. There's something else on the ground, though. You must have been able to see it. It's white; lighter than the sand on the surface. You'd have gone after it for some of your ice—"

"I didn't see anything of the sort. It's white to *your* eyes; we'll have to get a real reflection spectrum. Collect it, by all means. I can wait for *that*."

"Sure thing." Carol dropped to the ground, trotting behind the robot, and bent to scoop up some of the white material, bringing it close to her lamp. Then she stopped where she was.

"Molly! It's not snow or ice, or metal crystals. It's plastic—muddy—sticky—"

"Prelife?" came Jenny's eager voice.

"Jenny—Molly—it's *growing*. It's *alive*."

"I didn't see it!" said Molly firmly.

"Of course you didn't. Not on this planet." Joe's voice was equally firm.

"Carol!" Charley almost shrieked. "Are you on your robot?"

"No, but I can see it. Thanks, Charley, I forgot for a minute. There—it's just going into an opening in the cave wall. I'll be up to it in a moment—there. Back on board. You had me scared for a moment, but I knew better than to set this thing to go faster than I could."

"Does the place match Molly's description?" There was an impressive silence lasting several seconds before the Shervah's voice came back.

"No. Not in the least. She didn't find any life, either."

OF COURSE I DON'T SEE IT

"Better stop right now!" exclaimed Charley.

"Thanks. A good idea," replied the Shervah, almost as tonelessly as Joe's usual style. "I'll need to be careful with this rope as I retrace, though there shouldn't be enough of it to make a real tangle. Can you suggest whether I should go right or left when I get back to the big cave?"

"I take it we were too optimistic about the constancy of the wind," Molly opined before Charley could react as she feared he might. He could read sarcasm in words, with or without tones.

"That would seem to be it. I think I'll stop the machine and hunt on foot along the wall; that will be quicker than recoiling rope if I pick the wrong direction first time."

"Unless you encounter some of that sticky material Molly reported," interjected Charley.

"That's a point. I'll be very careful if anything but bare rock is underfoot. I'm back out of that tunnel and am stopping the robot. There."

"Bare rock, or more of this live stuff you just reported?" asked Jenny.

"Patches of both. Don't distract me now. I'm going along the wall, to my left as one faces it. The cave floor is dipping noticeably downhill, and the wall at my side is rough enough and slopes back enough so I think I could climb it in this gravity. You certainly could, Jenny. Now I'm at the bottom of the dip as far as the wall base is concerned, though the floor out to my left is lower still. I think I see a puddle of liquid there—you didn't spot anything of that sort, either, did you, Molly?"

"No, I'm afraid not."

"I don't see how you could have missed it. Our tracks diverged, all right."

"How deep is the puddle?" came Jenny's grating tone.

"I can't tell from here but will find out later if there's a chance. I'm heading uphill again. I'll go a little over a kilo this way, and if I don't find any match with what Molly saw I'll come back and do the other direction. It's all bare rock now, none of the living stuff and none of the crystals—I can't help wondering if they're alive, too. *Ddravgh!*"

"Symbol?" queried four voices politely.

"Sorry. Impolite. I stepped on something extremely slippery. Just a moment while I get upright again. Maybe it was water ice, Molly—remember those skating sessions? If one would only fall with decent speed here, there wouldn't be time for one's feet to get so far from underneath."

"What did you slip on? Please collect it!"

"All right, I guess Molly can spare a quarter of a minute. It's a very thin layer, and not easy to scrape off the rock, but—ah, I don't have to get it from the rock. I have some on my armor. It's slimy, not brittle; sorry, Mol, I guess it can't be your ice."

"With your mass, and the local gravity and temperature, would even water ice have been slippery?" asked Joe.

"I'm not sure," the Human replied thoughtfully. "That point didn't occur to me. I just think of water ice when I think ice, and I think of ice as slippery. Well, it was a nice hope while it lasted."

"Now relax, Jenny, we'll get it to you some time," Carol continued. "I'm traveling again." She fell silent, and for several minutes no one else found anything to say.

Then the Shervah reported again. "That's the limit I set to the left. I'm heading back to the robot. There was nothing but that slippery patch to watch out for, so I'm going a lot faster. I'll reach the machine in a minute or two."

Rather to Molly's surprise—her optimism was suffering another setback—this confidence proved justified and the small woman set out on the opposite leg of her journey. Molly's presumed path was not within this range, either; and once again back at the robot, Carol had to make a decision.

"You should come back and go out again when we make a mapping robot of the sort Joe suggested. It seems there is a complicated set of caves down there, that the winds change capriciously—or at least that we do not yet know the pattern of their changes—and a real map will be needed" was Jenny's firm opinion. Joe said nothing; rather to Molly's surprise, Charley was also silent. She herself did not feel very objective at this point. She very much hoped that Carol would not go back, but for purely Human reasons was embarrassed to say anything.

"I'm staying," said the Shervah flatly. "There is no way we could map this whole place fast enough to catch up with Molly while she's moving. If you want to come down yourself with such a machine, Jenny, I'm all for it; but I'm looking for Molly."

"I agree," said Joe. "I take it you will ride the robot now all around the cave wall. That place can't be too big. It would probably be best to leave the rest of the rope where you are now; unwinding it around the circumference of the cavern will accomplish nothing that I can see."

"Good point," agreed Carol. "It will be easier riding without it, too; I won't have to watch out for being caught as it pays out. There, it's off. Here I go. Any supernatural basis for a decision between left and right?"

No one proffered any, and she set out with no further remarks. There was little said in the boat, either. "Give this one a body that can be ridden comfortably, Joe," grated Jenny's voice, to tell Molly all she needed to know what was going on above. She reflected that the wind chart was still being made back at the tent, even if its designer wasn't there to watch. Poor Joe would get a look at it eventually, and of course she had no way of knowing that until that look was taken, she would be getting deeper and deeper into trouble.

A little rill of liquid, presumably ammonia since the surroundings were too cold for liquid water and much too hot for liquid methane even at this pressure, joined her path from one side and kept her company thereafter, picking up tributaries occasionally until it was a brook half a meter across. The passage she was following had widened gradually until she could see neither roof nor sides, and the wind dropped below her personal detection ability, though the robot still seemed to have an opinion about it. It was still coming from downslope, and the slope itself was getting much steeper; the stream was becoming a series of rapids and even falls of several meters height. She was carried some distance first to one side and then the other of the brook, but the latter never went out of sight. She kept the others informed of all this; Carol acknowledged with interest. They had seen no rivers at any point on the surface.

"Keep your light on and your eyes open for more life!" the Shervah exclaimed. "It certainly ought to be around any liquid. If the passage levels off and there are pools or lakes, be really alert."

"As alert as I can," replied the Human. "There's going to be another trouble before too long, though. I don't know how much longer I can keep awake; and if the wind isn't reliable, as it didn't seem to be in the big cave, any more gaps in my own recollection of where I've been could be pretty serious."

"That was one reason I stayed down here," replied Carol. "If we could think of a way for you to stop while you slept, things would be much less tense. It would be rather nice if that machine were to jam in a narrow passage for a few hours, wouldn't it?"

"It found its way around the only narrow passage I've seen so far, but I'm all for another," admitted Molly. "I'll look for that as well as your life forms; the more I have to think of, the better I can stay awake—I hope."

"I've been about four kilos along this wall so far. It's hard to believe the cavern wind could have changed so much. It probably means I started the wrong way. I'd be tempted to go back, only for all I know I may be more than halfway around this thing by now. As Jenny said, a real map would be useful. I wish I had some idea what could have made this space; I might be able to make an intelligent guess at its size. On any decent planet, gravity would prevent a cave from getting too big before its roof caved in, but this is not a decent planet. I could almost believe this was a big bubble, maintained by gas pressure."

"Except," pointed out Molly, "that there is direct communication with the outside air, and the pressure in here can't be significantly different."

"Not even from altitude difference?" asked Joe. "You could *really* be a kilometer or two down by now."

"And what difference would even five kilos make with this atmosphere at this temperature in this gravity?" asked Molly, who had had time to do some mental arithmetic since the question had come up earlier.

Joe took a second or two to run through the same figures. "Less than a thousandth of an atmosphere," he said at last.

"Which would not show on my suit gauge, I'm afraid. If I do get deep enough in this planet to read it there, I'm not sure I want to know it. I'll be facing a long, long trip back up again."

"How about a kame?" asked Charley.

"A what? Oh, I remember—"

"A place where a deposit of the ice you're looking for used to be, but melted or vaporized out, leaving your cave."

"Where did you learn about that? I didn't think ammonia behaved that much like ice."

"I don't know whether it does. I've done a lot of reading about your world since you people showed up. It's a fantastic place. I can't get over water's expanding when it freezes—"

"Neither could Carol when she found how slippery that made it," Molly remarked drily. "Say, I wonder—"

"Molly! I think I've found where you went in!" came Carol's excited voice. "Wait a bit, I'll check a few hundred meters around out in the cavern. Yes, your crystal region, and what seem to be your traces are here."

"About how far did you have to go to find it?" asked Molly.

"I'm estimating about six kilometers." The others knew that with the combination of depth judgment and memory possessed by the Shervah, this was probably good within ten percent. "That leaves another question. Am I most of the way around the cave, so that it will be quicker to go on for the rope than to go back, or not?"

"We'd better hope you are," said Joe drily. "If not, the rope is nowhere nearly long enough. With Molly getting farther away all the time, there is already some doubt about its reaching her."

"Right. I'll go on.

"Also," added Carol happily, "that will give us a good chance to find the actual size of this cave and maybe start some reasonable guessing about what formed it."

This rather barbed implication about Charley's suggestion was not taken up, even by the Kantrick.

"You're traveling as you talk, I hope," remarked Molly.

"Absolutely. I've gone about four hundred meters from the narrow end of the crack—the end you didn't go into—and you will be pleased to know that I remember this part of the cavern. The rope is a kilo farther along. I'll be with you soon."

"You mean if you'd gone only a little farther to the right on your original foot search, you'd have saved an hour or so?" asked Charley.

"You seem to have the picture. If Joe hasn't tied up all the tools, you might start some more rope in the shop while you're waiting. Jenny must have filed the specs. I hope we won't need it, but I certainly can't promise we won't."

Molly was tempted to express her annoyance at the lost time even more vehemently than Charley, but again found that she would rather not reveal such a feeling in Joe's hearing. It had happened; there had been no way to foresee it, and there was nothing to be done about it now. Complaint, or even remark, was meaningless. Leave that sort of thing for Buzz, until he outgrew it.

She was getting sleepy, and the surrounding darkness, relieved only by her own light, was more and more oppressive. She had used most of the rope Charley had loaded on the robot to fasten herself securely; she would not fall off even if she did go to sleep. Now, however, she began to wonder whether that were wise. If Carol were really close on her trail, was it best for Molly herself to stay with her own machine so faithfully—perhaps beyond the reach of the Shervah's kilometers of guideline? If she did fall asleep, she would be unable to report anything that might give warning of another branch in the trail; she might descend into another cavern as large as or larger than the first, with equally variable winds, without ever knowing it. She was certainly descending, much too fast for her own peace of mind when she thought of the length of Carol's line.

If only this tireless, indifferent thing that was carrying her would stop! If only—

She smiled and then grinned broadly as an idea took shape. For a moment she thought of calling Joe, but he must be busy on the mapping machine by now; and even if that weren't going to be needed for her own rescue, the Rimmore and Carol would be annoyed if work were delayed on it. No, there was no need for discourtesy yet; she could report in a few minutes. She remembered now what Joe had said about the pressure sensors on the robot—a point she had known herself during their construction, though she had forgotten it for the moment.

Her armor recycled everything chemical, of course, with negligible leakage; all it needed in any normal—or over ninety-nine percent of all abnormal—usage was replacement of energy. It had water and food buffers, some full and some empty at the start, to handle lack of uniformity in use versus production of these. In other words, she had spare water.

She could get at the spare water. The processing units of the armor were around her midsection, making her feel at times, where freedom of motion was concerned, a little as she had in the weeks before Buzz had been born. There was no risk of mistake, deadly as the environment around her was; she could have taken the armor apart and reassembled it blindfolded—Humans sometimes retired to Earth, but they grew up in other environments; and a Human who did not know armor was simply not adult. One was expected to design and build one's own.

The fact that she could open it without looking did not mean that she did. Carefully she unsealed a panel near her left hip, closed four valves, and removed a flexible container that held rather less than a liter of water. Two of the valves were on the container itself, the other two on the other side of the breaks with the armor tubing. Now, carefully, she reopened one of the former, and with gentle pressure began to squirt a fine stream of liquid over the front surface of the robot.

The metal was some forty degrees below water's freezing point, and a film of ice quickly formed over its surface. Well before the task was complete, Molly could tell her plan was working; the robot's direction of travel began to veer to one side. Using the brook as her direction guide, she covered the cylinder until the machine was moving back in the direction from which it had come.

She thought briefly of coating its entire surface and waiting where she was for Carol, but decided against it for several reasons.

One was economy of water. Another was the robot's computer; it was, as Joe had said, ready to allow for and discount plugged pressure ports. If she covered most of the surface with ice, she might miss a few tiny areas and find the machine moving in some unpredictable direction while she wasted even more water trying to find and block a single microscopic opening.

"I'm heading back toward you, Carol," she reported briefly. The response from three incomprehensibly mixed voices was completely satisfying. Carol, Jenny, and Joe all produced variations of "What did you do?" and "How did you do it?" Charley said nothing on the general channel; his voice came through on private. "I wondered when it would be. Are you sure the rope will still reach?"

The Human described her technique briefly, not trying to comment on Charley's words.

"None of us can feel too guilty for not coming up with that one," commented Jenny. "Who would have water in her armor?"

"I'm not bragging," assured Molly. "I should have gotten the notion long ago. Now, if you'll forgive, I intend to stop observing for a while. I'm not sure I can really sleep on top of this thing, but I'm going to try."

"Are you sure that's wise?" asked Charley.

"No, I'm not at all sure; but it's going to have to happen some time soon, and I feel safer right now than I have for some time past. I won't turn the light out, and if anything really out of the way happens, the chances are I'll notice—I hope. Right now, sleep is my prime order of business—unless I spot some life forms, of course, Carol and Jenny."

Joe, in the shop working on the new mapping robot, said nothing, and none of the others was in sight of him. If they had been, they would probably have been unable to guess his concern. Even Charley, who resembled him fairly closely in the eyes of the other three, was of a widely different body chemistry, physical engineering, and evolution, and would not have noticed or interpreted the suddenly increased effort the Nethneen put into his work as Molly finished talking.

Joe might have been worried, but Carol, presumably in far more danger at the moment, was not. She rode the rim of her robot, holding on with one hand and grasping a collecting can in the other. Like Molly, she had clipped her light to her helmet for convenience; unlike the two males, she could turn her head, though her eye arrangement made this unnecessary. She was noticing only incidentally where she was going; like her Human friend, she could not feel the wind that was guiding the robot. She was, of course, hoping for more life forms; in spite of Joe's emphatic denial of the possibility and her own knowledge that Enigma could not be a million years old and should not have evolved anything like the things she had collected, she knew what she had seen and had little doubt of its nature. A really close examination might prove her wrong, of course; she was burning to get the material back to the instruments in the boat and the tent, and the even more sophisticated equipment on *Classroom*, but she could postpone that while there was a chance of getting more data on Enigma. Her work, as initially planned, bridged that of Jenny and Molly; she was interested in the planet itself, physically, structurally, chemically, and biologically. She had not really expected the last aspect to appear, but since it seemed to have done so . . .

Carol's emotions were less obvious than Charley's, but she had them.

She had found a stream, presumably the one that Molly had reported, and confirmed its composition with some of the safety equipment on her armor; it was not pure enough for her to drink, being loaded with dissolved salts, but it was ammonia. The robot was following fairly close to it, as Molly's had done. The Human, when last heard from, had been following it back up, and it seemed likely that they would meet soon. Carol wondered in passing what Joe's program would do with two robots in collision, but she didn't waste any real time worrying about the matter. If anything of the sort seemed imminent, she could steer her own machine out of the way.

The only thing that caused her anything like worry was the rope. She had made no effort to go back to her first landing point in the cave and lay a straight line to the new passage, so about a kilometer of it had been wasted by the supposed wind change. There was not very much left in the coil now, and she had not considered what to do if it ran out before she met her friend. She found herself keeping one eye more and more constantly on what was left, and as this dwindled to a few hundred meters she slipped one of her tiny, almost human hands into the control access opening in the body of the robot.

"Jenny, Charley—I'm getting close to the end of the line and haven't met Molly yet. Should I wait there with the robot, leave the rope and ride on, or leave rope and robot and scout around on foot, do you think?"

Neither answer was surprising, but neither was very helpful.

"Wait," said Charley at once. "She should be back with you pretty soon."

"Scout on foot," grated Jenny. "You can get more done while you're waiting for her. She'll see the robot if she gets to it."

"Not if she's asleep," countered the Shervah.

"If she wakes up after passing it, she'll see the rope."

"I wouldn't count on it. It's not very big, and I don't know how its color contrasts with the rock to her eyes; do you?"

"No, of course not. You have a point. It still seems a pity just to wait there, though."

"How long has she been asleep? Maybe we should wake her up when I get to the end."

"Not much over an hour. Nothing like her usual time. Make that a very last resort, I'd say."

"Right. Well, here comes the end. I'm stopping the machine for a moment at least, because the rope is fastened to it and if we decide I should take the robot farther I'll have to untie it."

"How about pulling the rope straight?" asked Charley. "From what you said, there's a kilo or so been wasted by the false trail."

"If I could do it myself, I might take the chance," replied Carol. "With the robot doing the pulling, though, and its speed so firmly independent of outside factors, I'd never know until much too late if the rope caught on something and broke."

"Couldn't you set the robot to pull just so hard?"

"No. It has nothing to sense that. And don't blame Joe; there was never any reason why it should."

"I wasn't thinking of blaming anyone," said Charley with surprising mildness. "Why don't you scout on foot down the stream for a distance, after you park your machine? You'll see Molly even if she does happen to be asleep."

Neither of the women could find fault with this suggestion. Carol left the rope attached as it had been and powered down the robot. Then, making sure that she still had several empty collecting cans clipped to her armor, she set off down the brook.

It was not very deep, as she ascertained by wading in it. She was careful about this; her temperature tolerance was the narrowest of any of the group, and the present environment was about ten degrees below her minimum. Ammonia was her body fluid base, but was liquid at her temperature only because of the high pressure at which she normally lived. Her armor had good insulation, naturally, but she could feel the chill creeping into her feet before many minutes, and moved out of the stream.

As Molly had said, there was nothing remotely suggestive of life to be seen, a fact that would not have surprised any of the group had it not been for Carol's own find back in the big cave. Why it was there, and not here where liquid was available, was far from obvious. Several times the little Shervah knelt and examined the rock as closely as she possibly could, but it remained just rock. No glittering crystals, no slippery coating, no sticky material; nothing but rock. She announced as much.

"Get a specimen or two, anyway," advised Jenny. "Remember the planet has seasons. Maybe there are spores, or cell detritus, that we can find if we look hard enough."

"The hammer doesn't get it loose; I'll have to use the laser."

"Just don't cook the whole specimen."

Carol followed the suggestion, but with no great enthusiasm. Rock analysis was all very well, and she enjoyed it in its place, but life on a world like this was something *new*. There ought to be more of it if there was any; life didn't just occur in small, isolated bits. It came in whole ecologies, when it came.

"Any sign of Molly?" It was Charley, of course.

"Not yet." Carol swept her beam downstream as she spoke. "No, not in sight."

"Judging by times and speeds, it seems to me you should have met by now. You didn't get so absorbed in things that she might have gone by you without your noticing, did you?"

Carol was too honest to make an absolute denial, but felt pretty sure that nothing of the sort had happened, and said so.

"Did you get any distance from the stream?"

"No. I've been in sight of it all along."

"Then that's all right, I guess. Wait a minute, though! Since you left the robot, *are you sure the stream has been going into the wind?* Can you feel the wind yourself?"

The Shervah spun and began leaping back toward the robot as quickly as she dared. Her normal gravity was less than Molly's, but still far greater than that of Enigma, and she had the usual trouble coordinating her leaps so as to stay upright while off the ground. She answered as she ran.

"No, I'm not, and no, I can't. She could have gotten past me, at that."

Joe cut in. "I'm afraid it's worse than that. Carol, you would remember; Molly would not have been aware. Has the stream been perfectly straight while you have been following it?"

"No, not at all. I didn't worry about it; in fact, I was hoping it would turn out that the stream had something to do with eroding this passage. After all, the robots followed it going into the wind all the time, so the passage must have been guiding the wind pretty much the same way—oh!"

"Precisely. When Molly sealed one side of her robot to make it think the wind was coming from the other, in effect she would have caused it to fall back on its inertial system. That keeps the case of the machine oriented the same way, so it would have read pressure from the same inertial direction—"

"Planet's rotation, too!" interjected Charley.

"Not significantly, in this time interval. The point is that she wouldn't have followed back up the stream; she'd have gone straight in the direction that was upstream when she put on the ice coat. If she's anywhere near the stream, it's luck—of course, the passage can't be *too* wide if the wind has been turning along with the river, so she shouldn't be too far from it. Still, she could have reached the side and maybe worked into a side passage the way she did this one. Molly!"

Several seconds passed. The Human, in spite of the limited area of the cylinder top, had fallen deeply asleep; she was still lashed in place, and the feeble gravity permitted head and extremities to be over the side with no particular discomfort. It took several repetitions of her name, in several voices, to bring her back to awareness. She had been wise enough to leave her light on, and avoided the panic that might have come from waking to a combination of total darkness and near-total weightlessness.

"What's the matter?" she asked as she pushed herself to a more nearly upright position. "Is Carol in trouble? I don't see her."

"Of course you don't; I'm nowhere near you, I'm afraid. The real question is whether you see the stream."

It took perhaps a second for the points that Joe had just covered with the others to marshall themselves in Molly's mind, and suddenly she felt close to real panic.

"Of course I don't," she replied in an unsteady voice.

OF COURSE WE'RE LOST

Carol cut in promptly and incisively. "Were you right at the stream when you started back, Molly, or some distance to one side?"

"Ten or fifteen meters to one side—the right, in the direction I was going originally."

"All right. Joe?"

"Yes, Carol."

"Everything has been logged since Molly went underground, hasn't it? Instrument and conversation records?"

"Certainly."

"Please give me, as quickly as you can, the time between Molly's entering the crack—the one her robot almost didn't fit and I had so much trouble finding—and the time she reported starting back. Molly, can you judge how much time you spent putting the ice coating on your robot?"

"Fairly well. It was pretty quick—eight or ten minutes."

"How far did you travel between the time you started doing it and the time you finished and started back? Did your robot make any really wide or strange turns while you were doing it?"

"No, to the second question. Not more than fifty or a hundred meters, to the first."

"Good. I know, to within a few meters, how far into this passage I have come. Joe's time, when he gives it, should tell me how far upwind you traveled; and you are sure you never went very far from the stream going down it. I'll calculate where you made the turn and get my machine there as quickly as I can, checking the brook to make sure the wind hasn't changed too greatly. It shouldn't be very long. Maybe there'll be some trace of your work—some of the water you sprayed may be on the rock as recognizable ice. I'm not the chemist Jenny is, but anyone can recognize water by color. Just in case there isn't any trace, you can spend the time I'm on the way describing the area as exactly as you can remember it. I know that won't be very exact, but any data can help. From there, we'll have to—*I'll* have to—take a chance that what seemed like the opposite direction along the stream to you will seem the same to me, closely enough so that when I set my machine along a line it will be the right one."

"You'll be beyond the rope, Carol," Charley pointed out. "You already are."

"Can't help it. Can't wait. Molly's still traveling. I can remember what I see well enough to get back to it. I thought of going after her on foot for a moment—I'd be more able to spot any trail she might have left, or details she might remember—but it seems safer to keep the robot with me, and it should be able to go wherever hers has."

"Nothing very remarkable to report so far," Molly interjected.

"Since you woke up, you mean. All right, I'm ready to start as soon as I get Joe's log figures."

The Nethneen responded at once, and after a few moments of mental arithmetic Carol was traveling. "I should get to the place where you did your ice job in less than an hour at this rate, and if I manage to hit your line closely enough I should catch you in maybe an hour or an hour and a quarter more, Molly."

The Human acknowledged; she had not finished doing the arithmetic herself and didn't think she was getting quite the same answer; but of course Joe would have used either School or his own time and distance units, and her translator would have rounded both of these—no, that couldn't be it; Joe would have expressed himself quite precisely, and the computer on her wrist would have gone equally far in significant figures. Probably Carol was considering factors of her own, like time to reset her own robot's programming. Molly wasn't really awake yet, she began to realize, and this wasn't good. She *must* see and remember as much as possible of the route she was following, so that she could give the Shervah some sort of reasonable description if one were needed.

She swung her light around—that might serve another purpose; if they were still in the same cavern, Carol might see it. Certainly the place she was in was large, no wall was in sight in any direction. There must be a roof, but it was too far above to let her distinguish any real details. The floor, of course, was right below. Molly shone her beam alternately forward and backward, trying to decide whether or not the floor was level, but was unable to make up her mind. Presumably the cylinder's own attitude was erect, but it was small, and her own semicircular canals were of little help in this gravity. She found herself sure at one moment that she was going down a fairly steep slope and seconds later just as sure that she was climbing.

The floor was rock, not quite like any she had seen before on Enigma, but not very different; whether the change meant anything she could not be sure. It still seemed rather loose, friable stuff. Nothing resembling igneous rocks with which she was familiar had shown up so far on Enigma. She dismounted and took a closer look, reporting the nature of the material as precisely as she could to the others and cutting out a specimen at Carol's request.

"I know I can get one myself if I find you, but your dig will make a mark that will tell me I'm on the right track. We should have thought of this earlier. Make a hole in the rock every few minutes—use your laser if you have to."

"I haven't seen much that really needed it yet," replied Molly, "but I'll do better than that. I'll mark an arrow—does that symbol translate?—all right—to indicate which way the robot is going. I might even run off to the sides every now and then and make arrows pointing toward the trail, just to improve your chances of hitting it. There are occasional patches of dust now; I won't always have to use the hammer, even."

"Dust or salt?" asked Jenny.

"I couldn't say. Very, very fine powder; I don't have equipment to check the composition—I certainly don't intend to check whether it's water-soluble, and the ammonia brook is still out of sight. To forestall your next request, I have no more unused collecting cans, Jenny; you'll have to hope Carol hasn't filled all hers before she gets here."

Silence fell for some time, interrupted only by Charley's occasional check questions and, more rarely, by Molly's description of some change in her surroundings. She was almost, but not quite, sure now that her path was again descending quite steeply.

"Any wind that you can feel?" asked Joe.

"'Fraid not. That doesn't mean there is none—wait a minute; here's another patch that might be sand or dust. Let me try something—hey, Carol, there's a crust on this; the surface is hard. It looks like dried, cracked mud. There's fine stuff underneath, though. Just a minute. Joe, there's a very slight breeze, enough to carry some of the finest dust as I drop it, going roughly from right to left across my present path. Very weak indeed—in the centimeters-per-second class, I'd say, though at the rate things fall here my time sense is getting ruined, too."

"Note that, Carol."

"Don't worry, I wasn't going to use wind to follow her, Joe. I think I'm about at the place where she used the water now. You said you were a few meters to the right of the stream, Molly?"

"That's right."

"Well, I don't see any ice stains on the rock, but I suppose you'd have been careful not to waste any."

"I certainly was."

"Did the stream go perfectly straight for twelve meters, with a width varying from ninety-three to one hundred centimeters, then make a five-degree bend to the right, widening by twelve centimeters as it did so, and then take on a rather sinuous path for the next forty-five meters, making three oscillations with an amplitude of just under one meter, and—"

"As nearly as I can recall, that's about right; but I can't be sure how much is honest memory and how much is coming from your description."

"Of course," the Shervah remarked in an annoyed tone. "That was stupid of me. I should have let you do the describing, to avoid suggestion."

"I could never have done it to anything like that detail.

If you think the distance is right, you're probably as close as you'll get. The part of the stream I used for a back sight was just about perfectly straight; I do remember that."

"All right," agreed Carol. "That hasn't happened very often as I came along. We'll hope this is it. Stand by while I reset these keys—there. No pressure response, straight line along the stream section at about three quarters the speed I can run in this gravity. I'll flash a narrow beam straight ahead every little while; you look back when I do—I'll tell you—and let me know if you see it."

"Why not keep the beam steadily pointed ahead?" asked Charley. Molly and Jenny chuckled audibly; Joe was too polite.

"Because I'd have trouble looking at the rocks, of course," Carol answered patiently.

"And I'm not pointing mine back very often, because if I do run into anything I want some warning," added Molly. "I do hope you get here soon, Carol; I'm getting rather tired of this Juggernaut."

Even Charley needed an explanation of that symbol. Molly had to admit that the metaphor was slightly strained.

By the fifth time Carol's light had shone ahead without reaching her, Molly was becoming discouraged again. If both robots were following straight paths and the Shervah had picked the right direction, the distance between them should be quite small by now. The lights were powerful, and there was certainly no other illumination to compete with them—though when Molly turned her own lamp off, subjective glows and flashes swam around her field of perception. The rescuer's light, however, would presumably not move with the watcher's eyeball, and for the moment the Human felt some confidence in her ability to separate illusion from reality. She was beginning to wonder, however, how long she could expect this to last. The place was lightless except for her own lamp, soundless except for her friends' voices, and practically weightless. She knew that a nervous system without input, like a nervous system whose input was at the edge of its sensory limitations, tended to amplify and organize its own noise. So far she had heard no music and seen no canals, much less angels or faces, but she found herself looking forward more and more eagerly to Charley's voice checks and even calling one or another of her friends when she had nothing in particular to report.

On Carol's seventh try with her light, Molly saw something flashing from her backtrack direction and almost fainted with relief. She was doubtful enough about her own perceptions by then to ask her friend to flash the beam on and off several times, but the spark blinked in and out of existence in the same pattern as the sender's call.

"It's you all right! Can you see my light? I'm pointing it back at you."

"Yes. I'm glad you picked that straight bit of stream. We're a couple of hundred meters apart laterally; my direction was a trifle off to the right. I'm correcting and will be with you in a moment."

"Don't stop talking. My ears as well as my eyes were beginning to deceive me. I was beginning to hear faint rumbling noises, and deep hoots and bellows."

"That may not be illusion," Charley interjected. "There's another storm—a really wild one—going on up here, and you aren't so far from the surface, after all. Even Joe noticed it, though he doesn't really hear; the boat's been vibrating a bit."

"But would sound get through rock—I don't mean that; it would travel better in rock, of course—but would it get through the rock-air interface well enough to be audible down here?" Molly was more than doubtful.

"Carol, you can hear. Are you picking it up?" asked Charley.

"I think so, now that you call my attention to it. It wouldn't have to cross the interface, remember; there's a closed tube connecting us with the surface for a good deal of the distance. Anyway, it's not very important; when I get to Molly, we can check whether we're hearing the same sort of sounds, if she's still worried about her objectivity. I'll be with you inside of a minute, Mol."

"And there are only two people in the universe I'd rather see right now. Thanks, Carol."

"I'm not hurt. I have three. Set your light for diffuse; I don't need a beam now to spot you. I'm doing the same. Where will we have the party when we get back to our own? Pearl or Topaz? Your gravity and no air, or my gravity and your air?"

"Right now I'll settle for anyplace where water will stay liquid and in a tub."

"My place, then. I can melt water in the party wing, and you'll need the air. Taking a shampoo in armor is a bit pointless. You'd have to refrigerate for me and the Others on Pearl, and I want to play some more with water anyway. I can think of some really good party tricks with ice."

Molly watched the approaching patch of radiance containing the other robot and its tiny rider, and for the first time in what seemed like days felt really free to get off her own machine and walk along beside it. Carol pulled a few meters ahead, stopped her robot, and also dismounted, and the tiny humanoid leaped to meet her huge friend.

"Don't squash me!" she exclaimed. "I'm glad to see you, too, but let's not get overemotional." Molly set her back on her feet, and the Shervah turned her attention to the first robot. After a moment, she gave Molly more instructions.

"This may be a trifle awkward. You're going to have to walk or ride with the middle of your back, where your heat pump exhausts, as close as you can get it to this place here on the shell. Your ice coat has frozen the access panel shut, and we'll have to melt it away before I can get at the keys. I'm not sure the laser is controllable enough, and if it vaporizes any metal I might lose my eyesight even if the beam itself doesn't hit me."

"No problem," replied Molly. "I could walk on my hands in this gravity, and actually you could carry me in the best position, I suspect. How about trying it?"

"That's a thought. It never occurred to me that a living person could be used as a blowtorch, but we admit human beings are a bit special, don't we?"

By the time the ice had disappeared from the panel, both women were feeling a trifle uneasy; Carol's robot was some distance behind them. However, with the frozen water gone, she set her giant friend back on her own feet, opened the panel, and quickly manipulated the keys inside. The metal cylinder obediently stopped for the first time in many hours and, in response to further control, started back the way it had come at a somewhat higher speed. In two or three minutes it had reached the other machine, and Carol stopped it again.

"Relief mission accomplished," she reported. "We are together, and Molly and both robots seem to be all right. I can find our way back easily. I suggest we go quickly as far as the big cave where the life was found and learn what we can there; we'll need specimens. All right, Jenny?"

"Fine. I'm tempted to meet you there but have no intention of going outside in this storm. I might not be as lucky as Joe when I blow away. There are a fair number of hills around to make eddies, but I'm not sure I'd get close to one, and anyway there seem to be electrical discharges. My armor has metal in it."

"A good excuse for staying in the big cave for a while and collecting, if an excuse is needed," agreed Carol. "All right, I think you can trust us to pick up all you need—for a preliminary study, of course." The Shervah looked at her companion, who nodded wordlessly, and the smaller woman set first Molly's robot and then her own back into a traveling mode. She estimated a proper direction to bring them back to the stream, using the detailed mental picture she had formed of the parts of the cavern she had traversed so far. It was not straight back along the way either of them had come, but a little to the right of Molly's back track; it should, Carol judged, intercept the stream two or three hundred meters above the point where they had left it. She did not want to cut any farther to the right, since there was obviously something—wall or ridge—preventing the stream itself from coming in this direction. If anything, as far as she could tell, they were nearly under the first large cavern, though some hundreds of meters to the left of the path they had first followed from it. Like Molly, she was rather uncertain of slope, however, and would have been reluctant to claim real confidence about their position.

Her senses of direction and location, like those of human beings, were simply integrated memories of turns made and distances traveled; she knew that accumulating uncertainties in both would eventually put her badly off the truth. With only her own lights here in the caverns, there was little chance of long-range sighting, so direction errors in particular could accumulate quickly. Much too quickly for comfort.

The discomfort was vastly amplified when, at about the

time Carol expected to get to the stream, they reached what looked like a channel that had no liquid flowing in it. It was not completely dry; there were puddles, which she quickly identified as ammonia, along the depression, but in no sense was it a stream or brook.

She reported at once to the others.

"Check carefully against your memory," advised Joe. "The first thought to strike me is that it is your brook, run dry for some reason."

"The storm?" suggested Molly.

"Conceivably but not obviously. It is precipitating heavily here, and I would assume that the liquid must be ammonia. It would be easier to imagine ways in which your stream could have been overfilled from the surface."

"Streams and lakes are temporary things," Molly pointed out. "They cut new channels and dam old ones with sediment. I'd say we simply have another set of observations to make, if this does turn out to be the same stream."

"It is," Carol said firmly. "I remember a lot of what we see now. We are just about where I expected to be, a little more than two hundred meters upstream from where Molly and I both left it awhile ago. In another four hundred or slightly more we should reach the point where it first came in from the side. Just a moment while I reset the robots. Yours first, Molly; let me at the panel."

"Are the sounds you thought might be the storm any louder yet?" asked Charley.

"No," both women answered at once. "Dead silence outside the armor," added the Human.

"Was the change sudden?" asked Joe.

"I don't really remember. Probably not. Do you recall, Carol?"

"If anything, I am less sure than you, but inclined to agree. If I'd noticed at all, I'd certainly remember; it just didn't catch my attention. I'd hear better with no helmet, but I don't think—"

"You shouldn't risk taking that off!" exclaimed Charley in a horrified tone. Molly, feeling her usual pity for the Kantrick when he was taking things too literally, quickly changed the subject; fortunately, opportunity had arisen.

"Carol! Isn't that your rope?"

"It is. I was beginning to wonder—just a little—whether my own memory had been overpowered by suggestion, but that settles any possible argument about where we are. I knew we should reach it before we got to the place where the stream came in but didn't want to set you looking for it. We'll be back in the big cave almost at once; we're going faster than you were before, remember. Hold on a moment—it will be better if you walk, I think. I'm going to have to run from one of these machines to the other to keep resetting the guidance—no, I can use the wind again, can't I? Just set them to move away from ram pressure—"

"Not mine," Molly pointed out. "We didn't clear off all the ice."

"That's right. We should have washed it at one of the puddles we passed. Here's one now; let me stop the thing—there. I still have some empty specimen cans, and sloshing ammonia against it should do the trick. I haven't worked much with ice, but if polarity means anything it ought to be soluble."

The cleaning process took only a minute or two, and the robots resumed their journey in somewhat wavering fashion; "downwind" was a less definite direction than the inertial one Carol had been using. The passage narrowed, as even Molly remembered, and presently the women emerged into the vast open space where Carol had first lost her friend's trail. The fishline led off to the right.

"We'd better stay with it. I wouldn't want to guess how many openings there might be in the upper part of this hole, or where they might go, and I couldn't see enough for real guidance on the way down." Molly, who had never considered doing otherwise, fully agreed, and the robot controls were again reset. This time Carol did have to move back and forth for frequent readjustments; the wind was no longer a guide, and she had only a rough idea of the curvature of the rock wall.

As Molly knew from the earlier conversations, there was about a kilometer to go before the rope trail would turn out across the cavern floor, and both students paid far more attention to the floor itself. There were the sparkling crystals that *might* be alive, the slippery patches and other areas that almost had to be, or that at least could represent chemistry on its way to becoming alive—a more believable state of affairs. Carol had paid little attention to this kilometer of distance, though she had traversed it three times already—once searching for the passage Molly had taken, and again and back to get the rope after finding the way. The first time, her attention had been on the wall, and the other two she had been in a hurry.

Even so, she was aware of a difference as her light beam probed across the cavern floor. Then it had been irregular rock, sometimes bare, sometimes hidden by the mysterious growths and coverings they had both encountered. Now, however . . .

"Molly!" said the Shervah in a puzzled tone. "You never saw any liquid on the cave floor at all, did you—not even the little puddles I did?"

"Nothing. There might have been some under the crystals, but all I found was that sticky stuff. We have some of it, and if I don't encounter any more of it I'll be just as happy."

"But look out there now! That's not just a puddle!"

The Human swept her own light in the indicated direction and saw that her friend was right. It wasn't just a puddle. It was a lake, extending as far as the light could carry her eyesight. This was not too far—perhaps a couple of hundred meters, since she could not use really bright light with Carol beside her—but they had not yet come that far from "her" tunnel. She must have crossed this part of the floor only a few hours ago, and it was certainly no lake then.

"The glittery stuff was all over this place earlier," she pointed out. "We'd better see if it's still there, underwater—I mean under the ammonia. I can't really dive in this armor, but I should be able to see; how about you?"

"We'll both look. Come on."

The two explorers approached the edge of the lake cautiously, reporting the situation in detail to Charley and the others as they went.

"Both of you watch your temperatures" was the warning. Not even Charley tried to discourage the research.

Molly, fortunately, was ahead of her companion. "Watch out! Sticky!" she called suddenly, and with some difficulty retreated from the spot where her armored feet had tried to stay. She had not even reached the edge of the liquid, still half a dozen meters away. "This stuff was under the crystals before. I wonder what became of them?"

"The part you met was under the crystals. We don't know it was nowhere else," the Shervah pointed out cautiously.

"True. Let's try a little farther along." Molly approached the verge more carefully this time, but was able to wade ankle deep before encountering the same difficulty. She bent over and groped with a gloved hand, again finding no trace of the glitter before she reached the adhesive. "You'd better stay out of this, Carol," she advised. "I can pull free, but you'd find it harder. We should go back to the line I followed across here, as nearly as I can remember, and . . . no, the crystals didn't grow this close to the wall. We'd have to get well out in the lake to make sure they really aren't there any more. Let's go along the rope and check your line."

Carol agreed, and started the robots again. Twice they had to ride them, where the lake came to the very wall; one of these places, to Carol's annoyance, was where she had slipped on *something*. There was no way to check if it were still there; the liquid was too deep. She mentioned this to her companion.

The Human shrugged. "You got a sample before. If it had been ice, it would have dissolved in the ammonia anyway."

Then another problem claimed their attention. A little farther on, the rope turned and led toward the middle of the great cavern, as they had expected. Carol set the robot directions as precisely as she could from the lie of the rope. They mounted their machines, and Molly took the cord in one hand, allowing it to slip through her fingers as they floated slowly across the lake a few centimeters above the surface.

"You should have taken this thing," the Human remarked after a minute or two. "There's a lot of your slimy stuff stuck to it, and I don't have any collecting cans left."

"Let's see," said Carol from some two meters away. She turned her light on Molly as the latter held the line up for inspection. "Just a moment—I'll steer closer and get some."

Molly agreed, and as the other robot drew alongside, she held the slippery length of material out so that her friend could scrape the lip of a can along it.

"Of course, we could have waited and done this more

easily where it lifts out of the lake," the Shervah remarked, "but—"

"But that part wouldn't have been under the surface," Molly pointed out. "How fast are we going now? Can you judge when we should get back to that place?"

"Not too well. Even if I'd seen the lake before, it really hasn't any features to stick in memory."

"Are you sure?" asked Molly. "What's this stuff ahead of us?" Carol indicated the direction with her light but said nothing until they had drawn level with what looked like a patch of tall grass blades sticking through the surface of the liquid. Still silent, she took hold of one of them and tried to break it off.

"Tough and slippery," she reported. "Can you get a grip on it, Mol?" The Human tried, and after some effort managed to pull one of the stalks loose from whatever was holding it below. By this time, several voices were wanting to know what was going on, Charley's by no means the loudest. Molly explained briefly; she had handed her specimen to the Shervah, who was far too busy pulling it up the rest of the way and examining its base to talk to anyone.

"Something like swamp grass"—she had to be more explicit in description—"growing from the bottom of the lake. It's getting thicker as we go along. It must have started since Carol and I passed, probably since the lake filled. Something has changed the flow pattern down here, *and* the biology. I wish I could guess which was cause and which effect. Like it or not, Joe, there is complex life here, and I'd guess it's tied in with Enigma's seasons in some way."

"Is it interfering with your guide rope?" asked Joe, with his usual grasp of essentials.

"It seems to be dragging more, as though something were holding it to the bottom," replied Molly. "If I did lose my hold on it, it would be rather a nuisance; maybe you should take it, too, Carol, and just back me up. Put three or four meters between us; then I can warn you if something takes me by surprise and I lose it."

"Good idea." The smaller student, without really taking her attention from the grass blade she held in one hand and examined with one eye, worked her robot behind the other close enough to let her take hold of the cord trailing from her friend's glove; then she fell back a little, as suggested. Molly, of course, was still getting whatever tension was on the line.

"Any worse?" asked the Shervah after a minute or two.

"I think so, but the change is very gradual."

"Troubles?" came Charley's voice.

"Oh, no," the Human reassured him. "The rope's sticking to the bottom of this puddle, or maybe to the grass, a little, but we're in no danger of losing it. We'll be under the drop point soon."

"No, we won't," said Carol suddenly.

"What?"

"We've passed it. Look ahead." Molly sent the beam of her light into the region that the red-sun native could already see clearly enough.

The cave wall was a dozen meters ahead of them.

DATUM THREE: JENNY

It seemed a pity to have to be so quick. Hours or days would have been better, to look over the caves, decide something of the life pattern, and form some idea of a logical basis for selecting specimens. Still, she'd be back, of course.

Jenny slipped out of her mapper. It was tempting to try to walk on only the back three or four pairs of legs in this trivial gravity, and one *could* almost balance erect, Human or Shervah style, but it really took too much attention. It must be convenient to have eyes so far from the ground and be able to see so far without making a climbing or erecting project out of it; but on the other hand, it must be a nuisance to have to bend over or fold those long, rigid legs in order to give a close examination to something on the ground. Use what you have.

And there was work to do; one could philosophize later, though at least this was a time and place where one's theorizing could hardly result in embarrassment. She remembered with sympathetic amusement the degree holder who had stressed, during a lecture on, if she recalled correctly, Fire's inner planet Diamond, the universal tendency for the eyes of animals to be located close to their mouths. The unfortunate speaker had then noticed Joe in his audience. The Nethneen's environmental armor hid the fact that his mouth was at the lower pole of his nearly spherical body, but memory had been enough.

But this wasn't work.

There were lots of things growing here, but nothing moving. That did not mean, of course, that the things were all plants; it was already obvious that something radically different from the respiration-photosynthesis cycle of a typical sun-circling planet must be going on here. Jenny, like any imaginative being, was hypothesizing well ahead of data.

The growths in the patch which had caught her eye, only a meter or two from the mapper, were pulpy things which Molly would have compared to multiple links of sausage, some growing upward and some extending in segments along the cave floor. Jenny carefully sliced off end segments from a low and a high branch and stowed them in separate specimen cans. Colorless—to her eyes—ichor flowed copiously from the cut ends; she hoped she had not done excessive damage to the creature, and watched for half a minute, worried. If there were no animals, there might be no evolutionary provision for dealing with mechanical damage.

Then the penultimate segment shrank in on itself, the open end was pulled out of sight, and the flow ceased. The Rimmore went on, satisfied.

She could not budget much time; she was back at the mapper in ten minutes, specimen cans full. There was a puddle of material, presumably the spilled ichor, between the spot where she had made her first collection and the robot itself. Protected by her armor, she gave little thought to stepping in it; of course it might not be a good idea to contaminate the outside of her protective suit—but she would be cleaning it off when she got back to the tent, anyway.

The unexpected explosion hurled her into the air, completely over her robot, and sent the latter rolling sideways—she fortunately had powered it down completely when she emerged. If it had tried to hold position against the blast . . .

Jenny tested the last six legs on her left side, some of which were numb and some stinging from the shock. The armor had apparently done its job. She righted the robot, entered it, and checked its controls. Finding with relief that all was operating properly, she set out for the surface.

DATUM FOUR: CHARLEY

It was a jolt to his faith. The calm certainty that the Faculty would never allow anything serious to happen to a student had kept Charley steady through all of Enigma's unpleasant treatment of its visitors. When Joe had blown away, it had been frightening for a moment; when Carol had been trapped helplessly outside and had to be rescued, he had pictured himself in the same predicament. These had been tests, of course; students were supposed to solve them, to get out of the difficulty by their own ingenuity and intelligence. Joe and Carol hadn't passed, and would no doubt have to face others.

The trouble was that Charley himself wasn't sure what he would have done in either of those situations. He could foresee some of the tests—though perhaps it had been a mistake to mention the probable failure of the boat. Maybe they'd skip that now. Maybe he should be more independent of the Human. She was pleasant, and apparently imaginative, but that could be explained if she were the source of the test problems, or the observer who was grading them.

One couldn't be sure about that. There was reason to think it was Molly—but then there was Joe. Very different. Looked practically normal, if he were only larger and lacked those odd paired eyes and didn't seem to be made of rubber. How he dared to move around with no shell—maybe that had something to do with being the first victim of a failed test. But that failure didn't need to be real—

Would they realize that Charley's courage was really just faith? Would they have a test designed to undermine *that*?

He shouldn't think about that too much. The assigned problem about the planet was where his attention should stay. Worrying too much about what lay behind the assignment could unbalance anyone. Just do the job as it was planned, with any changes the extra tests might demand, and stop worrying about what the Faculty thought. If he didn't get rated this time, he could always try again.

He wondered what Molly's real rating was.

Or Joe's.

OF COURSE CAROL'S RIGHT

"Joe!" Neither of the women ever knew who had called out first, and neither was greatly calmed by the Nethneen's placid response.

"Yes?"

"Are you still getting any sort of position on us?"

"Yes. As you approached the surface once more, readings got clearer. I still can't trust them very well, though; the effect of the rock on direction and intensity—"

"But surely we're not too far from where we were!" It was Molly who asked.

"Not as far as I can tell. Will you clarify what has happened down there?"

The Human did so, summarizing events tersely.

"Any explanation?" asked Jenny at the end. "It's hard to believe anything has been moving the rope around, and a lot harder to suppose a new cave wall has formed."

"One." Molly spoke, after glancing at her companion. "The rope broke or was broken somewhere above and fell into the pool. For some time we've been dragging the bight and have now completely crossed the cavern."

"Wouldn't you have noticed that the line was slanting to your rear—that you were holding a bight—as you traveled?"

"I did. I assumed it was due to our speed. We were in too much of a hurry, I guess," replied Molly. "Carol wouldn't have noticed anything after we found that grass."

There were several seconds of thoughtful silence.

"That seems to fit what we know of the facts," Joe admitted finally. "The problem would now seem to be finding your entry tunnel without the aid of either the rope or Carol's memory. There could be a good many such passages, of course; it's looking more and more as though you had quite a labyrinth down there. If Charley's suggestion about kames is right, Enigma's crust could be riddled with those caves; and if they're connected enough for air currents to travel freely, there's a real problem."

"We'll have the wind," Carol pointed out. "We'd have the sound of the storm, but that seems to have died out pretty well. I take it it's ended up there."

"No, sand and dust are still blowing strongly. Visibility is very poor. When you get back to the surface, you'll have to be careful not to blow away as I did. All right, you'd better send the robots upward at one meter per second for six hundred fifty seconds—that will bring you to the level of the original entry tunnel—"

"Maybe. We don't know that the lake surface is at the level of Molly's first stop down here."

"Of course. Well, you'll still be somewhere near it, I'd think."

"Could be. But there's another point. I don't like the idea of moving from one robot to the other to reset their controls with a drop like that underneath. I might conceivably live through such a fall in this gravity, especially with a splash instead of a smash at the bottom, but if I did lose my hold while transferring, Molly and I would both be in trouble. I hate to suggest leaving one of the machines here even for a little while, but it's going to be a lot more practical for us to ride just one of them up."

"You have plenty of rope," Charley cut in testily. "Why should you be worried about falling? You could tie a safety line to each machine and another one to Molly, so you wouldn't even have to climb up by yourself if you did fall."

"And if I set up even a small difference in the flight courses of the robots, I could be breaking the ropes or pulling myself apart with no chance to correct it. Joe's machines are too independent of outside influence. No, thanks, Charley."

Molly wondered fleetingly how much of this objection represented a serious worry of Carol's and how much was reluctance to be corrected by the Kantrick. Even Joe hesitated before agreeing, but he did agree. Moments later, Molly had moved over to the Shervah's robot and was lashing herself to it while her little friend worked the inside keys. Before the knots were finished, they were rising. At Carol's suggestion, the Human kept playing her light on the nearby wall, and the smaller woman kept them keyed out of contact with it.

At what should have been about the right height, Carol stopped their ascent. The "wall" was not yet quite a ceiling, but had developed enough overhang to permit argument on the point. Distractingly, it was now covered with patches of something that reminded Molly of moss. The Shervah sent them drifting away from it reluctantly, until the rock was scarcely visible in their lights, and reset the machine to move downwind.

In the boat, Joe was hurrying as much as he dared on the final details of the mapping robot. Actual construction was no problem with the shop resources available, but even he was being corrupted by the notion that no possible emergency should be left unconsidered. He did not, as it happened, think of the facility as being particularly complete; it was the sort of thing one had in an auxiliary spacecraft. In a typical mechanical laboratory on any of the School planets he could have built a copy of the boat itself, complete with shop, with a few minutes of control adjustment and an hour's waiting. He would have been disappointed in an adolescent of his own or any other supposedly intelligent species who couldn't. He would, of course, have been a little quicker and less clumsy without the environment armor, thin as this was; but being Joe, he gave no thought to the negative aspects of the situation.

He kept adding equipment as thoughts occurred to him. He was genuinely concerned by now about the danger to the two explorers, and had put his own wind-mapping project well into the back of his mind.

This was unfortunate, as Molly was to point out later, though the data probably could not have been interpreted until later anyway.

Charley, without consulting anyone, had grounded the boat as nearly as he could manage to the point where Carol had attached her safety rope, but could see no sign of it through the blowing sand. He did not seriously consider emerging to make a personal search, but remained at the keys, straining his memory for any sort of handling equipment on board that might substitute for him to find the line and be sent along it to the point where the break had presumably occurred. A light left there, or even carried farther along the passage if there were no ambiguity about the path, might help the women identify the right tunnel.

Jenny, also without consulting anyone, had made another half kilometer of safety cord and was checking her armor with the intention of doing personally what Charley wanted to do by mechanical proxy. With her build, wind wouldn't get too much grip on her, she kept telling herself; and as long as she was firmly attached to the ship itself she couldn't blow too far even if it did. Unlike Joe, she came from a world where the concept of *wind* was very real to its people, and she was realistically scared; but if her friends were out of the physical touch Carol had so sensibly planned, something would have to be done. If anyone could climb that hill, it would be a Rimmore—maybe it would have to be from the upwind side, but she'd make it. Jenny checked her armor and made sure she had an extra light.

Charley knew, of course, when the air lock opened—he was preoccupied but still watching his instrument banks. His screen coverage did not include the lock area, and he wondered for a moment whether Joe had finished the mapping robot and were testing it without reporting to anyone. This seemed very unlike the Nethneen, but before Charley could decide on the propriety of interrupting work with a question, Jenny flowed into the field of one of his instruments. She was barely visible, half buried in sand, her numerous legs almost entirely out of sight as they worked her long body forward.

For just a moment her fellow student wondered about her sanity; then he caught a glimpse of the rope extending back toward the ship, bowed by the wind, and was quick enough on the uptake to grasp the whole plan before bursting into speech. When he did say anything, it was calm advice.

"If you're just heading for Molly's hill, Jenny, about five grads to your left would be better. If you're hoping to intercept Carol's rope before you get there, I'm not so sure, but would guess about as much to your right."

"I was thinking mainly of the hill" was the reply.

"The rope would help you climb it," pointed out the Kantrick.

Jenny had little of Carol's impatience and superiority where Charley was concerned. "Thanks; I hadn't thought of that. I suppose the real question is whether I'm likely to lose more time hunting for the rope in this sandstorm than I'll save by finding it. I'll try your shift to the right; the hill is big enough so that won't slow me down much in getting to it."

"Jenny, are you really outside?"

"Yes, Joe. I am not blowing away, though in this disgusting gravity I feel as though I ought to, but I have a rope connecting me to the boat if I do."

"Please come back! The robot is almost finished, and it will carry riders. You can take it on the track of the others much more safely."

"It isn't tested yet. You'd better combine a test run with backing me up. You consider time important now, or you wouldn't have dropped everything else to make that machine. If I come back and wait for you to finish it, we'll lose more time."

"True, of course. Very well. You or Charley please keep me informed of your progress. I'll be outside in, at a guess, a quarter of an hour." And in the shop, unseen by the others, handling tendrils moved even more rapidly.

"I've reached the base of the slope," Jenny reported a minute or so later. "I haven't seen or touched Carol's rope, and I'm not going to waste time looking for it. The sand is about at its angle of repose—I can't seem to climb it any better than Carol or Molly could—but I'm going around to the windward side. At least it won't be blowing down in my face there. The slope should be gentler, too, and the wind itself will help me up—no, wait—here's Carol's rope—I can haul myself up by that. Can you still see me, Charley?"

"Yes. Not clearly."

"You tell Joe how I'm doing, then—and me as well. I get less wind trouble if I stay mostly buried, and that keeps me from seeing very far. Let me know when I'm near the top."

"All right. Don't bury yourself entirely."

During the next few minutes, only Charley's terse remarks

connected the group. "You're about halfway." "You're digging in too deeply—I can hardly see you." "Are you following the rope? You seem to be working around to the other side of the hill." "You're getting buried again."

"I can't help it," Jenny replied to the last comment. "I'm not digging in; the hill is traveling like a dune, I think. The wind is trying to move it on top of me."

"Are you sure?" cut in Joe.

"Not sure, but it's the impression I get. Why?"

"Never mind." The Nethneen fell silent again.

"I hadn't noticed that the hill seemed any closer," said Charley thoughtfully, "but that would explain why the rope seems to be leading you around to the other side."

"So it—Oh! I get it! Joe! Nearly done?"

"Nearly. Get to the top as quickly as you can and report what, if anything, is left of the crater. Stay there as long as you can. Charley, get distance measures of her as exactly as possible at regular intervals after she gets to the top; we may want to know how fast that hill is traveling. Jenny, just do your best to stay on the crater rim, if there still is one, until I get to you. Carol? Molly?"

"Yes." It was the Human's voice.

"I take it you have not found your entry tunnel and that there is no wind to guide you."

"Plenty of wind. It led us to the wrong tunnel, which was blocked with vegetation—to classify hastily—before we got far anyway. We've gone back to the big cave and are checking its walls at this height for the right opening."

"How did you know it was the wrong tunnel?"

"We were pretty sure from the beginning because it was a lot lower than we thought it should be." It was Carol's voice this time. "Then it became a narrow, twisty tube of rock that finally got too narrow for the robot."

"Why didn't you tell us?" asked Charley.

"What could you have done about it? As long as we could get back to the big cave, there was nothing to worry about. It cost us only a few minutes, anyway. But, Joe—is there any point in trying to find the original tunnel now?"

"Possibly not, but what happened to your rope may still be useful data, and your memory will give us information on how much of the way is blocked."

"What are you talking about?" asked Charley.

"Their guiding wind has stopped. Your hill is a moving dune. They don't hear the storm any more. Jenny, are you at the top yet?"

"Nearly, I think. Charley, can you see me?"

"Yes, barely. Ten meters or so will bring you to the lip, as far as I can tell. I see what you mean now, Joe. But look—if they have a different wind, there must be other openings to the surface, even though this one may be blocked; and maybe we could dig through this sand—"

"That's why I want to have Carol check the inside and Jenny the out. It's too bad Jenny never saw the crater as it was before, but—wait; you did, Charley. Lift the boat and get a look into that hole yourself. Stay close to Jenny—you don't want to pick her up by her safety line. You can let down and collect her when you've checked the crater, unless it looks as though digging were going to be quick and easy and she wants to start in at it."

"I doubt that it will be" came the Rimmore's rasp. "The hole I can see now is less than half as deep as the hill looks high from outside. That's not what I remember the rest of you saying. I have no digging tools, anyway."

"Any luck from inside, Molly and Carol?" asked the Nethneen.

"Four holes that might be tunnel openings so far, all of them different in detail from the one we came through, none of them with any air currents, and each with different kinds of stuff growing in it" was the Shervah's answer. "We'll keep looking, but more for wind than for similarity. I'm beginning to guess what happened to the rope. Are you up where you can see the crater yet, Charley?"

"Just a moment. Yes. I was a little too high; this wind is increasing, or at least the visibility is getting worse. The hole is half full. Stay where you are, Jenny; I'll bring the boat down where you can reach it. You still have your own safety line, don't you?"

"Of course. It's fastened at the main personnel lock. Turn a quarter left—now straight down—ten meters to the right and about three aft—another two to the right—there. I have the lock open—I'm inside—outer door is closed, and I'm flushing the local air. You can do what seems good with the boat. Is the new machine ready, Joe?"

"Yes, but I'm not quite sure what we do with it now. Carol and Molly are blocked from us. We have no high-powered excavation equipment other than ordinary explosives, which it would be unsafe to use—for all we know of the local structure, we might bring the caverns down on them. We—"

"Pardon me, Joe" came Molly's voice. "I think there is a pretty clear line of action. Since there are winds down here—we've found another, much fainter current and are following it—there must be other connections with the surface. I think you'd better get back to your air-current maps, maybe concentrating on the local area more than you would have done, and see how many passages you can find with winds blowing out and with winds blowing in. At the moment, Carol and I really have no basis for a guess on whether we should go upwind or down. Back to your wind maps, little friend!"

"Which were you doing with that current that led you into a narrow passage?" asked Charley.

"Downwind. The only evidence we had at the time was that we'd come in against the wind."

"When its path got too narrow, did you backtrack?"

"Obviously." Carol's voice was a trifle impatient again.

"I mean past the point where you first found the current? I got the impression you went looking right away for other winds."

"Oh. Yes, that's right. We don't know where that one came from."

"Then you have at least one more lead if the one you're using now proves useless."

"I suppose we do. I suspect we have several hundred. What we really need is for Joe to find an incurrent passage and flood it with something nice and smelly that we could follow to its source."

"You're not going to take your helmets off to smell the air."

"I'm afraid not," agreed Molly before Carol could counter. "Even if I risked an occasional sniff, I don't suppose I could catch anything but ammonia—which probably doesn't have any odor to the rest of you."

"Actually, the idea has some merit," Carol pointed out. "The robots can do a certain amount of gas analysis, can't they, Joe? We might keep it in mind, if the right conditions arise. Anyway, I second Molly's motion. Back to your maps."

"I have a further suggestion," said Jenny. "In addition to the normal mapping, two of us could search the area for caves leading underground. Charley could use the boat and I the new mapping robot Joe has just finished. With this storm, vision won't be much help right around here, but we could head upwind to its edge and cover the topography in detail as it moves, following it back in this direction. We can map any promising places, and even if they seem too far from you to be very helpful yet, just getting an idea of their number and distribution should be of use."

"Joe!" Carol snapped suddenly. "The robot just stopped!"

"What was guiding it? Did you see or hear anything change?"

"We were following another air current, as I said—"

"Up- or downwind?"

"Down. It must have stopped. There's roaring ahead—I'm not sure what's happening—"

"The storm? You weren't hearing that before. Maybe you've gotten close enough to an opening to outside—"

"It wouldn't have been that sudden, Charley. Molly, can you see anything ahead? Use any kind of light you want—I'll cover my eyes with the regular flare lids."

"Nothing. The passage just goes on. But the racket is getting louder—back the way we came, Carrie! As fast as we can travel! It may not be falling rock, but I can't think of anything else that might sound anything like it. Move this thing!"

"You mean the tunnel is collapsing?" cried Jenny.

"I don't know. Not close enough to here for us to see, but that would explain the wind's stopping. Get back to the big cavern, at least, Carol, and do some more checking on its wind patterns—let's see whether the ones we found earlier still exist. If the structure of this labyrinth is changing much . . ." Molly left the sentence unfinished, and none of the others tried to complete it. There were several minutes of silence. The people in the boat could think of nothing useful to do, and even Charley was afraid of distracting the fleeing couple with a badly timed question. The boat, indifferent to the wind, hovered above the rapidly filling crater where the women had vanished. Its occupants could only listen to their translators.

"Back in the big place." Carol's voice came at last.

"Can you still hear the falling rock, if that's what it was?"

"No, Joe; that faded out within a few seconds. Whether we got away from it or it just stopped I don't plan to find out. I can't hear it, or the storm, or anything but your voices. You, Molly?"

The Human shook her head negatively, then remembered that only Carol could see her. "Nothing."

"What next? Search this level for more tunnels?"

"I don't think so. I say back down to the lake, or whatever it should be called, and find that passage we went along earlier. It had a wind, remember—so did the one you started into. Let's see whether those are still blowing. I'm beginning to think we'd be best off going upwind looking for places where air currents go underground."

"Why?"

"Well—"

"Going upwind is most likely to find your ice, isn't it, Molly?" Jenny's voice carried amusement.

"I hadn't thought about ice for a couple of hours at least," the Human replied, not even blushing. "It would be interesting to find it but wouldn't get us out of here. Right now I'm beginning to doubt that there is any."

"What?" This was Charley, of course. "You know the density of this planet as well as I do and have seen even more of the rock it's made of. It can't be all silicate—there must be hydrides."

"That's the logic," Molly agreed.

"Well, where's the hole in it? Don't you believe it any more?"

"There's a healthy doubt growing. This place could be a sponge rather than an iceberg. In any case, with no ice vaporizing, air would have to be blowing in to match what blows out, and we should have as good a chance going upwind as down—especially since two downwind searches have failed us now."

"Three, if you count the hunt for the original entry," pointed out Carol.

"All right, three."

"But going upstream, a river tends to subdivide into smaller and smaller streams," Charley pointed out. "Downstream it gets bigger. I'd think—"

"This isn't a river, which cuts its own path," Carol interrupted. "We don't know what made this labyrinth, and so far we've observed only one of its surface connections. Frankly, I'd rather be moving. There was a river in the other tunnel, and maybe it will give some guidance. The only other thing we have is wind; the only choices we have are with or against, and I'm with Molly for the moment—let's try against, as fast as the machine will take us."

"How about recovering the other robot?" Carol thought for a moment.

"If you can put up with its loss, Joe, I think I'd rather not commit myself to an endless running back and forth keeping the two together, even if we are near the ground most or all of the time. If a sudden drop takes us by surprise, the way it did Molly awhile ago, it might be hard to get back together. I think it would be best if we rode the same machine, however uncomfortable."

"If you think that's safest, do it that way. We can replace robots. Go ahead as you suggest. We'll follow, as nearly overhead as we can, in the boat as long as there is any contact with the one you're riding." The women agreed briefly, and Carol sent their mount downward more rapidly than she had risked up to this point.

Molly kept her light beamed below and gave warning as the liquid surface approached. They were out of sight of the cavern wall, and not even the Shervah was precisely sure of direction, but she sent the cylinder quickly in what she hoped was more or less the right one.

It took two or three minutes to reach the edge of the lake, grown thicker with the grass here; Molly wondered whether time or location had made the difference. The arrival brought no relief.

"Joe! Charley! The level is higher! There's no place along the edge to travel now. It's right against the cave wall and partway up—I can't tell how far."

"About three meters since we were last here. The passages we used—yours and mine both—are off to the right," Carol interjected.

"How far?"

"Yours, about seven hundred meters. We'd better hurry."

"Why?"

"Do you want to ride, swim, or get washed down that passage?"

"I'm not sure I want to go along it at all now."

"You'd rather wait until this place fills with ammonia?"

"It couldn't!"

"I'd like to believe that, too. Where's the stuff coming from? How big is the source? Maybe it's going to keep raining into the lakes in this neighborhood for the next twenty years. Maybe one of the lakes up above is draining into these caves."

"But—"

"Come." Carol said only the one word, and Molly regained her self-control. Of course her little friend was right.

Unless the ammonia turned out to be coming in from *below* . . .

Carol sent the robot on.

OF COURSE HE'D FAILED

"What if the passage you're looking for is already full of ammonia?" Charley asked anxiously.

"I don't see how it could be." Molly comforted him and herself. "There's a lot of space—I have no idea how much, but I'm almost sure it's more than this cavern here, judging by my own wanderings—to fill once it starts overflowing that way. The stream should be flowing again, though; maybe that will be some sort of guide."

"Not to the surface!"

"Well, no. But at least this particular place would have to be filling very fast indeed to cover that opening completely. We don't have to worry about being able to get into it, I'd guess."

"You mean you'll go down that passage, away from the surface, in spite of—"

"Unless," snapped Carol, "you can tell us that the storm up there, which is blowing sand fast enough to block our original entrance with a mountain-sized dune and apparently precipitating enough liquid to fill sizable caverns, is either a very small one or is about to end, yes. We are going down that passage if there is wind coming out of it. If not, we will go down any other passage we *can* find wind coming out of. I can't see anything else to do. If this idiotic ball of salt kept its surface features from one century to the next—at least we can see why there was no way to match our maps with the old ones—or had a magnetic field strong enough for an ordinary person to feel, or Joe had provided some way for a person riding this robot to read its inertial sensor—"

"I did, in the new one." An interruption by Joe was so startling that even Carol, playing straighten-out-Charley, was silenced for a moment.

Her attention shifted. "Good. Thanks. We'll still have to use air currents for a guide, though, and following rivers upstream doesn't seem very promising, as Charley pointed out awhile ago. For one thing, if this turns into a real river, it will probably have started out at the top from seepage; and I'm not *that* small. I also think we'll have to drop this policy of keeping the robot down to a speed we can catch on foot. We don't know how far we'll have to go."

"But if one of you falls off—"

"If Molly falls off, I can stop the thing and wait or go back for her. If I—I'd better not."

"I still have some surplus water," Molly said thoughtfully. "I'd rather not use it for glazing robots, of course. But maybe we could rig some kind of gadget that would let me stop the thing with a single key—I know the controls well enough; it's just that my hand is too big to get at them, even if I take off a glove and risk freezing my skin to the metal. All I really need is a piece of stiff wire about twenty centimeters long. I can see in as long as my light's working—at least the keyboard faces the opening in the body! That's luck. With Joe's tendrils, it didn't really have to. Sorry, Joe; that was unkind."

"Deserved, I fear. On a less painful note, what do you have in your armor or equipment that will let you reach the keys?"

"Until I figure that out, we'll keep multiple safety lines attached to Carol. Here comes the tunnel, doesn't it, Carrie?"

"Yes. This lake's draining into it, as you thought it might. We can get in at the farther side, where the opening is high enough for the robot, and see how full the stream is—"

"And whether there is any wind!" exclaimed Charley.

"And whether there is any wind," admitted the Shervah. "That first, actually. You'll have to duck more than I will, big friend; here it comes."

Charley, far above, waited tensely. He could not picture clearly how close the women would have to come to the flood he imagined spilling down into Enigma's bowels and was visualizing the worst. His faith that none of them, especially Molly, could be in real physical danger was eroding a trifle, to his own surprise, though he considered the underlying theory still valid. He continued to expect that the Human would report a new situation at any moment now, which would further complicate the group's assigned test, but he was finding it harder and harder to feel sure that this was all that would happen. He wished briefly that he could see, or even hear, directly what was going on so far below, instead of getting everything via translators.

If translators were all one could have, however, they might as well be used.

"Is your river there, Molly?" he asked.

"Very much so."

"Does it leave room for the two of you, or are you in danger of—"

"No danger. At least, none we can see." Carol's intrinsic honesty modified her impatient speech. "We're traveling fast—as fast as the robot will go, along a weedy river. There's life sprouting everywhere. I didn't think it was this early in the spring!"

"You have wind, then," another voice grated.

"A little, Jen, but actually we're not using it. Once we were sure it existed, we decided in favor of the stream. I know it's bound to take us down, but there must be a limit to that, and when we find its base level—underground lake or ocean, or Molly's ice, or whatever—we should be able to choose among winds reaching that region. The strongest will have the best chance of leading through passages big enough for us."

"Do I see Molly's thinking behind that?"

"Not entirely. There is also biology to check."

"Of course. I should have thought. I'm about to take Joe's new machine upwind to the edge of the present storm area and start looking for more ways into your cavern system. Charley will take Joe back to the tent and then do a similar search with the boat—we'll try to coordinate so as not to duplicate effort too much."

"Good." Molly was really relieved for a moment. "I'm glad Joe can get back to his maps."

"I don't think that would be wise just yet" came the Nethneen's voice.

"Why not?" asked several people at once.

"I have been thinking. It would be better, I am sure, if I stayed in the shop and made yet another mapping robot—possibly two. I haven't been able to forget Charley's prediction about the failure of this boat, though he would never supply us with his reasoning; and in any case it would seem better for all three of us up here to be in a position not only to locate possible entrances to your cavern system but to enter them. This craft is far too large for that."

"Far too large for any entrance we've seen so far—all one of them," pointed out Molly.

"Far too large for any passages likely to connect the caves, big as some of the latter are. I can accept big holes if they're really kames, but I see no reason to suppose that all the connections between them will be ship-size. Do you really expect to—"

"I don't know what to expect, but by all means make your extra bus!" exclaimed Carol. "When Molly and I get out of here, she and Jenny and I will all want to spend a lot of time in the caverns, and rather than ride one of these things we're on now, I'd rather—"

"Good point," Molly and Jenny cut in simultaneously. "But Joe," the Human went on, "don't stay away from your own work too long. I hate to see you kept away from it by all this."

"It's getting done, even when I can't watch it," the Nethneen pointed out calmly. "The longer I have to wait between looks, the more easily I can spot new trends when I do see it. You young people just keep alive, and don't worry about me."

"All right, Uncle." Molly knew the translators would handle the word and did not worry about how Joe or the others would take it. All four of their species used figurative speech, she knew.

Anyone who saw Charley's reaction to the exchange might have wondered briefly, but the Kantrick was alone, and his silence was not long enough to attract attention.

"We're past the place where Molly iced her robot," Carol reported. "New territory from now on."

"Cave or tunnel?" This was Jenny.

"I'd vote for cave. The river has spread out a lot and is flowing very fast—no walls or ceiling—"

"A lot of noise, considering the neighborhood," Molly supplemented. "Rapids—rocks in the stream, some of them loose enough to be rolled by it. At least some of this can be blamed on water erosion. Jenny—?"

"Water?"

"Pardon. Ammonia. *Stream* erosion. If either of us falls off now, Carrie, we'll never make good fossils; there won't be any bone fragments big enough to recognize. It's getting steeper, too; we're really heading downhill. I shouldn't have called these lazy swirls rapids; there isn't enough gravity to move anything rapidly. Should we maybe go by the side of this thing instead of right over it?"

"Then how could they damage your bodies, as you suggested?" asked Charley.

"A rock my own size has inertia, whatever it may lack in weight. You know that as well as I do; are you trying to be funny?"

The Kantrick made no answer, and Carol referred back to Molly's earlier suggestion.

"I suppose we should, though I was enjoying it. Have you ever been on Topaz? That's planet two of the brighter School sun, Fire. It's a wonderful place for being physical. Decent gravity and pressure—a little high for you in the latter, but you could probably stand it—and there's even oxygen in the air. I don't know why I've never seen a Human there. There's a wilderness park where I've spent hundreds of hours canoeing with my Others. Real white water. No really big lakes or oceans; like Jenny's world, of course. You can't have a lot of ammonia with free oxygen, but the life is active enough to keep rivers full. Jen's been there with us, and likes to swim while we paddle. You'll have to come some time, with your Others. We'll get away from over this stream for now; A little homesickness is good for me, but since my Others aren't here I may as well stick to the job."

The eyes of the two explorers met briefly. Molly smiled as images of Rovor and Buzz flashed across her mind, and Carol's grotesque features twisted in an expression that might have had the same meaning.

"I know what you mean," the Human said softly on private channel, "but it's just as well my son isn't here. He'd think it was fun to dive in merely because his father and I had said it wasn't safe."

"An independent thinker? Congratulations."

"Thanks. We're an independent species from early childhood. The thinking comes later. Let's get these rapids out from under us; they're getting even louder and scarier."

"And prettier." Carol maneuvered the robot to one side, however, and changed the subject. "Vegetation everywhere, if it really is plant life. I wish we dared go slower. We could be missing a lot."

"I've been thinking about that. It's spring in this hemisphere, as you said a little while ago; maybe we're running into seasonal changes—the storms, streams filling and emptying, life or something like it visible one moment and not the next. What we saw when the upper cave was dry may have been the last of the season's growth, wiped out right afterward by the flooding. In any case, there has to be a whole ecology, and we can't expect to examine every species. We'll find more, but let's not worry about missing a few items. What we need are Joe's new machines, so we can do it in more comfort and carry more of the stuff we need."

"Which means we need to get back to the boat. I'm in favor of that, but I still think tracing this river to its end will give the others their best chance of finding us."

"Or of providing you with information that will let you find yourselves." If the remark had been made by Charley, Carol might have found fault, but she agreed with Jenny.

"I wonder how far down you are now," the Rimmore continued. "I've been monitoring Joe's receivers, and there's no sort of signal coming back any more. You were at least three kilometers below the surface, making no allowance for refraction, the last time we got a reading."

"And we're heading down very steeply now," added Carol. "I'm surprised the stream can flow so fast in this gravity; it makes me wonder if my time sense is losing track."

"How about wind?" asked the Kantrick.

"I really don't know how much of what we feel is due to our own motion," Molly replied. "We should probably stop for a check some time, but that can wait awhile, I'd think. Jenny, you're outside now. Have you left the storm area yet?"

"Yes. It's a smallish cyclone only a couple of hundred kilometers across—rather surprising, considering Enigma's rotation. Maybe the topography is making eddies. I'm in sunlight, as far as the clouds permit, over very hilly ground."

"Hills or dunes?" asked Carol promptly.

"Hills. Quite solid. Not going anywhere."

"Folds? Blocks? Volcanoes? What?"

"I don't know. Folds, at a guess, with lots of erosion. Numerous dry streambeds."

"Any really long rivers, cutting across ranges of hills?"

"Not that I've seen yet."

"Good. Look *hard* for caves where the streambeds seem to enter or leave hills, particularly the former."

"Good idea. I'll be a long time covering the area, though."

"Assume we have the time, lengthy friend."

If Charley failed to grasp all the implications of this exchange, at least he asked no questions. He volunteered the boat's position—heading rapidly for a point a hundred kilometers west of Jenny's—and promised to start searching, too, as soon as he could see the ground. Joe said nothing.

For hours the two women raced through near-weightless darkness, not quite as helpless as roller-coaster riders. Jenny and Charley scanned Enigma's surface, producing an excellent topographic map in the boat's computer, but for a long time failing to find any caves with winds blowing either in or out. Joe completed another mapping robot, controlling himself in the face of the temptation to add even more safety and research equipment that might possibly be useful—yielding would have meant interrupting the work of the record-controlled shop equipment and adding much time to the project. Enigma rotated, but this made little difference to any of them; those who were on the surface were at a latitude where Arc never set at this season.

Molly slept again, and even Carol dozed, though she kept her great, side-placed, independent eyes open. It seemed unlikely that retracing their course would ever do them any good, but she was taking no risk of missing landmarks; everything her senses detected went firmly into memory, though her awareness was more concerned with earlier memories.

The dominant recollection during these hours was of her

first meeting with Molly and Jenny, perhaps because it, too, had involved a trip. Carol had carelessly allowed her physical fitness rating at the School to lapse and was in the process of earning it back with a rather dangerous eight-hundred-kilometer hike on Jet, Smoke's third planet; naturally, she had not been allowed to use a world with gravity weaker than that of her own. The Human colony was on Smoke's inner planet and the Rimmore one on the fourth, both for reasons of gravity comfort, and Molly and Jenny had been at the starting point. Courtesy had naturally prevented Carol from asking either of the others why they were making the same trip—it could not be for her own reason, since both women were used to greater natural gravities—but it might of course have been something else embarrassing; and neither had volunteered the information. It might have been simply an interest in Jet's native life, which like them was oxygen-breathing. In any case, enough had happened along the eight hundred kilometers, ranging from physically dangerous to merely interesting, to let each of the three be helpful to the others and lay the foundations of firm friendship. It had been Jenny who had suggested that they collaborate in the lab work still needed for their degrees, but the others had been enthusiastic.

The river was now too wide for their lights to reach across; whether rain seepage, lakes draining from the surface, or lakes already underground were feeding it none of them could guess. Wide as it was, it remained turbulent and presumably shallow.

The endless journey was taking nervous toll on everyone, not just the two travelers. Twice Charley called Molly on private channel to ask how long it was going to continue, and seemed surprised when she was irritated at the question. Charley was certainly not stupid, though these questions seemed to be; she had never suspected the theory behind his predictions and behavior. Had she even guessed at it, she would have been more tolerant of his seemingly senseless inquiries.

Then the Kantrick's voice came through with something more interesting.

"There's some sort of dust spout ahead!" he called. "I can't make out details yet—this air is murky enough anyway.

There's a hill at its base, so maybe it's a wind source like the cave you two went into. You should have been going downwind, I guess."

Molly was as gentle as possible, consistent with the need to get her words in ahead of her companion. "Don't guess just yet. Get a closer look, and make believe you're writing it up for the School."

"Oh, of course. It isn't really much of a hill—I can see it better now as I get closer. If it's piled up from underground the way yours must have been, it hasn't been piling for long. The dark column rising from its middle still looks like dust, though." He paused and keyed the boat still closer. "We need more of Joe's regular robots to see what the wind is doing. I can't tell whether there's any horizontal component at all. Just a moment while I land beside it and see whether the dust is blowing or not." No one said anything while this was accomplished. "The usual fine stuff; I'd call it drifting, not really blowing. Even Joe could walk around in it. I'll lift again and see about the hilltop; it *looks* like one of those sand volcanoes you went into—lower and broader, as I said—"

"No, you didn't."

"Sorry, Carrie. As I meant to say. I'll get right above it for a look straight down—there. Yes, there's a crater, but it isn't very deep, and the sand inside is churning violently—I'll let down toward it. It looks as though the wind were coming up through the sand, lifting the lighter particles but not the heavy stuff—maybe if I block part of it with the boat the way I did the other, the wind will be hard enough to lift the bigger grains too and clear the way—that would open a passage for you folks."

"Maybe by midsummer!" exclaimed the Shervah. "But try it if you like," she added more tolerantly. "It will be interesting to see the shape of those grains, wouldn't you say, Jenny?"

"Very" came the harsh answer. "I am tempted to interrupt the present search—but I won't. I could go back to your first trap and probably get the same thing, I suspect; the situation doesn't seem to be strange to Enigma. Be careful about getting too low, Charley."

"Why? What could happen?"

"How heavy did you mean by 'heavy stuff'? I don't suppose it really matters—the boat's pretty solid and nothing really big is likely to be carried by wind that hasn't yet cleared all the dust out of that neck. Or were you counting on something's happening? I was forgetting your prediction."

"No—nothing of that sort. But maybe you're right; I won't get too low. In any case, I don't see how the two of you could get through there unless the place was blown really clear—not in ordinary armor. Still, it's good to know that there *are* more places where winds come from inside. It's a pretty safe bet there are lots of them, if we've encountered three in such a short time." No one commented. "The main question, I guess, Molly, is whether the wind is going in somewhere else, or the ice you're hoping for is boiling somewhere below. I suppose it's that hope that has you heading into the wind."

"I'm not really good at psychology, either general or species," Molly evaded. "Consciously, I can assure you I'd be much happier to get back to the boat, get out of this armor for a while, eat and sleep decently, have a bath, and then explore down here properly in one of Joe's new mapping machines. What my subconscious is doing, if the translators can do that term real justice, I can't guarantee. It will not have escaped your notice, friend Charley, that a lot of the volume below Enigma's surface seems to be air, which is even better than ice at lowering the average density. Maybe this place is just a sponge."

"That's a thought—but we'd still have to find out, and there'd have to be another explanation for the wind. How far down in this gravity could the rock support caves?"

"I don't know. Dig something out of the boat's library and compute, I'd suggest. Just don't ask us to tell you yet what the compressive strength of this rock may be; we haven't had a chance to test it, you know!"

Charley took the suggestion at face value.

"Should I try to check that question out right now, or go on looking for more ways inside?"

Once again the women looked at each other, smiling. "Perhaps you'd better keep on with the search," Molly replied. "Maybe we can get some data at this end on the depth question, before you have to face any computation. Personally, I don't see how this downhill journey can go on much longer."

"I'm glad to hear you say that. You didn't seem to want to before," Charley came back happily.

The Human refrained, just barely, from saying something impolite about herself. Wishful thinking was bad enough; doing it out loud was worse; doing it where it would influence Charley's ideas was worst, or almost worst. Carol's glance, carrying what Molly recognized as sympathetic understanding on the features that she now knew far too well to consider hideous, almost brought the Human woman to tears. The Shervah's words on private channel, however, tempted laughter instead.

"I wonder what your Buzz would have said?"

For the first time, Molly gave some serious thought to what might be going on in Charley's mind. He *wasn't* a six-year-old; he was a competent adult, qualified—whatever Carol might think—as an advanced student at a major research facility; whatever his personal or racial peculiarities, he simply could not be stupid. Like Molly's own, his words and actions were based on some set of background ideas and beliefs. The fact that the words in particular were often irritating didn't necessarily mean his beliefs were wrong. It did mean that Mary Warrender Chmenici did not understand them as well as she should. Little Buzz, she reflected wryly, might actually do a better job than his supposedly intelligent mother at *that* if he were here. Most of his playmates were nonhuman.

For just a moment, she allowed her memory to flash pictures of her six-year-old holding his own with flying Parkemm children in that soupy-aired, low-gravity colony; with Nethneen in their nearly airless environment; even with Jenny's people—the child had learned quickly enough that gravity was no real problem if one stayed submerged, though ammonia furnished less support than water. She had quickly gotten over a mother's natural worry; the child care centers on the School planets were as good as Human ones, even when it came to teaching the very young about environments and environmental equipment.

For another second, Molly wondered whether she would

do as well, in the next few days, as her son had in the last few years. Would she ever see him and his father again?

She buried the question firmly. One could only do one's best.

"Thanks, Carrie." Molly shifted back to the common translator channel and went on. "If that sand spout, or whatever it is, has been mapped, Charley, I'd go on with the surface search for the time being at least. It seems to me more and more important that we get an idea of air flow out to the surface and, if there is any, in from it. Joe, is your map far enough along to give us any hints at all on that point? Could this cavern circulation be enough of the total to show on the planetary scale?"

"I have no basis for a guess, since I had not considered the possibility and haven't seen the map itself for some time. It occurs to me that it would be better for Charley to continue his search with the new mapping robot so that I can take the boat, with the shop, back to the tent. Will you please come back here, Charley? I think the matter important."

"All right, if you're sure the latest machine is really ready."

"As ready as the one Jenny is using. Controllable by any of us, electromagnetic location interlock with the boat and, through the computer, with all the other robots in touch; collecting equipment; power—"

"All right. I'm on my way to the shop. I've started the boat back toward the tent."

Many kilometers below, traveling at unknown speed in unknown direction, the two women listened to this conversation without expecting much new to come from it. Both were tired and getting heartily sick of darkness and recycled nourishment. Both knew that their armor was slightly less than perfectly efficient at the recycling process and that eventually it would not keep them alive, but neither was worried about this yet. Both were far too intelligent to let their minds dwell on the point. With work, they could also have kept their minds off simple discomforts, but only at rare intervals was there a chance to work.

Twice, as the hours passed, they stopped and made a close examination of the rock and pseudovegetation that formed the bank of their alien Styx, but neither study proved interesting. As far as either could tell, the former was a fine-grained, possibly amorphous matrix, possibly but not certainly silicate, possibly but not certainly modified both thermally and chemically, possibly but not certainly cemented by hydrates or ammates or both. Their eyes simply couldn't tell enough. Four times during the hours Jenny reported discovery of a cave from which wind was blowing; twice more Charley, now surveying with the new mapper, did the same. No sign of inflow had been detected. Joe, back at his map, had described verbally in great detail what was appearing, but neither he nor any of the others could recognize anything useful. It seemed like an ordinary planetary circulation, to those whose home planets had significant atmospheres, except for the presence of extraheavy dust clouds at the summer pole and relatively clear air at the other. If the clouds had been water or ammonia condensate, even that would not have been startling.

Maybe, Molly thought, when enough detail had been added—maybe, when they could see it themselves . . .

But if they could see it themselves, the main problem would be solved.

Even Charley was saying less and less as the hours wore on and Enigma crawled along its vast orbit. He had decided that Molly was not going to end this underworld Odyssey until someone else made an effective move; he remained emotionally certain that she could do so whenever she wanted. He was growing more and more afraid that he himself was the one who was expected to take the effective step—he remembered what Jenny had said, days earlier back on *Classroom*, about originality and his own failure to display it. This had to be a part of the test.

Should he take his robot into one of the caves he had found and start mapping the passages inside? Mathematically, this seemed poor policy; the women were traveling in more or less a straight line—at least, along *one* line—and only wild coincidence could bring him in touch with them that way.

Was there some painfully obvious step that he should have thought of and taken? Was the Human losing patience with him?

Should he—?

"The river's GONE!" came Carol's voice, in a near-shriek.

He should have. He couldn't now. Molly was taking new action herself. He'd failed, of course.

OF COURSE WE'LL WAIT

"You mean you moved away from it without noticing? How could that happen?" asked Jenny.

"We mean the river is gone," stated Carol. "So is the only wall we could see, and so is the ground under us."

"Stop and backtrack," said Joe quietly.

"Right. We are. I'm driving much more slowly just to play safe, but—yes. There it is again. The way we were following simply opened into a much larger cave, like the one above. The river is tumbling in through the ceiling; it looks really weird in this gravity."

"It could still pack momentum," remarked the Nethneen. "Be careful."

"Don't worry. The wind around it is plenty of warning, slow as the waterfall looks."

"Which way is the wind? Any guidance?" asked Charley.

"'Fraid not," replied the Human. "Random stuff; eddies set up by the moving water. We're holding motionless, if the inertial guidance can be trusted, and can feel this-way-that-way gusts trying to knock us off the robot."

"Then what will you do? Come back the same way you've been traveling?"

"Where would that get us? And when?"

"Closer to the surface, at least."

"Not good enough. All we know about the area around the original cave is your information that there seem to be no other surface openings near it. At least it seems sensible to be heading somewhere else—maybe toward one of the places you or Jenny have found. Heading down a river has something to be said for it, by itself; if any of you find one, doing the same is probably the best remaining chance of getting us together."

"If rivers tend to converge underground the way they do on a surface," Charley remarked.

"Do your own theorizing about that; I don't want to!" snapped the Shervah.

"You could be heading straight away from the region we're mapping."

"Maybe," agreed Molly. "This robot knows somewhere inside its crystal cerebrum, I suppose, but we can't ask it. Or maybe—Carrie, you've been using the inertial system telling this thing which way to go. It must have some reference direction of its own. If we let it sit quietly on a solid surface, how long would it take to tell itself, if it doesn't know already, which way and how fast this planet is rotating? Personally I'd guess about five minutes, but you know better than I do, probably."

"I'm not sure I do, but that seems a reasonable guess. Joe, I never knew—did you build the sensors in *Classroom*'s shop, or use standard ready-made ones?"

"Oh, I built them, of course. Slowly as Enigma rotates, five minutes will change attitude quite enough to measure. A good thought, Molly."

"Then we'll land beside the waterfall and let this thing decide which way is north, and then head in that general direction; that's where you two have been finding your wind vents, isn't it?"

"Yes," replied the Rimmore. "Should we bother to look for more?"

"Of course. Keep on mapping toward us, if the storm will let you."

"I have another suggestion" came Charley's voice.

"What is it, Charley?" Molly answered quickly, gesturing her small companion to silence.

"I propose to go underground at the nearest entrance I've found; perhaps Jenny might do the same thing, but if she wants to do that she should use one of the places near where I do."

"Why?" asked Carol impatiently, ignoring Molly's obvious wishes.

"You can program the robot to *stop* after it has gone a certain distance in a certain direction—it can keep track of all components of its travel, no matter how irregular its actual path. Even if it won't give any other signal, you can find out when you're close to this area, which is—" he paused to interpret instruments "—three hundred fifty-one kilometers distant and twenty grads right of north from the hole you two went inside by. Just arrange for it to go that far in that direction and stop. It won't be exact, obviously, but it will put you somewhere in this neighborhood. While you're making that trip, I, and Jenny if she wants, can be mapping the caverns under this area, within whatever radius seems smart, and as deep as we have time for. We will, of course, file the map in the boat's computer—no, we'll be out of electromagnetic touch once we're very far underground, but our own machines have enough capacity to record the planet, probably.

"Once you two know you're in the area, you can start examining it in detail, moving around as seems good to you, and describing it carefully. Sooner or later we'll find a match with one of our maps."

"Beautiful!" Molly made no attempt to hide her enthusiasm.

Carol didn't feel as happy, considering the source of the idea, but could not deny that it seemed a good one. "I'm not sure it's better than staying with the river, but it has possibilities," she admitted.

"There was a good windy cave only fifteen kilometers from here," Charley resumed. "That will make it three hundred sixty kilometers and almost exactly north for your robot setting, Carol. Are you going to come over and map, too, Jenny?"

"Yes, by all means. Let's see—my unit has copied from yours, so the maps are joined—there's another vent only a dozen kilometers from yours, just about east—that will make its distance about the same for Carol and Molly, and we'll be a broader target laterally. I'll start at that one, and we'll try to make our underground maps join up as quickly as possible at as many depths as we can."

"Fine." The Kantrick was in top spirits again. "I'm at the vent, and going underground. At least I'll be out of the glare of this murderous star." He shifted to private channel. "Was that the right idea, Molly?"

The Human couldn't quite see the point, either of the question itself or of his making it private, but she followed his lead. "There are probably hundreds, almost certainly dozens, of workable ideas. This seems a good one. There's only one thing that would make one 'right.' "

"Is it the one one of us was supposed to have?"

"Supposed by whom? I was hoping someone would think of something to get us out of this mess, and I'm happier than I've been for—it seems like weeks. Thanks, Charley."

"Molly." It was Carol, on general channel. The larger woman looked inquiringly at her. "I'd like to go fast, once we know which way to go, but I don't want to sail at full clip through an empty cave with no idea of when the far wall may come up. Shouldn't we find the bottom, if only to keep ourselves conscious of how fast we're going and a little more alert to what may be ahead?"

"Probably we should. But how fast do we dare go down?"

"That's no problem. The robot can sense its own height even if it can't tell us, and I can key it to stop on a downward trip before it hits anything." Carol refrained from mentioning how nice it would have been had the machine possessed similar horizontal sensing capacities. "As soon as we're oriented we'll move out far enough from the fall to feel safe, and I'll set up a fastest-downward."

"What if we're over another lake? This waterfall—excuse me, you know what I mean—must stop somewhere, and—"

"It will read that as a surface. Don't worry. Even if we splash, we're in armor."

Minutes later, the two were once more descending through Enigma's darkness. Molly had set her light to the narrowest, brightest beam possible without hurting Carol's eyes and was keeping track of the falling liquid a couple of hundred meters away, while the Shervah swept hers in the opposite direction and occasionally downward, using a broader focus.

"We'll have to be ready to move farther from the fall," the Human reported after a minute or two. "I suppose this is what happens to real water under decent gravity, too, but I've just never observed the detail. The fall reaches terminal velocity for this gravity and air density, which is pretty slow, and starts to break up into big drops, and those are blowing around randomly. I suppose they correspond to the spray under a real waterfall."

"How big are the drops?" Joe asked with interest.

"The smallest I see from here are a centimeter or two. They range up to blobs of a couple of meters, changing shape and orientation as they fall—if you can call that drift a fall. We're going down faster than all but the very biggest, so I haven't been able to follow any one of them for very long. They're pretty, Carol; have a look. I'll cut my light for a moment; yours should reach that far, with your eyesight."

The Shervah, unfortunately, followed the suggestion, and like her friend found the sight interesting. The drifting, shimmering, writhing blobs of fluid were indeed beautiful. Lacking cameras, they alternated with each other trying to describe what they saw to Jenny and the others. Not quite all their attention was thus employed—both were conscious that the "drops" were spreading farther and farther from the original fall and closer and closer to the robot, in their random wanderings—but neither was thinking of danger for the moment. Probably neither would have been able to foresee its details even with full attention.

Quite abruptly, the robot's descent stopped, or seemed to. Carol reached for the control keys, while Molly swept her light around to see whether they had reached a solid cave floor or a lake. She saw neither, and before Carol could finish her key work the descent resumed. The Human began to report the event to the others, while her companion swiftly considered possibilities. A likely one occurred to her immediately. A large drop might have drifted below them temporarily and been interpreted by the robot's sensor as ground. She suggested this to Molly, who interrupted her partially completed report with a brief "Wait a minute," and both turned their lights downward to check the possibility.

It seemed likely enough; there was a blob of ammonia only a meter or two below, whose motion suggested that it might have been right under them a few seconds earlier. Molly nodded and was about to resume her call to the others when Carol called her attention to another.

"Hold it; we'll check. There's one that should drift under

us in a few seconds—half a minute, maybe. We'll be nearly down to it by then; let's see if the robot does the same thing. If it does, we'll know, and can move out farther from this—would you call it 'spray'?"

"All right. Are you following, up there?"

"More or less," Joe replied. "Update us when you can; I get the impression you're busy."

"Thanks. A minute or so," replied Carol. "We have a check to make on what your height sensor responds to—yes. There. We *are* stopping again, Molly. Shall we get away from here right away, or—we'd better move; staying won't tell us anything more." She reached again for the keys but was too late.

Ammonia is less polar than water. It therefore has a lower surface tension and tends to wet a given surface less readily. The latter quality should have helped when a smallish, half-meter mass of the liquid touched Carol's shoulder, but the former was enough. The drop did not hold its shape but spread out, covering her helmet almost at once. She was not using her sight on the keys, naturally, but having that sense blocked was quite enough to distract her. She failed to key the new command.

She knew what had happened, of course.

"Molly! Get this thing off me!"

The Human was equally quick at seeing the trouble, but this was not quite the same as knowing what to do about it. Nothing remotely resembling a large sponge was on hand. Gloves, Human or Shervah, were quite inadequate wiping tools. The laser sampling cutters were as likely to boil the armor as the ammonia. It was several seconds before Molly thought of using the heat output from her armor's refrigerating system, and many more before she could get herself into a position to apply this usefully. By this time, Charley was asking frantically what the trouble was.

Molly was too busy at what amounted to a free-fall dance to be able to tell him, but Carol, who could do nothing but hang onto the robot and keep as motionless as possible, made it clear. Before she was finished, Joe made one of his rare interruptions.

"Carol or Molly! Close the access door to the robot's keyboard, if you haven't already!"

"*Gravdh! M'Kevvitch!*" No one asked for translation as Carol's glove slapped at the small panel. "Got it. But won't ammonia leak in through those pressure-sensing openings all over it?"

"I didn't overlook quite everything. They seal against liquids. I've heard of rain. If you have the port shut, it will be liquid-tight."

"But we're still in the spray area. More drops could hit us any moment. With the port shut, I can't move us out."

"When Molly gets you dry, you'll have to look around and try to spot a moment when nothing is going to get to you, and do a quick job of—"

"Another drop!" cut in Molly. "I'm falling behind. Who'd have thought we'd need bath towels in this operation?"

"Can you wave your arms, or something, to make air current that will move them away?" asked Charley.

"I'm trying. It works for the little ones, but I can't see in all directions at once, and Carol's helmet isn't clear yet so she can't either."

"But why can't she see through ammonia?" Charley asked almost plaintively. "It's transparent!"

"It's *ripply*!" snapped the Shervah.

Charley once again was visualizing the Human's battle with Enigma and wondering how many more tests there would be. Why had Molly put herself in the position where she, rather than one of the others, was having to take the physical action against the weird little world's environment, instead of staying in the boat or the tent and letting the others act as well as think? Maybe the presumptive Faculty policy against letting students get into really dangerous situations was operating, but that couldn't be the whole story. Carol was down there, too, facing the same risks, apparently.

And why had Molly come up with the idea of using her armor's heat pump to get rid of the ammonia, instead of letting Carol pass the test herself? The Kantrick, positive from the beginning that they were repeating a laboratory exercise that had been done thousands of times before, almost as certain that the Human was the Faculty member responsible for rating them, was beginning to have doubts about her as a teacher.

Molly, at the moment, was not even a student. She was

concerned with keeping the two of them alive, which seemed to mean finding the ideal time sharing between fending off more drops of ammonia and keeping the radiation from her armor's heat pump directed at Carol's helmet. Once the Shervah could see out, her side-placed, independently movable eyes could do a far better job than Molly's stereoscopic equipment at watching all directions for more of the amoebalike blobs.

Carol was waiting, and worrying. The robot was sealed against the ammonia, but had she done the job in time? She had been thrashing around thoughtlessly for a moment or two, and might have flung smaller drops of the stuff in any direction. The machine was safe enough in one sense—it had breakers that would shut down any part affected by short or sneak circuits. A fusion unit melt or blow was a possibility that not even laboratory experience brought to anyone's mind; the devices were as ubiquitous to all their cultures, both in School and on their home planets, as ballpoint pens had been to the Human's ancestors. They simply didn't think of them as dangerous under ordinary conditions—Molly's fear about the robot's driving into the cave wall, earlier in her adventure, had been a special case, like a child falling while carrying a pen.

Having power shut down at a time like this was not a pleasant prospect. Was liquid already spreading around inside? Would the device respond to its keys when she did manage to find a safe time to open the access port? Right now it was alternately stopping and resuming descent as drops moved into the path of its height sensor and out again. Each change in motion was a relief to the little Shervah. Neither motion meant safety from more collisions; stopped, they could be caught by the falling drops, and descending they were overtaking them; but changing motion meant the robot was functional. If only she could see!

Feeling turned out to be enough. Another descent started, and this time the metal cylinder failed to stay upright. Feeble as the gravity was, Carol could tell which way she was hanging in her safety ropes. So could Molly.

"Robot power is off," reported the Human as calmly as she could. "We're falling. Our terminal velocity seems to be faster than the smaller drops, but not as much faster as we were going down before. Maybe I can keep us clear of them long enough to get Carrie's helmet dry now."

"Is that worth doing?" asked Jenny. "Sorry, I didn't mean to sound quite that pessimistic. Any idea what you're falling into? That must be a really gigantic cavern; you've been going down for minutes."

"That doesn't mean too much here," the Human replied. "If we can get the inside of this machine dry and find our way to where you and Charley are mapping, this will have been just another interesting datum. Trouble is, if we land in a lake or river, we may have to swim this thing to shore. I wonder whether the robot-Carol-Molly system averages out less dense than liquid ammonia. I certainly hope so. The last two parts certainly are, but I don't know about this piece of metal."

Jenny was probably the most aware of the grotesque aspect of the situation, in spite of the fact that she could see it only by imagination. Her native world's gravity was nearly twice that of Earth, and the mental picture of her two friends carrying on a more or less reasonable conversation while falling through darkness toward some point they could not see and whose distance below they couldn't guess seemed dreamlike in some ways and irresponsible in others. Like most intelligent beings, she had a sense of humor. She had time to reflect how lucky it was that her normal expression of it was not audible and would not be carried by the translators; lucky, since the present situation wasn't really funny and a laugh like Molly's or a buzz like Joe's would be most inappropriate. Her friends might be dead in the next few seconds.

She controlled the body-ripple that would have corresponded to a giggle had another Rimmore seen it, and listened tensely. Falling took *so* long here!

"Good going, Molly! I can see!" came Carol's voice after what seemed minutes of silence.

"What's around you?" asked Charley.

"Large drops of juice, against a dark background. What else? We're still falling. Mol, we're going to hit that one; can we—good! I don't know if you moved it or moved us. Too bad we don't have a Parkemm here; your arms don't really make good wings, and mine are worse."

"The last time you wanted to fly was on Sink, when you were beginning to wonder whether our suits were going to keep us warm after all."

"Well, we practically did. The gravity was only a tenth of what it is here, and we could keep ourselves in the air—well, off the surface—nearly all the time by jumping. The main point was to keep out of contact with the ground."

"But even in that gravity a Parkemm couldn't have flown. A trace of helium won't—"

"Watch it—there's another drop! Anyway you're quibbling."

"I can't keep this up. I'm afraid we're going to have to put up with being wet—Lord, we certainly are! Look down there, if that's really down!"

"It's the way we seem to be going. It—"

"What is it?"

"Just listen, Charley. We'll report when we have time, and until then infer what you can from what we say to each other. I'd say it was too bumpy to be a lake, but with these big drops merging into it and taking awhile to settle, maybe it's just because I expect a wave on a lake to go away at a decent speed."

"It's too big to be called a puddle. I hope it doesn't rate as an ocean," replied Molly. "Here we go. Any bets on whether we float?"

"Not with my credit. I don't think there'd be room for an ocean in a cave, even with this gravity. Will you hold my hand? My brain trusts these ropes, but the rest of me doesn't, quite."

"Right. And hold the robot, too. You need it more than you need me."

"That's another point where my brain and the rest of me don't agree. We're not floating, are we?"

"We're not at any surface yet. I'd like to have seen our splash from outside; just a slow-motion replay of an ordinary one wouldn't cover the surface tension effects. There, that seems to be surface, a few meters that way." Molly pointed with her light.

"We can see all right now, Charley," Carol remarked rather savagely.

"How far?"

"Hard to tell." Molly took over. "Tens of meters, I'd say. There's nothing by which to judge the distance; we're just hanging here. Come on, Carol, let's see if we can swim effectively enough to drag this thing to the surface, if that is the surface."

"It must be. The bubbles that came under with us seem to be heading that way, though they aren't in much of a hurry. If it is, we're traveling; the bumps we saw from above are gone—we must be away from where the spray is falling." The women fell silent and concentrated on swimming, which is not easy in armor. Molly was good at it under more normal circumstances, and the Shervah caught on quickly watching her. The metal cylinder was certainly denser than the liquid, but Molly found herself able to drag it upward by herself even before her friend was able to offer effective help. Newton's third law, the inertial aspect of swimming, enjoyed considerable advantage in Enigma's gravity even if Archimedes' Principle didn't. Even so, it took some minutes for their helmets to break the surface.

"Nothing to report," Molly said after sweeping her light around. "I assume there's a current because we seem to be away from the fall already, but if this is a river we can't see any bank, we can't see any sides or top to the cave, and we don't know which way or how fast we're going. So much for finding your mapped areas."

"Then Jenny and I map southward and try to find your ammoniafall," replied Charley promptly.

"Which we probably won't stay anywhere near."

"Can you suggest anything better, Carrie?"

"No. Sorry, Charley. And maybe this will still be a river you can follow." Molly looked at her companion in some surprise, but her helmet was pulled below the surface by the robot at that moment and she missed whatever expression was on the Shervah's face. It took her half a minute to get up again, and some seconds more for the liquid to drain sufficiently from her faceplate to permit clear vision.

She decided that tact was more important than satisfaction of curiosity. So was survival.

"Carrie, we don't float. We can't stay up forever on muscle power. I hate to suggest it, but I think we drift to wherever we're going along the bottom of this brook."

"Why go anywhere?" asked Charley. "The robot isn't dragging you; why not wait for us to find you? It will no doubt take quite a while, but your armor will keep you alive."

"Of course. I'd gotten so committed to the value of keeping going that I'd forgotten we didn't have to!" exclaimed Molly. "We'll just wait! When you find the river, Charley, you can follow it down to the fall and over, and we can't possibly be very far from its foot. If we let ourselves sink to the bottom, we can probably stay put; and when you and Jenny get down here, you'll be able to see our lights even if we are underwater—I mean—"

"Sorry." The Shervah's voice was softer and more apologetic than any of them had ever heard it. "We can't wait here."

OF COURSE THERE'S INFLOW

"I don't think I can take the temperature," the Shervah explained. "I waded in that first brook for a while, and my feet were freezing even through the armor. If temperature gets too low, my air starts to condense."

"That's right; nitrosyl chloride has an awfully steep vapor pressure curve. All right, we'll have to find shore somehow, or think of a way to dry out the inside of the robot and get it going again while we're still swimming—that doesn't seem awfully practical, somehow. But wait a minute—the temperature is a lot colder for me than for you, and your armor should insulate as well as mine. I'm perfectly comfortable—well, as far as *that*'s concerned, anyway. I'd give a lot to get out of this suit and wallow in hot water. Are you really getting cold?"

"Not yet. I'm reporting what happened earlier. My feet nearly froze while I was wading."

"Did you measure the actual temperature of the brook?"

"No."

"Then the temperature of this puddle won't tell us whether you're really in trouble, but we'd better get it on general principles."

Molly was somewhat mystified by the situation. As she had said, the ambient temperature was much worse for Human than for Shervah, and the small humanoid's suit protection should be at least as good as Molly's. Indeed, it must be; a vivid picture from fairly recent memory and more recent conversation preempted her thoughts for a moment. It was of a black, airless sky, dominated by half a dozen blazing

O-type suns all within three or four parsecs. Much less impressive, though bright by Solar system standards at some seven hundred astronomical units, hung Fire and Smoke, the binary dwarves that formed the main mass of the School planetary system. None of their individual planets was noticeable at this distance. The foreground was a landscape of grayish, dirty methane ice, like the surface of Pluto. Molly and Carol had been together, just as they were now, with an assigned experiment. They had just reached Sink, the outermost common planet of the School suns, with its ten-Kelvin environment that was needed for their work, and this time it had been Molly who was uneasy. "Come on!" Carol had been saying. "It's safe enough. There's no gas to conduct; you can only lose heat to the ground, and there isn't much contact area even for you. Don't worry; I've been here before!"

Here on Enigma they did not have vacuum around them; maybe that made the difference in the Shervah's mind. Molly would have to be the support.

She attempted to bring her set of wrist instruments in front of her helmet while swimming hard enough to keep from being sunk any further by the robot. She was not very successful and was a couple of meters below the surface by the time she had a reading. Its value surprised her enough to take all her attention, and the two went down even further as she called the others.

"Joe! Charley! The temperature is up about ten Kelvins from the value I reported in that upper cavern. Either we've come down an awfully long way, or something is carrying heat to this liquid. Do you check with that, Carrie?"

"Yes. I still don't know whether it's warm enough so I can stop worrying, though."

"I'd think you'd be feeling cold already if your armor's heaters weren't handling the situation. I know ammonia doesn't have the heat capacity of water, but—"

"But if this were liquid water, I wouldn't be worried about the cold."

"Is your armor refrigerating or heating right now?"

"Heating."

"Which was it doing when you were freezing your feet?"

"I don't remember—didn't notice. I suppose it was heating, but now that I think of it, maybe it was just trying to hold an average. I don't know much about its heat distribution system or its internal sensing—"

"You should have made the armor yourself," pointed out Charley. Carol, for once, had no answer; the criticism was completely right, and she knew it. The suit was part of her field equipment, and she should have known all there was to be known about it.

"Tell the rest of us if you feel the slightest bit cold or your air pressure seems to be dropping," advised Molly. "We'll look for dry land, but maybe we needn't be as frantic about it as we thought. Let's get back to the surface and try to see if we're getting anywhere."

But the surface came back to them. They might have been falling for several seconds—perhaps half a minute—before either of them realized that surface was all around them; they were once more inside a large drop rather than a whole river. They must have gone over another fall. Molly reported the fact, resignedly, to the three so far above.

"We're trying to swim out of it, but the stuff is wet and sticks to us. It's huge, too—the biggest by far of any we've seen yet."

"Are your heads through the surface so you can see out?" asked Joe.

"We're sticking out," Carol replied, "but there's too much stuff on our helmets to let us see. Why is it important? There'd be nothing but more drops of river floating down around us."

"Different size drops, and different density objects like you and the robot, should fall at different rates—there *is* air, remember. I was wondering whether you were in front of most of the stream or behind it."

"I don't see how we could be anywhere but middle" was Molly's contribution. "What we need is to get to one side and dry out this piece of hardware. That's worth the effort of getting out of the drop for, though. Come on, Carrie—we'll give some momentum to the robot as long as it's in the liquid, and as it's about to emerge we'll try to get out ourselves. With luck, we'll be clear long enough for me to dry off your helmet again, and you'll have a chance to tell whether there *is* any direction that will get us clear of this stuff. I suppose we're in another cave."

"That's what I was taking for granted," agreed Joe.

"All right." Charley was practically authoritative. "You two try to get dry, and Jenny and I will get back to mapping. Now we look for *any* river, I'd say, and follow it down. Sooner or later we get to the same lake, or ocean, or something."

"One more delay," Joe said firmly.

"What?" grated the Rimmore.

"One more piece of apparatus for your mappers, and never mind remarks about whether I should have thought of it earlier. Come back here while we install radar units in your machines. Right now you have to explore any cavern you find visually and might still miss some connecting passages. This way you'll get every open space you enter, logged in detail the moment you're into it, and your computers will maintain a complete three-dimensional image set that you can display for your own convenience to help you see where you've been, how to get back, or where other things are—if you get a broad enough total picture. Head back here; I'll have the units ready for you when you arrive."

Not even Charley argued.

Twenty hours later, Molly woke. There had been no particular stimulus; there was still darkness except for her lights and Carol's, and at the moment not even translator voices. They were far enough from the river, for the moment, so that it was nearly inaudible, not that it made much noise anyway. The hours they had spent trying to win free of the falling drops when they were falling and to work their way out of eddies and other currents when they were flowing had been the main reason she had had to sleep. They had finally struggled to the bank at a point where the stream was practically horizontal, and carried themselves and the robot far enough from the weirdly writhing current to feel safe from it; there, even Carol had collapsed. The Shervah was still lying motionless; for the first time in Molly's recollection, her eyes were actually closed. For a moment the Human's heart almost stopped as she missed the robot; then she saw it parked on the rock a couple of meters away. Was it dry yet and the energy converter that was their life usable?

Probably not, since the control access port was still closed.

They had gone to sleep without unsealing it, she realized. Molly muttered something under her breath that she would not have said in Buzz' hearing, went over to the machine, and got it open. Whether the surrounding air was far enough below saturation to do them any good could not be checked by any of her armor's instruments, but at least it could now circulate inside the device. There was a fairly strong breeze; the feathery growths that had caught the Shervah's attention before she had remembered about the robot, and caused her to unfasten her safety line and leave Molly to carry the machine unaided the last few meters, were nodding and waving as the air moved by them. Carol had not had time for much of an examination; like her companion, she had been too exhausted and had fallen asleep even before reporting the new life form to the others. Molly had refastened the rope to her small friend's armor, stated only that they were ashore and perhaps drying off, and lost consciousness herself. She had made several thirty-kilometer swims, in reasonably warm water, in her time; she had twice done hundred-kilometer hikes carrying cooking and shelter equipment under the three-quarters-normal gravity of New Pembroke; but she had never in her life felt as exhausted as when she and Carol had emerged from the river. Armor made a difference that low gravity could not offset.

Sure that Carol's translator would not let anything but vital messages through as long as she needed sleep, Molly reported the present situation, including the new life, to the other students. A close look, taken at Jenny's insistence, revealed that there were several different organisms, or at least several different shapes. She tried to make sense out of their engineering, but had no real success. There were waving fronds, evidently maximum-area organs; they could hardly be intended to intercept light, like the leaves they resembled. Rootlike bases proved not to be roots—not only did they fail to penetrate the rock, they did not even cling to it. The things could be picked up easily and set down elsewhere without obvious effect. The "roots" hung limply even in Enigma's gravity during the transfer, and made no effort to rearrange themselves when the organism was put down again. The stemlike parts connecting roots and fronds did bend back and forth, without apparent aid from the wind, both while they were being held and while they were standing where she first saw them. None of it made sense to the Human. She reported as much.

Joe was unusually silent, even for him. The confirmation of highly organized life on Enigma had been hard for him to accept. However firmly an intelligent being may claim that it bows to facts, no mind accepts casually the readjustment of its basic beliefs; and Enigma *had to be* too young for this. Life might conceivably have gotten started—this seems to happen pretty early in the existence of most planets—but it could not by any recognized process have evolved so far in the time available. He badly wanted some of these organisms in Jenny's lab; they needed detailed explaining.

Molly's troubles, and later Molly's report, had done something Joe's work on the mapping robots had never managed to do; it had driven his wind-charting project entirely out of his mind for a time. With Charley and Jenny back underground busily but slowly building a three-dimensional diagram of the sponge that was Enigma's crust, Joe would ordinarily have been standing in the tent in front of his display to see how the wind map was getting on. Instead, he stood motionless in the boat's conning room before the controls, buried in thought, but doing nothing.

Even Carol's more detailed information, when she finally woke up and began to study the organisms, took little of the Nethneen's attention. He was already convinced of the facts and needed more details than Carol could supply to make them fit his ideas properly. The Shervah's deepish voice alternating with Rimmore gratings—or Joe's translator's equivalents for these identifying qualities—were merely background symbols, not information. It took a direct call from Molly to bring him out of the trance.

"Joe! I suppose you're back at your maps. Don't they make sense yet? It will be nice to hear about something that does!"

"Sorry, Molly. I was allowing myself to get distracted, I'm afraid. I'm not in the tent. I'll let you know as soon as possible what's developed."

The small being headed for the shop, however, not the tent.

Molly was too versed in Nethneen courtesy to pursue the

matter until Joe chose to continue it. She turned her attention back to their local problem.

"Do you think this machine is going to dry out in any decent time, Carrie?" she asked.

The Shervah had not given the robot a thought since she had awakened; the vegetation, if that's what it was, was much more interesting. She looked up with one eye and thought for a moment.

"I suppose so," she said. "The rock seems to be dry enough. Maybe you should sit on it, or lean against it, to provide a bit more heat from your armor and speed up the process, if you can bear to stay away from these things. They don't look a bit like the ones I saw up above."

"Or the metal whiskers I told you about, which are just as likely to have been alive, I'd say now. Of course we're a lot deeper, and it's a lot warmer, and there might be a whole different ecology. It's a pity we can't stay here long enough to study it carefully."

"Why can't we?" asked Carol in surprise.

"Because the moment this robot dries out, we've got to drive it along the river in the hope of meeting the others. If we don't make contact with some part of this rock sponge that they have mapped, none of the beautiful specimens you're collecting there will ever get to a lab. We may be able to come back, and I'm as curious as you are, but I want to keep on living, too. Come on, little friend, be sensible."

"I suppose you're right. All right, *you* turn your heat exhaust on the robot; I'll keep working on these things and collecting what seems best, while you get the machine dried out. All right?"

"All right. But I suspect your armor is using its refrigerator now, too, isn't it?"

"Well, yes; but yours is a lot bigger and working a lot harder with all the heat you generate. Find out from Charley and Jenny whether they've found any more quick ways down like ours."

"There was one, I thought" came Charley's voice. "It was a really terrific wind; but it led to a passage too narrow for my mapper. I didn't report it because I didn't want to disappoint you. I'm still going down wherever there's a choice, and so is Jenny; and we're working our way south."

"Which may not be the right direction any more," Molly couldn't help remarking.

"Maybe, but we have nothing else to go by. After all, we needn't worry; a lot of this planet seems to be open space, and the radars do a cavern very quickly. If it keeps the same average, we should be able to map the whole volume in barely two thirds of a million years—a good deal less if Joe will build another robot and join us." Charley's dead-pan remark completely silenced even Carol for a moment, and before either she or Molly could think of anything to say, the Kantrick went on. "The real need, of course, is another river to follow down. The farther down, the fewer the branches, one would expect. I'm getting more and more convinced there must be a sort of ocean somewhere below, and your river and any other must lead to it. If nothing else, working our way in what *was* your direction should get us to your river or one of its tributaries."

"That seems reasonable," admitted Molly.

"In that case," Carol pointed out promptly, "we might as well stay right here, as we wanted to do awhile earlier, and let them catch up with us."

"Two minor objections," replied her big friend. "They might not encounter the same river, and there should be more of this ecology to be seen as we keep going." Carol was silent but made a hand gesture of agreement. Molly, too, forbore to pursue the subject further; she did not want to admit how much more the first of the two points now meant to her. Not, at least, in Joe's hearing, and of course it would be going out of her way to shift to private channel just to make the remark to Carol.

The Nethneen's voice sounded on top of her thought of him.

"Molly, I don't suppose your robot's power is on yet. About how much time do you two have left in your batteries?"

"I'm about eighty hours," Molly replied promptly—she had no need to look at her gauges for that information. "Carol's batteries carry more energy, but her size gives her a poorer surface-to-volume ratio than mine, and she must have had to use more on temperature control. How about it, Carrie?"

The smaller woman had no need to look, either.

"About ten hours less than you. I'm taking it easy on eating until we can charge up again."

The Nethneen spoke thoughtfully. "It might be a good idea for me to join the underground mapping. It won't take long to finish another machine; I started the parts on automatic down in the shop as soon as I finished the radars for Charley and Jenny."

"You mean you aren't back at your map *yet*?" Molly asked with mock severity.

"I have just reached the tent for a quick look—I suppose the data might be useful, even in the present emergency . . ." His voice trailed off; none of the others could even guess what he was thinking.

"For Pete's sake—if that doesn't translate, never mind—get into the tent and look your own work over." Molly was not entirely mocking. "We've been guided by air currents most of the time since we've gone underground. We haven't the faintest idea what the rules about wind are on this silly world, except that there's something peculiar about them—Jenny found out before we got here that the high ones were circulating toward the summer pole, which I at least would expect the surface currents to be doing instead. Stay there for a few hours and see if you can figure out enough of the pattern to make a real guide for us. Rivers have their good points, but this one seems to be taking us toward the middle of the planet, and there's a limit to how far I want to go in that direction. *Get to your map and think!*"

The Human caught her breath and blushed; she hadn't meant to get so intense, and just what Joe did probably wouldn't make that much difference. Maybe nothing would. Was she, Mary Warrender Chmenici, getting *panicky*? Thoughts of Rovor, and Buzz, and planets where one could walk around without armor, and even swim or sleep outdoors, went flashing through her mind; she suppressed them sternly. Reality right now was Enigma.

"All right, Molly." Joe's voice was as quiet as ever; she couldn't tell how much he had read of her feelings. "I'll let you know how the map is doing; you can help in the analysis, perhaps. I'll be in the tent in a few seconds, but will no doubt be longer working up a meaningful description for you."

Carol looked at her huge friend curiously, but decided to say nothing. No doubt the Human would explain the thought behind her outburst in good time. The Shervah, with a real research problem holding her attention, was genuinely unable to get her mind onto the fact that she was in actual physical danger—though the suggestion that her mind was at all similar to Charley's would have been taken as a serious insult.

Molly, more aware of the danger than of anything else but quite ashamed of the fact, deliberately turned her attention to the robot. Carol might not have been serious when she suggested that the heat from the Human's armor might help dry the machine out, but the point seemed well taken anyway. She was beginning to wish that her heat pump exhausted almost anywhere except between her shoulders; she had used it so often as a tool lately that the problem of aiming its microwave beam was becoming a major nuisance. She seated herself, most uncomfortably, on the field disc of the robot in front of its control access port and bent forward as sharply as the armor itself permitted. She was reminded emphatically of a lab exercise she had had to do in crystallography, involving some hours of looking into a microgoniometer, the week before Buzz' birth. She couldn't see whether she was really throwing heat into the open port; she wasn't contortionist enough to see the port itself, or enough of a cold-worlder to detect the beam with her own senses. She comforted herself with the thought that the radiation had to be striking some part of the machine and producing at least a little effect.

"Carol," she remarked, very carefully on private channel, "I've just thought of another attachment for the next robot design. They should have internal heaters to dry them out automatically."

"I don't think even Charley would have suggested that seriously," the Shervah replied.

"I certainly hope not. You know, little friend, your suit must be refrigerating much more enthusiastically than mine at this point; the environment is really hot for you. Wouldn't you do as much, or more, good than I here—quite aside from the fact that you'd fit better?"

"Maybe. Let me finish checking out this stuff here, and I'll spell you."

Molly forbore to ask how long the checking out might take and settled herself for an indefinite wait. She never knew how long she sat there, but was not too surprised that it was not Carol who brought the session to an end.

"Molly, I have a problem." It was Joe's voice, calm as ever.

"With your map? Isn't it growing properly?"

"Very nicely, but very unexpectedly. Your remark that winds aloft were traveling from winter to summer pole, and that this surprised you, was what I checked first; the upper-level robots seem to be agreeing with you. Naturally I assumed that the surface circulation would be in the opposite direction, but the lower-level machines don't agree. Except for minor deflection one would expect from inertial effects—the rotation is slow, but Enigma *does* rotate—the air at all levels is going from winter to summer hemisphere."

"Then the return circulation must be underground—that must be the wind pattern we need for guidance!"

"No, Molly. Think. The air is coming *out* of every cave in your area that you, or Charley, or Jenny have found—there was even some coming up through the sand where Carol was trapped, and that was all in the summer hemisphere. Where does it come from?"

"And where does it go? You need a sink as well as a source!"

"Precisely. I think I have an answer to the sink, but not to the source question—or rather, I think that Jenny provided us with the sink answer."

"How?" grated the chemist. Molly simply waited for an answer. She was not surprised that Joe had one; he would probably not have mentioned the question until he did.

"You told us, when we first arrived, that a lot of the dust in the air was ammonium carbamate, which you would expect to form from ammonia and carbon dioxide since the two are quite unstable with respect to each other. The dust is solid and takes up far less room than the gas. If it forms primarily at the summer pole, it is using up gas and dropping the local pressure at all altitudes. The drop in volume would far more than offset the rise in temperature from the reaction heat."

"And why would it form primarily at the summer pole?" asked Jenny.

"I would suggest that Arc's radiation is supplying the activation energy for the reaction. I don't know how big that is, offhand, but carbon dioxide is stable enough so that a reasonably large kick must be needed."

"I agree," said the Rimmore at once. "I don't have the actual value in my head, either, but your point is a good one."

"All right, I see that, but where does the gas come from?" No one was surprised that the question came from Charley, but for once no one blamed him—not even Carol, who had been on the point of asking it herself.

"I can think of two possibilities," Joe replied, much more slowly. "I'm afraid I don't like either one very much, but—well, here they are. One is that Molly's ice, which made the kames you folks are exploring, is still below in large quantities and is still boiling out of the planet."

"And the other?" Carol thought she knew what was coming. She was right.

"The other is that your life forms are returning the gases to circulation, seasonally or constantly."

"Then we were wrong to go upwind; there are no inbound currents anywhere on the planet!" exclaimed Molly.

"I wouldn't say that. It's a quantitative question. Huge masses of atmosphere travel from winter to summer hemisphere; it seems quite possible that some of it goes below the surface."

"Of course! There must be inward currents at the winter pole!" cried Charley.

"You make my hearts leap out of time," Carol said, in a tone that needed no translation. "There's no 'must be' about it!"

"If my numbers are right, so is Charley," Joe's went on calmly. Carol silently came over to Molly and began to help heat the robot.

Molly wondered whether she could blush under her fur.

OF COURSE I WAITED FOR YOU

Molly was uncomfortable. It was dark. She had not seen or talked to Rovor or Buzz for weeks, and she was lonely, fond as she was of Carol. She had eaten nothing but recycled synthetics for more days than she cared to count. She felt grimy and itchy, and knew that the latter sensation was not entirely subjective; she had not been out of her armor for a long, long time.

But she was happier than she had been for a while. The feeling that her own carelessness had interfered with everyone's work, including her own, had gone; now there were useful, planned tasks for everyone that would not have existed without her mistake.

Joe's air-circulation project had been expanded to include underground currents; it was now evident that these were a significant part of Enigma's wind pattern. Joe was grateful for the discovery, and—surprisingly—visibly eager to set about the new work. Jenny and Carol were practically wallowing in the wealth of biological and biochemical information flooding in, or would be once they could collect and study it properly. Molly herself was still unsure about her ice hypothesis, since the likelihood of a spongy interior for Enigma was now pretty strong, but mineral analysis and dating as she had originally planned them were still very appropriate. She and Charley also had their activity lines clear, therefore.

The fact that she and Carol were still physically out of touch with the surface somehow was only an inconvenience now, rather than the major worry it had been. Inconveniences could be faced; they ended after a while. The whole School experience was an inconvenience of sorts; living in a dome on airless Pearl, with the endless, nagging fear that her child would make some mistake which his frequently nonhuman caretakers would fail to recognize in time and which could easily kill him was bad even for a stable, healthy Human. Though it had been generations since one of her species had been born or raised on Earth, most of them lived on colony worlds where one could at least stand the local environment for a few days rather than a few seconds. The School was worth it for her and Rovor; the present experience was probably going to be worth it for her; the upbringing would, beyond much doubt, be very good for little Buzz—in her saner moments Molly knew that he was not really in any great danger even when she and his father were parsecs away; but she was a normal parent, and the anxiety was there. She was glad—now that the immediate danger seemed to be moving toward resolution—she could relax a little.

Molly knew that this change in attitude had to be subjective, but she welcomed it anyway. Joe, now on his way to the winter pole with a third mapping robot to check on caves with inblowing winds, would expand the inside charting of the planet. The simple mathematical fact that the complete job should still take half a million years or so seemed less impressive than when the Kantrick had called attention to its magnitude. Somehow, Joe's being directly involved seemed to make things different. Her own rescue and Carol's, she now felt, would fit automatically into the new scheme of activities. Like the Shervah, she found herself paying nearly total attention to the research immediately before them.

With one exception. The robot was still powered down, and the hours of life remaining in their armor's batteries were growing steadily fewer. Carol, exploring on foot for new organisms, had found a small tunnel from which a relatively warm wind seemed to be coming. She had been impressed enough by their situation to help drag the metal cylinder to its mouth, and even spent some time debating with the others the advisability of following this passage when—she did not say *if*—they resumed powered travel; but she seemed still unworried as ever.

Jenny had found a small river and was following it downward, occasionally supplying the encouraging report that it seemed to be getting larger. Charley was methodically, and for him, silently, expanding his diagram of Enigma's interior downward and southward. At the moment the two were out of electromagnetic touch, and their mapping computers were working independently, but every few hours they found themselves close enough together so the machines could update each other's records. There were a number of points of overlap and connection; while it would have taken some hours of backtracking at the moment, either could have rejoined the other without going all the way back to the surface.

The Nethneen's voice broke a long silence. "You will be pleased to hear that I have so far located six caves of varying size. Four of them show no evidence of connection with any larger system, but two have strong inward flow of air."

"Then the ice theory is out," Molly replied promptly.

"It becomes very much less probable" was the cautious answer.

"Leaving biology as the surviving contender." Jenny made no attempt to conceal her satisfaction.

"If you mean the idea that life forms are responsible for reversing the gas-to-solid reaction and returning ammonia and carbon dioxide to the atmosphere, there is a very serious flaw." If Joe felt any pleasure at pointing this out, the fact was no more obvious than usual.

"What's that?" asked Jenny.

"The reaction would have to take place underground, judging from the direction of gas flow. Where would your life forms get their energy? The overall process is endothermic, obviously. If it is going on, you people should be much closer to the site than I am. What are your local creatures doing?"

"I . . . don't know," Jenny admitted. "I've found a lot of plantlike stuff along my route, but haven't collected any of it because it seemed to me that the search for Carol and Molly had to come first. If I had picked anything up, I don't suppose I'd be able to tell what it was doing chemically without getting it back to the lab."

"You could do that," Carol pointed out. "Charley could

follow the river you have there and make use of whatever chance it offers of getting to us."

"You wouldn't mind? And you, Molly?"

"Of course we wouldn't." Molly was partly delighted and partly resentful at not getting the chance to do her own answering. On the whole, she decided, it was better to be delighted; she wasn't sure just what she would have said.

Carol went on. "Pick up some specimens and get back to the tent. Joe's point is a very good one, and we need the answer. If life forms are breaking carbamates into gas down here, there's a local source of energy, and we need to know about it."

"You mean we could use that life instead of the robot's fuser?" asked Molly innocently.

"No, of course not. I meant—oh, you were joking, weren't you?"

"Not entirely. I admit, though, that whether Charley is looking for us alone or Jenny is helping him won't make any difference if we don't charge our armor pretty soon. Honestly, Carrie, what do you think the chances are of the robot's drying out?"

"I haven't thought much about it; there's been too much else to do. There can't be very much ammonia left inside. We tipped it and managed to get some liquid to pour out, so things can be only damp in there. I shouldn't think the air where we left it could be very close to saturation, so it *ought* to be drying and *oughtn't* to take very long."

"But it's been a lot of hours. If it's a lot more, and Charley doesn't get here with more energy for our suits, you'll never be with your Others and I won't see Rovor and Buzz again. It's as simple as that."

But Carol was emotionally incapable of taking the situation that seriously. Practically none of her species could have. Fond as Molly was of the little elf, she was certainly irritating company at times.

But so, of course, was Buzz—and, she had to admit to herself, even Rovor on occasion; and Carol had, after all, *done* everything that either of them had been able to think of that might lengthen their lives. It was just that she wouldn't worry. Which, Molly told herself firmly, was good.

Presumably. Probably. Obviously. The way to be.

But worrying wasn't quite the same thing as trying to think of other constructive lines of action. Maybe there were other tunnels, with dryer currents of air, or warmer ones—why was this one so much warmer, anyway? And since it *was* warmer, why wasn't it more effective in evaporating ammonia from the robot? The machine itself shouldn't be hard to heat up, and ammonia's temperature of vaporization wasn't great—not by the standards of anyone made of water. Naturally, Joe hadn't put packets of silica gel inside the machine—even if silica gel absorbed ammonia the way it did water, which seemed doubtful on what Molly remembered of the chemical structures involved. He hadn't put in the ammonia drinkers' equivalent of a dessicator, anyway. He hadn't expected the robots to get wet. Not inside, that is—he'd protected them against rain, he'd said.

Enigma seemed water-free, so far; would any of the salts lying around serve as driers for ammonia? *Non sequitur*—but this wasn't sequential thinking; it wasn't much better than worrying. They had a lot of collected material, between them, that might be tried out—but that would be an act of desperation; what chance would any one of a dozen or two naturally occurring salts have of being just the substance they needed at the moment?

Maybe an act of desperation was in order, of course, but Molly shrank from the idea of anything that might resemble panic. She cared what others thought of her, and cared about her own self-respect. If she were to put anything inside the robot with the intent of speeding up the drying process, it was going to be something with a good, solid reason for her to believe had the power to absorb ammonia vapor.

She drew a sharp breath, which Carol failed to hear because her translator made no attempt to handle it. The Human was startled, however, to hear Joe's voice.

"Molly! Is something wrong?"

"No. Why do you ask?"

"You said something I gathered to mean surprise."

"You've been doing some fancy work on your translator, haven't you? Well, I don't mind, as long as it's you and we stay on private. I just had another idea about drying this robot."

There was a brief silence before the Nethneen responded.

"Do you really think you should use any more of your water?"

"How long have you been waiting for me to think of that?"

"I haven't been. Your last sentence set me wondering what your idea could be, and that was all I could think of."

"Well, you're probably right. Yes, I see no reason not to use the water. My metabolism produces a constantly increasing amount of it anyway, if I can find anything at all for the food synthesizer to work on—anything with carbon, hydrogen, nitrogen, and such essentials, of course; it doesn't transmute. In any case, I have a fair amount of excess water, and if we don't get this unit going soon I won't need it anyway."

"Would Carol's nitrosyl chloride surplus be equally effective?"

"I don't know enough detailed chemistry to guess, and I wouldn't ask her anyway; she's too small, and an equivalent amount would be too much of her reserves. We'll use water." Molly switched back to the general channel by ceasing to whisper. "Carrie, I've thought of something else we can try to get the ammonia out of this machine. It bonds very tightly to water. If we seal it up with a liter or so of ice inside, any liquid that vaporizes should be taken care of fairly quickly."

"You can furnish that much water?"

"Yes. If we don't try, I won't need the water anyway." She couldn't make herself omit that point, though she knew it couldn't reach her companion's feelings. "Do you have any collecting cans I can use? Mine were full before you caught up with me." Molly was already opening the appropriate part of her armor.

The Shervah hesitated. "Mine are full, too. All with these life forms, unless that stuff I slipped on was something else. Yours have mostly just mineral samples, don't they?"

Molly was detached enough to be genuinely amused rather than indignant. "Yes, most of mine can be replaced easily enough. I'll dump one and use it for the water." She felt a slight temptation to use the can containing the metallic dust from the upper cave, but was not that childish. Besides, she wanted to know what it was herself, and as far as either of them knew it was *not* replaceable.

Carol watched with interest while the can was nearly filled with liquid. Molly waited a few minutes, until ice needles began to show across its surface, before placing it inside the robot. "There's no need to complicate matters with water vapor—or more of it than we can help. Even ice sublimes, but at this pressure it should be a slow process. Also, when this works and the robot starts up, it would be too bad if any motion spilled liquid water into its plumbing; we'd never get rid of that."

"The two together may be liquid at this temperature," Carol pointed out uneasily, "but the machine is standing upright; all it should do is lift to normal float height when its power goes back on. It shouldn't tilt."

"Better get yourselves on it, though, once the ice is inside and the port closed," Joe put in. "Power might come on when it was merely safe from the machine's standpoint, but with unknown and unpredictable commands sneaked in from the circuits shorted by the electrolyte. At the very least, Carol should be ready to open the access port and cut off main power manually the moment it shows signs of misbehavior."

"Good point." The elf crouched on the field ring, holding on by one of the ropes, her other hand at the port she had just closed, and the two women waited.

"I have found another cave with inflowing wind" came the Nethneen's voice. Molly acknowledged briefly but kept most of her attention on the robot and her companion. Charley and Jenny were equally terse, and long minutes of silence ensued.

"I'm back at the surface, heading for the tent." Jenny's rasp startled the Human. Carol was less visibly affected but did respond.

"I thought you were back there long ago, analyzing for high energy compounds."

"Charley and I were both quite a long way down, and I had to do a little collecting. Even knowing the way back up, or having our computers know it, didn't mean the journey could be a fast one; and what did you expect? I started up only a third of an hour ago."

"It seems a lot longer," Molly interjected. "Just waiting for something to happen, especially when you're not quite sure it will—"

"Of course it will. But you should be working!" Carol seemed almost indignant rather than reproving. "*I'm* the one who has to stand by this thing! If you can't get properly interested in the biology, check the rock structure, the passage topology, what you can tell of the wind currents—anything to get your time sense back to normal. Come on, Big Lady, make yourself useful to yourself!"

"I can't do much topology; if I get out of sight of you and the robot I'm likely to get lost. I don't have your memory, remember. I need lab facilities to get any further with the rock studies just as much as Jenny does for the life forms—and as you do, I should think."

"I can classify, on the basis of obvious structure."

"Only because you can remember the details so well."

"Jenny." It was Joe's voice, making one of his rare interruptions.

"Yes, Joe?" came the rough-voiced response.

"I should have checked with you earlier. You will be back at the boat and tent soon. I was taking for granted that you will be using laboratory facilities; is that correct?"

"That was my plan. Is there something else you want done first?"

"No. I was afraid an apology might be in order. If you happen to need the shop for anything, I'm afraid I have just about monopolized its facilities for a time. I have left things on automatic control, of course, and if necessary you may interrupt for work of your own; but if my additional material can be completed as quickly as possible, it may help."

"As far as I can see at the moment, I'll need nothing not already in my lab. If things turn out otherwise, I will call you before making anything, if the interruption will be allowable."

"Quite. There is nothing going on requiring my full attention here. That applies to the rest of you, as well—if anyone has been refraining from a call simply from courtesy, that is not necessary for a while. If I do get involved in really detailed work, I will report the fact to you all." He shifted to Human-private channel. "Molly, that was meant especially for you. I have suspected that you wanted to talk about one thing or another several times since you were trapped underground, and were afraid of interrupting my thoughts. You have been very careful about a courtesy code that I gather is quite exaggerated by your standards; I appreciate it. I assure you that, for the time being, it may be ignored."

"Thanks, Joe. It sometimes has been hard to bottle the words up. There's really nothing much to say right now, though; all we can do is wait on this piece of drying laundry."

She was not sure whether Joe's translator would handle that rather strained figure of speech; after the recent display of its powers she wanted to find out. Joe, however, made no direct answer, and she was left to wonder whether he had picked up enough knowledge of Humanity to grasp it unaided, or the equipment had done it for him, or he felt it would be discourteous to make a direct inquiry about her meaning. There was a lot she still didn't understand about the Nethneen, much as she liked and respected him.

"I can't repeat Carol's assurance that things will be all right" was all he said. "Neither of us can foresee with any certainty in that much detail. We are working, however."

Actually, it was Charley who took advantage of the permission to interrupt.

"What do you have growing in the shop, Joe?"

Even Molly was embarrassed; that was not merely interruption, it was downright snooping. If Joe had wanted them to know, he would have told—or, come to think of it, why hadn't he made the call to Jenny on their private channel? He must have wanted to *arouse* curiosity—

Her thoughts got only that far before the Nethneen answered.

"It is more mapping equipment, whose possible utility occurred to me while I was finishing this machine I am now using. It didn't take long to set up—it used units already designed for machines we have already put in service, with a minimum of modification to get them into a single device. I may want to put it to work quite soon, or possibly not for several hours. I hope it will be the latter."

Molly knew she was reading, probably too much, between Joe's lines, but his speech somehow comforted her. The little fellow did have a tendency to tend very strictly to business, but he was much more likely than Carol to include little problems like lost explorers in the list of current business. His saying as much, and as little, as he had in answer to Charley's query almost guaranteed that there was something he hoped not to discuss at all, but wanted Molly to know about . . .

Or was that just building on sand—or water?

"Molly!" a *whisper* from Carol caught the Human's attention as a shout never would have. "Molly! Look!"

She couldn't have looked anywhere but at the robot. For the first time in hours, it stirred without their pushing or lifting. Soundlessly, and very slowly, it straightened to a true vertical, so that only one side of its base touched the rock. It began to lift, and Carol tensed, ready to snap the access port open and shut it down if it seemed about to do more than rise to—

"Gravdh!!" the Shervah tore the little doorway open and reached in. Molly felt faint for a moment.

"Carrie! What's wrong?"

"We had it set for the long fall—to slow and stop a safe distance from the bottom. Even if everything is all right, the first thing it'll try to do is lift a couple of meters, and there isn't that much room overhead—there! You watch it, too! I *think* it's all clear, but I don't know."

"Better shut the door again. If there's still any ammonia, we want to get rid of it, and if there's anything we know it's that this outside air is pretty well saturated."

Carol hesitated; if anything were still wrong, delay in getting to the keys could be serious. Then she followed Molly's advice. Both watched, tensely at first, then gradually relaxing as the cylinder floated obediently a few centimeters above the rock.

"How much more time should we give it before we take out the can?" asked Carol. "We certainly don't want to move it around with that liable to spill. We'd be worse off than before."

"We worry about that later," replied the Human. "First things to the head of the line. Get up there and plug in your charging cable. I'll lift you if you're worried about jolting the cylinder."

"It won't be bothered by me." The small humanoid vaulted to the top of the robot, unclipped the appropriate plug from her armor, and established connection with the fuser. Five minutes later—the unit could have produced all the energy their accumulators could hold in as many seconds, but conducting it was another matter—Molly took her place, and a few minutes after that her sigh of relief reached Joe's translator.

"I take it your immediate danger is over, Molly and Carol."

"Yes. Now I can start thinking about a bath and a good meal again."

"Or maybe about the job," added Carol.

"Even the job. I think we may as well take that can out and remove one more immediate worry. Also, I'd like to know if it's liquid or not."

"Good," said Joe. "Then as soon as you reach the boat, Jenny, please set Exit Lock Five—the little waste-disposal one near the shop—for automatic cycling, and the shop master inside for Activation Code Two. I may as well put the new machines to work. There should be about three hundred of them ready—"

"*What?*" gasped Molly.

"—and about two hundred more to be finished. That will be enough, I hope. I made the bodies out of silicon and carbon compounds instead of metal, so the only raw material shortage is in electrical contacts; we're low on silver now. The shop equipment can handle them up to a few more than five hundred."

"But what *are* they?"

"You will have guessed, Molly. Small mappers, each with its own model storage unit, all interconnected electromagnetically, all radar equipped. They will be spread out through these caverns, plotting as they go, assembling a model of the interior of Enigma. Charley's estimate of the length of time it would take to do it by ourselves was very discouraging, and it seemed best to use equipment that wasn't limited by having to carry living operators. As soon as Jenny gets to the boat, she'll start sending them after me, and I can begin mapping from these incurrent caves inward. They should get to your end of the planet—I've programmed them to stay in touch, so they won't diffuse and try to map the whole sphere, and to go as far down as possible to make the trip a minimum-distance one—in a couple of weeks."

"But—" Molly started to vent her feelings, and fell silent. Carol was less restrained.

"You said this end was more likely to have the life forms that restored the gas. Why not send them here first?"

"Jenny has specimens of those and will be able to tell us fairly soon whether that hypothesis is right. Charley and you two are already mapping the summer end. If you hadn't managed to charge your batteries, naturally I'd have sent the new ones looking for you first. That was Activation Code One. Luckily, I was able to tell Jenny to key in Two; but I waited until I heard from you two, of course."

OF COURSE I COULDN'T KNOW

Once again, Molly was unable to find the right words. The vision of hot food and hot bath went glimmering as it had before.

Carol happily decided, aloud, that the next thing to do was resume their trip down the river toward Enigma's heart. It was only a matter of time before Charley made contact with them, and if for some reason the Kantrick failed, the new mappers would do the job. Five hundred certainly ought to be enough. With their armor batteries charged and the robot and its fuser standing by, there was nothing to keep them from work. Her beautiful brown fur might be sticky, matted, or even starting to fall out, but her armor would take care of any that did. She could shampoo later.

There were lots of questions to be answered. Was Enigma as spongy and cavernous as their experience was beginning to suggest, or was this something local? Were the caves really kames, and if so, were the original ice bodies that had molded them comet nuclei or something else? If they were comets, how had they incorporated themselves into Enigma's mass without blowing up in the process, since the kinetic energy of a typical interplanetary collision is more than enough to vaporize iron? If they were comets, were there still some of them at greater depths to be found in their original state, to justify Molly's ice hypothesis? If the basic idea was right, how had the silicates consolidated into rock hard enough to support these deep caves? Was Enigma really as young as its sun had to be? If so, how had it managed to develop highly complex life forms? Was biochemistry really the answer to the air-circulation problem? Was it also the answer to the problem of why the little world had air at all—their originally assigned research question? It could be; if gas precipitated as solid before getting far from the surface, it could hardly escape.

Even Molly, thinking all this over, was able to forget her personal discomfort and join in the planning. Clearly, they had to go deeper. However good Joe's new little robots might be, they would not be able to select biological specimens for detailed analysis; researchers would have to do that themselves. Furthermore, *geochemical* data were badly needed, too; the lasers and picks would have to be put to more use.

Perhaps it was no longer really essential to follow the river, as there was now another way for the others to find them and get the group back together; but since they were now frankly seeking for a route down, the river seemed the obvious guide. Also, it would clearly be much easier for even the new robots to find rivers than explorers.

With the anxiety about the robot allayed and the collecting can of ammonia water poured gratefully out on the rock where the machine had stood so long, Molly and Carol resumed their journey.

Charley, too, was following a river—Jenny's—but there was so far no evidence that it was either the same one as Molly and Carol's or one of its tributaries. He, too, was finding much life. His verbal descriptions irritated Carol; the organisms were either decidedly different in structure from those she and Molly had been seeing, or he was doing a very poor job of describing. He was collecting specimens, of course, so there was no point in being critical until these could be examined, and the Shervah managed to restrain herself.

Time went on, on the whole happily. Everyone but Jenny got deeper into the planet, though for Joe it was by proxy; he remained at the antarctic surface, finding and charting more and more wind-caves and sending a small swarm of mapping robots into each as he found it. The halo of fist-sized cylinders that accompanied his own craft was growing smaller, though replacements were still homing in on him from the boat's shop.

Even Carol and Molly were finding a gradual change in

the life forms around them, though not enough, the former insisted, to account for the discrepancies in Charley's descriptions. The temperature was rising significantly, though their armor prevented them from noticing the fact through their own senses. The real warning was the appearance on the rock around them of a faint, white mold.

Even Carol had reached the point where not *every* life form had to be examined closely, and neither had a container left in which to collect anything new, but this stuff got thicker as they progressed, and finally both felt that it deserved detailed attention. Molly scraped some from a convenient surface and spread it on her palm where they could both look at it. They saw a mass of needlelike crystals matted in a way that reminded the Human of the sparkling stuff she had seen in the first cavern.

This, however, was glassy rather than metallic. There was something else familiar about it, and as the women watched, the mass abruptly lost most of its whiteness and then slumped into a tiny puddle of liquid on the palm of Molly's glove. She didn't feel the local heat loss, as her suit had very efficient distributing apparatus even at the thin gloves, but what had happened was suddenly plain enough.

"Frost! Water!" the Human exclaimed. "What became of the ammonia? What's the river made of now?"

The river at the moment was a dozen meters away from the parked robot. Carol headed for it, eagerly but with caution bred by the low gravity, took a sample, and made the same standard test she had used on the stream so far above.

"It's not pure ammonia by a lot," she reported after a moment. "This gadget makes it about seventy percent. I don't know what the rest is."

Molly's armor lacked comparable testing gear, but she had a thermometer probe. She dipped this into the liquid on her glove and held it away from her suit, watching sample and reading as the substance froze again.

"Just under two seventy-two. Not pure, but mostly water. What's going on here?"

"What's the air temperature?" asked Charley.

"Wait a moment—it's still dropping, now the stuff's all frozen." Charley waited, to Carol's surprise. "About two sixty-four. Check, Carrie?"

"That's what mine's been saying."

"And the river?" Another brief delay while the women made the test.

"About two fifty-five. Much too high for pure ammonia, much too low for water. I couldn't begin to calculate percentage composition because it's probably not an equilibrium mixture, I don't know the constants for either association or ionization in those mixtures, and I certainly don't know what else may be there. So what's going on?"

"Very simple," said Charley. Carol rolled her eyes wildly but managed to keep silent. "There's heat below, warming the wind that comes up. Liquid is going down. The walls of the caves and passages connecting them give plenty of surface area and are rough enough for all sorts of turbulence. The planet is a countercurrent heat exchanger—"

"Better yet, it's a reflux condenser!" Molly jumped enthusiastically at the suggestion. Carol, with her conditioned skepticism for Charley-hypotheses, remained silent. "But there goes the last chance of my finding any ice—even water ice—down below. Wouldn't you say, Joe?"

"I gather you just found some."

"You know what I mean. Masses of it. Chunks that would explain these caves being kames, not just frost deposits on cold rock from vapor picked up from the river."

"I'm afraid so. I can't yet guess how far down the caverns extend, and I don't know how far down you are. My new robots have mapped downward a little over a hundred and fifty kilometers, but they're not equipped to take pictures or specimens, and I regret to say they can't measure temperature."

"Joe!" Molly hoped that Carol's shocked tone was not meant seriously. The Nethneen seemed unaffected; at least, he offered no further apology.

"To that depth," he went on, "the crust remains about the same. Between a quarter and a third of its volume is open space, as measured by the radar of the small units."

"How do you keep in touch with them for such a distance through rock?" Molly asked.

"I've programmed them to spread out in such a way as to be able to relay among themselves and all the way back to me. After the whole set of robots is completed and extended as far as practical, I'm going to have to go underground myself so that they won't have to use so many units in relay to the surface that their mapping front is too greatly reduced."

"So they each carry complete diagrams of the volume covered, and so does your own carrier."

"Right. I'll be able to follow down very quickly, when the time comes."

"Fine," said Molly happily. "Then downward to the warmth of the Underworld. This is starting to be fun. Oh—Carol, how about your armor's refrigerator? Is it all right? Is there any reason to worry about it? What sort of backup does it have?"

"It'll work. Standard equipment. No moving parts bigger than electrons to get out of order; I never heard of one failing. And I do wish you'd never given that word *worry* to my translator. Come along, and even if you can't help worrying about yourself, stop fretting over me."

Molly made no answer, though she wondered whether Carol or her own translator had come up with "fret". She came along.

No one had bothered Jenny for a long time. Joe would not have dreamed of it, since she was presumably working; Molly would not have as long as Joe might notice; Carol had managed to resist by reminding herself that any questions would have made her look too much like Charley; what had held the Kantrick back no one wanted to ask.

When the Rimmore finally did speak, Carol immediately keyed the robot to a stop; she wanted to give full attention.

"There's obviously a lot yet to check" came the grating tones, "but you'll all want to hear this much right away. The organisms I picked up represent at least two basically different life forms—that is, different in genetic coding. They are cellular in structure, which is not surprising, since that is the easiest way to engineer the nutrition-in and waste-out problem for any creature above microscopic size. The interesting point is that they do contain high energy compounds, as was suggested. There are hydrazine and hydrazine derivatives in all of them, nitrates in some, hydrogen peroxide in others with some overlap, and azides in a few. One had so much hydrazoic acid I'm a little surprised I'm not scattered around the cavern where I found it, so watch yourselves, all of you."

Carol reacted gleefully. "The next step is to find how they make the compounds. The primary energy source practically has to be the sun, but—"

"It's getting hotter as you go down," Charley interjected. Carol was silenced for a moment.

Molly decided to play safe, and made the obvious answer. "Another point to check as we go. I wonder how hot it will really get. Even in this gravity, there must be a limit before the rock creeps and these caverns close."

"Well, it's a young planet, we've been assuming. Maybe the creeping is still going on." Molly looked uneasily at the sections of cavern wall that her light and Carol's allowed them to see.

"I'm not sure I really like that thought. If you must dwell on it in conversation, please stress the word *creep*. Anyway, we'll look for more life, now that the liquid has changed to water. Things certainly ought to be different."

"But it isn't all water," Carol reminded her. "Ammonia from above is still mixing with it—which I suppose contributes to some of the heating that's been worrying us. The pure water has been vapor, condensing on cold walls."

"Right. Right. But do you know any life forms that operate anywhere near fifty-fifty ammonia-water mix? All I've ever heard of are either one or the other, with the one not the main solvent usually quite poisonous in more than trace amounts. My own body produces ammonia, but I have a couple of very complex organs we call kidneys whose main job is to get rid of it and some chemical machinery to turn it into something less toxic until they do. There are plants, if they are plants, growing *in* that river, Carrie. Are they water-based with evolutionary provision to avoid the ammonia, like me, or the other way around, or what?"

"Collect them. We'll see." Carol actually examined her own carefully labeled cans, selected one, discarded its contents, and replaced it with material from the river. She resealed the cover and redid the label, looking almost defiantly at Molly with one eye as she did so.

The Human said nothing to the implied challenge, but after a moment remarked, "We'll be back, you know."

"I know. Specific answers are more interesting than general ones, though." The giant had to agree, at least for the moment. They remounted the robot, and continued down river and through caves, sometimes more or less horizontally, quite often chasing another fall from top to bottom—much more cautiously now. They had less to go on but were inclined to agree with Joe's estimate that a quarter to a third of Enigma's volume was open. At the thought of the increasing thickness of planet above, Molly found herself less and less resentful of the negligible gravity. Maybe it was just as well that the rock didn't weigh much.

Wherever enough wall area could be seen, she checked carefully for evidence of faulting, hoping it would not appear. Sometimes she went to the length of sweeping mud out of the way to get a better look at underlying rock. She kept reminding herself that some of the laboratories on Think were over two hundred kilometers below the surface, and Think was an ice body, presumably less rigid than Enigma's silicate structure, and unless the hollows weakened the latter . . .

She put that possibility out of her mind, firmly. After all, Enigma had presumably had a million years or so to collapse in, if it were going to do any such thing; why should it pick the moment she was visiting the place?

"The last of the little mappers has arrived," Joe finally reported. "I'm going underground to get as wide a search front as I can. Things aren't going quite as fast as I hoped; apparently my machines aren't spreading out as widely as I had planned. Don't worry, though; the diagram is growing fast enough, and if it seems to slow too much, I'll come out and hit the planet from your end."

"I wasn't worrying, and I'm sure Carol wasn't," replied Molly. "Keep your eye open for life forms; we'll want to compare the two hemispheres."

"Certainly. I have entered a cave that, according to my recorded diagram, provides a relatively quick path to the lowest level my machines have reached so far. I have seen no living organisms yet but am keeping lights on all around me. I've set my controller to follow the passage recorded and can devote full attention to observing. I will report anything worthy of note."

Joe fell silent, and routine supervened. Molly, supposedly looking out for noteworthy material, was letting her mind wander once more; she was wondering who would be next to break the silence and trying to decide whether Charley deserved odds if she were to bet on the point. She hoped partly that it would be Jenny, with more details about the local life chemistry, and partly that it would be Joe.

She was also keeping rather close watch on her thermometer, since another thought had occurred to her. The local air was now well above the melting point of ice, but the last check had shown the river still to be somewhat below that temperature; it was evidently not yet pure water.

It was Joe who won, perhaps half an hour after he had started underground.

"There's something strange about my diagram," he reported. "It seems to be growing narrower at the lower end, as though the machines were finding fewer and fewer ways to go, and those were all funneling closer together. I find that both surprising and disturbing."

"So do I," admitted Molly. "If only the polar regions are porous, you'll really have to go back out and come for us the other way."

"And it will be necessary to rethink our ideas about planetary air circulation from the beginning. I shall investigate in person, of course, before committing us to any premature conclusions."

"Of course." Molly hoped she had kept sarcasm out of her voice; if she had not, she was sure now that the Nethneen would spot it. She maintained silence for more minutes, wondering what Joe's investigation would disclose.

"This is a bit embarrassing," the quiet voice resumed at length. "There seems to be no real change in the planetary structure. I made another thoughtless mistake in programming."

"Do you care to be specific?" Molly wasn't sure she should have asked even that much, but couldn't resist.

"Of course; it will serve as a warning for all. I had, of course, equipped the machines to detect and home to free metal, since the search for you and your robot carries high priority."

"Of course. That seems perfectly reasonable so far."

"True. My mistake was in failing to provide for shutting off all the other metal sensors when one had responded. It appears that one of the machines has found a metal object, and all are now converging on it. I regret to admit that I am going to have to reset them individually when I get there. This will take some little time; I trust you will forgive me."

"It seems a natural mistake. I wonder what metal they found? Offhand, I see no reason for there being anything of the sort—how far?—two hundred, nearly three hundred kilometers below Enigma's surface." Molly was not just being polite; even she was more curious about the discovery than amused or resentful at the Nethneen's planning slip. Not even Charley sounded superior as all chimed in with comforting remarks.

"I will certainly examine what they have found, but will be some time getting to it. I suspect the approaching passages will be somewhat clogged with my robots."

"Maybe it will be in a cave."

"Maybe. I will let you know. I assume you are still traveling."

"Yes. Nothing to report. You, too, Charley?"

"Nothing much. My river has joined a larger one; I am continuing to follow downstream." None of them asked Jenny, presumably busy in her laboratory.

It was more than two hours before Joe reported again.

"It is in an open cave, but my machines are so clustered around whatever they found that I can't see it yet."

"Maybe it's just as well they didn't find us," Carol remarked.

"Oh, they can't be in actual contact; they were set to stop a few meters away and keep reporting position. I'll have to reset a lot of them before I can see what's there, though; if I merely push them out of the way, they go back as close as they can without interfering with each other. I'm starting to work now. Five or ten seconds will be enough on each—I'll simply turn off the metal search."

With five hundred—but he won't have to do all of them before getting to the middle of the pile, Molly thought. Well, we've waited longer before. She kept the thought to herself; there are times when ordinary courtesy goes in line with mere decency.

The minutes passed, and the women resolutely kept their eyes and minds on the passing scenes revealed by their lights. There was still vegetation, if that's what it really was. Neither of them had seen anything resembling animal life, in the sense that it could move around under its own power. Bushlike, grasslike, and totally strange growths showed both beside the river and in it. Again they stopped to check liquid temperature and, as far as they could, composition. It seemed fairly certain that the water percentage was now nearly total; there was nothing obvious to tell what the plants were doing about this. There was no point in collecting anything else; they would have had to discard something else, probably just as informative. They went on.

Then Joe's voice sounded, with the near-whisper that indicated use of the private channel.

"Carol! Molly! There is a problem here. I am not sure what I should—no, I'll have to face it and solve it myself." He shifted to the general translator channel.

"I've found what attracted the robots, and it is a little disconcerting." He paused, long enough for Charley to get in his inevitable question.

"What is it?"

"It seems to be two suits of environmental armor, designed for different species. One I do not recognize by name, though I have seen members at the School. The other, while its design is not just like any I have ever seen, would fit a Kantrick. You could get into it, Charley, except for one fact."

"What's that?"

"It is already occupied, I regret to report."

"You mean there's a—a—" Charley produced a choking sound that Molly had never heard from him. Before she could begin to speculate on what her translator was doing, and what sort of signal her fellow student was actually putting out, Joe responded.

"Yes, I mean there are remains of the original occupants in both suits. I am not a good historian, but would guess from some of the more obvious engineering features of the armor that they have been here for perhaps a thousand years."

The stammering that had afflicted the Kantrick for a moment disappeared. "Have you examined them closely?"

"Not very, and only by eye."

"What's left of the bodies? Can you tell how they died?"

"Very little is left. The Kantrick's exoskeleton is there; soft parts such as eyes are not. The armor apparently remained functional long enough for biodegrading reactions to go well toward normal completion. The other being appears to have had a hard endoskeleton like Carol, Molly, and Jenny, and tissue seems to have shrunk around it. That may not be accurate; as I say, I am not really familiar with the species in question. The armor has no visible damage, and I would guess they died of chemical deprivation—suffocation, hunger, or thirst. What we feared was going to happen to Carol and Molly, before they managed to revive their robot. A power connection links the suits, which suggests that the two shared what resources they had as long as there were any. I would like to believe that, certainly."

"Any sign of how they got there?"

"None. None that I recognize, at least."

Charley was silent for perhaps half a minute. For the first time, Carol seemed to have had her emotional armor pierced; she was clutching Molly's arm tightly and breathing hard. The giant slipped her other arm around the small form and held her as close as their armor allowed. Molly herself had been afraid all along, but more afraid to admit it; the silence and darkness of Enigma's caverns, coupled with the knowledge that nothing there would supply her with usable food or safe drink, had haunted the edges of her mind from the time she had gone underground. She had envied Carol's ability to ignore the dangers, or inability to face up to them, whichever it was. Now the envy was gone, with real sympathy taking its place.

Well as the two knew each other, Molly realized that their attitudes toward death were still hidden. She knew nothing whatever of the customs or religious beliefs of a single one of the School species, not even the Nethneen. It occurred to her that in an institution of several tens of thousands of beings, most of them as far as she had heard with life spans comparable to the Human one, there must have been numerous deaths since she and Rovor had arrived; but she had not been aware of a single one of them. Some aspect of Joe's excessive privacy-consciousness? She couldn't even guess;

and she could not really tell how the Kantrick was reacting to the word of what appeared to be the death of one of his own people.

Charley's voice caught their attention again, and the Shervah released her grip on Molly. The Human kept her arm around the other as they listened.

"Is there any record of students being lost doing lab work here?"

"None that I know of."

"Molly, do you know?"

"Of course I don't. How could I? I'm among the first of my people ever to attend this institution; there hasn't been a human being in this part of the galaxy until a very few years ago. You said yourself the planet had been used as a student lab for thousands. I should think *you'd* know if anyone does, Charley. You kept telling us about earlier student results being sealed or destroyed so that the lab work could be done over by new classes, but it seems unlikely to me that accident reports would get the same disposal."

"Then you honestly don't know."

"I really and truly don't."

There were several more seconds of silence from the Kantrick. When he did speak, it was very slowly, and on private channel to Molly.

"I should have guessed."

OF COURSE THAT'S WHY

Once again, Molly found herself unable to understand the implication of the Kantrick's remark or his reason for making it privately. She was also quite unable to think of an appropriate answer, other than the obvious "Why?"

And Charley, as with his earlier prediction about the fate of the boat, seemed unwilling to pursue the matter further. He appeared content with making it clear to her and to her alone that he had an idea on the subject; its details might come later. Possibly after he had worked them out himself, Molly thought, and realized how unfair the thought might be. For the moment, he sounded almost like Joe being embarrassed by another oversight in planning.

"It's just something I should have thought of earlier. I'll tell you when things work out" was all he would say before returning to general communication. Molly could ask no more; Joe was speaking again.

"I don't quite know what to do about these remains. They would fit in the mapper here with me, I suppose, but I'm not too happy at the thought of carrying them inside for the rest of the trip, and I'm not sure I could fasten them outside effectively with what rope I have. Charley, do you feel strongly about what happens to the body of one of your people? We can arrange to recover it later, of course."

So Joe wasn't familiar with other peoples'—at least, with some other peoples'—funeral customs, either, but recognized that at least some groups did feel strongly about such things. Molly decided that perhaps her ignorance wasn't her own fault, after all.

The Kantrick responded promptly and with no sign of emotion. "It doesn't matter to anyone alive, if your guess at the age is right. We should probably bring them back eventually in order to figure out just what happened, but I don't see any reason for hurry. They've been here a long time and can wait awhile longer. I should think their translators would give some clue, but I suspect the archaeologists would shell us alive for separating those from the remains. I suppose there *are* translators with them?"

"I'm afraid I haven't made a close enough examination. They'd be hidden inside the armor, and your point about archeology is well taken. Very well. It's one of your people, as far as I can tell, and you have the say; with your permission we will leave them here for future attention."

"You have it."

Molly wondered what was going on in the Kantrick's mind. She had had the feeling, from his initial response to Joe's announcement, that he had been as shocked and bothered as she and Carol by the hard proof that death could actually strike a harmless student; like Carol, he had previously seemed unable to take in that fact on any but the coldly intellectual level. Now all signs of fear, or shock, or horror—whatever he *had* felt—had vanished, and he was treating Joe's discovery as though it had been news of an abandoned robot. The Kantrick was not cold-blooded, except in the most literal physical sense; she had met enough of his people to recognize an approximately Human tendency toward affection and fellowship in them. Had Charley popped an emotional circuit breaker somewhere? Probably not, but there was something about him she definitely did not understand.

"You have the location in your diagram." Thc Kantrick was stating, not asking. Joe confirmed that he had. "I will examine the site myself, later, if work permits; you have no objection?"

"Of course not." Molly would have asked why anyone could possibly object; Joe did not. Maybe he understood the Kantrick better—or maybe it was just Joe. But why should Charley anticipate objection?

Molly gave it up. Xenopsychology was interesting but unlikely to be useful right now. Back to work.

"The mappers are spreading out satisfactorily," Joe reported. "I should have them all back in service quite soon. There is no evidence that the makeup of Enigma's crust is changing greatly; their behavior was entirely due to their response to the armor here, I feel certain."

"How far down did all this happen?" asked Molly.

"Three hundred five kilometers below the cave at which I entered. That's radial component, not along the travel line."

"And what's the temperature there? I know your little robots can't read it, but surely you have a thermometer in the one you're riding." For just a moment, Molly's breath stopped; if Joe *had* forgotten that item, she had phrased the remark very tactlessly. Fortunately he had not.

"I read two hundred eight-three."

"That's only a little higher than we have. I wouldn't have thought we could possibly be anywhere near your depth."

"You may not be. I have a cold wind following me from the surface, and silicate is a poor conductor with a fairly low heat capacity. The temperature deep in the rock around me may be a great deal higher. You are getting air from inside—"

"But a river from outside."

"True." Except for the one-word response, Joe ignored the interruption; Molly blushed unseen even by Carol. "Nevertheless, I could be deeper. We will know in due time. I have all my mappers back in service now and am heading deeper myself. It will be interesting to learn whether this porosity extends all the way to Enigma's center."

"And what the temperature is *there*," added Carol. "I wonder how far down this river will last and how far down the life will go, even if they both turn to water. Onward and downward, comrade."

"And how stable the caverns at the center are, if they do exist," added Charley.

"I told people to accompany that thought with the word *creep*," Molly said firmly.

"Sorry. I'll be with you, if these rivers do join up. If we do get flattened, it will creep down on us together."

"Good try" was Molly's dry retort.

Joe, traveling by far the fastest, made the next report of

real interest, but this was not for several more hours. In the meantime the other three explorers had all gone deeper, presumably by several kilometers, and the river followed by the women was now well above the melting temperature of ice. Molly was following this phenomenon with interest that surprised even Carol, stopping for analysis and thermometer check far more frequently than the Shervah wanted. The Human was following another idea of her own, though she had kept it to herself so far. Ammonia was now below the detection limit of the simple instrument in Carol's armor. Ice had long since vanished from the rock, and living forms were becoming scarce and stunted.

"It begins to look as though they were ammonia rather than water types," Carol said thoughtfully, as she threw aside a tangle of filaments that might have been dead roots or a badly designed bird's nest. "With that disappearing, they aren't doing very well. Maybe Jenny's high energy compounds don't form this deep."

"You'd think the rivers would carry them at least as far as they themselves flow, if they form on the surface from stellar energy." Molly was equally pensive. "Ordinary evolution can do a lot, but I suppose it does have its limits. I never heard of a supersonic flyer on any planet, for example. Earth has things that can do with incredibly little water, and these may be the ammonia equivalents; maybe we should sacrifice another of our already collected items and put it in a can."

Carol hesitated, as Molly had expected. "You're pretty big. I don't suppose there's any space in your armor where you could tuck that thing, is there?"

"Well—" Molly picked it up and considered. "There is room around the removable water and chemical flasks—the ones I bled water from before, for example. Putting foreign matter in there is not exactly good procedure, but the compartments are sealed from the rest of the suit, of course, so I can open them while it's in use. Maybe—all right. I'll take a chance. It was my idea about the plants, I'd like to check it out. This thing looks very dry; if a valve leaks and the specimen gets contaminated with water, don't blame me."

"Remember the hydrazoic acid!" came Jenny's voice. Molly hesitated, then reassured herself.

"I've already handled this thing pretty roughly. It was growing in soft mud and didn't take much to pull up, but we dropped it on rock afterward. H-N-three would be liquid at this temperature, so there can't be enough to matter, anyway."

"You could have dropped glyceryl nitrate safely on rock in this gravity. Maybe putting that thing in your armor isn't such a good idea, Molly." Carol did not actually draw away, but giving danger as much thought as she had just uttered, and allowing the matter to weigh for a moment against the importance of the research, was her equivalent to some people's screaming and running. Molly was impressed.

Still, she opened the appropriate panel and stowed the tangle away, not entirely without uneasiness. "It's less likely to get jarred there than in one of the cans, after all," she said firmly. "Now another temperature check of the water, and we'll go on." Carol helped without comment; she had not really expected her big friend to take such a chance, and felt a little guilty. Still, Molly was adult and entitled to take her own risks if she felt the potential gain was worth it; and of course the specimen *was* worth some risk—why were they here, after all?

It was onward and downward again. For some time the river was just a river; then it fell for long, long minutes from top to bottom of what seemed to be the largest kame yet. The women outraced the drifting drops and found an extensive lake at the bottom. This had a few bits of floating detritus that might or might not have been alive. The edge of the body of water—it *was* water, according to a quick check—was nowhere in sight, and they set off at random, reaching a cavern wall with no sign of further passages in a few minutes. They followed this around to the left, as had become standard procedure with them, passing half a dozen tunnels but not stopping to investigate until they met one that was serving to drain the lake. They followed the new river without comment.

There was no visible life in or beside it. Its current was slow, though it slanted downward at a steep angle and frequently slithered around rocks that might have fallen into its bed from above. Sometimes there were enough of these to dam it into a pool, whose exit often took several minutes to find in the rubble.

At one of the smaller of these, Molly called for a stop.

"Another temperature check? We did one only a few minutes ago!" Carol's voice was definitely a complaint.

"Another temperature check. I have my reasons."

"Which you won't tell me."

"Which I'll show you. Park this thing, please." Carol stopped the robot, not quite happily, but at least curious.

Molly made a reading, and smiled, invisibly since all the light was concentrated on the instrument. "Three hundred seventeen. It has to be water. There couldn't be enough ammonia staying with it to smell at that temperature."

"You're using it to replace what you used? Why worry? Surely your recycling equipment would handle that sort of impurity."

"Yes, it would. Probably I *should* top off my buffer tanks; thanks. I hadn't thought of that."

"Then what are you going to do? Drink it? You'd be crazy. You can't be that tired of reprocessed stuff."

"I certainly could be, but I'm not yet. Help me get this suit off."

"You *are* crazy—oh! Of course."

"Yes. Of course. Sorry you can't join me, but you'd parboil in a few seconds." Molly had unclamped her helmet and now removed it carefully, keeping the mask and breathing connections tightly over her nose and mouth. Carol took the helmet and put it down for her, while the Human went to work on the body seals and presently opened and removed the waist-up section. Then she sat down and drew herself carefully out of the walking and recycling part, leaving it sitting on the bank of the pool.

"Keep your light and at least one eye on that stuff, please. In this gravity I can't help feeling it may blow away, and some of this mud seems soft enough to lose small pieces in. It all seems pretty wet, too; you'd think in this wind we'd find a dry surface occasionally."

"We didn't have the ammonia drying, up at that level."

"True. Our reflux unit doesn't get very far below saturation, does it?"

Molly sat down again with air recycler beside her, mask still on her face and the connecting tubing carefully laid out to avoid tangles. The most important part of the suit was still to be removed.

This was the "blubber," the skin-tight layer some four millimeters thick in most places that covered her entire body except face and hands and contained the lining that absorbed perspiration and body wastes and the capillary system that pumped it to the actual recycling machinery. None of this contained moving parts larger than molecules, and in theory should last for years of use and even abuse; but Molly peeled it off with the utmost care and spread it out beside the rest of the armor.

Then she entered the water and luxuriated for ten minutes. She climaxed the operation by holding her breath, removing the mask, and submerging completely for several seconds, rubbing the dried remains of sweat and, she admitted to herself, occasional tears from her cheeks. She stood up, accepted the mask handed to her by the Shervah, pressed it against her face, squeezed the tubing, and blew it clear around the edges; then she resumed normal breathing, only slightly afraid that she would detect the scent of ammonia.

She didn't. There was something else, very faint, that she failed to identify, but it did not worry her. The water could not be expected to be absolutely pure. She picked up the inner suit and immersed it in the pool, scrubbing its outer and especially its inner surfaces carefully and as completely as possible with her hands. Then, not worrying about drying—the suit would take care of that when repowered—she redonned the equipment, and presently stood fully accoutered in front of her small companion.

"That was worth it. I've never wanted a bath so much in my life."

"I can sympathize, but I think you were perfectly insane, just the same" was the response.

"Certainly I was, but that remark from someone who can pay more attention to a bunch of weeds than to the fact that her batteries are running down and the charger is out of action—"

Joe interrupted again. His exact words were not important, but they served to change the subject. Molly wondered if he ever felt any real emotion; it was possible that the embarrassment he occasionally seemed to show was just to keep his listeners from feeling inferior. She was soon to form a more definite opinion.

The journey was resumed, and they had been on the way for perhaps another two hours when the Nethneen's voice came through again.

"My computer seems to have failed."

"You have a backup, don't you?" asked Charley.

"Certainly, but it is behaving similarly. The diagram being relayed back is quite impossible."

"As impossible as the life on this planet?" asked Carol, perhaps too pointedly.

"At least. The model has just plotted a cavern nearly spherical in shape and approximately twelve hundred seventy-four kilometers in diameter."

"That's ridiculous, but not impossible."

"You've been computing, too, Charley?"

The Kantrick evaded the question by ignoring it.

"The biggest I've encountered so far was less than twenty, I admit, but even that means this gravity just doesn't count. We've known that all along. What's your record?"

"So far, just over thirty-five in greatest dimension; it was not very spherical."

"Your lead mapper probably has something wrong with its radar. Wait until some others reach the same point. What does your program do when two of them disagree with each other?"

"Checks against a third or a fourth, if necessary."

"Then wait a few minutes. The others will reach the same point, or points farther on, and straighten things out."

Joe made no answer, and everyone waited, except possibly Jenny, who might have been too absorbed in work to hear. After about ten minutes, Charley made himself heard again.

"Have any more mappers reached the area?"

"I would assume so. There is no easy way to check their location except by the model sections they have completed. There has been no change in the model."

"Then either a lot of your mappers have the same fault, or you've lost a lot of mappers. What could happen to them? What would rivers like the ones we've been meeting do to them?"

"Nothing, as far as I can judge."

"But there's no way you can identify individual signals."

"No. It could have been done, and I thought of it, but the arrangements would have been complex and time consuming. I was worried about Carol and Molly and wanted the devices ready quickly."

"There is one possibility Charley didn't mention," Carol cut in.

"What is that?" asked Joe.

"That there really is a twelve hundred-kilometer cave below you. No one has really calculated the strength of this rock. We know the gravity is weak and the planet young. It may have started as an ice body, a sort of giant comet nucleus, and accreted silicates later."

"And more comets," added Molly. "Consider the other caves. That would make the center just a super-kame."

"But how could such objects accrete without at least melting at the time?" Joe was more than doubtful; this was a worse blow than the life discovery.

"I don't know offhand; there's a lot of information to be collected before we do much calculating, let alone genuine theorizing. The first job would seem to be getting that machine you're riding down to where your model says the big cave is and checking for yourself whether it's really there. Maybe, if it is, we can get together more quickly than any of us were expecting. I certainly hope so. Have you met any rivers yet?"

"No. I don't expect any. The air going in from the surface would be warmed both by compression and from the surrounding rock. If any liquid were filtering down, I would expect it to vaporize long before reaching my present depth."

"I hope you're right. That's a very firm conclusion, and another mistake would be quite a jolt, wouldn't it?"

"Yes, Carol. Facts can be most tactless at times. However, I am learning to put up with them—perhaps a little late in life. I am following what seems the best path that my model shows to the central hollow."

"Central?" asked Molly.

"If real, yes. It commences eight hundred thirty-six kilometers below the surface and has a radius of six hundred thirty-seven. The planet, by our earlier measures, has a radius of fourteen hundred seventy-three. Unless the cavern is off-center on one of the axes at right angles to the rotation one, it is a hollow center to the planet."

"I don't really believe in hollow planets," Molly said thoughtfully.

"Neither do I, yet," replied Joe with what had to be genuine emotion, Molly was sure. "Suspend your judgment, young woman. I am trying to do the same. I am glad this machine can follow the indicated passage automatically; I am not sure I am in a state to guide it properly myself."

"How deep are you now?"

"Six hundred fifteen kilometers from my entry point."

"Two hundred twenty-one to go."

"If it were a straight line, Charley. It is far from that. I suppose I could get the machine to tell me the integral, but I will simply say that it looks more like five hundred on the model."

"How fast are you going?"

"Not nearly as fast as the little machines; this one is far less maneuverable, and as you must have noticed, many of these passages are rather tortuous. I would guess three and a half to four hours' travel time."

"It will take us a lot longer," Molly said thoughtfully. "At least, we know we only have to follow the river."

"If it lasts. Temperature may become too high even for water to stay liquid. Pardon me—I didn't want to give you another matter for worry."

"We'd already thought of that one," Carol assured him. "Don't worry; we'll face it if we have to. In the meantime, the river is here. You ride your car, we'll ride ours. Your river any bigger, Charley?"

"A lake, at the moment. I can't find the outflow."

"Good. That happened to us not long ago. Maybe you are on our track."

"It's the fourth time it's happened to me."

"Oh. Well, downstream is still the way; keep looking."

"I am."

Molly wondered whether the Shervah were coming to tolerate Charley a little better, or whether the teasing had been meant to hurt. She herself might have used the same words, jocularly; she was not sure at all how Carol meant them.

They went on, down the ever-slower stream. Gravity was weakening, too, though none of them had yet thought of this point, as more and more of Enigma's mass was left overhead.

Joe was aware of it; his travel was faster, and Enigma-normal was much closer to that of his natural environment. Carol and Molly weren't, since from the beginning they had felt on the point of blowing away, and even their armor wasn't much anchorage. The latter had, after all, been designed to be as light as possible, consistent with its other requirements. All the women really appreciated was the decreasing rate of flow of the water, and Carol was not sure whether that was an objective fact or that her time sense was getting out of order. Molly was more inclined by nature to trust her own senses, but near free fall put a severe strain on that inclination, space-trained though she was.

She did not actually get sick, fortunately. This would have put a heavy strain, though probably not an excessive one, on her armor's recycling capacity. She was, however, getting less and less comfortable. She was also beginning to itch again, in spite of the recent bath.

Joe's report was a relief to Molly, if not to the Nethneen; it took her mind off her mounting troubles.

"The hollow center is real." Once again his emotion seemed under control, but Molly felt quite sure that it was there. "It is not perfectly spherical, but very nearly so. The dimension is what I reported earlier. I am inside a hollow planet and am forced to believe it. I am grateful for your suggestion about its possible origin, Carol. I might not have been able to conceive one myself, and with none at all, I would have been most uncomfortable. I realize it is only a hypothesis, but at least it gives a foundation for more imagination and work planning. If someone could do the same for the existence of life here, which has been causing me acute discomfort ever since Carol first reported it—or at least, to be honest, after the later reports when I could not longer disbelieve it—I could be quite happy."

"You haven't seen that?" asked Carol in surprise.

"No. Have you?"

"Of course. You have the data, too. You've had it for hours. You've had some of it for weeks."

"Well?"

"The fact that this planet is a laboratory and has been for millennia. The bodies you found. Molly's bath, for School's sake! Obviously the life didn't start here; the School brought it!"

OF COURSE TIME'S NOT IMPORTANT NOW

"I have not felt more relieved, or more foolish, since Molly first reported the life. Thanks a lot, Carol. We can check that suggestion very easily, too. The life we find should show a wide variety of underlying biochemistry. Usually a given planet has one particular chemical system reach the self-replication stage, and that usually takes over completely; others either never develop at all or are destroyed by the competition. Any reasonably careful study of a single world's biology shows the evolutionary descent of all its life forms from a common molecule, and there are enough different ways to run life chemistry so that a particular basic commonly identifies a given world uniquely. Here we should find lots of different biochemistries competing with each other. It would be unlikely for any one to have eliminated the others, especially with frequent reseeding by new visitors."

Carol added happily, "That the metallic growths Molly found were doing well enough, and the more obviously organic ones the rest of us have encountered were also in active ecologies as far as we could tell, would support that. Also Jenny has already reported two different basic biochemistries, I recall."

"Right. Lab work is needed, but its nature is clearly indicated. I wonder whether Jenny has been listening."

That was as close as Joe would come, of course, to addressing the Rimmore directly, since she was presumably at work. The answer was prompt.

"I have been. Like you, Joe, I feel foolish. I got those

two and didn't see the implication; I just thought I wasn't to the real basics yet. I am going to have to redo some of this work, because I was taking for granted that there would be some one common chemical theme here, like double helix with a small number of coding units, or the positive against negative paired-sheet arrangement, or that amusing one which duplicates using absorption versus emission microwave spectra, or—"

"We get it, Jenny dear," Carol cut in as courteously as she could; even with Joe listening, she did not consider this the time for a general biology lecture. "I think there was a suggestion of starting with microscope work first."

"I did. With only one specimen, but don't—what's Molly's figure of speech, Charley?—don't rub it in. We now know why we're all students instead of Considered Words. Carol and Molly, the sooner you get back to this tent with what the two of you have collected, the better."

"I quite agree" was the Human's emphatic response. "Joe, I suppose you can fly your horde of miniature mappers right across the hollow and set them to working upward on our side. If there are rivers actually reaching the center, it will be a big help."

"It will also be a big surprise," replied Joe. "The temperature here is about three hundred thirty-seven, and the pressure one and a third atmospheres. I have never memorized the vapor pressure curve of water, but I'd rather expect the place to be dry."

"I haven't the whole curve in my head, either," admitted the Human, "but the pressure is greater than standard for me, if my translator can be believed, and the temperature well below what I consider the ordinary boiling point of water. I agree there should be no ammonia, unless the vapor makes itself obvious, but your hollow should have lots of liquid water if there are many rivers like this one feeding it."

"Good. I'll check. It won't be very obvious on this radar model I'm getting here, I fear; I'll have to fly around using a spotlight. That will be easy enough, though; at least the place seems to be very empty, and I won't have to worry about running into anything. I can fly as fast as I want. I'm heading for your hemisphere now."

"Hold it, Joe!" It was the Shervah.

The mapper came to an abrupt halt before the Nethneen answered verbally.

"What's the trouble?"

"Your mappers' radars show *nothing* in that space? It's empty except for air?"

"As far as every instrument I have indicates, yes."

"It shouldn't be. I know this is a young planet, but there has been some erosion—wind and water going through caves and tunnels have loosened material. We've all seen stuff like blowing sand and dust. That should accumulate at the center of your cavity. If you don't detect anything there, we need an explanation before you fly too fast."

"Why should anything accumulate at the center? There is no net gravity inside a hollow shell of matter," Molly pointed out. "Even if the hollow isn't perfectly centered in the planet, or the crust's density isn't perfectly symmetrical around it, any unbalanced attraction would be toward the greater mass concentration, not toward the center of the hollow."

"There is air," retorted her small companion. "Air has mass. There would be gravity—not much, but some—toward the center from any part of the inner surface. Any particle of solid or drop of liquid freed from that surface would eventually reach the middle. Joe should go cautiously. Maybe the dust is too loose, or too absorbent, to reflect the radar of his little robots; I don't know what sort of wave pattern he's using. I don't know why he doesn't see anything in his model—I don't really know that anything is there, for certain. There are probably factors I haven't thought of. All I'm saying is that I would *expect* something that was solid, liquid, or muddy to be at that point, and I wouldn't want to run into it too hard."

"There are traces of dust in the air," admitted the Nethneen. "A searchlight beam scatters enough to be followed by eye. I see no increase of concentration as I head toward the center, however. Thanks for the warning, though; I'll be very careful. I don't want even minor damage; going outside my mapper even in armor in this furnace doesn't appeal to me."

"Nor to me," replied Carol. "I hope you get to us before we get to you."

"If you hadn't told him to be careful, he might have been on your side of the hollow by now," pointed out Charley.

"And he might have been digging his way out of a mud satellite, if that's the word I want," was the sharp answer.

"I don't think it is." Charley remained mild, for him. "If there is anything there, it could hardly be said to be—"

"It would be in free fall, wouldn't it?"

Charley found himself without an answer, but not even Carol supposed she had convinced him.

"I am traveling slowly enough to stop if anything reasonably large comes within range of my lights, but should be across the hollow within an hour." Joe, not entirely to Molly's surprise now, took over the conversation again. "I am inclined to believe that my mappers are correct in reporting nothing large, but am holding them from getting too far ahead of me. This will not delay the search for rivers in your hemisphere very greatly, if at all; I am continually examining my model as I cross the opening, and while I don't see just what a river would do when it came out into this area, it should at least betray itself by moving."

"*Has* anything moved visibly, so far?" asked Molly.

"Nothing. This is rather surprising since you told me water would still be liquid here. I am not, of course, devoting all my attention to the surface ahead, in view of Carol's suggestion. I assume you two are still traveling with the river. It's too bad we have no way of telling how far you have yet to go; the temperature is certainly very unreliable."

"There's a pretty good approximation" came Charley's voice. "I thought of using it but didn't want to stop."

"What is it?" Carol didn't actually add "this time," but Molly felt very sure of this part of her work on the translator's tone. The "this time" was clearly implied.

"Gravity. It's about sixty-five centimeters per second squared at the outer surface and essentially zero at the inner. I know it's not quite zero, Carrie, but a ball of gas at the temperature and pressure and radius that Joe reported will give a good deal less than one millimeter per second squared. It's a nice low gravity that you wouldn't have to dilute with an inclined plane or an improvised pendulum to measure. Just drop something like a sampling pick the height of the robot, which you know, and time it. The change may not be perfectly linear as you go down, but I shouldn't think it would be very far from it. Joe said the sponginess of the crust didn't change much along the route he took, after all."

"A really good notion," Carol said slowly, rather to her companion's amazement. "We can make a more careful calculation later, if it seems necessary, of just how fast *g* changes with depth; but you're right, Charley—departure from straight line probably won't be much if any worse than our timing errors. We're waterfalling through another kame right now, but as soon as we come to a river with a bank, we'll go ashore and give that a try."

"Excellent," added Joe. "I have seen no signs of water yet, and it will be nice to learn how close to the central cavern your river does come."

"Joe, are you still feeling pessimistic?" asked Molly.

"Slightly. I find it hard to believe that any river could reach this space without giving some sign which my mappers would have found by now."

"Are you past the center yet?" asked Carol.

"I am just about at it, if this model can be trusted."

"Don't be pessimistic about that, too. If you can't see any dust or mud satellite from where you are, there can hardly be one, and your five hundred radar sets are probably right. You might as well speed up and take a close look at this side of the big hole. I think we're getting near the bottom of this one; we have another lake under us, but maybe it will have a shore somewhere."

"Won't it have to?"

"Not always, Charley. Some of them have water, or ammonia, or whatever right to the cave wall, with nothing to walk on anywhere; we've had to leave the cavern on, and sometimes under, a river." Molly was pleased. Carol had shown no trace even of sarcasm, much less of impatience, in her answer.

"I'm taking a chance and speeding up" came Joe's voice. "My radars have spotted two hundred or more indentations in the inner wall that may prove to be continuing passages. Nothing is moving in or near any of them, or anywhere else. It will take some time to check them all personally. I will have to decide what area to resume detailed mapping in three dimensions. I know, of course, the location where you went underground, and could find the spot directly below that easily enough, but with the shell thickness of this object well over half its total radius I'm not sure that would mean much. You've spent a lot of your travel in horizontal, or partly horizontal, motion and could be a quarter of the way around the planet from where you started by the time you reach the inner surface."

"Play it by ear, Joe" was Molly's not too helpful comment. The Nethneen understood her meaning without any need of Charley's promptly volunteered explanation, but he had already expected to be guided by events even before she had spoken. He was feeling even more pessimistic as he examined, with ever-improving resolution, the model of Enigma's inner surface and realized better and better just how irregular it was, how many different irregularities might prove to be passage mouths, and how many of the passage mouths might prove to be dead ends after one or ten or fifty kilometers. His count of two hundred had been at very low resolution.

Then something caught his attention. Not motion, just a difference. Much of Enigma's inner surface was very irregular, as the model showed, but there were two patches, roughly opposite each other, where it seemed to be a great deal smoother. The areas were not at all sharply defined, and were in fact so large that he only noticed them when the model scale was set to show practically a whole hemisphere at once.

Roughly, they corresponded to the arctic and antarctic regions on the outside of the sphere; the latitudes that alternated between decades of permanent sunlight and decades of permanent night as the hollow world swung around its vast, lazy orbit. He had actually emerged into the central space within one of the regions, without noticing anything strange about it at the time; there were lots of holes even in the smooth areas. It was the region between tunnel mouths that was different. He would have to be more attentive as he approached the other. He was hesitating whether to report the discovery and oversight now, or to wait until he had checked more details at the northern area, when he was interrupted.

"There—we can stop and make that check." Carol's

voice interested him but did not improve his pessimism. The women must have a long, long way to travel before they reached the core, and all sorts of things could happen to the river before then. There were no rivers to be seen here, on smooth areas or rough; the only question was not whether something happened, but what?

"Here" came the Human voice. "This will do to drop." Joe could not tell what she was talking about; Carol could presumably see. Some small tool, no doubt. "It would be better if we had a thread or fine wire to hang it from, so I could let go without any extra components, but I'll be careful. We'll each make several runs. Top of the robot—we know it's level, so we can sight along it—down to level with the field disc. Ready? Three, two, one, zero."

Joe listened, but not with full attention. He was well past Enigma's center now, though with some hundreds of kilometers still separating him from even the nearer side. Should he hold the mappers and look personally to see whether there was water *in* the tunnels? The little machines should not be harmed by it if there were. Their hulls were liquid and gas tight. No, waiting would be useless precaution and a waste of time; mapping should start at once.

The Nethneen keyed a set of general commands to his small slaves. These should have the effect of forming them into a disc some ten kilometers in diameter and sending it ahead along his present flight path at several times his present speed. He could not see the mappers even at this fairly small distance, but watched his model expectantly, looking for resolution to improve shortly in the area approached by the disc. Hundreds of observing machines, feeding new signals to his computer from constantly changing positions, should give almost microscopic detail to the region immediately in front of the antenna system.

To his satisfaction, this seemed to be working. He was less happy at the continued absence of water; he had now set his computer to note the presence of changing data at any given point in contrasting color, but only the shades he had assigned to geometric contour indication were visible so far.

Some twenty—no, twenty-three—concavities seemed to be tunnel mouths in the highly resolved region just ahead of the disc. A single key activated the principle mapping program, and three robots darted toward each of these. The others hovered for the moment, ready to form chains along the tunnels that could relay if necessary. It quickly became so, and once again mapping routine was underway.

"Forty-three centimeters per second squared." Molly knew better than to address anyone in particular. "About two thirds the surface value. That's discouraging one way, but better than I really dared to expect. It's not too much cooler than the central temperature; *that* can't possibly be changing linearly."

"Rock's a bad conductor. Even with this reflux condenser setup, most of the temperature change must occur fairly near the surface," Carol pointed out.

"And at your end of the planet, you're getting air currents from the central hollow," Charley added.

Molly agreed, rather shortly. She was feeling less and less comfortable. The itch seemed to be getting worse, and she was having trouble seeing; she wanted to wipe her eyes. Blinking had no effect. Once or twice she had considered taking her helmet off briefly to attend to the sensation—she could have stood the temperature and pressure for the few seconds it should take, she was sure—but judgment overrode temptation for the time being. She wondered whether Carol was experiencing anything similar but decided it was better not to ask, at least for a while. If either of them became unable to see, things would be awkward; if both were blinded . . .

The thought made her check her light once more. If Carol noticed this, or considered anything strange about it, she made no comment. The light itself seemed to be working properly, but the surrounding darkness suddenly seemed more oppressive. Darkness, and silence except for the sounds they made themselves and the voices coming through her translator—the river, in this gravity, seldom did anything audible—and the endless awareness of a planetful of rock surrounding them in all directions, ready to squeeze.

There was one good thing about this asteroidal gravity. She couldn't really make herself feel that much would happen even if the outer part of the planet *did* fall in on them.

That was silly, of course. Silly to suppose it would happen;

why should a hollow world, unstable by nature, pick the time *she* was visiting it to have its inevitable collapse? Sillier to suppose that if it did happen, it would have no personal effect. Even under this mere four percent of normal gravity, there were rocks she had seen on this trip, rocks that had certainly fallen from upper parts of the caves and passages they were traversing, which would have pressed Human and Shervah into thin films. They might have done it a little more slowly than on Earth or Nova Lidiska, but would that really be an improvement?

She twisted her mind firmly off that track.

There was no life, or anything she or Carol could recognize as life, now to be seen. Why? Temperature? Chemistry? Energy? There was no telling, nothing but guessing until the specimens in their collecting cans reached a lab. Even then there might only be more questions.

Charley, following what was evidently a different river, had reached a similar biological situation, he reported. He had not stopped to make a gravity check, but the temperature of the air around him was about the same as theirs, and he might well be closer to the center now than they were. Like them, he still had a river to follow.

But his river, he reported, was changing. He sounded puzzled.

"I took for granted that this stream must be getting deeper in this section, since it had become a good deal narrower." No, his voice wasn't so much puzzled as *wronged*. Someone was playing an unkind trick on him. "Now it's turned into rapids, if you can call them that, with rocks sticking through the surface all over the place and water oozing around them. It just can't be very deep, unless there was a channel ten or fifteen times as deep as it is wide that got filled by loose rubble and has water flowing between and around the rocks all the way down. That's hard to believe."

"Why?" asked Carol, predictably.

"I'd expect the rubble to fall, some decent fraction of the time, from the *sides* of the cut, and make it wider. I've seen canyons with pretty steep walls, but this is too much. Why would everything have come from above—especially when there isn't always enough clearance above to supply fifty or sixty meters of rubble?"

"I grant that's a better point," the little Shervah conceded. "If it really isn't so deep, though, what's the alternative?"

"Even less attractive. The river is shrinking. It's carrying less water."

"Why is that unattractive?" Joe's attention had been caught by Charley's report, and his pessimism vanished as his mind found something to work on. "You have hot air from the core blowing outward, against the flow of the river—your reflux condenser, Molly. The river is simply evaporating and getting blown back up to where it can condense. The fact that water's equilibrium vapor pressure is great enough to let it be liquid there, or even down here, is no guarantee that the actual vapor pressure is high enough in either place for the liquid to be present. My home world may not have air enough to give us weather, but even I know that much physical chemistry. Dynamic equilibrium is an interesting state to study and a useful one to produce industrially, but one never has the right to assume it's the actual, current situation."

"A point that I shouldn't have had to have pushed at me, since I am *very* used to weather," Molly conceded. "All right, then. Charley, like us, is a long way from the center, and his river is vanishing. Ours will probably do the same before very long, unless it's a much bigger river, or meets a much bigger one. When that happens, we either wait for your mappers to find us, or go back to traveling upwind when there's a horizontal component to follow and straight down when there isn't. Incidentally, Carrie, we'd better set this machine on solid rock again soon and let its inertial system have another feel for the planet's axis. We could have come a long way horizontally since it last had a chance to tell which way is up."

"Good point."

"How about the size of your river?" asked the Kantrick. "Does it seem to be shrinking at all?"

"We have no way to tell," replied Molly. "It's been a long time since we could see all of it at once. It should guide us downhill for a while yet; it's certainly pretty big."

"Mine's just a trickle now, with occasional drops up to brain-dome size being picked up by the wind and carried back upstream evaporating as they go. Several of them have hit my window—I see what you mean about what they do to the seeing, Carol. I have to slow down, or even stop, until they dry up. I'll be able to go faster when the river vanishes entirely."

"If you can decide which way to go."

"Upwind, of course. That must be coming from the central hollow, in this hemisphere."

"I hope you're right."

"I'm not worried. The main nuisance will be finding the wind direction. These mapping robots aren't built to sense it; I'll have to cut power every now and then and see where I get blown, if there's nothing else loose to show me. Score a point for low gravity."

Two, Molly thought, but kept the thought carefully to herself. Aloud she pointed out, "If you have rope with you, you can make some sort of wind flag. You'd still have to stop to use it, but it might be better than letting yourself get blown away."

"I meant the boat, not myself; I had no intention of emerging. Your flag idea is excellent—though I'll have to get out to set that up. I'll do it as soon as I figure out a way to hang it on some sort of support away from the mapper's hull. I may as well *try* to get an undisturbed wind."

Joe made no comment to any of this. For once, he did not feel guilty at having omitted wind sensors from the mappers; there was no obvious reason why they should have been needed. Actually, he was paying little attention to the Kantrick at the moment, because his own mapper was getting very close to the inner surface. He would have to decide very soon which mapped passage to follow himself and what region of the growing model to favor in guiding his small sensors.

The disc was now a set of tentacles probing into Enigma's crust once more. As the signal from any mapper advancing along a passage became weakened, another machine automatically positioned itself to relay and followed the same tunnel. The second would be followed by a third and still others as needed; Joe's problem was to decide how many tunnels to check at a time. The more he was mapping, the shorter the distance in any one that could be covered before running out of relays. There was no way he could think of to establish the perfect balance between reasonable probability of including the right direction and—

And what? Why was he worrying about time? The women could survive for weeks yet, as long as their energy source remained available, and there seemed little chance of another slip in that direction. Of course, research involves the unexpected.

Such as the realization that there had been changes over most of his recently mapped surface, he suddenly saw; and that less than half of the small mappers seemed now to be contributing signals to the model. He still couldn't spot individual sources, of course, but he could estimate well enough how many machines were committed to each tunnel.

After a little thought, he reworked his program to indicate by color change which passages were still increasing in length on his model. The picture was a complicated, bushlike structure, rather hard to appreciate in full, but it quickly verified his suspicion. Fully half the branches of the bush had ceased to grow. Something was stopping his mappers.

OF COURSE I CAN GET A SPECTRUM

Molly was more certain than ever that Joe could feel emotion as his latest report came through her translator.

"How do you know they're missing?" She put the question as calmly as she could, remembering how the Nethneen had been so careful of her own feelings earlier. "I thought you couldn't identify their individual signals."

"I can't. That's why I was so slow realizing what was happening. Several of the branches—the passages—in the present section of the model have simply stopped growing. Since others were extending normally and the pattern is fairly complex already, the frozen ones weren't obvious without careful examination. Carol, with her memory, might have spotted the situation more quickly; I could not."

"Couldn't the passages simply have reached dead ends?"

"That would have been indicated; a good many have been. Some things I did foresee clearly enough to program. I cannot see any interpretation for this other than a stoppage of incoming signals, though the fact that the height of the surface over much of the mapped area has changed slightly—a centimeter or two—may also be relevant. I am of course heading for the nearest of the frozen branches as quickly as possible, to see for myself what's happened."

Molly just managed to restrain a comment about possible danger. Joe would be careful, of course, but he could no more ignore the situation than could Carol or, basically, than Molly herself. It was Carol who actually spoke, and it was some time before Molly realized that the Shervah was also giving prime thought to analyzing the danger—the danger to the mappers, of course.

"Joe, don't go too fast. Please examine and describe as carefully as you can the nature of the rock, or whatever may form the walls of the passages you traverse. If you have time to stop and take samples, or even do a quick spectral analysis, do it."

"You have an idea of what may have happened?"

"Not a full scenario. A possible backdrop. Get the data to me, please."

"I will. I am just approaching the surface. I told you earlier that this area was much smoother, according to the radar model, between the actual tunnel openings than it is farther from the poles. I have not seen such material before on my own world. As I approach, the smoothness starts to show a pattern of cracks outlining polygons of usually five or six sides, anywhere from four or five centimeters across to eight or ten times that size, the edges rather curled up—pardon the word—*away* from the surface and toward Enigma's interior." One of Carol's eyes rolled toward her companion; Molly caught the glance and nodded.

The Shervah interjected a question. "Is that concavity true of all the polygons, or are some of them flatter, rougher, and set farther from the surface—as though a curved plate such as you are describing had been removed?" Joe gave no answer for several seconds; Carol and Molly waited patiently, knowing that he must be making a careful search for the sort of feature she had suggested. Charley's voice started to sound, and ceased again before he had completed a word.

"Your idea has substance," the Nethneen responded at last. "A great many of the markings—fully an eighth, in the area I can see clearly—are as you describe. The percentage is greatest close to the tunnel mouth."

Again Molly nodded. It was she who spoke this time. "Joe, can you take the time to stop and pry or kick loose a few of those polygons? We'd like to know where they go, and how fast."

"Certainly. One to two minutes, please, while I check my armor." Not even Charley made a sound this time.

"They are rather fragile." The voice finally resumed. "Most of them break, no matter how carefully I try to detach them. They are attached to the substrate with some tenacity. Not enough to make them difficult to remove, but enough to make them hard to remove intact."

"It doesn't matter whether they break or not. The pieces will be just as useful. They aren't falling, of course; but you didn't report any floating around as you approached, so they must be leaving somehow. Which way are they going?"

"Toward the nearest tunnel mouth. They are being carried by the wind."

"Right. Does your translator handle the word *mud*?"

"An approximation symbol comes through; I don't know how it would return to you. Is *slurry* adequate?"

"Fairly. Mud would have less liquid and more viscosity, generally speaking, but I couldn't give you a numerical boundary composition distinguishing the two. You've described a surface of mud that has dried, shrinking as it lost liquid, and some of the plates formed by the resultant cracking have been blown away. The rivers must get to the central hollow at some season or other of Enigma's year—"

"First from one pole and then the other!" Charley interrupted gleefully. "I see. The mud season has passed, the mud left in the center has dried, and rivers are drying too under the hot wind. It makes sense."

"Which does not necessarily make it true." Molly felt she had to say it; it was more properly Joe's line, but it was likely that he wouldn't want to interrupt. This was neither emergency nor incipient quarrel. "I agree, Charley. A stratigraphic study of the mud should tell us a lot about Enigma—it might even contain enough organic remains to let us reconstruct the life history. For that matter, it might even tell us why the mud, when it does come, spreads out in a fairly smooth layer over this part of the inner surface, with what gravity there is tending to pull it toward the center."

"Wind, of course," remarked Charley. Molly glanced toward her small companion. The latter's mouth was almost invisible even when she was not wearing armor, since her face did not include a chin, but silent lip motion could be discerned. Molly made a silencing gesture, and the Shervah nodded. Her friend went on, "I admit hydrogen bonds are stronger than gravity, but I have a very foggy mental picture there. The main point right now is that the mud flakes, when loosened, blow into the tunnels. There must be a lot of detritus there. Much of it may get reduced to the sort of powder we met blowing from the surface, much of it may get cycled through life forms, but some of it right now may be causing the trouble with Joe's mappers."

"How?"

"I don't pretend to know. With no gravity at all, practically speaking, it could hardly be any sort of tunnel collapse. You said there'd been some surface change. Just keep any eye on the passage walls as you go, Joe."

"Most assuredly." Joe was always happier with a working hypothesis around, even though he always expected it to need modification. "I'm entering the passage now."

"Are the walls still mud? Do they show any stratification?"

"To the first, apparently yes. To the second, I can't tell, Carol. I would expect to have to section the deposit to see."

"I was wondering whether there might have been a river through that passage to do the sectioning. How such a system would behave in weightlessness I can't guess. We'll have to come back two or three decades from now and try to catch this place with water reaching the inside, at one or another of the poles."

"I am sure that will be done. I wouldn't mind being one of those to do it, but if I manage my Respected Opinion rating I'll presumably be working somewhere else long before then."

"You don't have it yet, Joe?" Charley was clearly startled.

"Of course not. I was under the impression that none of us was even up to Considered Word. I did not, of course, inquire how far any of the rest of you had to go, but one more really successful project after this one—if this turns out as well as I'm beginning to hope—should satisfy my requirements. One must admit, of course, that a certain subjectivity occasionally shows in Faculty ratings, as even most Faculty members will concede, but one does not *worry* about facts beyond actual control."

Charley made no comment. He might have wanted to, but Carol rather pointedly repeated her question about the composition of the walls surrounding the Nethneen. Joe returned to business. The passage still appeared to be winding its way through dried mud, though whether this represented a thin covering over rock or a bore through kilometers of sediment could not be told by simple inspection.

"I'd vote for lots of sediment," Carol said thoughtfully. "It's an interesting bet whether this temporary hollow is going to fill first from rock creep or sediment transfer. There's no way it can last indefinitely. Yes, I said *creep*, Molly."

The mud itself was very salty and rather brittle; Joe stopped and emerged from his mapper long enough to ascertain these facts. He did not try to dig into it for any distance. The flare from his laser indicated, even to his eyes, that either the salt or the mud itself was very rich in sodium, but detailed information would have to wait until the fragments he collected reached the laboratory.

He had passed wind-borne flakes of what seemed to be surface mud other than those he had detached himself, and judged that the wind loosened these occasionally and bore them on up toward the outer surface. He wondered what would happen when gravity became strong enough to oppose the wind effectively for one of these, and began to get an inkling of what might be going on in the tunnels ahead. He thought of slowing his flight, then remembered the women and continued as he was.

The inactive branches were mostly well away from the inner surface, but one seemed to start less than twenty kilometers from the original passage mouth, measured along the route he had to follow. The path showed clearly enough in the computer model, but as he approached the indicated tunnel the Nethneen slowed somewhat and watched carefully ahead, using his mapper's lights and radar as effectively as he could. He had now set his computer to warn of any change in the tunnel shape or topology by the same contrasting color technique. If he had done this somewhat earlier, he would have been spared inconvenience and anxiety.

Nothing gave any warning, however, for nearly another ten kilometers. Then he reached a section where, according to the model, there was barely enough room for his own vehicle to pass. Had there been too little, the small machines would have interpreted it as a dead end and stopped mapping, but they had gone on. Joe did the same.

He had become a little remiss by now in checking the details of the passage walls; Carol had stopped reminding him. Molly insisted afterward that it would have made no difference. Even she, used to winds and their peculiarities, would not have expected to foresee just what happened; Joe, from a practically airless world, would hardly have had a chance.

Joe himself insisted that Charley's experience at the crater where Molly and Carol had entered the caverns should have been warning enough if he had kept properly alert.

He was never sure whether his vehicle actually brushed the loose mud of the passage wall as a result of careless piloting, or simply left such a narrow space for air to get by that the wind did the damage. Whichever happened, some of the sediment broke free, leaving a hole that gave the wind a real grip on the rest; and within seconds the passage ahead of him was full of blowing material ranging from fine dust grains to fist-sized clods. Joe's unfortunate reaction was to cut power for a moment to let the stuff get ahead of him; it was blinding in both visual and radar wavelengths. Unfortunately, the local gravity was still less than three millimeters per second squared, and the wind was quite able to move the robot he was riding. The shuttle-shaped polymer hull, a meter and a half in diameter and five in length, twisted erratically, and first one pointed end and then the other struck the passage wall, gouging out more clay and salt before jamming in place. Large fragments flying from the original disturbance site struck it. Some of these pulverized and were blown past, others proved more resistant and in many cases got themselves jammed between hull and passage wall. Before the Nethneen had a clear idea of an appropriate maneuver, the wind had stopped, blocked by a new plug composed of freshly moved sediment and his own mapping machine.

It did not seem a dangerous situation, particularly. He had lost his personal sense of direction for a moment, but there was enough gravity to tell him which way was down, after a little careful checking with loose items he had on board. He could not see outside, of course, being completely buried, but he was sure the burial could not be very deep.

If the robot's power would not push it through the deposit without damaging the hull, he could go outside himself and do some digging—with due precaution against being blown away again when he did get through and the air was once more free to move. Once was quite enough, even weightless.

At this point Molly, of all people, asked whether there were any evidence of what had happened to the mapping robots. Since it seemed clear that the tiny objects could never have triggered an event like this—their automatic controls would have prevented them from touching the walls, and their size would have kept them from changing wind speed significantly in any passage large enough for his own machine—he replied truthfully, he felt, that no evidence was yet forthcoming. He preferred to say nothing about his present minor predicament until he was out of it, of course.

He then applied driving power, gradually increasing the thrust until he began to worry about the strength of the robot's shell. There was no motion that he could feel in his craft or see in the surrounding sediment.

He thought briefly again of digging, but then remembered that the hatch opened outward. He did not even try to move it. He was strong—nearly as strong as Molly, in spite of the feeble gravity of his home world—but knew his limitations too well for that.

After a few seconds more of thought, he returned to the control keys, concentrating this time on attitude rather than motion. It proved possible, finally, to rotate the robot on its long axis—Joe remembered, with a slight shudder, that he had briefly considered giving the machine an elliptical rather than a circular lateral cross section merely for appearance's sake—and within a few minutes his equipment was boring its way gently out of its tomb.

Once free, he reported in full, including his reasons for doubting that this was what could have happened to the small mappers. "I'm a little bit unsure about whether to go back through this mess and continue checking this branch, or check out one of the others," he concluded. "I am sorry to say I dug my way out on the downward side of the block without thinking."

"You were thinking better then than you are now!" snapped Carol. "Your next maneuver is to get back out of the tunnels into the open and recall your machines. Count them out where you're safe, and incidentally where their radars will pick up Molly and me when we get through. Leave them out there, or most of them. Spread them to cover as much of that inner surface as possible. When that's done, you might take a few and go check one of your dead tunnels, if you like—well, of course you have to—but don't get all your mappers committed to an area that seems to be eating them, just yet. Get them out of there. I'm very glad we know about what this mud or clay can do in a high wind and no weight, and we will be extremely careful when we reach tunnels that seem to be made of it, but untie the knots in them before you stretch your arms any farther."

Molly sympathized with her companion, though she could never have brought herself to be that emphatic with Joe. She added a quiet "It would be nice to know just how many of those little mappers really are left" to Carol's diatribe, and waited for his answer, which was quite predictable.

"You are quite right; I should have withdrawn the other robots before starting this investigation. I'll go back and take care of that immediately."

"And please tell us when you're out in the open again," added the Human.

"There are no more such constrictions on the way out, but I will certainly report. It will take a little while to make even an approximate count of the robots; I should have included provision for individual monitoring."

"You can't either foresee or take care of everything, Joe. A fiction writer, years ago on my home world, complained that the trouble with writing adventure stories was that adventures happened only to the incompetent and he or she—I don't remember which it was—felt unhappy writing about incompetent characters. The readers, he felt, were bound to recognize each mistake as it happened and sneer at them. It just doesn't happen that way; if it did, none of us would make mistakes—and life could actually become boring. Horrid thought. Go on back to the hollow, Joe, check your machines, and keep in touch with us. Even there, things might happen that none of us has foreseen. I *think* we're in more danger at the moment than you are, but I'm far from certain of it."

Ten hours later, Charley reported a gravity of thirty in the usual units; presumably he was over halfway to the center. Jenny had found fundamental genetic biochemistry suggesting eight different planetary origins in the specimens she herself had found and brought back to the tent; there seemed no reasonable doubt that Enigma had been repeatedly seeded, and ordinary evolution been busily at work developing a fascinating ecology of the results. She was still working. The original atmosphere problem had been almost forgotten; objectively speaking, the guess that had been made toward a solution was still in the hypothesis class, but the flood of new questions had left the group willing to accept it so their attention could be freed for other things.

Joe had found that many of his robots were indeed missing, but fewer than he had guessed; there were still three hundred ten in service. This, of course, did not lessen the problem of what had happened to the other two hundred or so; he would long since have returned to the caves in search of them if another difficulty had not developed.

Molly and Carol were still following a river of unknown size. Gravity suggested that they might be nearly halfway to the inner surface by now, according to Carol's observations; but Molly was unable to check them.

Her vision had been getting progressively worse. The urge to blink and squint had increased, the blurring had grown more and more extreme, and occasionally she could feel liquid running down her cheek—slowly, and only when an accumulation that made seeing hopeless had finally been dislodged from her cornea by frantic blinking and head shaking. She had nothing to serve as a mirror and could not tell whether the liquid was ordinary tears or something else. Carol, who could see the drops, was not familiar enough with Human physiology to report anything useful. Her color sense was different enough from Molly's to make even basic description quite useless; there was no way for the translator to handle color symbols, and it simply reported the fact.

Both carried elementary first aid equipment in their armor, of course. Carol's was, except for purely mechanical items like wound dressings, incompatible with Human chemistry. Molly's seemed inappropriate to the present trouble, but she lacked the medical knowledge to offer more than a guess at her present trouble.

The Shervah could guess equally well, and with more conviction. "I told you it was insane to take that bath. School only knows what was in that part of the river besides water."

"But I didn't get any of it in my eyes. I had them shut tightly when I submerged."

"You didn't get *much* of it in your eyes. What's its vapor pressure at the temperature of that bath? What does it do to your chemistry? How much does it take to destroy your eyes?"

"Since I don't know what it is—"

"Precisely. All right, I'm sorry to overtrack; you know as well as I do how silly it all was—and I know as well as you do that I might have done the same under the same drive. Let's be reasonable. *If* you've been poisoned by something in that river, the stuff is water soluble. *You* will have to decide whether you can spare enough water from your armor system, and open your helmet long enough in this environment, to try swabbing your eyes out with a water-soaked dressing. I know it may be too late, and whatever happened will have to run its course; I know whatever caused the trouble may still be around us as vapor. I have wound dressings that will hold water if you decide to try it—so do you, I imagine."

"I do. Let me think."

"May I make a point?" It was Joe.

"Of course."

"If you have suffered chemically from the river, it might be well to get away from the river before you attempt first aid. This will delay your arrival at the hollow and therefore the time when we can get you back to the tent; but this may make little difference, since real treatment probably cannot be started until *Classroom* with others of your species returns. If you can wait without too much pain, it might be a good idea to hold off opening your helmet until your river has gone, as Charley's did. Is there very much pain involved, or is it a matter of the inconvenience of not seeing?"

"Mostly the blindness. I can wait, for a while at least. If you can do all the watching for narrow passages and low ceilings, Carrie—"

"I'll have to do that anyway. I don't expect just swabbing out will be a cure."

"It might let normal healing go faster."

"And it might expose you to another dose that would blind you permanently." Molly noted with gratitude that her companion refrained from adding anything like "if you aren't already," and wondered for a moment whether Charley might cut in with one of his infelicitous remarks. If he were so inclined, Carol gave him no chance. "I can keep alert as well as you, and for a lot longer, and even when I have to doze I can still stay on watch after a fashion. You know that. We won't have to stop. You relax—sleep if you can. I'll tell you if the river disappears, and you can decide then whether you want to try washing your eyes or not. Until then, let me run things, and be thankful it's your eyes instead of mine. Would you like to have to do the lookout job and face the delay of telling me what to do with the robot every time something came up?"

"Your logic is overwhelming. I am quite delighted." Molly didn't care whether Joe got the sarcasm, but rather hoped Carol wouldn't. If she did, she said nothing.

Charley came through, on private channel.

"I have a lot of Human information in my personal library but can't get at it until we're back in electromagnetic range of the boat. A lot of it's probably medical, and might help. Do you think it will be worthwhile for me to go back now to check it out?"

The offer was tempting. However, the likelihood that Charley had really detailed enough medical material available, even if he had simply transferred whole banks of information unselectively for later browsing, seemed too low to be worth anyone's time. Molly refused the offer with thanks, not guessing what that would do to confuse further the already undecided Kantrick.

Joe did not hear the offer, of course—the private channels were genuinely private—but the same notion had occurred to him. There was medical data appropriate to all members of the team in the boat, though he knew nothing of Charley's special collection. He could, with its aid, have set a bone for Molly, Carol, or Jenny, repaired even serious cracks in Charley's exoskeleton, sewn up or cemented wounds for any of them, treated burns and radiation injury, taken appropriate steps for lack of food or solvent or even air for those who used it; but chemical poisoning was a different game tank. There *might* be relevant and recognizable information. He *might* find it quickly enough to be of use. It *might* involve treatment that Molly and Carol could apply with what they had with them, following directions he could transmit. So he asked Jenny to check for the appropriate information and stayed where he was.

It was far more likely that the real need would be for transportation to the boat. Until Charley reached the interior, the only known way back to the surface was stored in Joe's mappers; and this meant that Joe could not risk his machine in the tunnels again until the women reached the hollow or were stopped so that he clearly had to go to them. He didn't like it, but he hung near the inner surface, doing a little very cautious tunnel mapping with his small machines, and otherwise simply waiting.

Charley raced through passages when there was only one way to go, stopped to check wind whenever there was a branch, and groped with his rope flag for appropriate exits when the course led through large caverns. His speed, so much greater than that of Molly and Carol when he had had a river to follow, averaged only a small fraction of its earlier value.

He envied Joe for being already in the hollow, where he could be useful. Joe envied Charley for having something to occupy his attention. Molly envied Carol for being able to see where they were going. Carol envied Jenny for being in the lab getting something practical accomplished.

Jenny, happy as a scientist can be only when the data are falling smoothly into a coherent picture, envied nobody. She made a run-through of the boat's Human information at Joe's request, found nothing that seemed relevant, and returned to the real work—properly concerned about her Human friend, but quite clear in mind and conscience that there was nothing more she could do about the matter just then. Joe, or conceivably Charley, would establish physical contact eventually; more effective steps could then be taken. In the meantime, a picture of a tightly coordinated ecology, involving life that seemed to have originated on at least nine different worlds and been interacting here for some unknown length of time, was beginning to emerge. Two fundamentally unrelated forms produced hydrogen peroxide; six contained considerable amounts of hydrazine in their body solvents; and one, with a genetic basis she had never seen or heard of, consumed both, apparently getting its energy by reacting the two to water and nitrogen. At least, this seemed to fit their structures; actual life processes would now have to be checked. Jenny kept happily at work.

"Joe!" Charley's voice came through the Rimmore's translator, but failed to catch her attention at first. "I've found another river—I think."

"Why is there doubt?"

"It's not traveling. I entered a big kame—irregular, over thirty kilometers one way, nearly forty at right angles, and over twenty-five deep—from about the middle of the north side. There was some radar ambiguity from near the top, and I went to check it. There are huge drops of what I suppose must be water just hanging here, drifting around, sometimes coming together and joining. When they do that they start to sink, but before they reach the bottom of the cave, they always break into smaller ones and start up again. It's sort of river's end, I'd say—maybe Carol and Molly's."

"Possible. Theirs seemed to be larger than your original one, and size would be needed to get that deep against rising hot air. It's a long way from certain, of course, but maybe you should make another gravity check to see how your depth compares with theirs, and if they aren't too different, you might wait for a little while anyway. If you can meet them, travel in your machine, especially for Molly, will be a lot better than on theirs."

"Right. I'll check."

Carol chimed in. "You know, if that's the real limit of the river, whether it's ours or not, the water or whatever it is ought to be loaded with salts; and if the drops are evaporating all the time and getting fed from above, there ought to be crystals around. Why don't you check the cave walls for that, too? It would be a pity to wait and do nothing."

"All right. The laser would give an easy check for dissolved salts; I could boil one of the drops, and if there is solid dust, vaporize it and get a spectrum. I'll—

"Charley! *DON'T!*"

The Rimmore's grating call was too late; Charley had been acting as he spoke.

OF COURSE I EXPECTED THAT

Fortunately the drop was small, as they went in that area, and there were no others really close by. Charley insisted later that this had not been a matter of luck alone; he had not wanted to waste time and energy boiling large amounts of water, or having his experimental results involved with other drops. Whatever the actual reason, the fact was fortunate.

The test laser was not a weapons-grade device but was quite capable of vaporizing small volumes of metal or rock. The present liquid target was more transparent, which meant that more of the material had to be traversed by the beam for a given amount of energy to be absorbed; but, as it turned out, very little energy was needed. The drop—not just the liquid in the path of the beam, but the entire drop—exploded violently.

The shock wave flattened other drops and reduced them to spray, but did not detonate them. Its most critical effect was on Charley's robot. This was supported and driven by the usual field effects, and guided and navigated by an inertial system. This, unless the guidance computer was set to respond to additional factors such as the approach of other vehicles or radar information, did its fusion-powered best to hold the machine in whatever position the driver had placed it.

The mapper did not, therefore, move under the impulse of the shock wave. Portions of its shell did yield to the pressure, some sections peeling away entirely and flying out of sight, some collapsing inward. Charley found himself, when he recovered from several seconds of daze, pressed down by what had been outer hull onto the ring-shaped seat cushion that normally surrounded his mouth. The polymer had bent to conform rather well to his own armored contours, but not perfectly; his forward arm and right leg seemed to be broken. One of his eyes, the front one, was also out of action. He could not localize the pain well enough to guess at the overall personal damage, but it certainly hurt.

"Charley! Don't!" the Rimmore called again.

He found himself able to answer clearly enough for his translator to handle.

"I'm afraid I did. It wasn't water, was it?"

"It might have been, but there were other possibilities. What happened?"

Charley reported as completely as he could.

"I see three possibilities—or rather, two and a combination," Jenny started thoughtfully. "Either it was—"

"Jenny! Charley's hurt! What can we do?" It was Carol, not Molly, who had interrupted. The Human was not too surprised at this; there is a difference between potential danger and actual damage.

"We consult medical information, get Charley to describe his damage in as much detail as possible, and tell him what to do for himself if he doesn't already know," the chemist replied calmly. "If he is actually on your river, you two may be able to do more shortly; listen carefully to any information I transmit."

"If he is on our river, we'd better find out what's in it besides water," the Shervah answered. "Your theories are important, after all; pardon my interruption."

"I'll get back to that later. Charley, are you losing body fluids at any serious rate?"

"Not as far as I can tell. I'm cracked in several places—leg, arm, probably right front upper body quadrant—but sac doesn't seem to be ruptured. I can't see my own head, of course, and one eye is out, so there is some damage there; but again, I don't seem to be leaking. Remember, I can't see through my armor; it's just inference. A bad leak would have me unconscious by now."

"Then from the summary of your physiology I have here, your main danger is starting to heal broken limbs without having them properly set."

"Right. If I can free myself from this robot's outer shell, I can take care of most of the trouble—the armor itself will do for splints, if I can find something with the leverage I need to straighten the limb sections."

"Will your robot travel?" asked Joe.

"It's still hanging where all this happened; its power must be on. At the moment I can't reach or nip the keys. I'll report when I can. I'm starting to feel stronger; maybe I can get out from under this envelope in a few minutes."

"I'd better come in for you," Joe started.

"Come in *where*? Stay where you are until we can figure out a useful action. Send those little robots back to their mapping, and if they all disappear we'll have to live with it and think of something else; but there's nothing else useful you can do from there right now."

"True, Jenny. I was getting ahead of my own thinking; thanks. If I can locate that river—or those rivers—the real problem is to get us back together and back to the boat."

"Get to it. You'll find me."

"I hope you're better with that guess than the one about the boat's not lasting. Are you ever going to tell us why you thought that?"

"Probably not. Just start mapping, please. I'm hurting."

"The robots are on the way."

"Charley, can you move yet?" called Molly.

"Yes, a little. The hull stuff that is pinning me down is very thin and should be easy to bend. I just don't have much leverage. There, I'm getting away from the pedestal and can move toward the rear of the mapper. I see what happened. The front part of the body was pushed back and wrapped around me, and most of the side and rear covering just peeled away like an outgrown shell. The interior doesn't seem to have suffered. I can twist this bent stuff out of the way and get at the keys. Wait a minute while I run them through. Yes. Good. I seem to have full control, and even my radar is working, though the lights are gone except for interior instrument ones."

"I hope your circuitry is still protected. With those floating drops, you might wind up in worse trouble than we did," Carol pointed out.

"True. My claw light is working—I'll fly away from the

neighborhood right away—if I can. My front arm doesn't work, and turning my body is awkward with a leg out of action, too, and I won't be able to nip keys as well with the rear hand."

"Why not?" Molly couldn't help asking. "Your front and rear look the same to me—I could never see why you cared which way you were going. Joe doesn't seem to."

"Your right and left look the same to me, but you seem to prefer to use your right," replied Charley. "Ouch! If we must talk, let's stick to essentials. I'll have to be careful moving; if that broken arm or leg shell cuts inner sac, it could be bad. There; I'm turned around. I've bent a piece of the hull sheeting to hold the light, since I can't do that and nip keys with the same digits. I'm traveling. Down, judging by large-drop motion. I trust that *is* the end of this river; traveling without them may be slow, but I feel better that way from now on."

"You're not going to wait for us, then?" Carol asked innocently.

"I don't think so. We don't know this is your river, after all, and I wouldn't be much help to you now if we did meet. If it is, maybe you'll catch up to me; I won't be going very fast. Jenny, I wouldn't mind hearing now what you think I ran into that looked so much like water."

"As I said, two guesses and a combination. I'd vote for hydrogen peroxide, but it might have been hydrazine or a mixture of the two. The first is most likely to have been really concentrated in that reflux system; as I recall, hydrazine gets to a constant-boiling mixture with water while still pretty dilute. Also, if there had been hydrazine in the river, it would have reacted with the peroxide pretty completely as the latter's concentration got high."

"Joe!"

"Yes, Molly." The Nethneen didn't need to have her thought specified. "That's what could have gotten them, perhaps. Of course—"

"We haven't thought of everything!" All three women chanted this practically in unison, as it came to the Human's ears. She assumed Carol and Jenny must actually have been slightly ahead of her, allowing for translator delay.

"We've thought of enough." It was Carol who continued.

"There is a reasonable chance, approaching certainty, of higher-boiling things than water getting concentrated toward the bottom of this big condenser, and there's a demonstrated certainty of explosives being around whether that's how they originate or not. I say we still follow the river since it remains the best guide downward; it must have done a reasonable amount of erosion, after all, no matter how young the planet is. We treat it very respectfully, though. If we find it shrinking, we assume that little if any of it is water, and get even more careful. The main thing is *we keep going down*. So does Charley. As long as we can travel, and as long as we can tell which way *is* down, we travel down. Joe does *not* come to meet us unless something else happens and we get stopped; and if he does have to do that, Jenny, I strongly advise that you leave your lab, much as I hate to suggest it, and take his route to the big cave and be there to back him up."

"I agree. I admit I hope that does not become necessary."

"Don't we all. But, Joe, you'd better send one of your little machines—maybe several for safety—back to your entrance and have them wait there so they can feed the model to Jenny's mapper if she does have to come. You can treat them that independently, can't you?"

"Yes." Molly wondered whether Joe was as relieved at being able to give that answer as she was at hearing it. "I will send back six. As far as I know, there was no danger to them along that path, but—"

He stopped. This time no one made the obvious completion. Carol simply approved.

"All right. Let's move. I want a shampoo as much as Molly wanted her bath, but someone's got to stay in shape to complete this tour."

Four hours.

"I'm out of touch with them, of course, but the mappers should be back at the surface by now, Jenny."

"They are. My own computer has received and stored the model they were carrying. I am returning to the tent. I would return your machines to you if I could control them."

"Beam out five zeros, five ones, then five ones and five zeros on Band 2471. I still foresee a few things."

Twelve hours.

"Molly, I think I do see the other side of this river."

"Are we flowing or falling right now?"

"Flowing, more or less. Just a minute while I swing us over that way. Yes, there is an opposite bank; the whole thing is less than a kilometer wide."

"How big is the cave we're in now?"

"No idea. I can't see roof or walls, no matter what I do with my lights."

"Anything ahead?"

"Just more river, right now."

Fifteen hours.

"There's not much in this machine close enough to its original shape to measure the fall distance with, but gravity is less than ten. The real problem is finding a place where wind isn't blowing, so I can let something fall, now that this robot doesn't have a hull anymore."

"We've been having some wind troubles, too, Charley," replied Carol. "We never did have a hull, but now an occasional big drop is being lifted off this river and carried back upstream, and I don't always see it coming as soon as I should. Since there isn't much left of the river now, I'm really afraid of hitting the drops. You at least had some protection and a little distance when yours went off."

"Still flow, or some straight fall?"

"Two straight-down sessions since we last checked in, but nothing like your terminal region. The very small drops got blown back up, but the big stuff kept falling."

Twenty-two hours.

"Joe." Charley's voice was little more than a whisper, but it went out on the general channel. Joe acknowledged. "I think the passage walls around me are different. I never saw the mud you and the others were talking about, but I have seen mud. Maybe I'm getting there. Keep your radar hot."

"We're still rock, but the river is practically gone," Carol came in. "I think I see it disappearing over another fall ahead. I'd almost bet it won't reach the bottom. I wonder if we've joined your path."

"There'll be no easy way to tell," answered the Kantrick. "I haven't had many very good looks at the route I've been following since then; I've simply done my best to go upwind. Even if I'd seen it all, I couldn't remember the details well enough to give you a helpful description."

"I know. Don't worry. We'd never be really sure anyway. The real worry is the explosive river; once we're away from that we'll just use the wind, too."

"Why did you follow the river if you feel it's so dangerous?" asked Jenny.

"Speed. Almost certainly the quickest way downhill. I want to get Molly to help as fast as possible. I'll be less scared once we're past it, but no less worried. There—I was right. We're into another kame from somewhere near the top, and the stream is falling. Slowly. Very slowly. There aren't any really small drops any more; the waterfall, or peroxidefall, or whatever it is just comes gradually apart and big shimmery blobs of liquid spread out through the cave. Over toward the side they fall a little faster—some of them faster than I've seen anything but us go downward for a long time. Maybe eddies—downdrafts. I have to keep alert, but they're not too hard to dodge. I hope the bottom isn't too far down, though."

"Joe, I can't see very well. Another eye seems to be quitting, and my head hurts. I can't see the mud walls any more, and I don't want to run into them—I remember what happened to you, and I could never dig what's left of this machine out if I got buried—my light doesn't show anything—Joe, what can I do?"

"Don't do anything, Charley. You're on my model, a hundred and eighty-four kilometers from my mapper. I'll be with you in fourteen minutes. Just stop where you are."

"How about Molly and Carol? They're still somewhere in that rock sponge. How can we find them?"

"They're doing a pretty good job of finding themselves. Relax."

"It hurts."

"Do you have any pain-killers in your armor kit?"

"Sure."

"Then get something out, and tell me how to use it. I'll be there. You needn't worry about the others."

Twenty minutes later Charley was tranquilized, and Joe reported the fact to the rest.

"Good. I'm on the way," replied Jenny. "One of us can take him back to the boat as soon as I get there—I've left it on the surface just outside your antarctic entrance, to save time. I'd say you should start back with him right now, but we don't know when the others will come through, and someone should be waiting to spot them."

"You may as well start back, Joe." Carol's voice came quietly. "We won't be out very quickly."

"Why not?"

"I didn't want to report until Charley was taken care of, since he seemed so worried about us, but there's a problem here. We've been all over the lower part of this cavern, and I mean *all* over it. It's covered with mud, some of it fairly wet—drops must have been reaching the bottom, and sticking, and soaking in fairly recently, though I haven't seen any do it since we got here. The wind is coming through at pretty high speed, but through hundreds of small vents all over the floor. None of them is big enough for our robot to get through—few of them are big enough for me, even if I were to leave Molly. We could go back—I guess we'll have to go back—and look for another downward track, but we're not going to be there very quickly."

"Wait. Don't start back yet; we'll try to think of something else."

"I wasn't going to. I'm awfully tired."

"All right, rest. We have some work here and will be back with you soon."

But Carol did not rest. She drove the robot slowly and carefully twice around the perimeter of the cavern, a few meters above the surface of the mud. Not finding what she wanted, she repeated the maneuver fifteen meters higher. This time she located four openings that might conceivably lead to additional tunnels. Explaining to Molly what she was doing, she parked the robot at the mouth of each in turn and explored it briefly by herself. She was not exactly on foot, though her status was not yet quite free fall.

Two of the passages seemed to go on indefinitely; she followed each for a hundred meters or so before returning. One of the others went horizontally for some fifteen meters and reached a dead end, the barrier closing it formed apparently of hardened mud. The last of the four slanted sharply downward and also came to an early end, but for some reason was entirely free of sediment.

Carol sternly suppressed the urge to stop everything and try to figure out how this could have happened; she did not even look for small drains or wind vents. After some thought she brought the robot to the mouth of the last passage, helped Molly untie herself, and guided her inside. For the moment she left the machine at its mouth.

"Stay here, and sleep if you can," she said briefly. "I have something to try out. I'll be back soon. Call if you're worried; I won't be far."

"All right." Molly did not like to ask for details; her work and friendship with Joe had instilled a good deal of the Nethneen courtesy code into her. In any case, she was quite willing to sleep. Nothing could happen while they weren't traveling, of course.

The Shervah half floated, half walked out toward the center of the cavern. The mud floor, pierced with the wind vents that repeatedly tried to pick her up when fatigue made her careless, was nearly three kilometers across. Again she was tempted to stop to figure out the feedback mechanism that must have existed to cause the vents to form so uniformly. Something to do with drying rates? The way in which the liquid returned—no, Carol. Stick to business.

The nearly nonexistent gravity both helped and threatened to spoil her plan. She had a digging tool of sorts: her sampling hammer, an ordinary geological pick. She approached one of the vents, as nearly at the cavern center as she could judge, and began swinging.

Her cut was a nearly circular groove over a meter across, wide enough for her small hands to work to some depth. She was hoping that the surface of the mud would be harder than that lower down, and was relieved to find that this was the case. When she thought the groove was deep enough, she worked both hands and the hammer down one side and pried.

A small part of the edge cracked out, giving her a fragment of hardened mud massing perhaps five or six kilograms. This was not what she wanted, and she tried again, digging deeper before she pried. This time the entire circle lifted, though it broke in two before she had it quite out where she wanted it. She accepted that. There was one more test.

She carried one of the pieces over to the nearby vent and used it as a cap, circulation overspeeding and breathing stopped as she waited to see whether the wind would lift it against the feeble gravity.

It stayed. She gave her grotesque equivalent of a smile and began digging again.

Three and a half hours later, nearly exhausted, she had twenty-five of the mud caps or reasonably large fragments of mud caps each lying beside a vent.

She swept her light around to make sure she knew the direction to the robot and Molly, and began placing the caps, one after another as quickly as she could, over wind vents. In ten minutes or less, there was an area at the center of the cave free of updraft, and a quick glance upward warned her that gravity was doing what she had hoped. The drops—School grant they were peroxide, but she hadn't dared make the obvious test—were settling in the center. She got out of their way quickly, but stopped near the edge of the plugged area to watch the results of her work in detail.

Her tiny fists clenched as the first of the blobs of liquid touched the warm mud. It stuck, and began to soak in, and slowly she relaxed. More drops were coming, and slowly she retreated toward the robot and her blinded friend.

Long before she got there, the supply of liquid was exceeding the capillary capacity of the mud, but hydrogen bonding was doing its work. The drops that touched the surface, or touched other drops on the surface, stuck, and a growing, pulsing dome of liquid was swelling where the wind had been stopped.

Satisfied, Carol made her way back to the side cave in a few careful leaps.

"All right, Molly? Get any sleep?"

"Some. What have you been up to?"

"You'll see in a moment."

"See?"

"Quite possibly. Joe, you still there?"

"Yes. Jenny has not reached the hollow yet."

"All right. Your computer is set to detect any change in the surface, didn't you say?"

"Yes."

"Your mappers are covering as much of the polar mud cap as possible?"

"Yes."

"All right. I'm going to give a quick countdown. At zero, start timing and start watching your model for changes. There may be more than one, and at more than one time, so if you see something don't stop watching. Are you ready?"

"Yes."

"All right, give me a few seconds to get our machine as far inside this hole as possible. That isn't very far, but we may need the shelter. There. Where's my light? I can see the liquid—yes, clearly enough. Here comes the count. Four. Three. Two. One. Zero." Carol's testing laser unloaded.

Even Molly saw the flash through her closed lids and from deep in the tunnel. The ground shock took over a second to reach them and was not very energetic; the mud, as Carol had hoped, transmitted the wave very poorly. The sound, arriving slightly later, was much worse, but their armor held.

"I took a seismology course once," the Shervah remarked complacently. "How about it, Joe?" There was a pause.

"Most of the mud cap is moving. The area is spreading out—"

"*Gravdh!* Did you spot where it *started*?"

"Oh, yes. About forty-five kilometers northwest of where Charley emerged. You couldn't have been on the same river, I guess. And now there's more. Four sites near the starting point are changing further—there is material erupting from several of the tunnel mouths."

"I hadn't counted on that. I suppose there was enough mud knocked loose all the way along the tunnels to supply the material, but I didn't expect it to travel far upwind. It couldn't have. Surely it's already blowing back toward the tunnels?" Again there was a pause.

"Yes, it seems to be."

"All right. Actually, that's very lucky. I was expecting the seismic jolt would zero the area where you could resume your mapping with a really good chance of meeting us, but I didn't think there was going to be quite such a perfect guide to where we are. It's just as well. I'm afraid our robot is out of action from the blast wave; you'll have to come and get us. Just follow any of the four passages that erupted, and don't worry about getting buried. There can't be anything left in them that your mapper could possibly knock loose. We'll be waiting for you out in the open, once we've gotten around the remains of this machine. It's kind of jammed into our shelter, but your radar should spot it all right. Be sure you map the route, so Jenny can follow you if she has to. She shouldn't, of course, but . . ."

Nobody said it.

DATUM FIVE: MOLLY AND OTHERS

Molly walked comfortably into the chatter room. Buzz was straddling her neck and bouncing violently, but she didn't mind; real weight, even the three-quarters gravity of Topaz, was heavenly just now. The light was dim but adequate; Fire had set some hours before, but its distant companion provided much more illumination than Earth's full moon. Carol was a good hostess; the space had been tented, and the air had enough oxygen for her Human and Rimmore guests. The Shervah herself wore a transparent breathing suit that permitted her freshly washed fur to show to full advantage. The Humans were similarly protected from the cold.

"Done?" Jenny, draped over the jungle of bars and ropes in her personal corner, put the rhetorical question.

"Done," Molly said, "if the word applies to a preliminary write-up. It's nice to know this will be studied instead of sealed."

The Rimmore chuckled. "Enigma is still a study site. It's merely moved up a few levels, with higher-degree types doing the studying, instead of a minor lab exercise for beginners. You're going back, too, I see."

"I was intending to; now there are complications, and I still don't see why there's a Faculty recommendation that I coordinate the next study session. I can't see that I showed up better than anyone else. I've been redesigning my armor as well as I can, but I'm certainly not going to be able to do field work for the whole time."

"Any of the group might have been selected; the general report commends the students collectively. The Faculty looks for imagination at the start, and a whole spectrum of other things thereafter. I rather think the fact that none of us was ever formally in charge impressed them. Even Charley showed up well after he broke out of his initial mold."

"You know what his trouble was?" asked Molly.

"Some of it was obvious, and he told me more," replied the Rimmore. "He just didn't believe there was any danger. He was firmly convinced not only that the Faculty wouldn't put students to personal risk, but that one of the group was a Faculty member whose main job was to watch out for us and give us spot tests. He was perfectly sure that we were going to have to get our job done and keep ourselves alive in the tent, because the Faculty would have arranged for the boat to go out of action—it would make things too easy if it were available. He'd planned heavily around that and was quite disappointed when the machine kept working."

"I did catch onto that." Molly nodded. "The amusing part was that for some of the time he thought I, of all people, was the Faculty member."

"I know. Then he decided it must be Joe, and was shifting back and forth between the two of you, trying to make up his mind, never once thinking that *both* ideas might be wrong, until he was approaching real imbalance. When Joe found those bodies, he even thought for a while that it was an attempt to deceive him. He was dangerously close to paranoia at that point. Nearly getting himself blown to pieces was about the best thing that could have happened to him."

"So even Charley is going back to Enigma," remarked the squarely built Human male sprawled on a floor mat.

"With a huge crowd of biological bigwigs," agreed Molly. "I can't help wondering how many of them are interested in finding Enigma's energy-fixing life and how many merely want to be there when Wendy gets born. Maybe we were a little hasty in starting her."

"After having it hammered into our emotions as well as our brains that either of us could get killed without notice? We do it now, my one and only. And does it matter about why the biologists are interested? Being curious about your friends' physiology is perfectly normal. We tend to think of it as childish because back when there was only one species to make friends with, we usually satisfied a lot of that curiosity during childhood. You were pretty interested in Charley's repairs, once you could see again."

"He couldn't have been thinking very carefully." Molly smiled reminiscently. "I made some of the silliest imaginable mistakes—"

"So did everyone else there," Rovor retorted. "Your taking a bath and picking up a case of hydrazine poisoning that could have blinded you permanently wasn't much worse than Joe's shortsighted robot planning or walking out of the boat without armor—"

"That's my point," returned his wife, tossing their child to him. Buzz, already used to a range of gravities, crowed triumphantly as his hands met his father's.

Carol rolled her eyes. "That settles it. I'm setting up a water-ice rink, and Bobby and I are going to practice figure skating. If a Human child can coordinate like that . . ."

Molly smiled at her small friend. "We'll be glad to help, though I won't be as agile as I might be for the next few months. But, honey," she said, returning to the earlier subject, "Charley's idea about having Faculty with the group was just silly. I don't say no teacher would have made such mistakes, but wouldn't he or she have used them better for teaching? Of course, Joe did analyze his errors to us pretty carefully, now that I think of it. Maybe—but no. He wouldn't have told an outright lie, and he did say he didn't have his degree yet, didn't he?"

"Of course he did," said Jenny.

ABOUT THE AUTHOR

Hal Clement (Harry Clement Stubbs) was born in Massachusetts in 1922. He has been a science lover from early childhood, at least partly as a result of a 1930 *Buck Rogers* panel in which villains were "headed for Mars, forty-seven million miles away." His father, an accountant, couldn't answer the resulting questions, and led little Hal to the local library. The result was irreversible brain influence.

He majored in astronomy at Harvard, and has since acquired master's degrees in education and in chemistry. He earned his basic living as a teacher of chemistry and astronomy at Milton Academy, in Massachusetts, until his retirement in June, 1987. His first two stories, "Proof" and "Impediment," were sold when he was a junior in college; their impression on Harvard's $400 per year tuition secured family tolerance for that crazy Buck Rogers stuff.

He has since produced half a dozen novels, of which the best known are *Needle* and *Mission of Gravity*. His reputation among science-fiction enthusiasts is that of a "hard" writer—one who tries to stick faithfully to the physical sciences as they are currently understood. Like Arthur C. Clarke and the late Willy Ley, Clement would never dream of having a spaceship fall into the sun merely because its engines broke down. He can do his own orbit computing, and does.

He leads a double life, appearing frequently at science-fiction conventions as Hal Clement and spending the rest of his time in Milton as the rather square science teacher with a wife of thirty-four years and three grown children, Harry Stubbs. He does occasional merit badge counseling for the Boy Scouts, has served on his town's finance committee, and is a sixteen-gallon Red Cross blood donor.